W9-BNX-549

KYDD:
The Admiral's Daughter

JULIAN STOCKWIN

KYDD:

The Admiral's Daughter

HODDER &
STOUGHTON

Copyright © 2007 by Julian Stockwin

First published in Great Britain in 2007 by Hodder & Stoughton
A division of Hodder Headline

The right of Julian Stockwin to be identified as the Author
of the Work has been asserted by him in accordance with the
Copyright, Designs and Patents Act 1988.

A Hodder & Stoughton Book

I

All rights reserved.
No part of this publication may be reproduced,
stored in a retrieval system, or transmitted, in any form
or by any means without the prior written permission of the publisher,
nor be otherwise circulated in any form of binding or cover other than that
in which it is published and without a similar condition being imposed
on the subsequent purchaser.

All characters in this publication are fictitious
and any resemblance to real persons, living or dead,
is purely coincidental.

A CIP catalogue record for this title
is available from the British Library

Hardback ISBN 978 0 340 89859 8
Trade Paperback ISBN 978 0 340 89860 4

Typeset in Garamond MT by Palimpsest Book Production Limited,
Grangemouth, Stirlingshire

Printed and bound by Clays Ltd, St Ives plc

Hodder Headline's policy is to use papers that are natural, renewable
and recyclable products and made from wood grown in sustainable forests.
The logging and manufacturing processes are expected to conform to the
environmental regulations of the country of origin.

Hodder & Stoughton Ltd
A division of Hodder Headline
338 Euston Road
London NW1 3BH

Ye gentlemen of England that live at home at ease
Ah! Little do you think upon the dangers of the seas

– Martyn Parker ca. 1635

Chapter 1

Nicholas Renzi nodded to the man sharing with him the warmth of the log fire at the Angel posting-house and regarding his deep tan with suspicion. It was not an attribute often seen in England after a hard winter. Renzi was newly returned from tumultuous experiences on the other side of the world that had left him questioning his reason. He had sailed to New South Wales as a free settler, determined to forge a new life there, but it was not to be. And now, in just a little while, he would see Cecilia . . .

The ship that had brought him home had docked three days ago and, having signed off on the voyage, he and Thomas Kydd had made for Guildford. It had been cowardly of him, Renzi acknowledged, to have asked his friend to arrive first to prepare his sister for their sudden reappearance. Cecilia had nursed him through a deadly fever and touched his heart, but such was his respect for her that he had vowed to achieve something in the world before he made his feelings known to her, and had left without a word.

He had laboured long and hard to try to create an Arcadia

of his small landholding for Cecilia, in that raw land. Eventually Kydd had rescued him: he had suggested that Renzi make use of his education by devoting himself to the elucidation of natural philosophy from a new standpoint. Where Rousseau and his peers had pontificated from the comforts of rarefied academia, Renzi's studies would be rooted in the harsh reality of the wider world, which he had encountered at first hand in places as varied as the Caribbean and the vast South Seas, the sylvan quiet of Wiltshire and the alien starkness of Terra Australis.

He would distil his observations and experiences into a series of volumes on the extraordinary variety of human response to the imperatives of hunger and aggression, religion and security – all the threats and challenges that were the lot of man on earth . . . That would be an achievement indeed to lay before Cecilia and, it must be confessed, it was a prospect most congenial to himself.

This he would owe to Kydd, who had said he would employ his friend as secretary aboard whichever ship Kydd might captain.

For Renzi, performing this role – more of a clerk than anything – was a small price to pay for the freedom it bestowed on him; he had learned the tricks in Spanish Town long ago and knew that his duties would not be onerous. He had never set store by the petty vanities of rank and was glad to withdraw discreetly from the hurly-burly of tasking and discipline to be found on deck. Above all, he and Kydd, old friends, would continue to adventure together . . .

A boy brought the other man's pot of flip, beer spiked with rum, and looked doubtfully at Renzi, who shook his head and stared into the fire. It was all very well to have found for himself an agreeable position but the wider world was now filled with menace: the recently concluded hostilities had ended with the worst possible consequences. Prime Minister William Pitt had been replaced by Henry Addington, whose panicked response to the spiralling cost of the Revolutionary War was to trade away all of England's hard-won conquests round the world for peace at any price. And Napoleon Bonaparte, now squarely atop the pyramid of power in France, was energetically accruing the means to succeed in his greater goal: world dominance.

The King had recently delivered an unprecedented personal message to Parliament. In tones of bleak urgency, he had pointed to the First Consul's naked aggression since the peace – his occupation of Switzerland, his annexation of Savoy and more: there was little doubt now that Addington's gamble of appeasement had failed, and that England must brace herself to renew the struggle against the most powerful military force the world had ever seen.

Kydd, an experienced and distinguished naval officer, would not languish in unemployment for long and Renzi felt a stab of concern: might his friend be prevented from keeping his word on their arrangement?

He glanced at his pocket watch, his thoughts now on his imminent meeting. Cecilia's image had gone with him in his mind's eye on his long journey and stayed with him to be burnished and cherished: soon he would face its reality. He drew a long breath.

Kydd's mother handled the capacious muff of kangaroo skin dubiously; its warm, fox-red fur divided pleasingly to an underlying soft dark grey – but might not other ladies disdain it as an inferior substitute for fine pine marten?

'T' catch 'em boundin' along, Ma, it's so divertin' t' see!

They hop – like this!' To the consternation of the house-maid, Kydd performed a creditable imitation of a kangaroo's leap.

'Do behave y'self, son,' his mother scolded, but today Kydd could do little wrong. 'Have y' not given thought, dear,' she continued, in quite another tone, 'that now you've achieved so much an' all it might be a prime time t' think about settlin' down? Take a pretty wife an' sport wi' y'r little ones – I saw some fine cottages on the Godalming road as might suit . . .' But her son was clearly not in the mood to listen.

The commotion of his arrival began to subside a little as the rest of the knick-knacks expected from a voyage of ten thousand miles were distributed. His father, now completely blind, felt the lustrous polish of a Cape walking-stick fash-ioned from walrus bone and exotic wood as Kydd presented Cecilia with a little box, which contained a single rock. 'That, sis, y' may not buy, even in London f'r a thousan' guineas!' he said impressively.

Cecilia examined it quietly.

'It's fr'm the very furthest part o' the world. Any further an' there's jus' empty sea to th' South Pole – th' very end of everythin'.' He had pocketed the cool blue-grey shard when Renzi and he had gone ashore for a final time in the unspeak-ably remote Van Diemen's Land.

'It's – it's very nice,' Cecilia said, in a small voice, her eyes averted. 'You did promise me something of your strange land in the letter, Thomas,' she said, 'I do hope the voyage wasn't too . . . vexing for you.'

Kydd knew she was referring to his captaincy of a convict ship and murmured an appropriate reply, but he was alarmed by her manner. This was not the spirited sister he had known and loved since childhood: there was a subdued grief in her taut, pale face that disturbed him. 'Cec—'

'Thomas, do come and see the school. It's doing so well now,' she said, sounding brittle, and retrieved the key from behind the door. Without another word they left the room and crossed the tiny quadrangle to enter a classroom.

For a space she faced away from him, and Kydd's stomach tightened.

'T-Thomas,' she began, then lifted her head and held his eyes. 'Dear Thomas . . . I – I want you to know that I – I'm so very sorry that I failed you . . .' Her hands worked nervously. Her head drooped. 'You – you trusted me, with your d-dearest friend. And I let him wander out and be lost . . .'

'Wha—? Cec, you mean Nicholas?'

'Dear brother, whatever you say, I – failed you. It's no use.' She buried her face in her hands and struggled for control. 'I – I was so tired . . .'

Kydd reeled. He had sworn secrecy about Renzi's feelings for his sister and the logic that had impelled his friend to sever connection with her. They had prepared a story together to cover Renzi's disappearance: it had better be believable. He took his sister's hands and looked into her stricken face. 'Cecilia, I have t' tell ye – Nicholas lives.'

She froze, searching his eyes, her fingers digging painfully into his own.

'He's not lost, he – he straggled away, intellect all ahoo, y' see.' It seemed such a paltry tale and he cursed yet again the foolish logic that had denied her the solace of just one letter from Renzi.

'He was, er, taken in an' attended f'r a long time, an' is now much recovered,' he ended awkwardly.

'You know this?'

Kydd swallowed. 'I heard about Nicholas in Deptford an' hurried to him. Cec, you'll be seein' him soon. He's on his way!'

'May I know who took him in?' she continued, in the same level voice.

This was not going to plan. 'Oh, er, a parcel o' nuns or such,' he said uncomfortably. 'They said as how they didn't want thanks. Th' savin' o' souls was reward enough.'

'So he's now recovered, yet was never, in all that time, able to pen a letter to me?'

Kydd mumbled something, but she cut in, 'He tells *you* – he confides in his friend – but not me?' A shadow passed across her features. She stiffened and drew back. 'Pray don't hold my feelings to account, Thomas. If you are sworn to discretion then who am I to strain your loyalties?'

'Cec, it's not as ye're sayin'—'

'Do you think me a fool?' she said icily. 'If he's taken up with some doxy the least he can do is to oblige me with a polite note.'

'Cec!'

'No! I'm strong enough! I can bear it! It's just that – I'm disappointed in Nicholas. Such base behaviour, only to be expected of – of—'

Her composure was crumbling and Kydd was in a turmoil. Where *did* his loyalties lie? The words fell out of him. 'Th' truth, then, sis, an' ye may not like it.'

Now there was no going back. She waited, rigid.

'Ye have t' understand, Cec, that Nicholas is not like y' common sort o' cove. He has a rare enough headpiece.'

'Go on.'

'An' at times it leads him into strange notions.' She did not stir. 'Er, very strange.' There was no help for it: she would have to know everything. 'He – he cares f'r you, sis,' Kydd said. 'He told me so himself, "I own before ye this day that Cecilia is dearer t' me than I c'n say." This he said t' me in Van Diemen's Land.'

She stared at him, eyes wide, hands at her mouth. 'He was *there* with you? Then what . . . ?'

'Y' see, Cec, while he was abed wi' the fever he was thinkin'. Of you, sis. An' he feels as it would be improper for him t' make it known t' ye without he has achieved somethin' in th' world, somethin' he c'n lay before ye an' be worthy of y'r attention. So he ships out f'r New South Wales as a settler, thinkin' t' set up an estate in th' bush by his own hands. But I reckon he's no taut hand at y'r diggin' an' ploughin', an' he lost his fortune and reason toilin' away at his turnips.'

Kydd took a deep breath. 'I offered him passage home. Now he'll come t' sea wi' me an' work on an ethnical book. It's all a mort too deep f'r me, but when it's published, I'll wager ye'll hear from him then.'

Cecilia swayed, only a slight tremor betraying her feelings.

Kydd went on anxiously, 'He made me swear not t' tell a soul – an' it would go ill wi' me, y' understand, Cec, should he feel I'd betrayed his trust.'

'Nicholas – the dear, dear man!' she breathed.

'We conjured up th' story, sis, as would see ye satisfied in th' particulars, but . . .' He tailed off uncertainly.

'Thomas! I *do* understand! It's more than I could ever . . .' A shuddering sigh escaped her and she threw her arms round him. 'Dear brother, you were so right to tell me. He shall keep his secret, and only when he's ready . . .'

'Why, it's Mr Renzi. Just as y' said, Thomas!' Mrs Kydd was clearly much pleased by Renzi's reappearance and ushered him into the room. His eyes found Cecilia's, then dropped.

'Why, Nicholas, you are so thin,' Cecilia said teasingly, 'And your complexion – anyone might think you one of Thomas's island savages.' She crossed to him and kissed him quickly on both cheeks.

Renzi stood rigid, then pecked her in return, his face set. She drew away but held his eyes, asking sweetly, 'I'm so grateful to the nuns who ministered to you. What was their order? I believe we should thank them properly for their mercies to our dear brother restored to us.'

'Oh, er, that won't be necessary,' Renzi said stiffly. 'You may be assured that every expression of gratitude has been extended, dear sister.'

'Then a small gift, a token – I will sew it myself,' she insisted.

Kydd coughed meaningfully, then grunted, 'Leave him be, Cec. Tell us *your* news, if y' please.'

She tossed her head. 'Why, nothing that might stand with your exciting adventures.' She sighed. 'Only last week—'

'Oh dear!'

'What is it, Mama?'

'I've jus' this minute remembered.' Mrs Kydd rose and went to the sewing cupboard. 'I have it here somewhere – now, where did I put it?'

'Put what, pray?'

'Oh, a letter f'r Thomas. From London, th' navy, I think.' She rummaged away, oblivious to Kydd's keen attention. 'I thought I'd better put it away safely until – ah, yes, here it is.'

Kydd took it quickly. From the fouled anchor cipher on its face it *was* from the Admiralty. He flashed a look of triumph at Renzi and hastened to open it, his eyes devouring the words.

'The King . . . orders-in-council . . . you are required and directed . . .' Too excited to take in details, he raced to the end where, sure enough, he saw the hurried but unmistakable signature of the First Lord of the Admiralty – but no mention of a ship, a command.

Renzi stood by the mantelpiece, watching Kydd with a half-smile. 'Nicholas, what do ye make o' this?' Kydd handed him the letter. 'I should go t' Plymouth, not London?'

Renzi studied it coolly. 'By this you may know that your days of unalloyed leisure on half-pay are now summarily concluded and you are, once again, to be an active sea officer. If I catch the implication correctly, Lord St Vincent has knowledge of your far voyaging and therefore is not sanguine as to your immediate availability for service. He directs you, however, to repair at once to Plymouth where, no doubt, the admiral will be pleased to employ you as he sees fit.' He frowned. 'Yet within there is no mention of the nature of your employment. I rather fancy you should be prepared for whatever the Good Lord – or the admiral – provides.'

'Then we should clap on all sail an' set course f'r Plymouth, I believe!' exclaimed Kydd.

'Just so,' said Renzi, quietly.

Cecilia's face set. 'Nicholas, you're sadly indisposed. You need not go with Thomas.'

With infinite gentleness Renzi turned to her. 'Dear sister, but I do.'

'Come!' The voice from inside the admiral's office was deep and authoritative.

Kydd entered cautiously as the flag-lieutenant intoned, 'Commander Kydd, sir,' then left, closing the door soundlessly after him.

Admiral Lockwood looked up from his papers, appraised Kydd for some seconds, then rose from his desk. He was a big man and, in his gold lace, powerfully intimidating. 'Mr Kydd, I had been expecting you before now, sir. You're aware we'll be at war with Mr Bonaparte shortly?'

'Aye, sir,' Kydd replied respectfully. It was not the navy way to offer excuses, whatever their merit.

'Hmm. The Admiralty seems to think well enough of you. Desires me to give you early employment.' The gaze continued, considering, thoughtful.

'Now I *can* give you an immediate command –' Kydd's heart leapt '– in the Sea Fencibles. The whole coast from Exmouth to the Needles. Eighty miles, two hundred men. Immediate command! What do you say, sir?'

Kydd had no wish to take a passive role ashore with a body of enthusiastic amateurs and fishermen watching and waiting on the coast. He clung stubbornly to his hopes. 'Er, that's very generous in ye, sir, but I had hoped f'r a – f'r a command at sea, sir.'

'At sea!' Lockwood sighed. 'As we all do, Mr Kydd.' He came round the desk and stood before Kydd, legs braced as though on a quarterdeck. 'You've come at it rather late for that. For weeks now I've had all the harum-scarum young bloods to satisfy and you as commander and not a lieutenant . . .'

It had come back to haunt Kydd yet again: as a lieutenant he could be put instantly in any one of the large number of cutters, brigs, armed schooners and the like, but as a commander only a sloop as befitting his rank would do. 'Ah

– I have it. Command? How do you feel about taking *Brunswick*, seventy-four, to the Leeward Islands, hey?'

A two-decker ship-of-the-line to the Caribbean? Kydd was dumbstruck. Was the admiral jesting? Where was the joke? Then he realised: the only way he could captain a seventy-four was if she was going to sail *en flûte* – all her guns removed to make room for troops and stores, a glorified transport, which would effectively remove him from the scene of action. 'Sir, if y' please, I'd rather—'

'Yes, yes, I know you would, but almost everything that swims is in commission now. Don't suppose *Volcano*, fire-ship, appeals? No? Oh – I nearly forgot. *Eaglet!* Fine ship-sloop, in dock for repair. Confidentially, I rather fancy that, after the court meets, her present commander may find himself removed for hazarding his vessel and then we'll have to find somebody, hey?'

Kydd realised he had probably reached the end of the admiral's patience and, in any case, a ship-rigged sloop was an attractive proposition. 'That would suit me main well, sir, I thank—'

'But then again . . .' Lockwood seemed to have warmed to him. His brow furrowed and he faced Kydd directly now. 'It's only proper to tell you, *Eaglet* will be long in repair. There is one other in my gift – but again, to be fair, no one seems keen to take her. That's probably because she's a trifle odd in her particulars, foreign-built, Malta, I think. Now if you'd be—'

'Sir, her name's not – *Teazer?*'

'As it happens, yes. Do you know her?'

'Sir – *I'll take her!*'

Chapter 2

Kydd's face was sore from the spray whipping in with the dirty weather disputing every foot of *Teazer*'s progress, but it bore an ecstatic smile as he braced against the convulsive movements of his ship.

It would be some time before they could be sure of clearing the Cherbourg peninsula in this veering sou'-sou'-easterly, but it would be an easier beat as they bore up for Le Havre. Kydd couldn't help but reflect that it was passing strange to be navigating to raise the enemy coast directly where he had every intention of anchoring and making contact with the shore.

Earlier, he had eagerly claimed his ship and set about preparing her for sea. Then, in the midst of the work, urgent orders had been hurried over from the admiral's office: it was His Majesty's intention to respond to the repeated provocations of Napoleon Bonaparte by 'granting general reprisals against the ships, goods and subjects of the French Republic' within days. It would be the end of the fragile peace.

England planned to steal a march on Napoleon by declaring

war first and any vessels, like *Teazer*, that could be spared were dispatched urgently to the north coast of France to take off British subjects fleeing the country before the gates slammed shut.

Teazer had put to sea within hours, terribly short-handed and with few provisions, little in the way of charts and aids to navigation, and neither guns nor powder. In the race against time she had left behind her boatswain, master and others, including Renzi, who was ashore acquiring some arcane book.

Still, miraculously, Kydd was at sea, in his own ship – and it was *Teazer*, bound for war. What more could he ask of life?

Warmly, he recalled the welcome from the standing officers who had remained with the vessel all the time he had been far voyaging; Purchet the boatswain, Duckitt the gunner, Hurst the carpenter. And, in a time of the hottest press seen that age, the imperturbable quartermaster Poulden had appeared on the dockside, followed some hours later by the unmistakable bulk of Tobias Stirk, who was accompanied by another, younger seaman.

'Thought as how *Teazer* might need us, Mr Kydd,' Stirk had said, with a wicked grin, and pushed forward the young man. 'An' has ye need of a fine topman as c'n hand, reef 'n' steer, fit t' ship aboard the barky?'

Kydd had grunted and sized the man up; in his early twenties he had the build and direct gaze of a prime deep-water sailor. Of course he would take him – but why was the man wearing a grin from ear to ear that just wouldn't go away? Then it dawned on him. 'Ah! Do I see young Luke, b' chance?' The ship's boy of long ago in the Caribbean had grown and matured almost unrecognisably and was now Able Seaman Luke Calloway.

But as Stirk and Calloway were trusted men, Kydd had allowed them to go ashore and they were somewhere in the dockyard when he had sailed.

'Sir!' *Teazer*'s only other officer, Kydd's first lieutenant, Hodgson, pointed astern. Twisting in his streaming oilskins Kydd saw the dark outlines of questing scouting frigates emerge through the blurred grey horizon and then, behind them, lines of great ships stretching away into the distance.

He caught his breath: this was Cornwallis and the Channel Fleet – ships-of-the-line on their way to clamp a blockade on the great port of Brest and thereby deny Napoleon the advantage of having his major men-o'-war at sea on the outbreak of hostilities. The grey silhouettes firmed; the stately seventy-fours passed by one after another, only two reefs in their topsails to *Teazer*'s own close-reefed sail and disdaining to notice the little brig-sloop.

The grand vision disappeared slowly to leeward across their stern. Kydd felt a humbling sense of the responsibility they held, the devotion to duty that would keep them at sea in foul conditions until the war had been won or lost.

'We've made our offing, I believe,' Kydd threw at Hodgson. 'Stations t' stay ship.' Now was the time to put about to clear Start Point for the claw eastwards.

Kydd was grateful that a brig was more handy in stays than any ship-rigged vessel but he had to make the best of the situation caused by their hasty departure. 'You'll be boatswain, Mr Hodgson, an' I'll be the master.' As well as the absence of these vital two warrant officers, he had a raw and short-handed ship's company.

They wore round effectively, though, and set to for the thrash up-Channel. With no shortage of wind, they would be in position to seaward off Le Havre at dawn the next day.

However, Kydd was uncomfortably aware that nearly all his sea service had been in foreign waters; the boisterous and often ferocious conditions of these northerly islands were unfamiliar to him. The morning would tax his sea sense to the limit: all he had of the approaches was the small-scale private chart of Havre de Grâce of some forty years before, published by Jeffreys, with barely sufficient detail to warn of the hazards from shifting sandbanks in the estuary.

Daybreak brought relief as well as anxiety: they were off the French coast but where? Small craft scuttled past on their last voyages unthreatened by marauders and paid no attention to the brig offshore under easy sail. Kydd had ensured that no colours were aloft to provoke the French and assumed that if any of the vessels about him were English they would be doing the same.

He steadied his glass: rounded dark hills with cliffs here and there, the coast trending away sharply. From the pencilled notes on the old chart he realised that these were to the south of Le Havre and *Teazer* duly shaped course past them to the north. They would be up with their objective in hours.

His instructions were brief and plain. He was to make the closest approach conformable with safe navigation to Honfleur further up the river, then send a boat ashore to make contact with an agent whose name was not disclosed but whose challenge and reply were specified. It would mean the utmost caution and he would need to have men with a hand-lead in the chains as they entered the ten-mile-wide maze of channels and banks in the estuary.

They closed slowly with the land; the wind was now moderating and considerably more in the west. Then he spotted a sudden dropping away and receding of the coastline – it was the sign he had been looking for: this was where a great river met the sea, the mouth of the Seine. Paris, the centre for the storm that was sweeping the world into a climactic war, was just a hundred miles or so to the south-east.

In the forechains the leadsman began to intone his endless chant of the fathoms and deeps below: the Baie de Seine was a treacherous landscape of silted shallows and other hazards that could transform them into a shattered wreck, but that was not Kydd's greatest worry. As *Teazer* busily laid her course into the narrowing waters, who was to say that the peace had not ended while they were on passage, that behind the torpid quiet of the just visible fortifications ahead soldiers were not casting loose their guns and waiting for the little brig to glide past?

The firming heights of Cap de la Hève loomed on the north bank of the estuary; the chart noted the position closer in of the Fort de Sainte-Adresse, which lay squat atop the summit of its own mount, but their entry provoked no sudden warlike activity. The huddle and sprawl of a large town at its foot would be the main port of Havre de Grâce; their duty was to pass on, to lie off the ancient village of Honfleur on the opposite bank and make contact with the shore.

Uneasily Kydd conned the ship in. His chart was at pains to point out the menace of the Gambe d'Amfard, a sprawling, miles-long bank that dried at low water into hard-packed sand, lying squarely across the entrance. He glanced over the side: the turbid waters of the Seine slid past, murky and impenetrable.

He straightened and caught Hodgson looking at him gravely, others round the deck were still and watching. If the venture ended in failure there was no one to blame but the captain.

Kydd began to look for little rills and flurries in the pattern of wavelets out of synchrony with their neighbours, the betraying indications of shoaling waters. A deep-laden cargo vessel was making its way up-river and Kydd fell in to follow, carefully noting its track. A passing half-decked chaloupe came close to their stern and the man at the tiller hailed them incomprehensibly; but his friendly wave reassured Kydd as they passed the batteries into the confines of the river mouth.

Honfleur was five miles inside the entrance, a drab cluster of dwellings round a point of land. Kydd sniffed the wind: it was still unsettled, veering further, but if it went too far into the west they stood to be embayed or worse. 'Stand by, forrard!' he snapped.

He turned to the set-faced Hodgson. 'Take th' jolly-boat an' four men. There'll be one in th' character of an agent looking f'r us somewhere in th' town.' He moved closer, out of earshot of the others, and muttered, 'Challenge is *"peur"*, reply *"dégoût"*, Mr Hodgson.'

'S-sir? *Purr* and *day-goo*?' the lieutenant asked hesitantly.

'That's "fear" an' "loathin'" in the Frenchy tongue,' Kydd said impatiently.

'Ah, I see, sir. Fear and loathing – yes, sir.'

'*Peur* and *dégoût*, if y' please!'

'*Purr* and *day-goo*. Aye aye, sir!'

Kydd smothered his irritability: it had not been so long ago that he was equally ignorant of French, and if the agent was wise allowances would be made for uncultured Englishmen.

'And, sir,' Hodgson held himself with pathetic dignity, 'perhaps it were best that I shift out of uniform while ashore?'

Kydd hesitated. 'Er, I think not. How will th' agent sight ye as a naval officer else?' He refrained from mentioning that in uniform it was less likely Hodgson would be mistaken for a spy.

It was unsettling to order another into danger, particularly the harmless and well-meaning Hodgson, who had been almost fawning in his gratitude to be aboard – he had spent the last five years on the beach – but there was no other with the authority. 'Send th' boat back wi' the agent. We'll keep the rest o' the boats manned ready to ship th' refugees as y' sends 'em.' Kydd stood back while Hodgson called for volunteers. There were none: *Teazer* had yet to acquire that sturdy interdependence within her ship's company that would develop into a battlefield trust, and even the most ignorant could see the danger. Kydd picked the only names he could remember, 'Harman, Joseph,' then pointed at a nearby pair, 'an' you two.' Later the rest would find themselves manning the other boats.

In deference to the unknown tide condition the anchor went down a quarter-mile offshore and *Teazer* swung immediately to face up-river, a disquieting measure of the strength of current. 'Ye may leave now, Mr Hodgson,' Kydd said encouragingly. 'Red weft at th' main is y'r recall.'

The little boat leant jauntily under a single spritsail, bobbing through the hurrying waves in a series of thumps of spray. It disappeared round the headland to the small port beyond, leaving Kydd under a pall of apprehension, now the rush and excitement had settled to danger and worry.

It seemed an age before the jolly-boat hove into view; the busy river still had no apparent interest in the anchored brig with no colours and the boat wove tightly through the other vessels. Hodgson was not in it but a dark-featured man with an intense expression boarded quickly and hurried to Kydd.

'*M'sieur le capitaine?*' he said in a low, nervous voice. '*Nous devons nous déplacer rapidement!'* Then, glancing about, he exclaimed, *'C'est la guerre! Le tyran a choisi de se déplacer contre l'Angleterre!'*

Kydd went cold, and the agent continued. Napoleon had suddenly declared war himself on the pretext that Britain had not ceded Malta under the terms of the 1801 treaty. The news was not yet public but dispatches were being sent even now all over France – and the worst was that, contrary to the rules of war and common humanity, the First Consul had ordered the instant arrest on the same day of every citizen of Britain, including civilians, on French soil.

It could be days, hours or the next minute that the orders came, and when the origin of the unknown brig off Honfleur was revealed the guns would open fire. They were inside the ring of forts and in full view: the time to leave was now. But ashore there were desperate people who had made a frantic dash to the coast. Their only hope was *Teazer*. Kydd could not just depart.

'Every boat in th' water. We're not leavin' 'em to Boney,' he yelled, and challenged the seamen with his eyes. 'Do ye wish t' see the ladies taken b' the French soldiers? An' th' gentlemen cast in chokey?' There were growls of unease, but they came forward.

'Well done, y' sons o' Neptune,' Kydd said heartily, 'There's those who'll fin' reason t' bless ye tonight.'

The first boat returned. The sight of the packed mass of forlorn, wind-whipped creatures brought mutterings of sympathy from those still aboard who helped them over the side, but Kydd did not want to waste time in introductions and waited apart.

Poulden dealt manfully with a tearful hysteric while the

gunner took the brunt of a tirade from a foppish young blade. An animated babble replaced *Teazer*'s disciplined quiet until the first passengers were shooed below at the sight of the cutter coming with others. More arrived, including a tearful woman who had been separated from her husband, and an older man with a strong countenance who looked about watchfully as he boarded.

How much more time would they be granted? A muffled crump sounded ominously from across the estuary, answered almost immediately from the Ficfleur battery further up the river. A horrified lull in the chatter on deck was followed by excited speculation, then alarm as another thud was heard. This time the ball could be seen, the distant plume of its first touch followed by an increasing series of smaller ones as it reached out towards them.

'Send up th' signal weft,' Kydd ordered. There was no longer any doubt about French intentions: the news had got through and they must now know of *Teazer*'s origins. 'Be damned to it!' he said hotly, 'Hoist th' ensign, if y' please.' They would go out under their true colours. 'Hands t' unmoor ship.' There was every prospect of the situation turning into a shambles; so many were away in the boats still, yet he needed men to bring in the anchor, others to loose sail.

'Silence on deck!' he roared at the milling crowd, as more boatloads arrived in a rush.

Where was the damned jolly-boat? Was Hodgson having difficulties disengaging from the other frantic refugees who, no doubt, had arrived? His mind shied away from the memory of a similar plight in Guadeloupe and he tried to focus on the present. One more thud, then another – shots from cannon ranging on them. Distances over sea were deceptive for land-based gunners but sooner or later they would find the range and then the whole battery would open up on them.

He needed time to think: most forts faced the wrong way to be a serious menace at this stage but that didn't mean *Teazer* was safe. Any warship hearing gunfire and coming to investigate would end their escape before it began.

A ball skipped and bounced not more than a hundred yards away to screams of fright from those who had never been under fire before. Kydd knew they had to go – but should he wait for Hodgson? Send someone back for him? There was still no sign of the jolly-boat but to put to sea now would condemn both the officer and the four seamen with him to capture and incarceration – or worse. Could he bear to have this on his conscience?

In a whirl of feeling and duty he made the decision to leave.

He lifted his face to sniff the wind again; it would dictate how *Teazer* should unmoor and win the open sea. Then he realised that while he had worried over other things the wind had shifted westwards and diminished – the arc of navigability for a square-rigged vessel was closing. Already their entry track was barred to them; more mid-channel and tightly close-hauled on the larboard tack was the only way out – and be damned to the half-tide banks.

He sent a hand forward to set axe to cable as others loosed sail on the fore alone. Tide-rode and therefore facing upstream, *Teazer* began rapidly to make sternway, and under the pressure of full sails on the fore, and a naked mainmast together with opposite helm, she wore neatly around until able to set loose at the fore, take up close-hauled – and proceed seaward.

A ripple grew under her forefoot: they were making way

at two or three knots, and with the current from the great river this was increasing to a respectable speed. They had a chance. Kydd trained his glass on the fortifications. They seemed to have been caught unready by *Teazer*'s smart pirouette and were silent, but the penalty for making mid-stream was that they were opening the bearing of the closer Villerville guns – and shortening the range for those on the opposite bank.

It would be a near thing; Kydd shied at the mental image of Hodgson and his seamen watching hopelessly as they left but he needed to concentrate on the sea surface ahead for any betraying cross-current and tried not to notice the renewed activity of the cannon. The fall of most shot could not be seen but several balls came close enough to bring on a fresh chorus of shrieks; he bellowed orders that the decks be cleared, all passengers driven below. It would give them no real protection but at least they would be out of sight of the gunfire – and *Teazer*'s commander.

Poulden took several sailors and urged the passengers down the main-hatchway; a lazy dark stippling in the sea to larboard forced Kydd to order the helm up to pay off to leeward and skirt the unknown danger. Suddenly there was an avalanche of crumps from the far shore; they were losing patience with the little brig that was evidently winning through to freedom. But would the artillery officer in charge of this remote coastal battery be experienced enough to direct the aim with deadly effectiveness?

More sinister rippling appeared ahead; *Teazer* bore away a few points further to leeward. More guns sounded.

The last of the people were being shooed below, and in an unreal tableau, as though it happened at half the speed, Kydd saw a well-dressed lady take the rope at the hatchway and her arm disappear. She stared at the stump in bewilderment. Then the blood came, splashing on her dress and down the hatchway ladder. She crumpled to the deck.

Chaos broke out: some tried to force passage down the hatchway as others sought to escape the madness below. The fop tore himself free and beseeched Kydd to surrender; the man with the strong features snarled at him. It may have been just a lucky shot but who were these folk to appreciate that? Kydd reflected grimly.

Others joined in a relentless assault on his attention and his concentration slipped. With a discordant bumping *Teazer* took the ground and slewed to a stop. Sail was instantly brailed up but, with a sick feeling, Kydd knew his alternatives were few.

As far as he could tell they had gone aground on the southern edge of the Gambe d'Amfard tidal bank. The critical question was, what was the state of the tide? Would they float off on the flow or end hard and fast on the ebb?

He looked about helplessly. Virtually every vessel in the estuary had vanished at the sound of guns, the last scuttling away up-river as he watched. The battery rumbled another salvo and he felt the wind of at least one ball. It was now only a matter of time. Was there *anything* at all? And had he the right to risk civilian lives in the saving of a ship-of-war? Did his duty to his country extend to this? If only Renzi was by his side – but he was on his own.

'T' me! All Teazers lay aft at once, d' ye hear?' he roared against the bedlam. Frightened seamen obeyed hurriedly, probably expecting an abandon-ship order.

Kydd became aware that the strong-featured man had joined him. 'Captain Massey,' he said simply. 'How can I help ye?'

After just a moment's pause, Kydd said, 'That's right good in ye, sir. I've lost m' only l'tenant and if you'd . . .' It was breathtaking gall but in the next instant HMS *Teazer* had a full post-captain as her new temporary first lieutenant, in token of which Kydd gave him his own cocked hat as a symbol of authority. Together they turned to face the seamen as Kydd gave out his orders, ones that only he with his intimate knowledge of *Teazer* was able to give, and ones that were her only chance of breaking out to the open sea.

In any other circumstance the usual course would be to lighten ship, jettison guns and water, anything that would reduce their draught, even by inches. But *Teazer* had not yet taken in her guns and stores and was as light as she would get. The next move would normally be to lay out a kedge anchor and warp off into deep water but he had neither the men nor the considerable time it would take for that.

And time was the critical factor. As if to underline the urgency another ripple of sullen thuds sounded from across the water, and seconds later balls skipped past, ever closer. 'Long bowls,' Massey grunted, slitting his eyes to make out the distant forts. A weak sun had appeared with the lessening airs and there was glare on the water.

The last element of their predicament, however, was the hardest: the winds that had carried them on to the bank were necessarily foul for a reverse course – they could not sail off against the wind. And Kydd had noticed the ominous appearance of a number of small vessels from inside the port of Le Havre. These could only be one thing: inshore gunboats. A ship the size of *Teazer* should have no reason to fear them but with empty gun ports, hard and fast . . .

What Kydd had in mind was a common enough exercise in the Mediterranean, but would it work here?

From below, seamen hurried up with sweeps, special oars a full thirty feet long with squared-off loom and angled copper-tipped blades. At the same time the sweep ports, nine tiny square openings along each of the bulwarks, closed off with a discreet buckler, were made ready. The sweeps would be plied across the deck, their great leverage used to try to move *Teazer* off the sandbank.

'Clear th' decks!' Kydd roared, at those still milling about in fear. Through the clatter he called to Massey, 'If ye'd take the larboard, sir . . .' Then he bellowed, 'Every man t' an oar! Yes, sir, even you!' he bawled at the fop, who was dragged, bewildered, to his place. Three rowers to each sweep, an experienced seaman the furthest inboard, the other two any who could clutch an oar.

'Hey, now – that lad, ahoy!' Kydd called, to a frightened youngster. 'Down t' the galley, y' scamp, an' find the biggest pot an' spoon ye can.'

Kydd, at an oar himself, urged them on. The ungainly sweeps built up a slow rhythm against the unyielding water. Then, with a grumbling slither from beneath, it seemed that a miracle had happened and the brig was easing back into her element – in the teeth of the wind.

To the dissonant accompaniment of a cannon bombardment and the urgent, *ting-ting-ting clang* of a galley pot, His Majesty's Brig-sloop *Teazer* slid from the bank and gathered way sternwards and into open water. The sweeps were pulled in, the playful breeze obliged and *Teazer* slewed round to take the wind on her cheeks. With sails braced up sharp she made for the blessed sanctuary of the open sea.

After this, it seemed all the more unfair when Kydd saw the three gunboats squarely across their path, a fourth and fifth on their way to join them. Clearly someone had been puzzled by the lack of spirited response from *Teazer* and had spotted the empty gun ports. One or two gunboats she could handle but no more, not a group sufficient to surround and, from their bow cannon, slowly smash her into surrender.

It was senseless to go on: they could close the range at will and deliver accurate, aimed fire at the defenceless vessel with only one possible outcome. This could not be asked of innocent civilians and, sick at heart, Kydd went to the signal halliards and prepared to lower their colours.

'I'd belay that if I were you, Mr Kydd,' Massey said, and pointed to the bluff headland of Cap de la Hève. Kydd blinked in disbelief: there, like an avenging angel, an English man-o'-war had appeared, no doubt attracted by the sound of gunfire. He punched the air in exhilaration.

Chapter 3

'Aye, it was as who might say a tight-run thing,' Kydd
said, acknowledging with a raised glass the others round
him in the King's Arms. He flashed a private grin at Captain
Massey, who lifted his eyebrows drolly – their present coming
together in sociable recognition of their deliverance was due
to his generosity.

'I own, it's very heaven to be quit of that odious country.
And poor Mrs Lewis – is there any hope for her at all?' a
lady of mature years enquired.

'She is in the best of hands,' Massey said, and added that
she was at Stonehouse, the naval hospital.

Kydd looked out of the mullioned windows down into
Sutton Pool, the main port area of old Plymouth. It was
packed with vessels of all description, fled from the sea at
the outbreak of war and now settling on the tidal mud; it
took little imagination to conceive of the economic and
human distress that all those idle ships would mean.

However, it was most agreeable to sit in the jolly atmosphere of the inn and let calm English voices and easy

laughter work on his spirits. The immediate perils were over: *Teazer* now lay in the Hamoaze, awaiting her turn for the dry-dock after her encounter with the sandbank. Her grateful passengers were soon to take coach for their homes in all parts of the kingdom, there, no doubt, to relate their fearsome tales.

A couple from an adjoining table came across. 'We must leave now, Captain,' the elderly gentleman said. 'You will know you have our eternal thanks – and we trust that your every endeavour in this new war will meet with the success it deserves.'

Others joined them. Pink-faced, Kydd accepted their effusions as he saw them to the door. In a chorus of farewells they were gone, leaving him alone with Massey. Kydd turned to him. 'I have t' thank ye, sir, for y'r kind assistance when—'

'Don't mention it, m'boy. What kind of shab would stand back and let you tackle such a shambles on your own!'

'But even so—'

'His Majesty will need every sea officer of merit at this time, Mr Kydd. I rather fancy it will be a much different war. The last was to contain the madness of a revolution. This is a naked snatching at empire. Bonaparte will not stop until he rules the world – and only us to stand in his way.'

Kydd nodded gravely. The dogs of war had been unleashed; destruction on all sides, misery and hunger would be the lot of many in the near future – but it was this self-same conflict that gave meaning to his professional existence, his ambitions and future. No other circumstance would see his country set him on the quarterdeck of his own ship, in a fine uniform to the undoubted admiration of the ladies.

'I shall notify their lordships of my presence in due course,'

Massey said affably, 'and you will no doubt be joining the select band of the Channel Gropers.'

'*Teazer* was fitting out when we put t' sea,' Kydd responded. 'I'm t' receive m' orders after we complete.' This was probably a deployment with Cornwallis's Channel Squadron off Brest.

'Yes,' Massey said slowly. 'But hold yourself ready for service anywhere in these waters. Our islands lie under as grave a threat as any in the last half a thousand years. No more Mediterranean sun for you, sir!'

At Kydd's awkward smile he added, 'And for prizes the Western Approaches can't be beat! All France's trade may be met in the chops of the Channel and on her coasts you shall have sport aplenty.' A look suspiciously like envy passed across his face before he continued, 'But of course you shall earn it – it's not for nothing that the English coast is accounted a graveyard of ships.'

'Yes, sir.'

'And a different kind of seamanship, navigation.'

'Sir.'

'You'll take care of yourself, then, Mr Kydd. Who knows when we'll see each other again?' He rose and held out his hand. 'Fare y' well, sir.'

Kydd resumed his seat and let the thoughts crowd in.

'Admiral Lockwood will see you now, sir.' Noiselessly the flag-lieutenant withdrew, leaving Kydd standing gravely.

'Ah.' Lockwood rose from his desk and bustled round to greet him warmly. 'Glad you could find the time, Kydd – I know how busy you must be, fitting for sea, but I like to know something of the officers under my command.'

Any kind of invitation from the port admiral was a

summons but what had caught Kydd's attention was the 'my'. So it was not to be the Channel Fleet and a humble part of the close blockade, rather some sort of detached command of his own. 'My honour, sir,' Kydd said carefully.

'Do sit,' Lockwood said, and returned to his desk.

Kydd took a chair quietly, sunlight from the tall windows warming him, the muted rumble of George Street traffic reaching him through the creeper-clad walls.

'*Teazer* did not suffer overmuch?' Lockwood said, as he hunted through his papers.

'But three days in dock only, Sir Reginald,' Kydd answered, aware that in any other circumstance he would be before a court of inquiry for touching ground in a King's ship. 'Two seamen hurt, an' a lady, I'm grieved t' say, has lost an arm.'

'Tut tut! It's always a damnably distressing matter when your civilian is caught up in our warring.'

'Aye, sir. Er, do ye have news o' my L'tenant Hodgson?'

Lockwood found what he was looking for and raised his head. 'No, but you should be aware that a Lieutenant Standish is anxious to take his place – asking for you by name, Mr Kydd. Do you have any objection to his appointment in lieu?'

'None, sir.' So Hodgson and the four seamen were still missing; the lieutenant would probably end up exchanged, but the unfortunate sailors would certainly spend the rest of the war incarcerated. As for his new lieutenant, he had never heard of him and could not guess at the reason for his request.

'Very well. So, let us assume your sloop will be ready for sea in the near future.' The admiral leant back and regarded Kydd. 'I'll tell you now, your locus of operations will be the Channel Approaches – specifically the coast from Weymouth to the Isles of Scilly, occasionally the Bristol Channel, and you shall have Plymouth as your base. Which, in course, means that you might wish to make arrangements for your family ashore here – you may sleep out of your ship while in Plymouth, Commander.'

'No family, sir,' Kydd said briefly.

The admiral nodded, then continued sternly, 'Now, you'll be interested in your war tasks. You should be disabused, sir, of the notion that you will be part of a great battle fleet ranging the seas. There will be no bloody Nile battles, no treasure convoys, and it will be others who will look to the Frenchy invasion flotillas.'

He paused, then eased his tone. 'There will be employment enough for your ship, Mr Kydd. The entrance to the Channel where our shipping converges for its final run is a magnet for every privateer that dares think to prey on our shipping. And in this part of the world the wild country and filthy state of our roads means that four-fifths of our trade must go by sea – defenceless little ships, tiding it out in some tiny harbour and hoping to get their hard-won cargo up-Channel to market. Not to mention our homeward-bound overseas trade worth uncounted millions. Should this suffer depredation then England stands in peril of starvation and bankruptcy.'

'I understand, sir,' Kydd said.

'Therefore your prime task is patrol. Clear the Soundings of any enemy privateers or warships, safeguard our sea lanes. Other matters must give best to this, Mr Kydd.'

'Other?'

'Come now, sir, I'm talking of dispatches, worthy passengers, uncommon freight – and the Revenue, of course.'

'Sir?'

Lockwood looked sharply at Kydd. 'Sir, I'm aware your service has been for the most part overseas—' He stopped, then continued evenly: 'His Majesty's Customs and Excise has every right to call upon us to bear assistance upon these coasts should they feel overborne by a band of armed smugglers or similar. Understood?'

'Sir.'

'Now, I say again that I would not have you lose sight of your main task for one moment, Mr Kydd.'

'Security o' the seas, sir.'

'Quite so. For this task you are appointed to a command that puts you out of the sight of your seniors, to make your own decisions as to deployment, engagements and so forth. This is a privilege, sir, that carries with it responsibilities – should you show yourself unworthy of it by your conduct then I shall have no hesitation in removing you. Do you understand me, sir?'

'I do, sir.'

'Very well. No doubt you will be acquainting yourself with navigation and its hazards in these home waters. I suggest you do the same soon for the other matters that must concern you.'

'I will, sir.'

The admiral leant back and smiled. 'But then, of course, you will have a splendid opportunity in the near future.'

'Sir?'

'I shall be holding a ball next month, which the officers of my command will be expected to attend. There will be every chance then for you to meet your fellow captains and conceivably learn much to your advantage.'

He rose. 'This I'll have you know, sir. Your contribution to the defence of these islands at this time stands in no way inferior to that of the Channel Fleet itself. If HMS *Teazer* and you, Mr Kydd, do your duty in a like manner to the other vessels under my flag I've no doubt about the final outcome of this present unpleasantness. Have you any questions?'

'None, sir.' Then he ventured, 'That is t' say, but one. Do ye have any objection to my shipping Mr Renzi as captain's clerk? He's as well—'

'You may ship Mother Giles if it gets you to sea the earlier,' Lockwood said, with a grim smile. 'Your orders will be with you soon. Good luck, Mr Kydd.'

So this was to be *Teazer*'s future: to face alone the predators that threatened, the storms and other hazards on this hard and rugged coast, relying only on himself, his ship's company, and the fine ship he had come to love – not in the forefront of a great battle fleet but with an equally vital mission.

Poulden brought the jolly-boat smartly alongside. The bowman hooked on and stood respectfully for Kydd to make his way forward and over *Teazer*'s bulwark as Purchet's silver call pealed importantly.

Kydd doffed his hat to the mate-of-the-watch. The etiquette of the Royal Navy was important to him, not so much for its colour and dignity, or even its flattering deference to himself as a captain, but more for its outward display of the calm and unshakeable self-confidence, rooted in centuries of victory, that lay at the centre of the navy's pride.

Purchet came across to Kydd. 'I'll need more hands t' tackle th' gammoning, sir, but she's all a-taunto, I believe.'

Kydd hesitated before he headed below; the view from where *Teazer* was moored, opposite the dockyard in the spacious length of the Tamar river, was tranquil, a garden landscape of England that matched his contentment.

He turned abruptly, but paused at the foot of the companionway. 'Mr Dowse,' he called.

'Aye, sir?' The master was tall, and had to stoop as he swung out of his cabin.

'Might I see ye f'r a moment?' They passed into the great cabin and Kydd removed a bundle of papers from his other easy chair, then offered it. 'Have ye had service in this part o' the world, Mr Dowse?'

'I have that, sir. Not as you'd say recent, ye'd understand, but I know most o' the coastline hereabouts an' west t' the Longships. Can be tricky navigation, an' needs a lot o' respect.'

'That's as may be. Our orders will keep us here f'r the future, an' I mean t' know this coast well, Mr Dowse. Do ye find the best charts an' rutters, then let me know when ye're satisfied an' we'll go over 'em together.'

'I've sent out f'r the new Nories an' I has Hamilton Moore ready set by. F'r a Channel pilot he can't be beat.'

More discussion followed; Dowse was new to Kydd, but was of an age and had experience. His wisdom would be vital in a small ship like *Teazer*. 'Thank ye, we'll talk again before we sail.'

With a sigh, Kydd turned to his paperwork. Fielding, the purser, had carefully prepared his accounts for signature. Tysoe entered silently with coffee, his urbane manner in keeping with his station as the captain's servant and valet: Kydd congratulated himself yet again on having sent Stirk ashore to find his servant of *Teazer*'s last commission, whom he had necessarily had to let go when he had lost his ship with the brief peace of the Treaty of Amiens. Tysoe had raised no objections to quitting his situation with a local merchant and had slipped back easily into his old post.

Kydd completed a small number of papers but found he was restless. All over the ship men were working steadily on the age-old tasks of completing for sea and all he could find to do was address his interminable load of reports. There was one matter, however, far more agreeable to attend to.

He got up quickly, passed through the wardroom and emerged on to the broad mess-deck. There were surprised looks from the seamen but his hat was firmly under his arm, signifying an unofficial visit, and he crossed quickly to the tiny cabin adjoining the surgeon's that extended into a corner of the mess space.

It was new, the thin panels still with the fragrance of pine and with a green curtain for a door. It had cost him much debate with the dockyard but *Teazer* now had a cabin for her captain's clerk, an unheard-of luxury for one so humble. Kydd tapped politely. After some movement the curtain was drawn aside and a dishevelled head appeared.

'Nicholas, is this at all to y'r liking or . . .' Renzi pulled back inside and Kydd could see into the tiny compartment. The forward bulkhead was lined with books from top to bottom as was the opposite side, with each row laced securely; in the middle a very small desk stood complete with a gimballed lamp, and a cot was being triced up out of the way. It was definitely a one-person abode but if the sea-chest could be made to suffer duty as a chair, and movements were considered and deliberate, there were possibilities.

Renzi gave a rueful smile, grateful that his years of sea service had prepared him for the motion here. 'Should we meet with a seaway of spirit, it may require our stout boatswain to exercise his skills in the lashing of myself to my chair, but here I have my sanctum, thank you.'

The contrast with Kydd's own appointments could not have been greater, but this was all that Renzi had asked for.

'Er, should ye be squared away b' evening, m' friend, might we sup together?'

'Nicholas, dear friend, it does m' heart good t' see ye aboard.' The cabin was bathed in the cosy glow of twin candles on the table.

'*Your* chair, Nicholas,' Kydd said pointedly, pulling forward one of an identical pair of easy chairs.

Renzi gave a half-smile but said nothing.

'Who would've thought it?' Kydd went on. 'As ye'd remember, come aft through th' hawse an' all.'

Renzi murmured something and reclined, watching Kydd steadily.

Tysoe filled the glasses and left noiselessly. 'And now we're shipmates again,' Kydd concluded lamely.

Renzi unbent a little. 'This is true and I'm – gratified that it should be so, you must believe, brother.'

Kydd smiled broadly and handed him a glass. 'Then I give ye joy of our friendship, Nicholas!' He laughed. 'If it's t' be half o' what it was when we were afore the mast, then . . .'

'Yes, dear fellow. Here's a toast to those days and to that which lies ahead,' Renzi answered softly.

But Kydd realised in his heart that there was no going back. In the years since they had been foremast hands together too much had happened: his elevation to the majesty of command, Renzi's near-mortal fever and subsequent striving for significance in life – and all that had passed which had seen them both pitched into bloody combat and fear of their lives. They were both very different men. 'Aye, the old days.'

'More wine?' Renzi said politely. 'I can only applaud your taste in whites. This Portuguee is the gayest *vinho verde* this age.'

'Yes – that villain in town can't stand against Tysoe,' Kydd said shortly. 'Nicholas, may I know if ye've set course ready for y'r studies?'

'There may *be* no studies,' Renzi said, his face taut.

Kydd's stomach tightened. 'No studies?' Did Renzi see the great gulf in their situations as a sick reversal of the relationship that had gone before?

'We gull ourselves, brother,' Renzi said evenly, 'if we believe that the world will abide by our little conceit.' He shifted in his chair to face Kydd squarely. 'Consider: you are captain and therefore lord over all, and may direct every soul in this ship as you desire. But that is not the same as the unthinking obeisance of your redcoat or the sullen obedience of the serf in the field. Our Jack Tar famously has an independence of thought.'

He smiled thinly. 'You might set me at an eminence and sup with me. I may pace the quarterdeck in your company and be seen to step ashore with you. This is all within your gift – you are the captain. Yet what will our honest mariner perceive of it? And your new lieutenant –'

'T' arrive t'morrow.'

'– what construction will he place on our easy confidences, our privy conversations? Am I to be in the character of the captain's spy?'

Renzi was right, of course. The practicality of such a relationship was now in serious question: any interpretation might be placed on their conduct, from the bawdy to the felonious. Kydd's position was fast becoming untenable and it would seem he risked his ship for the sake of an innocent friendship.

'Nicholas.' To have the prospect of resolution to the loneliness of command snatched away was too much. 'Answer me true, m' friend. Are ye still resolved on y'r achievin' in the academic line? For the sake o' Cecilia?' he added carefully.

'Were it possible.'

'Then it shall be so, an' I'm settled on it,' Kydd said firmly. 'It is th' world's perceivin' only,' he added, 'an' the world must know how it is.'

He paused, framing his words with care. 'The truth is always th' safest. In society you shall be introduced as a learned gentleman, guest o' the captain, who is undertaking interestin' voyages f'r the sake of his studies, an' who f'r the sake of appearances in the navy takes on himself th' character of clerk – secretary – to th' captain.'

This should prove the easiest task: it would be assumed in the time-honoured way that Renzi would not, of course, be expected to sully his hands with the actual clerking, which would be handled by a lowly writer.

'In the navy, we take another tack, which is just as truthful. Here we have th' captain takin' pity on an old sea-friend, recoverin' from a mortal fever and takin' the sea cure, who spends his hours wi' books an' worthy writin'.' He paused for effect. 'I spoke with th' admiral,' he continued innocently, 'who told me directly that he sees no objection to Mr Renzi shippin' as clerk in *Teazer*.'

'You discussed my health?' Renzi said acidly.

'Not in s'many details,' Kydd replied, and hurriedly made much of Tysoe's reappearance signalling dinner. 'Rattlin' fine kidneys,' he offered, but Renzi ate in silence. Even a well-basted trout failed to elicit more than grunts and Kydd was troubled again. Was Renzi finding it impossible to accept their new relationship, or was he appalled by the difference in their living accommodation?

Kydd tried to brighten. 'Why, here we lie at anchor in Devonshire, th' foremost in the kingdom in the article of lamb. Our noble cook fails in his duty, th' rogue, if he cannot conjure some such meat.'

The cutlets were indeed moist and succulent and at last Renzi spoke. 'I can conceive of above a dozen matters that may yet prove insuperable rocks and shoals to our objectives.'

Kydd waited impatiently for the cloth to be drawn, allowing the appearance of a salver of marzipan fruits. 'Crafted y'r Chretien pear an' Monaco fig damn well, don't y' think!'

'Just so,' Renzi said, not to be distracted. 'You will want to be apprised of these preclusions, I believe.'

'If y' please, Nicholas.'

'The first is yourself, of course.'

Kydd held silent: there was no point in impatient prodding, for Renzi would logically tease out a problem until a solution emerged – or proved there was none.

'Very well. Some matters are readily evident, the chief of which is that this scheme requires I be placed in a condition of subjection to you, which the rule and custom of the sea demands shall be absolute. You shall be the highest, I . . . shall be the lowliest.'

'Nicholas! No! Not at all! I – I would not . . .' Kydd trailed off as the truth of his friend's words sank in.

'Exactly.' Renzi steepled his fingers. 'I journey on your fine bark as a member of her crew – if this were not so there would be no place for me. Therefore we must say that the Articles of War bear on me as scrupulously as upon the meanest of your ordinary seamen and with all the same force of law.'

Kydd made to interrupt but Renzi went on remorselessly: 'As captain you cannot make exception. It therefore necessarily demands that I should be obliged to make my obedience to you in all things.' There was a finality in his tone.

'Does this mean—'

'It does. But, my dear fellow, it is the most logical and consequently most amenable to sweet reason of all our difficulties.' A smile stole across his features. 'To leave issues unsaid, to be tacit and therefore at the mercy of a misapprehension is pusillanimous, thus I shall now be explicit.

'I do not see fit to vary my behaviour by one whit in this vessel. I see no reason why I should be obliged to. Do you?'

At a loss for words, Kydd merely mumbled something.

'I'm glad you agree, brother. Therefore from this time forth I shall render to the captain of HMS *Teazer* every mark of respect to his position in quite the same way as I allowed the captain of *Tenacious, Seaflower, Artemis . . .*'

'Aye, Nicholas,' said Kydd, meekly.

'Splendid! In the same vein I shall, of course, discharge the duty of captain's clerk in the fullest sense – any less would be an abrogation of the moral obligation that allows me victualling and passage in *Teazer*, as you must surely understand.'

'Y'r scruples do ye honour, m' friend – but this at least can be remedied. Cap'n's attendance take precedence: ye shall have a sidesman o' sorts, a writer, fr'm out of our company.' Even before he had finished the sentence he knew who. Luke Calloway, who had learnt his letters from Kydd himself in the Caribbean, would be completely trustworthy and on occasion would not object too strenuously to exchanging the holystone for the quill.

'But then we must attend to more stern questions.' These had to wait as the table was cleared and the brandy left, and the captain and his visitor had resumed their easy chairs.

'Stern questions?'

'Some might say of the first martial importance. You wish to be assured of the conduct of every member of your company in the event of a *rencontre* with the enemy, including that of myself. This is your right to ask, and I will answer similarly as before. As a member of *Teazer*'s crew I have my duties in time of battle as has everyone aboard.'

'As a clerk? This is—'

'As a clerk, my quarters are strictly specified, and these are to attend upon my captain on the quarterdeck for the period of the engagement. I shall be there – this you may believe,' he said softly.

Kydd looked away, overcome.

'And if *Teazer* faces an assault upon her decks from without, I shall not feel constrained in defending myself and my ship. This also you may believe.' He paused. 'But in any affair that calls for noble leadership, the drawn sword at the head of a band of warriors – there you will see that, by our own devising, we are denied. I am a clerk, not even a petty officer, and no man can thus be made to follow me. As bidden, I might carry a pike or haul on a rope but otherwise ...'

Renzi was laying down terms for his continued existence in *Teazer*, or more properly defining limitations that tidied things logically for his fine mind. Kydd hoped fervently that there would be no situation in the future that tested the logic too far.

He found the brandy and refreshed their glasses. 'Ye spoke of – preclusions, m' friend. Here is one!' Renzi regarded Kydd steadily. 'How can it be *right* f'r a man o' letters, sensible of th' finer points, t' be battened below like a ... like a common foremast jack?'

It was said.

To Kydd's relief Renzi eased his expression. 'Do you not remember my time of exile in the company of Neptune's gentlemen? It was my comfort then to remark it, that the conditions were to be borne as a necessary consequence of such a sentence.

'I now take notice that there is a similarity: in like manner to your monk or hermit scratching away in his cell in his sublime pursuit of truth and beauty, there are conditions contingent on the situation that may have to be endured as price for the final object. Should I not have the felicity of voyaging in *Teazer* then I fear my purse would not withstand an alternative course, and therefore I humbly accept what is so agreeably at hand.

'Fear not, dear fellow, I have years at sea that will inure me and, besides, this time I have a *sanctum sancti* where at any time I may take refuge to allow my thoughts to run unchecked – I need not point out to you that the keeping of sea watches now, mercifully, will be a memory for me.'

'That's well said, Nicholas – but you, er, will need t' talk out y'r ideas, try out some words or so . . .'

'Indeed I will. We shall promenade the decks in deep discussion – as the disposition of the ship allows, of course – and should you be at leisure of an evening it would gratify me beyond words to dispute with you on the eternal verities. Yet . . .' Kydd's soaring hopes hung suspended '. . . we both have calls upon our time. It were more apt to the situation should we both inhabit our different worlds for the normal rush of events and perhaps rely otherwise on the well-tried rules of politeness – which places so much value on invitation, rather than crass assumptions as to the liberty of the individual to receive.'

Kydd smiled inwardly. This was no more than Renzi securing to himself the ability to disappear into his 'sanctum' when he desired to. 'By all means, Nicholas. Er, might I know y'r station f'r messin' . . . ?'

It was a delicate point. The need for a captain to keep his cabin and table clear for ship's business was unspoken, and therefore a standing arrangement for dining *à deux* was not in question. This had now been dealt with, but where Renzi took his victuals had considerable social significance. A lowly clerk in a brig-sloop could usually expect the open mess-decks; it was only in weightier vessels that the captain's clerk would rank as a cockpit officer and berth in the gunroom.

'I have been led to believe that steerage will be open to me.' This was the open area below bounded on both sides by cabins and aft by the captain's quarters. It would be where the first lieutenant would hold court over the lesser officers – the master, surgeon and purser. The gunner, boatswain and carpenter had their own cabins forward.

'Why, this does seem a fine thing we've achieved this night,' Kydd enthused, raising his glass. 'Here's t' our success!'

Renzi gave an odd smile. 'As it will rise or fall by the caprice of your own ship's company,' he murmured.

'Aye. We'll find a way, Nicholas, never fear. So, let's drink.'

An apologetic knock on the door sounded clear. 'Come!' Kydd called.

It was the mate-of-the-watch. 'Sir, we have Lieutenant Standish here come t' join.' Behind him a figure loomed. Both streamed water; rain must have swept in unnoticed on the anchorage as they dined.

'L'tenant Standish? I hadn't thought ye'd join afore—'

'Sir. M' apologies and duty but I've been afire to be aboard since I heard I'm to be appointed.' His figure was large but indistinct in the darker steerage. 'Ah, I'm sorry, sir, I didn't know you'd got company.'

'Oh – that's no matter, Mr Standish. I'd like ye t' meet Mr

Renzi. He's a learned gentleman who's takin' berth with us th' better to further his ethnical studies. In th' character of captain's clerk, as it were.'

Standish looked mystified from one to the other, but Renzi got quickly to his feet. He inclined his head to the newcomer, then turned to Kydd and said civilly, 'I do thank you for your politeness and entertainment, sir, but must now return below. Good night.'

'Y' see, sir?' Duckitt held out a horny palm. In it was a tiny pyramid of harsh dark grey particles, the early-morning light picking out in curious detail the little grains, smaller than any peppercorn. 'This is y' new cylinder powder – throws a ball jus' the same range wi' a third less charge,' he said.

'Or a third further if y' charge is th' same,' Kydd retorted, but his curiosity was piqued. It was seldom he came across the naked powder: guns were served with it sewn safely inside cartridges of serge or flannel to be rammed home out of sight, and priming powder had a different grain size.

'Ah, well, as t' that, sir, ye must know that it's an Admiralty order as we takes aboard twenty per centum fewer barrels.' A sceptical look appeared on the hovering boatswain's face, which disappeared at Kydd's sharp glance. 'And, o' course ye'd be aware we gets less anyways, bein' Channel duties only.'

'Are ye sayin', Mr Duckitt,' Kydd snapped, 'that we must land the powder we now has aboard?'

'Not all of it, sir. We keeps a mort o' White LG for close-in work an' salutin'. For th' rest it's all Red LG powder, best corned an' glazed, charge a third y'r shot weight and a half f'r carronades, one fourth for double-shottin'. It's all there in m' orders jus' received.'

It would take time to discharge from their magazine,

cramped into the after end of the hold. Then there was the swaying inboard of the lethal copper-banded barrels from the low red-flagged powder-barges, no doubt only now beginning their slow creep down from the magazines further upstream. 'Very well. I'd have wished t' know of this afore now,' Kydd growled.

Purchet turned anxiously. 'Shall I rouse out th' larbowlines below now, sir?'

'No, no, Mr Purchet, th' forenoon will do. Let 'em lie.' The thought of breakfast was cheering.

As he turned to go below he saw Standish emerge on deck, ready dressed for the day against Kydd's shirt and breeches.

'Sir – a very good morning to you!'

'Oh – er, thank 'ee.' He had asked that his new first lieutenant present himself in the morning. Clearly the man had taken him literally and was prepared for the morning watch, which started at four. 'I had expected ye later. Has all y' dunnage been brought aboard?'

'It has, sir – all stowed and put to rights. Cabin stores coming aboard this afternoon.' He glanced up into *Teazer*'s bare masts. 'If we're to get to sea this age it were better I begin my duties directly,' he said briskly.

Kydd paused. Was this an implied slight at *Teazer*'s untidy state or the sign of a zealous officer? 'It does ye credit, Mr Standish, but there's time enough f'r that. Shall we take breakfast together at all?' he added firmly. There was no reason why he should be cheated of his own repast and it would give him proper sight of the man for the first time.

'Why, thank you, sir.' Standish seemed genuinely flattered and followed Kydd respectfully to the great cabin.

'Another f'r breakfast, Tysoe,' Kydd warned. His own meal was ready laid at one end of the polished table – wiggs, dainty

47

breakfast pastries, and sweet jelly, quiddany of plums, in a plain jar, the coffee pot steaming gently. 'Well, Mr Standish, the sun's not yet over the foreyard but I'm t' welcome ye into *Teazer*, I believe.'

Tysoe brought napery and cutlery and set another place.

'Pleased indeed to be aboard, sir. You'll understand that to be idle when your country stands in peril sits ill with me.' Standish was well built, his strong features darkly handsome, hair tied back neatly in a queue, like Kydd's, but with a studied carelessness to the curly locks in front.

Kydd helped himself to one of the wiggs, added a curl of butter and a liberal spread of the conserve, then asked casually, 'Tell me, sir, may I know why y' asked f'r *Teazer* especially?'

Standish seemed abashed. 'Oh, well, sir . . .' He put down his knife and paused, turning to face Kydd. 'Do you mind if I'm frank, sir?'

'Do fill an' stand on.' The man held himself well and Kydd was warming to his evident willingness.

'You'll be aware that you, sir, are not unknown in the service,' he began respectfully. 'Your boat action at the Nile has often been remarked and, dare I say it, your courage at Acre has yet to see its reward.'

'That's kind in ye to say so.'

'I will be candid, sir. My last post was a ship-o'-the-line, and while a fine enough vessel, she was to join Cornwallis before Brest.' He went on earnestly, 'For an officer of aspiration this is, er, a slow route. A frigate berth is too much sought after to be in prospect – then I heard of L'tenant Hodgson's misfortune.'

Kydd nodded for him to continue.

'Sir, my reason for requesting *Teazer* – you'll pardon the direct speaking – is that I believe you to be an active and enterprising captain who will see his chance and seize it. In fine, sir, prospects of a distinguished action for all will be better served in *Teazer* than another.'

It was true that the only sure path to glory and promotion was distinction on the field of battle and subsequent recognition above one's peers. Standish had heard something of Kydd's history and had made a cool calculation that this captain would not hold back in the event of an engagement, so his chances were better for a bloody victory in *Teazer* than in a battleship on blockade duty.

'Thank ye f'r your frankness, Mr Standish. But it may be that within a short time th' Channel Fleet will meet the French an' their invasion fleet. Glory enough f'r all, I would say. Coffee?' The officer looked sincere and was clearly eager to be an active member of *Teazer*'s company. 'Tell, me, Mr Standish, have ye been fortunate in th' matter of actions?'

'I was at Copenhagen, sir, third o' the *Monarch*,' he said modestly, 'and was fourth in *Minotaur* when we cut out the *Prima* galley.'

This was experience enough. In Nelson's squadron during the bloody affair against the Danes, and before, in the fine exploit off Genoa that saw the difficult capture of the heavily manned vessel. 'Were ye in the boats?'

'I had the honour to command our pinnace on that occasion, yes, sir.'

This was no stripling learning his trade in a small vessel. Standish was going to be a distinct asset – if his other qualities were as creditable. 'Well, I hope *Teazer* c'n afford ye some entertainment in the future.'

'Thank you, sir. May I ask it – do we have our orders yet?'

'None yet, but Admiral Lockwood assures me we'll have 'em presently. Do help y'self to more wiggs.'

'If I might be allowed to make my excuses, sir, I feel I should make an early acquaintance with our watch and station bill.' Kydd noted the 'our' with satisfaction. 'If there is fault to be found I'm anxious it shall not be mine,' Standish added. He rose to leave, then hesitated. 'Did I hear aright, sir, that your friend, our learned gentleman –'

'Mr Renzi?'

'– is he not also in the nature of a – a clerk?'

Kydd allowed his expression to grow stern. 'In HMS *Teazer* he is captain's clerk, Mr Standish. He is b' way of being a retired sea officer and brings a deal of experience t' the post. You will find him of much value when he assists ye, as he will.'

'Aye aye, sir,' said Standish uncertainly.

It was while the powder hoy was alongside, and the ship in a state of suspended terror at the sight of the deadly barrels swaying through the air, that *Teazer*'s two midshipmen arrived. Awed by the tension they sensed in the manoeuvres around them, they stood bare-headed and nervous before a distracted Kydd.

'Andrews, sir,' squeaked the younger. His wispy appearance was not going to impress the seamen, Kydd reflected.

'Boyd, sir,' the other said stolidly.

'Ye're welcome aboard, gentlemen, but f'r now, clew up wi' Mr Prosser. That's him by th' forebitts. Say ye're to take station on him an' I'll attend to y' both later.' Prosser was *Teazer*'s only master's mate.

The lads trotted off and Kydd turned back to events. Purchet was in charge: his style was to give few orders and those quietly, forcing the party of men to a strained quiet in case they were missed, the boatswain's mate standing by meaningfully.

The morning wore on, and with the last of the powder aboard and securely in the magazine, the atmosphere eased. 'Carry on, if y' please, Mr Prosser,' Kydd said, and turned to go below.

At the bottom of the steps he nearly bumped into Standish. 'Ah, sir, do you have a few moments?' He was carrying a sheaf of papers, and in the subdued light of below-decks Kydd saw Renzi standing politely a few paces back.

He hesitated, caught between courtesy to his friend and a captain acknowledging a mere clerk in front of an officer, and compromised with a civil nod. The two officers went together to Kydd's cabin, leaving Renzi alone.

Standish spread out his papers: it was the watch and station bill and he had, no doubt with discreet hinting from Renzi, made sizeable inroads into the task. 'Two watches, I think you requested, sir,' he said, with businesslike vigour, smoothing out a larger paper made of two sheets pasted together. 'With a complement of eighty-two men in a brig this size I see no difficulty here, sir. I will stand watch opposite Mr Prosser and we will apportion the men to divisions in like wise.'

It was a good plan: both would see the same men every watch they would lead in detached service or for which they would take domestic responsibility.

Standish added, 'As to petty officers o' the tops and similar, as you have been to sea once with them I respectfully seek your opinion.' He handed over his list of stations for each seaman in the various manoeuvres that *Teazer* must perform; mooring ship, taking in sail, heaving up the anchors.

This showed a reassuring technical confidence. Discussion continued; mess numbers had been assigned and Standish had a useful suggestion about hammock markings and location.

It was always a tricky thing to find a man at night in the press of off-watch humanity below, and men did not take kindly to being clumsily awakened as the carpenter's crew or others were found and roused out.

'We stand eighteen short o' complement,' Kydd said – it was a nagging worry as they had to be fully prepared for war. 'I'm trusting t' snag some local men,' he added doubtfully. It was unlikely but not impossible: there must be a fair number of sailors thrown ashore from the crowds of coastal shipping he had seen lie idle on the mud in Plymouth. They might be glad of the security of a King's ship known to be on service only in home waters.

Standish left as the purser came for more signatures. Suddenly, from the deck above there was a bull roar. 'That pickerooning rascal in the foretop, ahoy! If you think to take your ease, sir, we can accommodate you – Mr Purchet?' It seemed *Teazer*'s new first lieutenant was losing no time in making his presence felt.

Teazer's orders arrived, and Kydd sought the solitude of his cabin to open them. There were no surprises: the whole coastline between Portland Bill and the Isles of Scilly would be his responsibility '. . . to cruise for the protection of trade of His Majesty's Subjects, particularly of the coasters passing that way, from any attempts of the Enemy's Cruisers, using your best endeavours to take and destroy all ships and vessels belonging to France which you may discover or be informed of . . .'

He was to call regularly at Falmouth, Fowey and other ports to acquire 'Intelligence, Orders or Letters', and further it seemed he should neglect no opportunity to procure men for His Majesty's Fleet who should then be borne on the

Supernumerary List for victuals until conveyed to the nearest regulating captain.

There was, however, no mention of Customs and Excise but if any trade or convoy in the Downs bound to the westward should eventuate he was to 'see them safely as far as their way may be with yours'.

All in all, it was eminently suited to *Teazer*'s qualities and vital to the country's survival. And it left full scope for a bold action against any enemy daring to cross her bows.

Kydd grunted in satisfaction, gathered up the papers and reviewed what had to be done now in the way of charts, victualling, manning. A small folded paper that he had overlooked slipped out. It was watermarked and of high quality and he opened it carefully. 'Admiral Sir Reginald and Lady Lockwood request the pleasure of the company of Commander Thomas Kydd at a June Ball . . . at the Long Room, Stonehouse . . .'

Kydd caught his breath. There was no escape, he must go, and if Standish were invited separately he must make sure he accepted as well. It would be his first formal occasion in home waters as captain of a ship and because of his long overseas service it was, as well, his first entry into proper English society on his own terms – the Guildford assemblies paled into insignificance beside this.

This was something for Renzi. He knew all the finer points, the way through the social quicksands and the subtleties of conversational byplay, the rules for bowing and scraping. Kydd's grasp of the fundamentals of politeness was adequate for the usual run of social events but if at this level he were to bring disgrace on *Teazer* with an unfortunate gaucherie . . .

Kydd stood up and was on the very point of passing the word for Mr Renzi when he stopped. How in the name of friendship could he summon Renzi to appear before him simply when it suited? It would risk alienating him and fundamentally affect their delicate arrangement; it was important for the future that Kydd find a way to achieve the same object in a manner that did not offend sensibilities.

Of course! In Renzi's very words – the rules of politeness, the value of invitation: 'Tysoe, do inform Mr Renzi that I request th' pleasure of his company when he is at liberty to do so . . .' As it was done in the best circles.

'M' friend, I'd take it kindly if ye'd give me a course t' steer in this matter.' Kydd handed over the invitation.

Annoyingly, Renzi did not display any particular admiration or surprise. He merely looked up and asked calmly, 'An invitation to a ball – is there an exceptional service you therefore wish of me?'

'I'm concerned t' put on a brave face f'r *Teazer*'s sake – that is, not t' appear th' drumble as it were. Y' understand, Nicholas?' Kydd said warily.

'I think I do,' Renzi said evenly. 'This ball. It is given by our admiral and to it will come all the officers under his command in order that he might make their social acquaintance and allow the same to discover each other's wit and shining parts.'

'Aye – this is what vexes me. Shall I be found wantin' in polite company? I've not attended a regular-goin' society ball in England. What is y'r advice, Nicholas? What c'n ye tell me of how to conduct m'self? What have I t' learn?'

'Dear fellow! You have the graces – polite conduct is the same in Nova Scotia, Malta and Plymouth. If you acquit yourself creditably there, then a mere ball . . . And be assured that as the captain of a ship you will not lack for admirers among the ladies and will command respect and attention from the gentlemen. I would not fear an ordeal.'

'That's kind in ye to say so, m' friend. So they'll take me f'r who I am?'

'You may be quite certain they will not,' Renzi said immediately. 'This is England and they will take you as they see you – an uncultured boor or salty son of Neptune. Your character will be fixed only as they perceive it.'

'But—'

'I will be clear. If the prescripts are not observed then, quite rightly, they will conclude that you are not of their ilk, their social persuasion, and would therefore not be comfortable in their company. In fine you would in mercy be excluded from their *inner* circle.'

Kydd remained stubbornly silent, but listened as Renzi continued, 'You would no doubt wish to exhibit the accomplishments of a gentleman in order not to frighten the ladies. Among these that you lack at the moment I might list dancing, cards and gallantry.'

'I'm said t' be light on m' feet and—'

Renzi looked at him kindly. 'On the matter of dancing, I dare say that you may well have been considered of the first rank, but I have to confide to you that those wretches the dancing masters, to secure their continued employment, are always inventing quantities of new dances. These you must surely hoist aboard, as unaccountably your female of the species sets inordinate store on their confident display. I would suggest some lessons without delay.'

'Cards? Ye know I'm no friend t' gamblin'.'

'Cards. Do you propose to spend the entire evening stepping it out with the ladies? This would surely be remarked upon. It would be much more the thing from time to time to sit at a table with your brother officers being amiable to the ladies at loo, *vingt-et-un* or some such. To hazard a shilling a hand would not be noticed.'

'Then m' gallantry . . .'

'Ah – gallantry. This is not so easily won and may be said to have as its main objective the reluctance of the lady to quit your enchanting company. The science you will find in the worthy tomes such as your Baldwin, and the art – the art you must discover for yourself at the first hand.'

'Baldwin?'

'My constant companion in youth, *The Polite Academy, or, School of Behaviour for Gentlemen*, which will repay you well in the studying. Now, if there is nothing else you desire of me I should return to my new acquaintance the Abbé Morelly, whose views on the origin of social ills is quite startling and – and interesting.'

'Please do, Nicholas!' Kydd said warmly, then caught himself and added, 'I find that ye're not t' be invited, m' friend. You should know this is not as I'd wish it . . .' He trailed off, embarrassed.

'No matter, brother,' Renzi said quietly. 'You have earned your right to enter in upon society – I seek quite another felicity.'

There was a warm softness on the evening air, a delightful early-summer exhilaration that added to Kydd's heightened senses. He tried to maintain a sombre countenance before Standish, who sat next to him in the hired diligence as they clipped along Durnford Street, but it was difficult; this was the night when he would discover if he had it within him to claim a place in high society.

They passed the last elegant houses and across an open

space to approach the curiously solitary single edifice of the Long Room: it was ablaze with light in every window, and the sight brought on in Kydd a fresh surge of excitement. They drew up before the stately entrance – flights of steps ascending each side of what was plainly the ballroom.

Handed down by a blank-faced driver, Kydd clapped on his hat and fumbled hastily for silver, aware of the gawping crowd standing about to see who was arriving in their finery. He turned and saw a young lieutenant in full-dress ceremonials approaching. 'Good evening, sir, and welcome to the ball. Might I . . . ?'

'Kydd. Commander Thomas Kydd, captain of *Teazer* sloop-o'-war.' He would not yet be known by sight, of course.

'If you would accompany me, sir, the admiral is receiving now.' There was a guilty thrill in being aware of the respect he was accorded by this flag-lieutenant and Kydd followed with his head held high. As a lesser mortal, Standish would have to wait.

His boat-cloak and hat were taken deftly in the small anteroom and after a nervous twitch at his cravat he stepped from the small foyer into noise, light and colour.

'Thank you, Flags. Ah, Kydd. Glad to see you, sir.' The admiral was in jovial mood, standing in the splendour of full-dress uniform, an intimidating figure. He turned to the two ladies who flanked him. 'My dear, Persephone, might I present Commander Kydd, now captain in one of my ships here? He's much talked about in the Mediterranean, you must believe.'

Kydd turned to the admiral's lady and bowed as elegantly as he could and was duly rewarded with a civil inclination of the head. 'I do hope you will enjoy this evening, Commander, I did have my fears of the weather,' she said loftily.

'An' I'm sure it will back westerly before sun-up, ma'am,' Kydd replied graciously. He was uncomfortably aware of straight-backed dignity and hard, appraising eyes. He tried to smile convincingly when he turned to the daughter.

There was a quick impression of a willowy figure in a filmy white high-waisted gown that bobbed decorously in response to his bow; when she rose, Kydd's eyes were met by amused hazel ones in a fashionably pale, patrician face. A neat gloved hand was extended elegantly.

'Miss L-Lockwood,' Kydd said, taking the hand. Renzi's polite words, learnt so laboriously, fled from his mind at the girl's cool beauty. 'M-my honour, er, is mine,' he stuttered.

'I do trust that you don't find England too dull after the Mediterranean, Mr Kydd – they do say that Naples is quite the most wicked city in the world.' The well-bred voice had an underlying gaiety that Kydd could not help responding to with a grin.

'Aye, there's sights in Naples would set ye –' Something warned him of Lady Lockwood's frosty stare and the admiral's frown and he concluded hastily '– that is t' say, we have Pompeii an' Herculano both rattlin' good places t' be.'

'Why, I shall certainly remember, should I ever have the good fortune to visit,' the daughter said demurely, but the laughter was still in her eyes. After a brief hesitation she withdrew her hand gently from Kydd's fingers.

The orchestra's subdued airs went almost unnoticed among the hubbub. While he waited for Standish to be received Kydd looked about him. The room was filled with laughter and noise, the occasional splash of military scarlet, and to Kydd the much more satisfying splendour of the blue, white and gold of the Royal Navy. Tiered chandeliers hung low from the lofty ceiling, shining brightly to set eyes and jewellery a-sparkle and lightly touching every lady with soft gold. He looked back: there were still some to be received but Standish was not among them – he had disappeared into the throng.

Kydd was alone. Glances were thrown in his direction but no one ventured to approach: he knew why – he had not been introduced to any other than the admiral's party and he was unknown. Purposefully, he strode into the room, neatly avoiding knots of people in just the same way as he would on the mess-deck in a seaway, clutching to his heart Renzi's strictures about politeness and genteel behaviour.

Then he found what he was searching for: a jolly-looking commander who was holding forth to a fellow officer and his shy-looking lady while controlling a champagne glass with practised ease. Kydd hovered until the reminiscence was concluded but before he could step forward the man turned to him. 'What cheer, m' lad? Are you here for the dancing or . . . ?'

'Oh, er, dancing would be capital fun,' Kydd said stiffly, then added, with a courtly bow, 'Commander Thomas Kydd o' *Teazer* sloop.'

'Well, Commander Thomas Kydd, first we must see ye squared away wi' a glass.' He signalled to a footman discreetly. 'Bazely, sir, Edmund Bazely out o' *Fenella* brig-sloop, and this unhappy mortal be Parlby o' the *Wyvern*.' The handshake was crisp, the glance keen. 'Are ye to be a Channel Groper, b' chance?'

Kydd loosened; the champagne was cool and heady and his trepidation was changing by degrees into an irresistible surge of excitement. 'Aye, so it seems, f'r my sins.'

'An' new to our charming Devonshire?'

'Too new, Mr Bazely. All m' service has been foreign since

– since I was a younker, an' I'm amazed at how I'm t' take aboard enough t' keep *Teazer* fr'm ornamentin' a rock one day.'

'All foreign? Ye're t' be reckoned lucky, Kydd. As a midshipman I can recollect mooning about in a seventy-four at Spithead and with no more sea service than a convoy to the Downs for all o' two years.' He mused for a moment, then recollected himself. 'But we have a whole evening looming ahead. If ye'll excuse us, Mrs Parlby, I want to introduce m' foreign friend here to some others.' As they moved slowly towards the side of the room he chuckled. 'No lady in tow – I take it from this ye have no ties, Kydd?'

'None.'

'Then where better to make your acquaintance wi' the female sex than tonight?' They reached a group of young ladies with fans fluttering, deep in excited gossip. They turned as one and fell silent as the two officers approached, fans stilled.

'Miss Robbins, Miss Amelia Wishart, Miss Emily Wishart, Miss Townley, might I present Commander Kydd?' Bazely said breezily. 'And be ye advised that he is captain o' the good ship *Teazer*, now lying in Plymouth shortly to sail against the enemy!

'Miss Townley is visiting from Falmouth,' he added amiably.

Kydd bowed to each, feeling their eyes on him as they bobbed in return; one bold, another shy, the others appraising. His mind scrambled to find something witty to say but he fell back on a feeble 'Y'r servant, ladies.'

'Mr Kydd, are you from these parts?' the bold-eyed Miss Robbins asked sweetly.

'Why, no, Miss Robbins, but I do hope t' make y'r closer acquaintance,' Kydd replied, but was taken aback when the young ladies fell into a sudden fit of smothered giggles.

· Bazely laughed. 'If ye'd excuse me, m' dears, I have to return. Do see my friend is tolerably entertained.'

Kydd took in their waiting faces and tried to think of conversation. 'Er, fine country is Devon,' he ventured. 'I've once been t' Falmouth, as pretty a place as ever I've seen.'

'But, Mr Kydd, Falmouth is in Cornwall.' Miss Robbins laughed.

'No, it is not,' Kydd said firmly.

They subsided, looking at him uncertainly. 'Not at all – Falmouth is in Antigua – the Caribbean,' he added, at their blank looks.

'Mr Kydd, you have the advantage over we stay-at-homes. Pray tell, have you seen the sugar grow? Is it in lumps ready for the picking or must we dig it up?'

It was not so difficult, the ladies showing such an interest, and so pleasantly was time passing that he nearly forgot his duty. 'Miss Amelia,' he enquired graciously, of the shyest and therefore presumably safest, 'c'n you find it in y'r heart t' reserve th' cotillion for m'self?'

Gratified, he watched alarm, then pleasure chase across her features. 'Why, sir, this is an honour,' she said, with a wide smile. A pity she was so diminutive – not like the admiral's daughter, who, he had noted, was nearly of a height with himself – but Miss Amelia had a charmingly cherubic face and he could not help swelling with pride at the image of the couple they must present.

A disturbance on the floor resolved into the master of ceremonies clearing a space about him and the hum of conversation grew to a noisy crescendo, then died away. 'M' lords, ladies 'n' gentlemen, pray take your partners – for a minuet.'

Kydd offered his arm: it had seemed so awkward prac-
tising in the great cabin of HMS *Teazer* with Renzi but now
it felt natural. It was to be expected that a stately minuet
would open the ball, but the dance's elaborate graces and
moves were too intimidating to consider until his confidence
strengthened, and they stood together on one side as the
lines formed. He nodded amiably to the one or two couples
that had seemed to notice him and glanced down at his young
lady: she smiled back sweetly and Kydd's spirits soared.

It seemed that the admiral's formidable wife was being led
out by his flag-lieutenant to open the dancing, and Kydd,
conscious of Miss Amelia's arm on his, sought conversation.
'A fine sight, y'r grand ball, is it not? Do ye have chance f'r
many?'

Her eyes grew wide. 'Oh, sir, I have come out only this
season,' she said, in a small voice that had Kydd bending to
hear.

'That's as may be – but I'll wager ye'll not want f'r admirers
in the future, Miss Amelia.'

The cotillion was announced: Kydd led her out with pride
and they joined the eightsome opposite a star-struck maiden
and her attentive beau, a young lieutenant who bowed respectfully to Kydd. He inclined his head civilly and the music
began.

Miss Amelia danced winsomely, her eyes always on him,
the more vigorous measures bringing a flush to her cheeks.
Kydd was sincerely regretful when it ended and he escorted
her gallantly back to her friends.

Somehow he found himself in the position of requesting
that Miss Robbins grant him the pleasure of the next dance,
which luckily turned out to be 'Gathering Peascods', a fashionable country dance that he had only recently acquired.

Between the changes Miss Robbins learnt that he was widely travelled, had been moderately fortunate in the matter of prize-money and was unmarried. Kydd was made aware that Miss Robbins was from a local family, much spoken of in banking, and lived in Buckfastleigh with her two younger sisters, single like herself.

There was no question but that this was the world he might now call his own. He was a gentleman and all now knew it! At the final chords he punctiliously accorded Miss Robbins the honours of the dance, then with her on his arm wended his way back to her chair.

Happy chatter swelled on all sides; he was conscious of the agreeable glitter of candlelight on his gold lace and epaulettes, the well-tailored sweep of his coat, and knew he must cut a figure of some distinction – it was time to widen his social connections.

He threaded his way through the crowded ballroom and headed for the upper floor, where there would be entertainment of a different sort – cards and conversation. At a glance he saw the tables with card-players and others politely attendant on them but also couples promenading, sociable groups and forlorn wallflowers.

'Mr Kydd, ahoy!' A remembered voice sounded effortlessly behind him and he wheeled round.

'Mr Bazely,' he acknowledged, and went over to the table. Curious eyes looked up as he approached.

'Mrs Watkins, Miss Susanna, this is Commander Kydd, come to see how prodigious well the ladies play in Devon. Do take a chair, sir,' he said, rising to his feet.

'May I know how the pot goes?' Kydd asked courteously, remaining standing.

'Why, four guineas, Mr Kydd,' one of the ladies simpered.

Sensing that Bazely would not be averse to respite, he replied sadly, 'Ah, a mort too deep f'r me, madam.' Turning to Bazely, he bowed and asked, 'But if you, sir, are at liberty t' speak with me of the country for a space, I'd be obliged.'

Bazely made his excuses and they sauntered off in search of the punch table. 'Your Mrs Watkins is a hard beat t' windward, Kydd,' he sighed gustily, 'Mr Watkins being a fiend for dancing and always absentin' himself,' he added, with a glimmer of a smile.

'Tell me,' Kydd asked, 'how do ye find service in these waters, if I might ask ye?'

With a shrewd glance Bazely said, 'For the learning of seamanship an' hard navigation it can't be beat. The coast to the sou'-west is poor, remote, devilishly rock-bound and a terror in a fresh blow.' He pondered for a moment. 'The folk live on fishing mostly, some coastal trading – and free trading, if they gets a chance.' Kydd knew this was a local euphemism for smuggling.

'So what sport's t' be had?'

'As it dares,' Bazely grunted. Now at the punch table he found glasses and poured liberally. 'Getting bold and saucy, y'r Johnny Crapaud. Sees his best chance is not b' comin' up agin Nelson an' his battleships but going after our trade. If he can choke it off, he has us beat. No trade, no gold t' pay for our war, no allies'll trust us. We'd be finished.'

The punch was refined and had none of the gaiety Kydd remembered from the Caribbean. 'But ye asked me how I find the service.' Bazely smiled. 'Aye, it has to be said I like it. No voyage too long, home vittles waiting at the end, entertainments t' be had, detached service so no big-fleet ways with a flagship always hanging out signals for ye – and doing a job as is saving the country.'

'True enough,' Kydd agreed.

'Come, now, Mr Fire-eater, should Boney make a sally you'll have all the diversion ye'd wish.'

'Why here you are, Mr Kydd,' a silvery voice cooed. 'For shame! Neglecting the company to talk sea things. I'm persuaded a gentleman should not so easily abandon the ladies.'

'Miss Lockwood! I stan' guilty as charged!' Kydd said, and offered his arm, his heart leaping with exultation. The admiral's daughter!

Chapter 4

'Help y'self to the Bath cakes, Nicholas – I did s' well last evenin' at supper.' Kydd stretched out in his chair. The morning bustle of a man-o'-war sounded from on deck but, gloriously, this was the concern of others.

'Then your appearance in Plymouthian society may be accounted a success?' Renzi asked. 'I did have my concerns for you in the article of gallantry, it being a science of no mean accomplishing.'

'All f'r nothing, m' friend. The ladies were most amiable an' I'm sanguine there's one or two would not hesitate t' throw out th' right signal t' come alongside should I haul into sight.'

Kydd's broad smile had Renzi smothering one of his own. 'Do I take it from this you find the experience . . . congenial?'

'Aye, ye do. It's – it's another world t' me, new discovered, an' I'm minded t' explore.'

'But for the time being you will be taking your good ship to war, I believe.'

Kydd flushed. 'M' duty is not in question, Nicholas. We

sail wi' the tide after midday. What I'm sayin' only is that if this is t' be m' future then I find it agreeable enough. We're t' expect some hands fr'm the Impress Service afore we sail,' he added briskly. 'This'll please Kit Standish.'

Their eighteen men shortfall translated to a one-in-four void in every watch and station; he was uncomfortably aware that the first lieutenant had found it necessary to spread the crew of two forward guns round the others to provide full gun-crews. The Impress Service would try its best, but after the hullabaloo of the hot press on the eve of the outbreak of war every true seaman still ashore would have long gone to ground.

Kydd finished his coffee – in hours *Teazer* would be making for the open sea. Out there the cold reality of war meant that the enemy was waiting to fall upon him and his ship without mercy, the extinction of them both a bounden duty. Was *Teazer* ready? Was *he*?

He nodded to Renzi. 'I think I'll take a turn about th' deck – pray do finish y'r breakfast.'

At two in the afternoon the signalling station at Mount Wise noted the departure of the brig-sloop *Teazer* as she passed Devil's Point outward bound through Plymouth Sound on her way to war. What they did not record was the hurry and confusion about her decks.

'M' compliments, an' ask Mr Standish t' come aft,' Kydd snapped at the midshipman messenger beside him. Battling *Teazer*'s exuberant motion Andrews staggered forward to the first lieutenant who was spluttering up at the foretopmen.

'Mr Standish, this will not do!' growled Kydd. Their first fight could well take place within hours and their sail-handling was pitiful. 'I see y'r captain o' the foretop does not seem t'

68

know how t' handle his men. We'll do it again, an' tell him he's to give up his post t' another unless he can pull 'em together – an' that directly.'

'Sir.'

'Only one bell f'r grog an' supper, then we go t' quarters to exercise gun crews until dusk.' He lowered his tone and continued grimly, 'We're not s' big we can wait until we're strong. Do ye bear down on 'em, if y' please.'

While they were exercising on a straight course south and safely out to sea, they were away from the coast and not performing their assigned task. Kydd kept the deck all afternoon. He knew that the sailors, so recently in the grog-shops and other entertainments of the port, would be cursing his name as they laboured. The occasional flash of sullen eyes showed from the pressed men – there had been only nine men and a boy sent out to *Teazer* before she sailed, all of questionable worth. There were so few of her company he knew and trusted.

When eight bells sounded at the beginning of the first dog-watch sail was shortened, and after a quick supper it was to the guns until the long summer evening came to a close, *Teazer*'s bow still to seaward. Kydd would not rest: one by one the seniors of the ship were summoned to the great cabin and, over a glass of claret, he queried them concerning the performance of their men, their strengths and prospects. It was not to be hurried, the intricate process of turning a collection of strangers into a strong team that would stand together through the worst that tempests and the enemy could bring. Kydd knew that any weaknesses would become apparent all too quickly under stress of weather or battle.

The following day broke with blue skies and a clear horizon; both watches went to exercise and at the noon grog issue

Kydd saw the signs he was looking for – the previously wary, defensive responses were giving way to confident chatter and easy laughter that spoke of a shared, challenging existence. This would firm later into a comradely trust and reliance.

Already, characters were emerging: the loud and over-bearing, the quiet and efficient, those who hung back leaving others to take the lead, the ones who made a noisy show with little effect, the eager, the apprehensive, the brash. His seniors would be picking up on them all and he in turn would be taking *their* measure – it was the age-old way of the sea, where the actions of an individual could directly affect them all.

In the early afternoon they wore about to reverse course back to Plymouth but Kydd was determined that his ship should take up her station without the smallest delay. When the misty, rolling Devon coast firmed again, there was only one decision to be made – with his home port at the mid-point of his patrol area, should he go up-Channel or down?

The weather was fair, seas slight with a useful breeze from the Atlantic. 'Mr Dowse to set us t' the westward, if y' please,' he ordered.

Ready or no, *Teazer* was going to war. For him, it would be a much different conflict from those he had experienced so far. There was no specific objective to be won, no foreign shores with exotic craft and unknown threats: it would be a challenge of sea-keeping and endurance that might explode at any time into a blazing fight that must be faced alone.

Kydd recognised the massive triangular rockface of the Great Mewstone, the eastern seamark of Plymouth Sound. That and the sprawling heights of Rame Head on the other side he knew from before, but then he had been a distracted captain about to set forth on his urgent mission to France.

70

Now his duty was to close with the land, to go against all the instincts of his years at sea and keep in with this hard, fractured coastline. There were other sail, some taking advantage of the flurries and downdraughts from the cliffs and appearing unconcerned at the hazards sternly advised in the chart and coast-pilot. No doubt they were local fishermen who had lived there all their lives.

Once past Penlee and Rame Head, the ten-mile sweep of Whitsand Bay opened up. Dowse moved closer. 'If'n we wants t' clear all dangers between here 'n' Looe, we keep th' Mewstone open o' Rame Head.'

Kydd noted the tone of careful advice: it would be easy for the master to slip into condescension or reserve and he needed this man's sea wisdom in these waters. 'Aye, then that's what we'll do, Mr Dowse,' he responded, and glancing astern he watched as the far-off dark rock slid obediently into alignment with the bluff face of Rame Head. With *Teazer* a good three miles offshore, this left a prudent distance to leeward in the brisk winds. Kydd relaxed a little: he and his sailing master would likely get along.

The early-summer sun was warm and beneficent; it set the green seas a-glitter and took the edge off the cool Atlantic winds. With *Teazer* eagerly taking the waves on her bow and held to a taut bowline, Kydd could not think of anywhere he would rather be. He gazed along the decks: his first lieutenant was standing forward, one foot on a carronade slide as he observed the topmen at work aloft; the watch-on-deck were busy tying off the lee lanniards as new rigging took up the strain. Purchet had a party of hands amidships sending up a fresh main topmast staysail, and Kydd knew that below the purser was issuing slops to the pressed men, with Renzi and young Calloway preparing the recast quarters bill.

Somewhere under their lee were the first tiny ports of Cornwall – Portwrinkle and Looe, then the remote smuggling nest of Polperro. This was quite different country from the softer hills of Devon and he was curious to set foot in it.

The afternoon wore on. The big bay curved outwards again and ended in precipitous headlands and steep rocky slopes. With a little more south in the wind Whitsand Bay could well be a trap – embayed, a square-rigged ship would not be able to beat out and would end impaled on those same rocks.

'Makin' good time, Mr Kydd – that's Fowey ahead, beyond th' inner point.' The visibility was excellent and Kydd lifted his telescope: presumably the port lay between the far headland, and the near landmass. He picked out the dark red of the oak-bark-tanned sails of inshore craft – but nowhere the pale sails of deeper-water vessels.

'Fowey? Then I believe we'll pay a visit, Mr Dowse.' Fowey – Dowse had pronounced it 'Foy' – was one of the Customs ports and well situated at the half-way point between Plymouth and the ocean-facing port of Falmouth. No doubt they would welcome a call from the navy and it was his duty to make himself known and check for orders.

'Mr Standish, we'll moor f'r the night – no liberty t' the hands, o' course.' There was no point in sending the men, so soon to sail, into temptation. 'I shall make m' call on th' authorities, an' I require ye to keep the ship at readiness t' sail.'

'Aye aye, sir,' Standish said crisply.

'An' find me a boat's crew o' trusties, if y' please.'

The busy rush of the waves of the open sea calmed as they passed within the lee of Gribbin Head, the looming far headland. 'Leavin' Punch Cross a cable's length berth – that's th' rocks yonder – until we c'n see the castle,' Dowse told

72

him. Kydd gratefully tucked away all such morsels of information at the back of his mind.

They glided through the narrow entrance and into the tranquillity of the inner harbour in the evening light and let go the anchor into the wide stretch of water that had opened up. A twinkle of lights began to appear in the small town opposite through the myriad masts of scores of ships.

'Nicholas, do ye wish t' step ashore or are books more to y'r taste?' said Kydd, as he changed from his comfortable but worn sea rig.

Renzi looked up. He had taken to reading in the easy chair by the light of the cabin window when Kydd was not at ship's business. This was more than agreeable to Kydd as now his cabin had lost its austere and lonely atmosphere and taken on the character of a friendly retreat, exactly as he had dared to imagine.

'When the Romans invaded these islands, brother, the native Britons who did not succumb to the blandishments of civilisation were driven to the remote fastnesses of Cornwall and Wales, there to rusticate in barbarian impunity. Thus we might account the natives here foreigners – or are *we*? I have a yen to discover the truth of the matter.'

'And add this t' your bag o' ethnical curiosities, I'd wager.'

'Just so,' Renzi agreed.

'Then I'd be obliged if ye'd keep sight o' the boat once we land – I've no notion how long I'll be.'

It was Stirk at the jolly-boat's tiller, Poulden at stroke, with Calloway opposite, and a midshipman at each of the two forward oars. Kydd gave the order to put off.

Andrews struggled with his big oar and tried his best to follow Poulden while the larger Boyd handled his strongly but with little sense of timing. Poulden leant into the strokes theatrically giving the youngsters every chance to keep with him as they made their way across the placid waters towards the town quay.

'Stay within hail, if y' please,' Kydd called down from the long stone wharf after he had disembarked. This left it up to Stirk to allow a small measure of freedom ashore for his crew but as Kydd and Renzi moved away he saw the boat shove off once again and savage growls floated back over the water. The trip back would be more seemly than the coming had been.

Nestled against steep hills, the town was compact and narrow. The main quay had substantial stone buildings, some medieval, to Renzi's delight, and all along the seafront a jumbled maze of small boat-builders, reeking fish quays and pokey alleyways met the eye. They were greeted with curious stares along the evening bustle of Fore Street – word would be going out already in the Fowey taverns that a King's ship had arrived.

The harbour commissioner's office was at the end of the quays, before the narrow road curved away up a steep slope. Inside, a single light showed. Renzi made his farewell and Kydd went up to the undistinguished door and knocked. A figure appeared, carrying a guttering candle. Before Kydd could say anything the man said gruffly, 'The brig-sloop – come to show y'self. Right?'

'Aye, sir. Commander Thomas Kydd, sloop *Teazer*, at y' service.' His bow was returned with an ill-natured grunt.

'As I've been waiting for ye!' he grumbled, beckoning Kydd into what appeared to be a musty waiting room illuminated by a pair of candles only. 'Brandy?'

'Are ye the harbour commissioner, sir?' Kydd asked.

'Port o' Fowey t' Lostwithiel an' all outports – Bibby by

74

name, *Mr* Bibby to you, Cap'n.' The spirit was poured in liberal measure.

'Might I know why ye've been waitin' for me?' Kydd said carefully.

Bibby snorted and settled further into a leather armchair. 'Ye were sighted in the offing afore y' bore up for Fowey – stands t' reason ye'll want to make y' number with me.' He gulped at his brandy. 'So, in course, I'm a-waiting here for ye.'

Kydd sipped – it was of the finest quality and quickly spread a delicious fire. 'I don't understand. Why—'

Bibby slammed down his glass. 'Then clap y' peepers on those! Y' see there?' he spluttered, gesturing out of the window into the dusk at the lights from the multitude of ships at anchor. 'We're all a-waiting! For you, Mr damn Kydd!'

Kydd coloured. 'I don't see—'

'War's been on wi' Boney for weeks now an' never a sight of a ship o' force as will give 'em the confidence t' put to sea! Where's the navy, Mr Kydd?'

'At sea, where it belongs. An' if I c'n remark it, where's the spirit as keeps a ship bailed up in harbour f'r fear of what's at sea?' Kydd came back.

Bibby paused, then went on gruffly, 'Ye're new on the coast. Let me give ye somethin' t' ponder. Here's a merchant captain, and he has a modest kind o' vessel, say no more'n four, five hunnerd tons. Like all, he's concerned to see his cargo safe t' port, as it says in his papers, but in this part o' the world he's not doin' it for a big tradin' company – no, sir, for in his hold is bulk an' goods from every little farm an' village around and about. Brought down b' pack-mule, ox-wagon and a man's back t' load aboard in the trust it'll get to the Cattewater, Falmouth, the big tradin' ports up-Channel.

'He sails wi' the tide – an' gets took right away by a

privateer. That's bad, but what's worse is that these folk o' the humble sort have put all their means into the cargo and now it's lost. No insurance – in time o' war it's ruinous expensive and they can't afford it. So they're done for, sir, quite finished. It may be the whole village is ruined. And the sailors from these parts, their loved 'uns 'll now be without a penny an' on the parish. The ship? She'll be on shares from the same parts, now all lost.

'So you're going down now t' the quay an' tellin' our merchant captain to his face as he's a cowardly knave for preservin' his ship when he knows as there's at least three o' the beasts out there?'

Kydd kept his tone even. 'There's three Frenchy privateers been sighted in these waters? Where was this'n exactly?'

'Well, three ships taken these last two days, stands t' reason. Anyways, one we know, we call the bugger Bloody Jacques on account he doesn't hesitate to murther sailors if'n he's vexed.'

'Then it's one privateer f'r certain only. And I've yet t' see a corsair stand against a man-o'-war in a fair fight, sir,' Kydd said stoutly. But a hundred and fifty miles of coastline defended by himself alone?

However, there was something he could do. He took a deep breath and said, 'An' so we'll have a convoy. I'm t' sail f'r Falmouth presently an' any who wishes may come – er, that is, only deep-water vessels desirous o' protection before joining their reg'lar Atlantic convoy there.'

This was going far beyond his orders, which called only for his assistance to existing convoys chancing through his area. Convoys were formed solely by flag-officers and were complex and troublesome to administer, with their printed instructions to masters, special signals and all the implications of claims of legal responsibility upon the Admiralty once a vessel was under the direction of an escort. By taking it on himself to declare a convoy he had thereby assumed personal responsibility for any vessel that suffered capture and in that case would most surely face the destruction of his career and financial ruin.

'I shall speak with th' masters in the morning, if ye'd be s' good as to pass the word,' Kydd said.

'Nicholas. I've declared a convoy,' Kydd mumbled, through his toast.

'Have you indeed, dear fellow?' Renzi replied, adding more cream to his coffee. 'Er, are you sure this is within the competence of your sloop commander, however eminent?'

Despite his anxiety Kydd felt suddenly joyful. At last! The decision might have been his but never more would he have to face one alone. 'Perhaps not, but can y' think of aught else as will stir 'em t' sea?'

'*Teazer* is a fine ship, but one escort?'

'I saw a cutter at moorings up-river off Bodinnick – she'll have only a l'tenant-in-command and thusly my junior. Shortly he'll hear that he's now t' sail under my orders.' She would help considerably but it would be little enough escort for the dozen or so deep-water vessels he could see at anchor. If they could get away to sea quickly, though, word of them would not reach the jackals on the other side of the Channel in time.

'So, would ye rouse out every hand aboard c'n drive a quill? I've some instructions f'r the convoy t' be copied, an' I mean to have 'em given out after I talk.' Kydd pushed back his plate and began jotting down his main points: a simple private identifying signal, instructions to be followed if attacked, elementary distress indicators. Vanes, wefts and other arcane features of a proper convoy were an impossibility, but should he consider the customary large numbers painted on each ship's quarter?

HMS *Teazer* led a streaming gaggle of vessels, all endeavouring eagerly to keep with her in the light winds, past the ruins of Polruan Castle and the ugly scatter of the Punch Cross rocks.

In the open sea, and with the rounded green-grey headland of the Gribbin to starboard, she hove to, allowing the convoy to assemble. Kydd's instructions had specified that *Teazer* would be in the van, with *Sparrow*, the cutter, taking the rear. Her elderly lieutenant had been indignant when prised from his comfortable berth and had pleaded lack of stores and water, but Kydd was having none of it and the little craft was now shepherding those at the rear out to sea.

The wind was light in this first hour after dawn. Kydd's plan was to make the safety of Falmouth harbour before dark but a dazzling glitter from an expanse of calm waters met him to seaward.

The light airs were fluky about Gribbin Head and Kydd shook out enough sail to ease away slightly. He looked back to check on *Sparrow* but she was still out of sight, and the narrow entrance was crowded with vessels issuing forth in an unholy scramble to be included in the convoy.

The little bay would soon be filled with jockeying ships, which in the slight breeze would have little steerage way, and before long there would be collisions. There was nothing for it but to set sail without delay. *Teazer* bore away in noble style as if conscious of her grand position as convoy leader.

An excited Andrews pointed high up to the rounded

summit of Gribbin Head where an unmistakable flutter of colour had appeared.

'Signal station, sir,' said Standish, smartly bringing up his glass.

Kydd's eyes, however, were on the ships crowding into the bay – there were scores. He swivelled round and squinted against the glare of the open sea. Now would be a sovereign opportunity for Bloody Jacques to fall upon the unformed herd and take his pick. It was fast turning into a nightmare.

'Can't seem to make 'em out,' Standish muttered, bracing his telescope tightly. They must have been perplexed to see the port suddenly empty of shipping and were probably wanting reassurance. A small thud and a lazy puff of gunsmoke drew attention to the hoist. But it hung limp and unreadable in the warm still airs.

'Hell's bloody bells!' Kydd snarled. There was no way he could conduct a conversation by crude flag signals at this juncture.

'God rot th' pratting lubbers for a—' He checked himself. 'We didn't see 'em, did we?' he bit off. 'Tell Prosser t' douse his "acknowledge" – keep it at th' dip.'

Standish gave a conspiratorial grin. 'Aye aye, sir!'

It was perfect weather for those ashore enjoying the splendid view of so many ships outward bound. The mists of the morning softened every colour; where sea met sky the green of the water graded imperceptibly into the higher blue through a broad band of haze, an intense paleness suffused by the sunlight.

'Take station astern, y' mumpin' lunatic!' Kydd roared, at an eager West Country lugger trying to pass them for the wider sea. His instruction to the convoy had been elementary: essentially a 'follow me' that even the most stupid could understand. He took off his hat and mopped his brow, aware that he was making a spectacle of himself, but not caring. The milling throng began to string out slowly and at last, in the rear, Kydd saw *Sparrow*, but she was not making much way in the calm air and was ineffectual in her task of whipping in the stragglers.

Indeed, *Teazer* found herself throwing out more and more sail; the zephyr that had seen them out of harbour was barely enough to keep up a walking pace. However, with Gribbin Head now past, and the wider expanse of St Austell Bay opening up abeam, they had but to weather Dodman Point and would then have a straight run to St Anthony's Head and Falmouth.

Apart from the insignificant inshore craft, the sea was mercifully clear of sail, but who could know, with the bright haze veiling the horizon? Looking back astern again Kydd saw a dismaying number of ships strung out faithfully following in his wake. By turns he was appalled and proud: the undisciplined rabble was as unlike a real convoy as it was possible to be but on the other hand he and his fine sloop had set the argosy on its way.

'How d'ye believe we're proceedin', Mr Dowse?' Kydd said.

Dowse's significant glance at the feathered dog-vane lifting languidly in the main-shrouds, followed by a measured stare at the even slope of the Dodman, was eloquent enough. 'I mislike that mist in the sun's eye, I do, sir. I'd like t' lay the Dodman at th' least two mile under our lee.'

'Very well, Mr Dowse.' The band of haze had broadened but, charged as it was with the new sun's splendour, Kydd had paid it little attention. But if this was a sea-fog it was unlike any he had seen – the dank, close ones of the Grand

Banks, the cool, welcome mists of the Mediterranean. Surely this summer haze should give no problem?

'Hoist "keep better station",' Kydd called to the pair at the signal halliards. *Sparrow* seemed to have recovered some of the sea breeze but was crossing about behind their flock to no apparent purpose. After a few minutes she drew back to the centre of the rear but it was clear they were going to get no reply: either the humble cutter did not possess a full set of signal bunting or her captain did not see why he should play big-fleet manoeuvres at Kydd's whim.

'Sir.' Dowse nodded meaningfully at the haze. It was broader and the luminous quality at its mid-part now had an unmistakable core, soft and virginal white.

Kydd glanced at the Dodman – St Austell Bay had swept round again to culminate in this historic point ahead, one of the major sea marks for generations of mariners over the centuries. It was now far closer: the menace of Gwineas Rocks to starboard showed stark and ugly – and the band of misty haze was wide enough now to touch the lower limb of the sun.

'Early summer, sir. In a southerly ye sometimes find as after it passes over th' cool seas it'll whip up a thick mist quick as ye'd like, specially if'n the wind veers more t' the west.'

The sun was now reduced to a pearlescent halo, the foot of the advancing mist clearly defined. Things had suddenly changed for the worse. Kydd glanced at the looming precipitous bluff. It was so unfair: another mile and they would have weathered the point but they would be overtaken by the rolling mist just as they reached the hazards to the south of the Dodman, the heavy tidal overfalls of the Bellows, stretching out for a mile or more into the Channel. To fall back from where they had come with his unwieldy armada in an impenetrable fog and a lee shore was impossible and a dash north for Mevagissey or one of the other tiny harbours marked on the chart was out of the question for a complete convoy.

Kydd bit his lip. He could not return; neither could he go on and chance that unseen currents and an onshore wind would draw *Teazer* and the convoy on to the deadly Bellows. Should he anchor and wait it out? That would risk his charges, who, expecting him to press on, might blunder about hopelessly looking for him.

The first cool wisps of the mist brushed his cheek. The world changed to a calm, enveloping, uniform white that left tiny dewdrops on his coat, and rendered nearby vessels diaphanous ghosts that disappeared. Kydd took a deep breath and made his decision. He was about to give the orders when he saw a still form standing back. 'Why, Mr Renzi, I didn't notice ye on deck before,' he said, distracted.

'You will anchor, I believe.'

'I never doubted it,' Kydd replied, nettled at Renzi's easy observation. Then he realised that the words were intended as a friendly contribution to the burden of decision-making and added, 'Aye, the greater risk is t' go on.'

He took a few paces forward. 'Mr Dowse, way off the ship. Mr Purchet, hands t' mooring ship. We'll wait it out.'

Their bower anchor splashed noisily into the calm and the wind died to a whisper. Dowse had previously recorded careful bearings of the shore and had now himself taken a cast of the lead and was inspecting the gravel and broken shells at its base.

A sepulchral *dong* from close astern was answered by their own bell, struck enthusiastically by a ship's boy. There was an occasional muffled crack of a swivel gun from a nervous vessel. Other sounds, near and distant, came flatly from all round them.

The mist swirled gently past as Kydd peered over the bulwarks. He could see the water was sliding along on its way aft equally on both sides; the tide was on the make and at her anchor *Teazer* was headed into it and therefore would be facing into the currents surging round the Dodman. They were as safe as it was possible to be in the circumstance and could only wait for the sun to burn off the mist.

It was little more than an hour later that the forms of vessels could be made out once more and the sun burst through. Kydd scanned about anxiously and his heart lurched as he saw that of the dense mass of ships that had followed him to sea there were only ten or fifteen left. Had they failed to notice him anchor? Had they drifted ashore? Been taken by a corsair in the fog?

'Such a practical race of sailors,' Renzi murmured.

'What?' Kydd said sharply.

'Why, I'm sure you've made notice that these vessels remaining are your deep-sea species only. The small fry, being local, have navigated clear and, inspired by your actions, have for a surety pressed on to Falmouth.'

His friend was right, of course, Kydd acknowledged grudgingly, then smiled. In brilliant sunshine and a strengthening breeze, what remained of the convoy won its anchors and rounded the Dodman. They took little more than an hour in the fine south-easterly to lay the dramatic Gull Rock to starboard, and by early afternoon they made Falmouth Bay.

Kydd, however, had no intention of going ashore at Falmouth and possibly having to make explanation, so he rounded to well off the entrance. His charges passed into the harbour, some with a jaunty hail of thanks. The cutter tacked about smartly and disappeared without ceremony.

It had been an experience but *Teazer* was accounting herself well in this, her first war cruise. 'Mr Standish, course south, an' all sail abroad. I mean t' clear the Manacles before dusk an' then we snug down f'r the night.'

'Aye aye, sir,' the first lieutenant confirmed. His orders were chalked on the watch-keeper's slate and *Teazer* shaped her course.

'Er – an' pipe hands t' supper with a double tot f'r all,' Kydd added. There was no reason by way of service custom for the generosity but he felt his little ship and her company had reached a milestone.

Dawn arrived overcast; the ship had stood off and on in the lee of the Lizard throughout the night and was now closing with the coast once more; the massive iron-grey granite of Black Head loomed.

There was nothing around but fishing craft and, in the distance, a shabby coastal ketch. Kydd decided to send the men to breakfast, then put about to press on westward. This would mean a closer acquaintance of that most evocative of all the sea marks of the south-west: the Lizard, the exact southerly tip of Great Britain and for most deep-ocean voyages the last of England the men saw on their way to war or adventure, fortune or death. It was, as well, the longed-for landfall for every returning ship running down the latitude of 49° 20' finally to raise the fabled headland and the waters of home.

Kydd had seen the Lizard several times, and each experience had been different – watching it emerge leaden and stolid from curtains of rain, or seeing it dappled dark and grey in the sunshine and sighted twenty miles away – but always with feeling and significance.

'Do ye lay us in with th' coast, Mr Dowse,' Kydd ordered. Curiosity was driving him to take a close-in sight of this famed place. 'Oh – younker,' he called to a rapt midshipman, 'my compliments t' Mr Renzi an' I'd be happy t' see him on deck.' He would never be forgiven if it were missed.

The master pursed his lips. 'Aye, sir. A board to the suth'ard will give us an offing of somethin' less'n a mile.'

'Thank ye,' Kydd said gravely. With the south-westerly strengthening it was a dead lee shore around the point and asking a lot of the master to approach. They stood away to the south until the last eastern headland was reached; beyond, the Atlantic swell crowding past the Lizard was resulting in ugly, tumbling seas that put *Teazer* into violent motion, the wind now with real strength in it, producing long white streaks downwind from the crests.

The land receded as the offing was made, then approached again after they went about on the other tack, the seas almost directly abeam causing the brig to roll deeply. 'Call down th' lookouts,' Kydd snapped. Even at forty feet, with the motion magnified by height, the situation for the men in the foretop would be dangerous and near unendurable.

Dowse pointed inshore where the sea met the land in a continuous band of explosions of white. 'Man-o'-war reef, the Quadrant yonder.' He indicated a cluster of dark rocks standing out to sea and in furious altercation with the waves. 'An' Lizard Point.'

There it was: the southernmost point of England and the place Kydd had always sighted before from the sanctity and safety of the quarterdeck of a ship-of-the-line. He clung to a weather shroud and took it all in, the abrupt thump of waves against the bow and a second later the stinging whip of spray leaving the taste of salt on his tongue.

They eased round to the north-west and into the sweeping curve of Mount's Bay, the last before the end of England. The scene was as dramatic as any Kydd had met at sea: completely open to the hardening south-westerly and long Atlantic swell piling in, the rugged coastline was a smother of white.

Kydd said nothing when he noticed the quartermaster was edging imperceptibly to seaward from the dead lee shore, but turned to the master. 'I think we'll give best t' this sou'-westerly, Mr Dowse. Is there any haven short o' Penzance to th' west'd?'

'None as we c'n use, sir – this is a hard piece o' coast.' He gazed thoughtfully at the busy seas hurrying shoreward. 'Porthleven? Opens t' the sou'-west. Nought else really, Mr Kydd.'

'Then Penzance it'll have t' be. Mr Boyd? Compliments t' Mr Standish an' I believe we'll send th' hands t' dinner after we moor there.' Most would prefer the comfort of a hot meal later than a scratch one now. The midshipman looked uncomfortable. 'Come, come, Mr Boyd, lively now!'

Reluctantly the lad released his grip and lurched to another handhold. Kydd realised that his order sending the boy below would probably condemn him to the seasickness he had so far manfully avoided. As *Teazer* leant closer to the wind to clear a small island Boyd slid down the canted deck to finish well soused in the scuppers.

The islet passed under their lee; a tiny scatter of houses huddled together under dark, precipitous cliffs at the head of a small patch of discoloured sand. Who lived in this impossibly remote place?

'Mullion Cove, sir – an' there?' Dowse had noticed a big,

three-masted lugger at anchor riding out the blow in the lee of the island, the only vessel they had sighted since the Lizard. No doubt all smaller local craft had scuttled off prudently to find a harbour.

'A wise man,' Kydd replied, but something niggled.

They plunged on. An indistinct hail came from forward, then Calloway hurried aft and touched his forehead shyly. 'Sir, I saw . . . over on th' land in them cottages . . .'

'Yes?'

'It were red, like. Fr'm the windows.' He trailed off, dropping his eyes.

Those nearby looked at each other in amusement, but Kydd knew Calloway from the past. His young eyes were probably the best in the ship. 'Tell me, if y' please,' he said kindly.

'Well, as we was passin' I saw somebody hold somethin' red out o' the window. An' as I watched, I swear, one b' one they all has red out o' their windows.' Doggedly he went on, 'An' then, sir, they all starts shakin' it, like.'

The amusement was open now, titters starting from the waisters who had fallen back to hear. 'I swear it, Mr Kydd!' Calloway blurted.

At a loss, Kydd looked about the little group on the quarterdeck. All averted their eyes, except Renzi. 'Ah, there is *one* conceivable explanation. Supposing our unlettered country-folk were to recognise us as a King's ship. Equally suppose that they have a guest, an unwelcome one, who holds them in deadly thrall from where he lies at anchor . . .'

'The lugger!'

'. . . how then should they signal their disquiet? A red flag of some sort for danger. I can see no other interpretation of such—'

'Helm a-lee!' Kydd bawled to the wheel. 'Luff 'n' touch

her – Mr Dowse, once we have th' sea-room we wear about an' return!'

In an instant the atmosphere aboard changed and activity became frenzied. Braces were manned by seamen slipping and sliding in the crazy bucketing as *Teazer* was sent clawing offshore as close to the wind as she could lie. Only when they were at a sufficient distance from the dangerous shore could they risk a turn inwards to the land.

Kydd's mind raced: a bloody engagement – in these conditions? It was preposterous but the logic of war demanded it. He was now sure in his own mind that the anonymous-looking fine-lined lugger was an enemy – and it was his duty to destroy him.

A dishevelled first lieutenant burst out on deck.

'Mr Standish, I believe we've surprised a Frenchy privateer an' I mean t' take him. We'll go t' quarters only when we have to, but I desire ye to bring th' ship to readiness now.'

'Aye aye, sir!' There was no mistaking the fierce gleam in the officer's eye.

Kydd took out his pocket telescope and trained it aft on the lugger, but the wild jerking made it near impossible to focus. Once he caught a dancing image of a vessel quite as big as their own, a long bowsprit, raked mizzen-mast and a line of closed gun ports the whole length of the ship.

He forced his mind to coolness: what were the elements in the equation? He had never seen a northern French privateer lugger, a Breton *chasse-marée* or others of this breed, but he had heard of their reputation for speed on the wind and the daring impudence of their captains. But no privateer worth his salt would take on a man-o'-war: their business and profit were in the taking of prizes, not the fighting of battles.

Kydd lifted the telescope and tried to steady it against a

shroud but the brisk thrumming thwarted his efforts and he lowered it in frustration. But by eye there was some movement aboard; someone must have correctly interpreted *Teazer*'s move as the precursor to a return and most likely they were now busy preparing a hot defence – with all the lugger's men sent to the guns.

'*Haaaands* to stations t' wear ship!' The manoeuvre of tacking was tighter but anything going wrong would result in their being blown rapidly ashore; even so, in wearing ship, the act of deliberately turning their backs to the wind this close inshore had its own dangers.

Kydd threw a final glance at the lugger. Held by his anchor directly into the wind there was sudden jerky activity at his prow. They were cutting the cable! Exactly at the moment the vessel swung free, a jib soared up from the long bowsprit and instantly caught the wind, slewing his bow round. Then sail appeared on all three masts together, evidence of a sizeable crew.

It was neatly done. The lugger was now under way close inshore, paralleling the coast – and thereby closing with *Teazer*. The realisation hit Kydd with a cold shock: they were going to have to fight in the open sea and any advantage they had at the guns would be nullified by the wild circumstances. What was the enemy thinking, to try conclusions in these conditions, when any victor would be unable to board and take their prize?

'Belay that!' he roared at the seamen ready at the braces. 'Stand down th' men, Mr Purchet.' The obvious course for the lugger was to throw over his helm at the right moment to take up on the other tack and, with the advantage of his fore-and-aft rig, slash straight out to where the close-hauled *Teazer* was striving desperately to get to seaward.

And then what? It was clear when he thought about it: the privateer needed only to bring about some little damage to their rigging and the weather would do the rest. In these winds the square-rigged *Teazer* would be driven out of control on to the white-lashed crags and be destroyed as utterly as if she had been cannonaded into ruin.

Kydd's grip on the shroud tightened. It had changed so quickly – and only one could see them through: *Teazer*'s captain. He raised his eyes and met Renzi's; his friend did not speak but gave a half-smile. Standish gazed hungrily at the oncoming lugger while the others about the deck watched silently.

They must hold their course seaward: the only question now was when to send the men to the guns – but with the leeward bulwarks so low and seas swirling aboard any pretence at serving a gun there was futile. On their lee side they were essentially defenceless.

The privateer gathered speed, rolling wickedly with the seas abeam but making good progress a half-mile closer inshore. Kydd allowed reluctant admiration for the unknown seaman in command of her: he must possess considerable local knowledge to feel so confident close to this grim coast.

Kydd decided that the men would go to the guns precisely when the privateer put down his helm to tack in their direction; he waited tensely for the lugger to find *Teazer* at the right angle for that sudden slash towards.

Minutes passed, and still the privateer held her course down the coast. 'The villain's making a run f'r it, Nicholas!'

Once again the situation had changed, but Kydd was beginning to appreciate his opponent's clear thinking: he had declined battle for good, practical reasons and was now using his lugger's superior rate of sailing to make off, using that local knowledge to stay close inshore, knowing his antagonist dared not do likewise.

'We're going after th' rascal.' *Teazer* eased away three points or so and no longer tight to the wind stretched out in fine style, on the same course parallel to the coast but further seaward. Kydd guessed the privateer's intention was to use his speed to pull far enough ahead to chance going about across their bows, then to escape seaward with no risk of battle damage to cut short his cruise.

It was a shrewd move – but there was one essential not within their control: the winds. *Teazer* was from the Mediterranean, the home of the savage *tramontana*, and with just a single reef in her topsails was handling the bluster with ease, her sturdy design well able to take the steeper seas close inshore. The lugger, on the other hand, was making heavy weather of it. With lugsails taut on all three masts, he had not attempted topsails, at the cost of his speed advantage.

The result was that *Teazer* was more than holding with the privateer and paced the vessel. The long sweep of Mount's Bay ahead ended suddenly at Penzance and as long as they could keep sail on, there would be a conclusion before the day was out.

It was an exhilarating charge along the white-streaked waves, rampaging towards the dour coastline, the lugger tapping every resource of knowledge about rock and shoal in keeping so close in with the shore, while *Teazer* kept tight watch far enough offshore to have warning of any sudden move and in prime position to intercept a break for the open sea.

Dowse pointed out the little settlements as they passed. Poldhu, Chyanvounder, Berepper and then Porthleven. Foreign-sounding, exotic and untouchably remote. A headland loomed, its steep grey crags half hidden in misty spume. Beyond, a beach all of a mile long stretched away with another, larger promontory at its end. Now, more than half-way to Penzance, was this where the attempt would be made?

As if in direct response to the thought Dowse gave a sudden shout. The aspect of the privateer was altering rapidly – he was making his move and it was to seaward. Kydd's stomach tightened. To serve a gun in the insane rolling was madness. Yet how else was he going to fight?

Then, without warning, every sail on the privateer disappeared and the bare-masted vessel fell back, still bows to sea, until it was just clear of the breakers rolling into the beach.

'Well, I'll be— He's thrown out an anchor, sir, an' hopes t' ride it out till dark!' Dowse said, in open admiration.

If in fact that *was* the intention, Kydd mused. He'd already led them on a merry dance. 'Mr Dowse, heave to, if y' please,' he ordered. It would give him time to think and for a short time preserve his superior position.

Lying awkwardly diagonal across the line of white-caps, *Teazer*'s motion changed from a deep rolling to a vicious whip as the waves passed at an angle down the pitching hull, making it difficult to concentrate. If the privateer—

Muffled shouts from forward – an urgent '*Man overboard!*' Kydd saw the fall of a sheet uncoil out to leeward and staggered to the side. At first he saw nothing but foam-streaked waves in vigorous progression towards the shore but then he made out a dark head against the foam and an arm clutching frantically at air, not five yards off.

It must have been a foremast hand caught by the sudden change of motion and pitched overboard. Kydd could not recognise him from the flailing shape but he was being carried by the waves' impetus ever further from his ship.

'Poor beggar!' Standish handed himself along to stand next to Kydd. But his eyes were on the enemy.

Kydd said nothing; his mind furiously reviewing his alternatives. 'Mr Purchet, secure a dan buoy to th' kedge cable and—'

'Sir! You're not proposing a rescue?'

'Why, yes, Mr Standish, o' course I am.'

Face set, Standish confronted Kydd. 'Sir, the lugger might take the opportunity to escape.'

'He might.'

'Sir, it is my duty to remind you that we are in the presence of the enemy – that man is as much a casualty of war as if he had fallen from a shot.'

The sailor was now several waves downwind and thrashing about in panic; like most seafarers, he could not swim.

What Standish had said was undeniable, but Kydd's plan would give the man a chance and still have them in some sort of position to—

More confused shouting came from forward, then a figure rose to the bulwarks and toppled into the sea. 'Get forrard an' find out what th' hell's goin' on,' Kydd snarled at Standish: with two in the water his plan was now in disarray – were they to be the first men to die in *Teazer*?

'Clear away th' cutter,' he bawled, at the gaping mainmast hands. It was the biggest boat they had and was secured up in its davits. 'Cut th' gripes away, damnit!' he shouted, as they fumbled with the ropes. This was a desperate throw – he would have the boat streamed off to leeward at the end of a line and hauled back bodily. If it capsized, the men could cling to it.

Standish worked his way aft, his face expressionless. 'Sir, I have to report that Midshipman Andrews took it upon him to cast himself in the sea in an attempt to save the man.'

'Four volunteers f'r the boat,' Kydd snapped, 'each with a lifeline t' a thwart.' What was the boy thinking, to take such a risk? It was madness, but a noble act for one so young.

It was a fearsome thing to set the cutter afloat with the rocketing rise and dizzying fall of the seas under their stern but at least this was in *Teazer*'s lee and temporary protection. The seaman was out of sight downwind, hidden by the driving combers, but the midshipman could occasionally be seen striking out manfully for him in the welter of seas.

'He's seen our boat,' Standish said coldly, watching the lugger. A jib was jerking up in the privateer and when it had taken the wind the other sail was smartly hoisted. Kydd refused to comment, obstinately watching the cutter as line was paid out and it drew near to Andrews.

'Sir! He's under way and going round our stern. We've lost him.'

Kydd glanced once at the lugger as it leant to the hammering south-westerly and made its escape, derisory yells coming faintly over the tumult accompanied by rude gestures from the *matelots* along the decks.

The privateer was still in sight, driving southwards towards France under all sail possible when the boat was hauled in, half full of water, with a soaked and subdued Andrews. The sailor had not been found.

'Will you follow him, do you think?' Renzi asked softly. Kydd had not seen his friend come up but now Standish had moved away and was standing apart, trying to catch the fast-disappearing lugger in his glass.

'Not today,' Kydd said quietly. It was over for the poor wretch who had reached out obediently to do his duty and found instead a lonely death. In an hour or so a dark shape would appear in the line of breakers at the sea's edge, carelessly rolled about by the swash of surf. They would retrieve it and give it a Christian burial in Penzance.

Kydd's eyes pricked: no matter that he had seen so many lose their lives following their profession of the sea – this had occurred on *Teazer*'s first commission in home waters and he as captain. Things could never be the same.

Feeling the need to be alone, he left Standish to lay *Teazer* to her anchor, went to his cabin, sprawled in his chair and stared moodily out of the stern windows. There was a soft knock at the door and Renzi appeared. 'Come in, old friend,' Kydd said. Renzi made his way cautiously to the other chair, the lively movement becoming more unpredictable as the ship felt her anchor.

'You would think it fatuous of me should I remark that the sea is a hard mistress.'

'Aye, I would.'

'Then—'

'But then, o' course, it doesn't stop it bein' true, Nicholas.' Kydd heaved a sigh and continued softly, 'It's just that – that . . .'

'"They that go down to the sea in ships . . ."' Renzi intoned softly.

'True as well.'

Renzi broke the moody silence. 'Is the Frenchman to be blamed, do you think?' he asked.

'No,' Kydd said decisively. 'He has his duty, an' that he's doing main well.' He levered himself upright. 'What takes m' interest is that not only does he shine in his nauticals but he knows too damn much of th' coast.'

He reflected for a moment, then said quietly, 'He's goin' t' be a right Tartar t' lay by the tail, m' friend.' Pensively he watched the shoreline come slowly into view as *Teazer* snubbed to her anchor, then added, 'But we must account him our pigeon right enough. What will I do, Nicholas?'

There was no reply, and when Kydd turned to look at Renzi he saw his friend with his arms folded, regarding him gravely. 'I find I must refuse to answer,' Renzi said finally.

'You . . . ?'

'Let me be more explicit. Do you accept the undoubted fact that you have your limitations?'

There was no use in being impatient when Renzi was in logic, Kydd knew, and he answered amiably, 'That must be true enough, Nicholas.'

'Then you must hold that this must be true for myself also.'

'Aye.'

'And it follows that since you have advanced so far and so rapidly in the sea profession, you must be gifted far beyond the ordinary to have achieved so.'

Kydd shifted uncomfortably. 'If ye mean—'

'For myself, I accept this without rancour, that you are so much my superior in the nautical arts. You have the technical excellence, the daring and – if I may make bold to remark it – the ambition that places you at such an eminence, all of which sets my own small competences to the blush.'

'Nicholas, you—'

'Therefore the corollary is inescapable, and it is that if I were to venture an opinion in such matters then it will have sprung from so shallow a soil that it may not stand against one cultured to so full a bloom. It would be an impertinence to attach weight or significance to it and from this we must accept therefore that it were better not uttered – I shall not be offering a view on how you will conduct your ship, nor praise and still less blame. Your decisions shall be yours to make, and I, like every one of *Teazer*'s company, will happily abide by them.'

So there would be no private councils-of-war, for there was no shifting Renzi's resolve, logically arrived at. But then it dawned on Kydd. Close friends as they were, nothing could be more calculated to drive a wedge between them than the holding of opposite opinions before an action, only one of which would be proved correct to the discomfiture of the other – whoever that might be.

Renzi was putting their friendship before self, Kydd recognised. For the future, the decisions would be his own but unconditional warmth of the companionship would always be there at the trifling cost of some defining limits. 'Why, that's handsomely said, Nicholas,' he replied softly. He paused, then began again in a different tone: 'We have t' put down the rascal, that's clear, but where t' find him? That's the rub.'

Renzi waited.

'An' I have notion where we might . . .'

'May I know your reasoning?' Renzi said carefully. Evidently discussion was possible but advice and opinions were not.

'I feel it in m' bones. Our Bloody Jacques is *not* going home. He's lost not a single spar in th' meeting of us – why should he give it away while he c'n still cruise?' Unspoken was the feeling that, be damned to it, he was going to have a reckoning for his own self-respect.

'So where . . . ?'

'Just as soon as we're able, we clap on sail to th' suth'ard – I mean t' make Wolf Rock b' sunset.'

'Wolf Rock?' said Renzi, in surprise. The dangerous single outcrop well out into the entrance to the Channel was feared by all seafarers.

'Aye.'

'And, er, why?' Renzi prompted.

'Pray excuse, Nicholas, there's a mort t' be done afore we sail.'

There was now just enough time to punish Andrews for breaking ship and hazarding his shipmates, then deal with Standish.

With Penzance under their lee they left Mount's Bay for the south. Kydd had dealt kindly with Andrews, even as the letter of the law judged him guilty of desertion and, what was worse, that his captain had been presented with a situation not of his intending or control. The crestfallen lad was given the thirty-fourth Article of War to get by heart before claiming his supper.

Standish, however, was a harder matter. Clearly quite sure of his opinion, he had become cold and reserved in his dealings and would need careful handling if this were not to turn into something more charged.

Within the hour they had left the shelter of the bay and headed out into the Channel, first to the south and, the winds proving favourable, further towards the open Atlantic. The seas moderated, and as the afternoon continued the sun made an appearance, setting all in their path a-glitter in a last display before dusk.

'Tide'll be an hour earlier'n Falmouth hereabouts, sir,' Dowse said laconically.

'Aye.'

'It's high-water springs, sir,' he added, with more feeling.

'That'll be so, I believe.'

Kydd didn't want any discussion about his dash for Wolf Rock, for while his reasons could be explained logically – the rock's position as a fine place of lookout squarely athwart both the east–west and north–south shipping channels – his conviction was based on intuition only. In some way he *knew* that the privateer captain would head for friendly waters for the night but then turn about and, believing *Teazer* to be continuing her patrol along the south coast, round the tip of Cornwall to resume his depredations, this time on the north coast. But first he would have to pass within sight of Wolf Rock – and there *Teazer* would be waiting.

'Sir,' Dowse went on heavily, 'Wolf Rock covers at high-water spring tides.'

Kydd had seen the ugly rock several times from seaward but what Dowse was saying meant that his plan to lie off with it in sight as a means of keeping his position during the dark hours – and by knowing where it was, guard against coming upon it unawares – was now questionable.

As if mocking him, a pair of seagulls keened overhead while Dowse waited with dour patience. Dusk drew in and somewhere out there just under the surface was a deadly crag – it could be anywhere beneath the innocent waters ahead. Attempts in the past had been made to erect some kind of warning mark but the sea had always swept it away.

They could not continue into such danger. 'Ah, it seems—' Kydd stopped. Away on the weather bow there was a discontinuity in the wan light on the sea, a black object that had appeared, vanished, then reappeared in the same place, where it remained. He stared at it, eyes watering.

Standish made a play of raising his telescope and lowering it again. 'Naught but a seal,' he said, with studied boredom, 'as we might expect this time of the year. I remember—'

'That will do,' Kydd said with relish. 'The beast sits atop th' rock. Clear away th' best bower an' stream anchor an' we moor for the night.'

'Why, sir, I hardly think—' Dowse seemed lost for words.

'Mr Purchet, be sure an' buoy th' cables, we may have t' slip without a deal of warning.'

'Anchor, sir? Y' knows that Wolf Rock is steep to. Seabed drops away t' – what? Twenty, thirty fathom?' the boatswain said uneasily.

'He's right, sir,' Standish interjected. 'If we were—'

'Silence!' Kydd roared. 'Hold y' tongues, all o' you! T' question me on m' own quarterdeck – I'm not standin' f'r it!' He waited until he felt his fury subside, then went on frostily, 'Th' bower cable's seven hundred 'n' fifty feet out to its bitter end, so with th' usual allowance f'r three times the depth o' water we c'n moor an' with cable t' spare.' It would be damnably little, but the greater peril lay in blundering about a dangerous shore in the blackness of night.

'By mooring f'r the night we'll be in position ready in th' morning, an' no danger of bein' cast up on the rock.' He glared round defiantly and left the deck for Standish to carry out his order.

'An hour before dawn, sir, and, er, nothing in sight.'

Kydd struggled to wakefulness at Tysoe's gentle rousing. He had spent a restless night even though at this distance offshore a spacious and soothing ocean swell had predominated over inshore fretfulness. He dressed hastily and made his way to the dimness of the quarterdeck, where Prosser was on watch. 'Brisk mornin',' Kydd said, slapping his sides in the cold early-morning breeze.

'Sir,' Prosser said, without emotion, standing with his arms folded next to the empty helm.

'Do ye think we'll be lucky t' day?'

'Sir.'

The watch on deck were forward, rehanking falls and squaring away in the grey morning light. Kydd caught the flash of glances thrown in his direction – he needed no one to tell him the topic of their conversation.

The light strengthened: it was uncanny to be anchored in the middle of the sea, for while land was in sight from the masthead, in accordance with Kydd's plan to be both invisible and all-seeing, there was nothing at all from deck level except an unbroken expanse of water and the disfiguring sea-washed black of Wolf Rock away on their beam.

The men were piped to breakfast. An hour later, with nothing on the horizon and *Teazer* lying to single anchor, hands were turned to for exercise. Kydd paced along the deck.

Time passed, and apart from a small merchantman and a bevy of morning fishermen, the coast remained clear. Standish wore a look of pained toleration as he went about the deck, and Renzi kept out of the way below.

'*Sail hoooo!* In wi' the land – a big 'un!' There was no mistaking the animation in the mainmast lookout's voice. Kydd threw his hat to the deck and scrambled up the main-shrouds.

'Where away?' The lookout pointed to the distant dark band of coast, and there indeed was a vessel of size on the bearing – the three pale blobs had to be sail on three masts. Kydd fumbled for his glass. A lugger sprang into view, and with that oddly raked mizzen there could be little doubt.

'*Deck hooo!*' he yelled in exultation. '*Enemy in sight!* Buoy an' slip this instant, d' ye hear?' He swung out and descended hastily, thinking of what he might say to Standish but nothing clever came to mind, and he contented himself with the brisk orders that sent the men to their stations for rapid transition from quiescence to flying chase.

He had been right! His intuition was sound and the privateer had returned to the place Kydd had reasoned he would. At anchor far to seaward and without sails abroad, they were invisible to the unsuspecting Frenchman who had passed Gwennap Head and was therefore now committed to the passage round to the north. He was due an unpleasant surprise.

The buoy with the anchor cable secured to it splashed away to set them free and sail dropped from the yards. As if in sudden eagerness *Teazer* caught the wind and leant towards their quarry, who must now be in complete astonishment at the man-o'-war that had appeared from nowhere, like a magic spell, and was now hot on his heels.

It would be a tight chase: again, they were well to windward of their prey in a south-westerly and again the privateer could not contemplate putting about to return, for that would require tacking round and right into the path of his pursuer. But this time *Teazer* was perfectly positioned and conditions could not have been bettered: the winds were strong and in her best quarter for sailing while the privateer was being forced against the coast as it trended to the northwest to Land's End, which must first be rounded before they could bear away along the north coast.

In less than an hour the two ships would reach a point of convergence somewhere close to the Longships lighthouse, which stood atop a group of wicked rocks extending out from this final promontory.

How to open the action? There was little need for lengthy planning, however: the lugger would lie under their guns to leeward in a very short time and his gun-captains would know what to do then. Kydd sent for his sword, remembering to speak encouraging words to those for whom this would be a first taste of powder, and in good time HMS *Teazer* went to quarters.

The tumbling mass of grey rock that was the very tip of England drew closer – so did the lugger, sailing perilously in with the cliffs and rolling uncomfortably from the seas on her beam. Every detail became clear: the faded black sides, soaring pale lugsails with odd, off-square topsails straining above and no colours of any sort flying.

A point of red at her bow had Kydd reaching for his telescope – under its bold bowsprit was a figurehead, a crimson fighting cock with spurs extended in ferocious challenge.

'I own I stand rebuked for want of faith, sir,' Standish said quietly. He stood in front of Kydd and bowed awkwardly. 'That is Bloody Jacques for a surety – I heard a lot of him in Fowey.'

'Ah, I had th' feeling,' Kydd said lightly. 'We open fire t' st'b'd,' he went on, and resumed his hungry stare at the privateer, 'when we're within pistol-shot.' *Teazer*'s carronades were deadly at close quarters but not to be relied on for accuracy beyond a few hundred yards.

It would not be a one-sided fight, that much was certain. While *Teazer* outgunned the similarly sized vessel, her company would be so much less than that of a privateer crowded with prize-crew and she must at all costs remain out of reach of the torrent of boarders. Yet she must close the range – and risk any sudden lunge to grapple.

'I can almost feel pity for the Frenchman.' Renzi's calm, reassuring voice came from behind him; Kydd had not noticed his clerk take up his station for battle. His half-smile was in place and he wore a plain fighting hanger, but in accordance with duty held a regulation notebook to record all significant events.

The privateer lay no more than seventy yards ahead and Kydd could see the small group round the helm clearly: one was certainly the shrewd captain, looking back at *Teazer* and weighing his chances. The Longships with its lighthouse now lay close ahead, and with rising exhilaration, Kydd began to estimate distances and sea-room on what must soon be the field of battle.

They had successfully crowded the lugger against the coastline and now it must shape course towards them to get round the Longships – that would be the time to let the seven starboard guns do their work. Kydd drew his sword and raised it high. 'Teazers!' he roared – then stopped in bafflement.

The privateer was not altering course: while *Teazer* was hauling her wind to round the Longships, the big lugger carried on with a full press of sail, heading for the narrow band of open white water between the shoreline and the lighthouse.

'Be damned! Throw up y'r helm, Poulden, an' follow in his wake!'

'Sir!'

'Where he c'n swim, so can we, Mr Standish.' Kydd tried not to think of *Teazer*'s keel, cleaving the water a couple of fathoms below them as they bore off into the narrowing space between the lighthouse rocks and the cliffs. What if the lugger had been specially designed with a light draught for just this inshore work?

Kydd clutched the shroud he was holding as they plunged through – dark shadows of kelp-strewn rock in the sea flicking past under them, the wind gusted and flawed so close to the shore. Another, smaller, outlying group of rocks surged white off to port – and Bloody Jacques opened fire.

Admittedly they were four-pounder chase guns only but

both of *Teazer*'s were aft for defence and in Kydd's cabin. The manoeuvre through the channel had brought both vessels into line and now as they bucketed madly along *Teazer* must suffer the vicious slam of shot across her decks.

With the wind now dead astern they swept through together and on the other side it became clear that in these conditions *Teazer* had the edge – the lugger was slowly but surely being overhauled. As soon as they had established an overlap . . .

The move was as unexpected as it was effective. Like a dancer pirouetting, the privateer threw down his helm and came up into the wind as close as he could lie, in the process bringing his entire broadside to bear. The gunsmoke was whipped away quickly downwind but Kydd felt the sickening crunch in the hull where balls had struck – and not a gun could they fire in return.

The lugger was now away on the wind, the distance increasing by the second. 'Follow!' he bellowed directly at the quartermaster, Poulden, who spun the wheel furiously. *Teazer* moved round more slowly – her square rig needed men at the braces instead of the guns now.

It was lunacy: close-hauled, the privateer was now headed to pass the Longships and reach open sea where presumably *Teazer* would find sea-room to force a conclusion. But was this a desperate attempt to shake off a pursuer or . . . ?

Kydd glanced at Dowse. The master was tense and his white face told Kydd he had knowledge of perils that he was keeping to himself while in contact with the enemy. Renzi was looking up from noting the change of course but everyone else was gazing after the lugger whose deck seemed crowded with men, the occasional glint of steel among them giving point to their threat.

The privateer captain was wily and kept a fine discipline to handle his ship as he had – there had to be a reason for his strange move. And there was: at precisely the right place the lugger's bow swung, passing through the wind's eye, took up on the other tack and stood away to the south-east.

It was a master-stroke. The square-rigged *Teazer* needed room to manoeuvre if she wanted to tack about and must go beyond the Longships. The fore-and-aft-rigged lugger had gone about neatly enough but additionally he had taken advantage of the rocky outlier and was now threading between it and the Longships to return the way he had come, and would be long gone by the time *Teazer* could follow.

'Sir! No!'

But Kydd had no intention of trying to emulate the corsair. They had to let him go. He let out his breath in a sigh of appreciation at the princely display of seamanship, watching the lugger thrashing southward, and turned to Standish. 'A right devil! Should we have—'

'We could do no other, sir, I'm persuaded. And if I might make remark, our motions must have given him pause. He may well decide to prey on less well-defended shores.'

'Why, thank 'ee, Mr Standish, but I've a feelin' we'll be meetin' again. I'll not forget this day.'

The ship's company of HMS *Teazer* gathered beside an open grave. The vicar of the ancient Gulval church had performed this office so many times – the sea giving up its dead from shipwreck, foundering, piracy and war. These at least had a Christian burial. Far more had been removed from human ken and had not returned from a voyage; they had died far from home of disease, a fall from aloft, any one of the multitude of hazards lying in wait for every seafarer.

The young foretopman shyly added his handful of earth to the rest on the coffin, conscious of the sombre eyes of his shipmates, packed closely about the grave. He stepped back and raised his eyes to his captain. Kydd understood, and looked at the vicar, who nodded solemnly. 'Er, "They that go down t' th' sea in ships . . ."' he began, and stopped. He was the captain; their ship had suffered her first loss to the sea and they were looking to him for words of strength. The trouble was that he himself had been affected by the death, more so for its occurring not in the heat of battle but in the course of the seaman's obedience to his own commands.

He gulped and tried to concentrate. 'We all who use th' sea . . . the unseen perils . . . must find courage . . . our duty . . . to th' end.' The unblinking eyes watching him gave no indication of the seamen's thoughts. When he clapped on his hat they returned down the little road to Penzance.

Kydd stood for a moment longer by the graveside. Then his eyes met Renzi's. Wordlessly they turned and followed.

Chapter 5

With six sail-of-the-line at anchor in Cawsand Bay, and Plymouth Sound alive with wartime shipping, it was probably too much to expect any to notice the arrival in port of so modest a vessel as the brig-sloop *Teazer*, but Commander Kydd didn't care. Pacing his own quarterdeck in his best coat and breeches, he was ready for any summons from the admiral after a not uneventful first war cruise.

The challenge flag fluttered up the mast of the signal station at Mount Wise and *Teazer*'s reply shot up the lee halliards as she eased to larboard to avoid an ungainly Indiaman working her way seaward. Then, within a few hundred yards of the grassy sward of Plymouth Hoe, *Teazer*'s helm went over for the final mile to the notorious Devil's Point and the entrance to the Hamoaze – and rest.

Kydd concentrated on the approach. The vicious currents in the narrows had claimed many victims – their bleached timbers could still be seen on the banks.

In the fine weather people were thronging the pleasant gardens on the point. 'Why, there's a beauty wants to be noticed!' Standish exclaimed. He had his telescope trained on one particular lady who was waving both arms enthusiastically. Distracted, Kydd turned back to the conn but something about that figure . . .

'If y' please?' he asked, and took a peek. It was Cecilia.

'Mr Prosser, dip th' ensign!' Standish looked at Kydd with alarm. 'My sister,' he said defensively. Obediently *Teazer*'s colours lowered six feet and proudly returned.

He had no idea why she was there but her gaiety did not seem to indicate a family crisis. After *Teazer* had picked up her moorings, he penned a quick note to go ashore with the first boat, inviting her aboard after the flurry of official business, which always awaited a warship returning from a cruise.

'*Boat ahoy!*' blared the mate-of-the-watch, at the approaching pinnace – there was really no need, for it plainly bore only an assortment of passengers, but its coxswain Poulden bellowed the required '*No, no!*' to indicate that no naval officer was coming aboard.

Cecilia climbed daintily over the bulwarks, handed across by an attentive Kydd, who tried not to notice the look of admiration she received from Standish. His elaborate bow, however, was lost on her: she threw her arms determinedly round her brother and kissed him soundly, to the delight of the seamen on deck. 'Dear Thomas! I'm so thrilled – you have no idea! Captain of your ship—'

'Why, yes, er, welcome on board HMS *Teazer*, Cecilia,' Kydd said hastily. 'An' this is . . . ?' He turned to the two other passengers stepping aboard.

'Oh, you must remember Jane! She invited me to stay, and how could I refuse?' The lady dimpled with pleasure at the introduction and shyly held out her hand as Cecilia continued,

'In Jamaica, I helped at her wedding to William. And we all had dinner together that time . . . ?'

The thickset man grinned broadly. 'I was a lowly ensign o' Foot.' He chuckled, clearly impressed to know the captain of a King's ship and apparently not recalling that in Jamaica Kydd had been but the quartermaster's mate of a tiny cutter.

Cecilia took his arm with determination. 'Do take us about your ship, Thomas,' she said, with an impish smile.

Kydd cleared his throat importantly. 'Mr Standish, let me know if ye have any troubles – I'll be takin' these people f'r a tour.'

His visitors showed every delight at the sights to be had in a man-o'-war: towering masts with their incomprehensible tracery of rigging; the soaring, naked bowsprit so immensely long at close quarters; the deadly fascination of the line of guns at either side; the compass binnacle and spoked helm, now motionless.

Heads were bumped on the deckhead below but they were able to see for themselves the clean expanse of the mess-deck with its tables triced up and ditty bags against the side. The boatswain affably displayed his store and they witnessed at first-hand the procedure for the issuing of victuals to the mess-cooks for preparation.

Finally they entered the great cabin of HMS *Teazer*, and admired the noble appointments accorded the ship's captain. Cecilia's eyes shone as she looked up at her brother. While her friends peered hesitantly into Kydd's sleeping cabin he whispered, 'An' ye're invited t' the captain's table at eight bells tonight, sis.'

It called for sherry all round before Kydd had regretfully to announce that, owing to pressure of work, he must conclude their tour and send them ashore. They returned on deck, blinking in the sunshine, but Cecilia hung back. 'Thomas,' she said in a small voice, 'we haven't seen Nicholas.'

'Aye, well, he doesn't like t' be disturbed, y' see,' he said uncomfortably. Renzi's instructions had been clear.

She met his eyes levelly but said nothing.

'Ah, b' chance he might be at leisure t' see you,' he said, and excused himself to his visitors and went below, hearing Cecilia's footsteps tapping behind him.

The tiny cabin had its curtain pulled across but Kydd cleared his throat and said brightly, 'Nicholas – er, here's someone desirous o' speaking with ye.'

There was movement and Renzi's head poked out. He paused when he saw Kydd's sister, then turned and looked accusingly at Kydd. Cecilia gave an encouraging smile and said sweetly, 'So kind in you, sir, to receive us without notice. Do I find you in health?' Her eyes were already straying beyond the curtain, and Renzi, with a curious air of dignity yet defiance, answered, 'I do thank you for your politeness but as you may see I cannot in all civility invite you to enter.'

Kydd hastened to say, 'Oh, er, you'll understand, Cec, we don't have an overplus o' room aboard, an' this *is* how Nicholas wants it.'

Cecilia stooped to see inside, ignoring Renzi's pained expression. 'Why, this is nothing but your monk's cell,' she said, taking in its Spartan simplicity. 'It's just the right place for you, I vow. And will we be seeing you tonight, Mr Renzi?'

'I – I'm desolated to find that on this occasion there is ship's business ashore that has the prior claim upon me, Miss Kydd.'

'Oh? Aye, this c'n be so, Cecilia,' Kydd said hastily. 'Y' remember he acts in th' character of ship's clerk an' always knows his duty, I find.'

*   *   *

'Miss Cecilia, sir.' Tysoe held the door as she entered the great cabin, awed now by the effect of the candlelight's tawny gold on the naval splendour within.

'Good evening, Thomas – how kind of you to invite me.'

Tysoe accepted her pelisse with the utmost courtesy, his approval of the quality of Kydd's visitor barely concealed.

'Oh, sis, I don't think ye've made y'r number with Tysoe here. He's been m' personal servant since before Canada an' gives the greatest satisfaction.'

Tysoe exchanged a pleased inclination of the head for Cecilia's wary interest. 'My brother is in good hands, then,' she said, and allowed herself to be conducted to one of the two easy chairs, set to take full advantage of the view from the stern windows in the gathering dusk. Kydd sat companionably in the other.

'Our dinner'll be alongside presently, Cec. The cook's warned off ye're aboard. Can I help ye t' the wine afore we eat?'

'That's so kind, but I will decline for now, Thomas,' she replied delicately. The incongruity of his younger sister deploying the arts of politeness for his sake touched a chord and he laughed, evoking in her a pleased smile.

'Just think,' she said, with childish warmth, 'it was only a few years ago . . .' Her face shone. Then she turned and said eagerly, 'Tell me what it's like, Tom! The captain of a King's ship – how does it *feel*?'

Kydd affected not to notice the deep glow of the gold lace on his coat. 'Why, it's so fine a thing, I find it hard t' remember when I was aught else – but I c'n tell ye now, ye must believe th' biggest thing in life was t' be removed fr'm the fo'c'sle to th' quarterdeck.'

Cecilia remained silent as he continued. 'Y' see, sis, when

ye're only a foremast jack, y' peep aft an' see officers who're calm 'n' strict, looking down at ye, all the power an' discipline ... an' when I heard I was t' join 'em I didn't know what I must expect. F'r me, the big surprise was t' find that in th' wardroom all th' rank an' ceremony is left on deck, not an order given except it's on the quarterdeck, never below.

'It means we're all equal, y' see. We share like brothers an' this means that in battles an' such we understand an' trust, one wi' the other. It's – it's ...'

'But now you're captain!'

'That's what I'm tryin' to say. I've been plucked out o' their comp'ny now, Cec, an' not a one c'n speak t' Tom Kydd but he's addressin' his captain, an' we both know it.'

Her eyes grew round. 'Then this is why Nicholas is ...'

'Aye – I own that I'm truly fortunate t' have his company aboard, even if it's a mort hard t' hoist in his meanings at times.'

Tysoe interrupted an introspective silence. 'Dinner is served, sir.'

Cecilia regained her vivacity as the meal progressed. 'To think it – do you eat in such ceremony every day, and all alone?' Reassured on the practicalities, she persisted, with a shy giggle, 'Does it not cross your mind, ever, what your sailors must be feeling as they look at you? I mean, once you were one and you must know what they're thinking.'

'That's a question I've often asked m'self, sis. An' the answer is that, yes, I do have a notion what's in their minds. It was th' same f'r me, that ye see th' captain afar off an' know he's the one set over us all, an' there's no quarrel wi' that.

'Now respect, there's another thing. If ye hasn't their respect then y' hasn't their confidence, an' that way ye lose battles.'

Looking intently at her wine Cecilia said carefully, 'If I might be so bold as to remark it, when you speak of respect I am obliged to mention that while it may be said that you have advanced far in life, do you not find the sailors might resent being commanded by one of your – er, *our* origins?'

Kydd gave a wolfish smile. 'Men like t' have a captain who's a swell cove, an' to have a lord is prime – but always they'll like a fighter best.'

He put down his glass. 'Y' know, Cec, there's not too many in th' sea service from forrard like me. We call it "coming aft through th' hawse", an' I doubt there's above a hundred reached th' quarterdeck that way. There's some o' these – right good seamen all – who glory in where they've come from and these are y'r "tarpaulin officers".

'Now, I'm not, as who might say, ashamed o' bein' a fore-mast hand – I'm proud t' have been one – but, sis, f'r me, what's chalked up on my slate is not where I've come from but what I c'n look forward to as a gentleman o' conse-quence.' Self-consciously he went on, 'It was at th' admiral's ball, Cec. I was Cap'n Thomas Kydd, honoured guest, an' I met th' ladies an' everyone, an' they took me as one o' them. I have t' tell ye, it was very pleasing t' me – very agreeable indeed.'

Cecilia smiled sweetly and Kydd went on, 'Except that I had the feelin' I was a – a visitor, if ye gets m' meanin', welcome f'r all that, but a visitor t' their world just the same. Now, Cec, what I want t' be is – not a visitor. I want 'em t' take me as their own, y' see, just th' same as when I came aft t' the wardroom. Is this s' wrong for such as I?'

'Bless you, Thomas, no, it is not! But – but there are . . . difficulties, which I feel obliged to point out.'

'Fire away, then, sis.'

'You will understand that I speak from the kindliest motives, and some years in the employ of Lord Stanhope, where I've been privileged to move in the highest levels of society . . .'

'Aye, that I do!'

'Then kindly attend, Thomas,' she said seriously. 'The first point I will make is that you ask to enter society as a waif and stray – without you have an establishment, a lodging at the very least, you cannot expect to receive visitors or hold the usual polite assemblies.'

It was a novel thought: 'home' had always been his ship, the centre of his world, and failing that, then Guildford where his parents lived. He and Renzi had briefly shared a residence there, it was true, but they had always known it would be temporary. Cecilia was now telling him to have life outside his ship – to put down roots for the first time.

'I've been staying with Jane and her husband, who is something in a financial way in Plymouth. She will tell us where distinguished sea officers might find suitable accommodation.' She regarded Kydd's splendid full-dress commander's uniform doubtfully. 'In course, you will not often be in uniform on the land, Thomas. You will need to consult a tailor. Coat and breeches simply will not answer any more. Pantaloons and cravat are all the thing.'

'I'll not be made—'

'Then shall you meet us for an expedition on the strand tomorrow? Or . . . ?'

'Aye – at eleven,' Kydd muttered.

'Now, pray don't take it amiss, brother, but I'm bound to observe that your speech is not at all that is to be expected of a high officer. It smacks too much of the old ways and simply will not do. You must try to speak more slowly, to pronounce every word to its full measure, to use circumspection in your language. Surely you don't want to be mistaken for some kind of sea bumpkin?'

Kydd felt a flush rising. 'The sea's a hard enough place. Y' need plain-speakin',' he growled.

'But we're not at sea when we're on the land,' Cecilia replied firmly, 'and on shore we do as others do. I will give you a poetry book, and you are to read it aloud every morning to Tysoe, trying very hard to make the words beautiful.'

Utterly lost for something to say, Kydd snorted.

'And, Thomas,' she said primly, 'I cannot help but note that you speak to me in too familiar a manner. I may be your sister, but that is no excuse for omitting the usual delicacies of converse. Do, please, try to be a little more polite in your address to me.'

'If this'n pleases y'r ladyship,' Kydd said sarcastically, and instantly regretted it. Cecilia was right: the eighteenth century had gone, and with it, much of the colour and vigour he remembered from his youth. Now, in the year 1803, times were more sombre and careful. Appearance and manner were valued over spirit and dash. 'That is t' say, ye're in the right of it, o' course.' The warmth of her smile touched him and he felt ashamed of his obstinacy. 'I'll try, sis,' he said sincerely.

'Well, now, there's the matter of deportment – but you already cut a fine figure of a man, Thomas. I think we might accept your qualities in this. But there are other skills of a social order that you'll find indispensable: ability at cards, the arts of gallantry—'

'Be damned! You're beginnin' t' sound too much like Nicholas.'

Her face shadowed.

'Oh, er, Cec, I didn't mean to . . .' But there was no going

117

back. 'May I know ... how is it wi' Nicholas an' yourself? Are you ... ?'

At first she did not answer; she crossed to the windows and stared out into the darkness. Then she spoke: 'He is a man like no other, Thomas. I will wait for him, whatever his reasons, but you are never in life to tell him of my – my feelings for him. When he's ready ...'

She found a handkerchief and dabbed her eye. 'Is he – is he happy, do you think?'

Floundering at the change in subject Kydd gathered his thoughts. 'Nicholas? Well, I – but then he's a fathom an' a half too deep for me t' know f'r certain, but I can tell ye – that is t' say, you – that he's taken aboard s' many books and scratches away in his little cabin all th' hours God gives that it must be givin' him satisfaction.'

'You're such a good friend to him, Thomas,' she said softly. 'You'll both take care, won't you?'

Kydd saw her eyes had filled. Out of his depth in the presence of female emotion, he reached for the brandy. 'Cecilia, let's toast. T' the future, sis, as who knows what's lyin' in wait for us both?'

'Mm, yes. I do see what you mean, Cecilia, dear.' Mrs Mullins was in no doubt about Kydd's shortcomings in the way of dress and twirled her parasol in exasperation. 'Men are such tiresome creatures to encourage when it comes to matters of appearance.'

'Quite so, dear Jane,' Cecilia said comfortably, on Kydd's arm for the short walk up Fore Street to the Plymouth diligence stand. 'But Thomas has promised, and he shall bear his lot with patience until his dress may match his station in life – is this not the case, Thomas?'

'Aye, Cec,' he said reluctantly.

'I do beg your pardon, Thomas?'

'Er, I meant t' say, that is so, Cec – Cecilia.' Be damned to this wry way of talking – but she was right. Kydd accepted that in some ways his sister had advanced much further into polite society than he, even to familiarity with the ways of the nobility and landed aristocracy. If he was to be fully accepted, there was no alternative but to follow her strictures and conform to the way things were at those levels.

'Jane has very kindly brought a newspaper with her, and after we have finished at the tailor we shall consult her concerning a suitable district for your residence.' Cecilia informed him firmly, 'We are fortunate, Thomas, that we have a friend living here who is to advise us.'

They climbed into the diligence and set off for Plymouth town. The ladies happily chattered about sartorial possibilities while Kydd stared out over the Sourpool marshes, scattered pine houses among their melon and cucumber pits. There was no question but that he was going through with whatever it took to enter fully into society. Fortune had brought him this far but he had to fit himself properly to take advantage of the next big stroke.

He allowed his fancies to soar: as a commander he had the respect of the world, but most probably it would be as far as he could reasonably expect to go in naval service and he should then be content with an honourable retirement as a gentleman. In the navy, the next and final step was to post-captain with an automatic but slow rise by seniority to admiral, but for this he had either to succeed in a particularly spectacular feat of arms – unlikely in a brig-sloop – or benefit by the workings of interest on his behalf.

Interest: embittered officers, envious of others' rise, blamed a system whereby if it was possible to secure protection from one of lofty rank at the centre of power one's name would go forward over others of equal merit. Kydd, however, saw that at least it was an open and recognised form of favouritism that carried its own check and balance: the favouring would be clearly seen so no senior figure would allow his name to be associated with that of a fool – and if his *protégé* went on to glory, he would bear the credit also. This was how a daring young man such as Nelson had been given his chance. A post-captain at twenty!

The rattling, jolting conveyance left the potholes of the open country for the smart clatter of cobblestones as they reached the Frankfort gate and the Old Town. Kydd's mind, however, sped on. The key to interest was first to come under notice; but even to come within sight of a luminary he should be able to move in social circles that would intersect on the right occasions. And having achieved this, nothing could be more disastrous to his cause than to be seen as an outsider, however characterful.

His course was set, the way ahead clear.

The tailor was most obliging, promising a first fitting in two days, and Kydd found himself in prospect of showing quite a different face to the world. Gone were the gorgeous colours and lace of before. Mr Brummell had decreed that gentlemen would now be choosing the plain but exquisitely cut over satins and brocades; light-coloured pantaloons with cuffed-top boots in place of breeches and buckles.

It would take some getting used to but Kydd persevered. In the end he allowed himself satisfied; a dark-green coat that swept back rakishly into tails with not a peep of lace, a buff double-breasted waistcoat cut high and a pair of what felt like indecently close-fitting cream nankeen pantaloons.

'Sir'll require some gallowses wi' his hinexpressibles?' Of course: pantaloons were cut generously at the top for comfort when horse-riding and would need reliable suspending. At the bootmaker, orders were put in train for the latest style of pointed-toe black boots with brown tops, despite Kydd's objections that they resembled a jockey's, and at the gentleman's outfitter much care was given to the selection of a black beaver hat with a white silk lining. It was odd to feel its round bulk in place of the sensible navy bicorne, but he could tell it would be much more convenient in the bows and flourishes of polite ceremony.

'Now, Thomas, we have time to inspect one or two prop-erties for you. Jane is insistent that officers of rank do favour Stonehouse above Plymouth for its salubrious air and genteel neighbourhood. Will we visit, do you think?'

Commander Kydd, lord of sixteen guns and suzerain of near a hundred men, agreed meekly and followed his sister. They reached Stonehouse and turned south down the main street, which he recognised as leading to the Long Room, but stopped, well before the open fields, in Durnford Street, which consisted in the main of substantial terraced mansions.

After a flash of glances between herself and Jane, all lost on Kydd, Cecilia announced that number eighteen might repay the visiting, and shortly Kydd found himself before the sturdy pale façade of a half-mansion three storeys high. Appalled, he turned to Cecilia. 'No! It's too—'

'Nonsense, Thomas! You will need to entertain. Come along.'

The landlord's agent sized Kydd up and, with a well-prac-tised smile, took them in. The front door opened into a small hallway and a passage with rooms on either side. The ladies sniffed politely in unison – the kitchen and scullery apparently passed muster. At the end of the passage a fine staircase mounted invitingly up.

· Ushered impatiently, Kydd ascended to the first floor – a fleeting impression of a jolly dining room on one side and a full-length drawing room on the other – then to the second, with a capacious main bedroom and a children's room.

'Should you desire to view the servant's quarters?'

'Aye – er, yes,' Kydd said hurriedly. It was the navy way always to ensure that the men were taken care of before consulting one's own comfort. The final attic floor, with its sloping ceilings and two sizeable rooms, would be more than adequate for any level of domestic manning that Kydd could consider.

A last quick look and they were on the street again, with Cecilia possessively on his arm. 'Well, Thomas, I do declare – a fireplace in every room, an entirely splendid drawing room. We shall need to change that odious curtain colour of course, and the floor rug is rather disgraceful, but your bedroom is quite the most commodious I have seen.'

It was for Kydd too – he remembered it hazily as nearly the size of *Teazer*'s quarterdeck. 'Now, sis, afore we go much further, this is jus' too big f'r me. I don't—'

'Don't be such a silly,' Cecilia said impatiently, 'One drawing room, one dining room, a bedroom for yourself and another – how can you live with less?'

A glance at the serene expression of her friend seemed to suggest that an understanding of sorts had already been reached and in these matters it were best to follow along. 'But, Cec, the cost must be—'

'An arrangement in the short term would be ruinously expensive, I'll agree,' she said, 'But an annual lease will be had for, say, twenty pounds or so?' she added, with suspicious confidence.

That was a substantial portion of his pay but less than he had feared; and the thought of being master in his own home to do as he pleased, to return invitations, to announce an assembly, have dinners to be talked about for months afterwards . . . 'Y' may be right, Cecilia. I'll think on it.'

'Nicholas, I'd be greatly obliged if you'd assist me in a small matter.'

Renzi looked up from his book. 'By all means, brother.'

The morning light reflected up from the water was playing pretty patterns on the cabin deckhead but Kydd's mind was on other things. 'Y' see, I'm thinkin' on takin' a lease – in a small way, of course – in a lodgin' ashore. If you'd be so kind as to step off wi' me to inspect it . . .'

Courteous and patient, Renzi toured number eighteen with Kydd, admiring the staircase, commenting on the number of floors and forbearing to point out that Kydd's observation on the felicity of having cooking country on the lowest floor and the servants safely aloft in the highest was quite in keeping with general practice.

'Might I know the asking price for this lease?' he murmured.

'Twenty guineas,' Kydd answered stoutly.

'That will be unfurnished, I believe. Shall we say about twenty-three if semi-furnished, which I earnestly recommend?'

'Ah, just so, I'd think,' Kydd replied hastily, and sought to bring himself to a proper state of seriousness. 'Nicholas. I have a proposition I'd like ye to consider.' Choosing his words carefully, he went on, 'In the matter of y'r own situation – I know how scant y'r means are as a captain's clerk wi' no other. As a man o' learnin', you'll need a place to rest your books an' things. I'm offerin' such a place for you here – but I have m' price.'

'I'm flattered to receive your offer,' Renzi said equally carefully, 'but as you may see, I'm fully provided for aboard the fine ship *Teazer*.'

'Ah, but here you would have an address you can give to people that will stop 'em thinkin' ye're a singular cove as lives all his life in a ship . . .'

Renzi paused.

'. . . and y'r grateful assistance at times of m' social duty such as dinners will be well remarked.'

'I see.' He stroked his chin. 'You mentioned a price, as I remember.'

'I did. One shillin' a month – and I shall see m' name, Thomas Kydd, printed for all the world to see, in y'r first book.'

Renzi looked away. When he had regained his composure he turned with a smile and said lightly, 'Then it seems that, not content with topping it the captain over me, you shall be my landlord as well.' He held out his hand. 'And here's my word on it.'

It was amazing, the amount of work that was apparently needed before they could claim their domicile. Drapery of fashionable colour replaced darker hangings at the windows, tastefully painted and varnished sailcloth lay over plain-edged floorboards in all but the drawing room, where an only slightly worn green-patterned carpet complemented the restful sage of the walls.

When it came to his bedroom, Kydd refused strenuously to contemplate the larger room, contending that he felt uneasy in any but ship-sized quarters and, besides, Renzi would need

drollery. I suspect he's not to be deprived of sociable occasions.'

Kydd's daily visits to *Teazer* as she lay under repair were not onerous and the success of the party the previous night combined with the warmth of a long friendship to produce a glow of satisfaction. 'Aye, that it was, Nicholas,' he mused, with a sigh, remembering these very drawing-room walls resounding to laughter, the soft candlelight on flushed cheeks. 'Do y' think we should make th' next by way of a fancy dress?' If six made a rousing evening they could probably stretch to eight and have a glorious rout. 'An' Miss Robbins tells me there's quantities o' ladies would favour us with a musical evenin', if begged.'

Renzi pursed his lips. 'This is an agreeable prospect, my friend, and I'm desolated to intrude – but have you given thought to the unfeeling demands of Mammon?'

'Y' mean, Nicholas, where's the pewter as will pay for it?'

'Have you by chance perused your books lately?'

'Books?'

'Of account. Household books of account as may readily be seen in both the greatest and meanest houses in the land.'

Kydd bristled, but Renzi continued remorselessly, 'As will detail to the prudent the ebb and flow of income and expenditures so as to give comfort that any projected enterprise will be within—'

'When I have th' time, Nicholas,' Kydd said curtly.

'As I suspected,' Renzi said, 'your lofty duties spare you no time for this necessary chore, and therefore I will make you a return proposition. Should you see fit to reduce my monthly lodgings to sixpence, I should be happy to assume the character of bookkeeper for you – for us both, as it were.'

'No!' blurted Kydd, appalled.

'Pray, may I know why not, as I already perform the function in part for your fine vessel?'

'But – but you're a learned gentleman fit f'r more than—'

'It were folly to despise the importance of keeping one's accounts, my friend, even for a scholard.'

Kydd smiled reluctantly. 'You're in the right of it, o' course. Very well, Nicholas,' he said humbly, 'Thank you, an' I honour ye for it.'

The door squeaked as Becky entered, bobbing to each. 'Draw the curtains, sir?' she asked timidly.

'Please do,' Kydd replied, with an absent-minded nod, and turned to his friend. 'Nicholas, I've been wonderin': would y' tell me how your work is progressin' now?'

'Certainly,' Renzi said, with a pleased smile, steepling his fingers. 'As you know, my study is ethnographical in nature. At its heart I will be trying to extract universals from the differing response around the world to the same challenges, be they grand or petty.

'To this end I will be on quite another tack from your usual philosopher, for I shall look only to the assembling of observations at the first hand to support my truths, my own and others, not the cloistered ratiocinatings of the ivory tower! And for this I have started down two trails: the first, that I must gain a thorough acquaintance of what passes for knowledge in the subject at present, and the second concerns the amassing of my facts. This is a difficult and complex task, which I've yet to structure satisfactorily, but it is clear that in essence it will require two storehouses – one, truths, which *are* so because I or another have seen them to be so, and two, suppositions, which are *said* to be so and which, therefore, I cannot accept until verified.'

He smiled diffidently. 'Your kind service in allowing me a

berth in your ship does, of course, mean that many observations will be possible that are unavailable to the landbound,
and your other kindness in affording me a place ashore to
lay my head is of increasing value to me for as I acquire
correspondents they will need an address. Dear fellow, your
name will most certainly be inscribed in the preface as principal benefactor, you may be assured.'

Kydd sat back. This was a far greater project than he had
understood; no wonder Renzi had been closeted for hours each
day with little to show for it so far. 'If there's anything . . .'
he began hesitantly.

'Thank you, no. But on quite another subject, did I not
spy a certain invitation arrive this morning?'

Kydd reddened. 'Er, yes, y' did, Nicholas.' How to include
his ship's captain's clerk in anything with a naval connection
was still not settled in his mind. 'From Admiral Lockwood's
lady, a picnic t' be held next week over in Lord Edgcumbe's
estate,' he added, as off-handedly as he could, and handed it
over.

'It will be a social event of some significance,' Renzi
admitted, after studying the card. 'All the notables will be there
and yourself – but I fear that this, of course, will be by ulter-
ior design.'

Kydd paused. 'Er, design?' he said suspiciously.

'Why, yes! You are fresh blood, a personable young man
of good nature who is at present unattached and shows no
immediate prospect of being otherwise. Therefore a prime
choice to make up numbers as the hostess has a requirement.'

'Oh, I see.'

'Do bear the disappointment with fortitude – it would seem
that your prospects for many further invitations will be bright,
should you acquit yourself amiably enough on this occasion.'

'Ah, the invitation says, "and friend". Um, Nicholas, would you—'

'It seems to me that here is your opportunity to impress your sister with your social standing. She would be delighted to venture abroad on a picnic, I shouldn't wonder.'

Cecilia serenely on his arm, Kydd joined the group assembling at the Mutton Cove jetty in some trepidation, conscious of being under eye and, in his new pantaloons and boots, feeling more than a little conspicuous.

There, in the centre, was the admiral's wife, the formidable Lady Lockwood, and Kydd set course resolutely to approach. 'Madam, might I be allowed t' present m' sister, Cecilia,' he managed, remembering to remove his beaver hat in an elegant sweep as he bowed.

It appeared to satisfy: conversations stilled as the newcomers were noticed, but the admiral gave an encouraging smile and Lady Lockwood replied imperiously to Cecilia, 'So glad you could be here, my dear. I'm sure you will enjoy yourself.' Her eye rested briefly on Kydd before she moved on to the next arrival.

Kydd glanced about furtively; there was not a soul he recognised but Cecilia steered him subtly to an apprehensive-looking middle-aged woman on the arm of a florid gentleman in blue whom she had met recently at a rout. 'Do forgive the impertinence, but I cannot help remarking that adorable bonnet,' Cecilia said gaily, 'The ribbons do so suit your complexion.'

The woman started in pleased surprise, and after Kydd was introduced to her husband the two ladies were soon deep in converse. The short trip across the water to Cremyll in the admiral's barge passed in a blur of impressions. They stepped out to a picture of rural charm: rolling parkland kept in immaculate order, acres of greensward interspersed with pretty groves of English trees and a double avenue of spreading elms that stretched away up the rise to a grand mansion with curious octagonal towers.

'If there are any who feel unequal to the ascent I'm sure we could send for a chair,' Lady Lockwood declared. However, it was pleasant in the bright summer sun, passing slowly under stately chestnut trees to sylvan glades, and Kydd's fears slowly eased.

A picnic was laid out on the level expanse of lawn before the great house, servants standing behind hampers with sunshades at the ready, and after the admiral's party had decorously draped themselves over the spread rugs there was a general move to do likewise.

'You must try to be more entertaining in your talk, Thomas,' Cecilia whispered sharply, as she smiled politely at the acquaintance who had claimed her attention once more.

Obediently, Kydd turned to the man, one Mr Armitage, a landed relative of the admiral's wife and from Ireland, and whose conversation seemed to consist chiefly of ill-natured grunts. Nothing in common was evident, and Kydd's despairing talk about Pitt's chances of returning to government, the shocking price of tobacco and a juicy local murder all left the man unmoved and he lapsed into silence.

Cecilia had been taken away by Mrs Armitage to meet a friend, leaving them both alone, and while elegant conversations swirled round him, Kydd reflected mutely on the trials of a society occasion. Then he sensed movement and looked round.

It was the admiral's daughter, Persephone, now stooping to offer him a plate. 'Mr Kydd, might I press you to try one of these little olive pies? They're quite the most toothsome.'

Her gay voice, however, had a cool patrician ring that might have been intimidating.

Her dress – a sweeping filmy gown in sprigged muslin – did nothing to conceal her willowy figure, and a single pink coral necklace complemented a smart beribboned bonnet.

Covered with confusion, Kydd scrambled to his feet. 'Miss Lockwood! How g-good to see you again!' His foot caught in the rug and he stumbled, dropping his new hat in his anxiety not to lose the pie he had accepted from her.

She laughed and picked up his hat for him. 'This is a smart beaver indeed. It's not often a naval officer displays such good taste.' There was a disarming warmth in her tone and the laughter had stayed in her eyes.

'Oh, er, the hat. For that I must own it's my sister is m' pilot in matters o' fashion.' He looked about for Cecilia but she was not in sight. 'Y' should meet her, Miss Lockwood. All the men do think her the prime article.'

'I shall, Mr Kydd,' she said, amused. Her glance strayed to the stolid form of Kydd's acquaintance and she added loudly, 'If this is your first visit here, you'll be entranced by the views to be had. Do let's see.'

Other couples were promenading or talking together and Kydd walked forward stiffly, trying hard to appear fashionable. He felt sudden pressure on his arm as Persephone, stifling a giggle, said softly, 'Armitage can be such a bore when he wants to be, and I did feel so sorry for you on your own. Can you bear to forgive me carrying you off?'

'Miss Lockwood! I – I thank you for y' service to me and I do confide it would be of some interest t' me should we sight the Sound.' This was a small distance across the rise to the thin line of trees veiling the view eastwards, but still within plain sight of the picnic gathering.

'Then so we shall.' They walked slowly together until the rise fell away to reveal the wide, glittering expanse of Plymouth Sound past the Hoe to the busy Cattewater and a sweep on out to sea.

'I never tire of this prospect,' Persephone said. 'It's always so animated, so ever-changing. But, then, you must have quite another perspective, I'm sure.'

Not possessed of a witticism worthy of such a lady Kydd fell back on a simple recounting of a mariner's experience when entering the great port. It seemed to satisfy, for Persephone remained attentive throughout. 'Papa tells me you were with Nelson at the Nile,' she said.

'Well, not really, I'm afraid – y' see, I was in a different ship fr'm his and we fought in the dark. I couldn't see much o' the flagship.'

She looked at him oddly. 'And at Acre the same year?'

Kydd gave a wary smile; this was not really a fit subject for fine ladies. 'Yes, but I don't care f'r y'r land-fightin'. It's so . . . so disagreeable,' he finished lamely.

After a space she said quietly, 'Do you know, Mr Kydd? You're quite unlike anybody else I've met – that is to say, for a sea officer. You may believe that an admiral's daughter does not lack for men's company, but you— Anyone else would have delighted in telling me of their victories in the face of such perils, and you . . . are different.'

Kydd found he had to look away from her frank gaze. 'I heard Admiral Lockwood went t' London to attend the court. Did you b' chance go as well and see, er, their majesties?' he asked tentatively.

Persephone paused and looked at him kindly. 'Papa's brother is Groom of the Stole and one of Prinny's set. And Mama is remembered as lady-in-waiting to Princess Charlotte

– she's now the queen consort of Frederick of Württemberg, of course – so you may be sure it's quite impossible to stay away,' she said, with a sigh.

'Prinny?' said Kydd, awed.

'The Prince of Wales is such a spendthrift and coxcomb, of course, but I do believe his heart is in the right place.' Suddenly she looked down. 'I think we should return now, Mr Kydd. I thank you for your company, and I do wish you well for your next voyage.' Then, with the flash of a sweet smile, she walked ahead of him back to the picnic.

Chapter 6

'D id y' find entertainment enough along shore, Mr Standish?' Kydd asked the figure in glistening black oilskins standing next to him as another slowly drifting rain squall passed over the little sloop.

The first lieutenant shook himself in a shower of droplets and allowed a smile. 'I do have my hopes of the young ladies here, sir.'

Kydd kept his eye on the swirling current lapping noisily round the rocks in the narrows of Devil's Point. On the ebb, and with this mild south-westerly, there should be no difficulty with the sharp turn before Drake's Island on their way out to sea.

Standish raised his speaking trumpet and blared at the forebrace hands as *Teazer* straightened for the run past the Hoe. 'I believe, sir, you now have an address in Stonehouse.'

'I have,' Kydd said, with satisfaction. 'Durnford Street. There – can y' see the darker roof o' the third house along? A view o' the Hamoaze on one side an' Plymouth Hoe th' other.' It was an unreal thought that there he had a home of his own making.

'Sir!' The quartermaster's voice was sharp with alarm as he pointed at the bulk of a large merchantman ahead, emerging from the rain squalls and about to cross their bows on its way to the Mill Bay docks. It was unfortunate: the lookouts had probably assumed that his attention was on the task in hand and had refrained from pointing out the obvious.

Annoyed with himself, he snapped the orders that took the way off the sloop to pass astern of the ponderous vessel. 'It seems we're in some need of a sea breeze t' clear our heads. As soon as we're t' seaward o' Jennycliff, let's see th' hands lose some sweat. Both watches t' exercise then, Mr Standish.'

'Aye aye, sir,' he acknowledged. 'Er, and, sir – if you'd excuse the impertinence – I did learn as well that our captain's clerk is now, er, of the same address?'

'Aye, he is,' Kydd said firmly.

'Sir.'

'Then am I t' understand that he's easy in his duties – as who's to say backward in diligence – when assistin' you?'

'Why, no, sir,' Standish answered hastily, 'He is very amiable and obliging.'

'Mr Renzi is a learned gentleman o' shinin' qualities as is acceptin' th' convenience of this vessel by th' admiral's express permission, and who finds the value of an, um, *pied à terre* in this place an obligin' thing.

'If your philosophicals are lofty enough you'll have th' chance t' quiz him as y' please, for I'll be invitin' you an' Mr Renzi both t' dinner soon.'

*   *   *

The afternoon brought an improvement in the weather, and with the wind backing to a pleasant westerly, Kydd decided to patrol the eastward half of his area.

There was no need for haste, as who was to say where any trouble might lie? The admiral's office had received no recent reports of predation and Kydd wondered if he would ever again get the chance to face Bloody Jacques at bay.

Meanwhile his contentment continued to build, with warm thoughts of his progress in society mingling with enjoyment of the tumbling green Devonshire coastline and the clean, sparkling summer seas ahead.

Renzi had received the news of Kydd's successful first foray into *real* society politely and had been cautiously approving when he had heard in some detail of his encounter with an admiral's daughter. Kydd had no idea how he had done, but the very fact that she had stayed to talk implied that his presence was not altogether uncongenial. She was certainly of a quality far above his, yet she had singled him out – this was surely proof of his acceptability in gentle company. He hugged the conclusion gleefully to himself and turned on his heel to pace the quarterdeck.

The line of coast was beginning to take on meaning and character – Kydd recognised the mouth of the Erme river: it had been there, so long ago, that he had been one of the party that had crept ashore to discover the truth of the great mutiny, learning of the worst in the pretty village of Ivybridge below the moor.

As the coast trended south past the Bolt Tail and Head it peaked with Start Point. One of the major seamarks for the winter-beset battleships of the Channel Fleet fleeing a ferocious gale, it promised calm and rest at Tor Bay, beyond.

Teazer's patrol limit was at the other end of the long sweep of Lyme Bay at Portland and nearby Weymouth. There were no seaports of consequence in the bay beyond Exmouth and he determined to stretch out for Portland.

'Mr Standish, tomorrow is Sunday an' we shall have Divisions. If you'd be s' kind?' It was a little unfair; the ship was still being squared away after three weeks in dockyard hands, but what better way to pull *Teazer* into shape than to have a captain's inspection and bracing divine service? Anyway, it would give him a good idea of the temper of his men. It was the duty of the first lieutenant to prepare the ship and Standish would be held to account for any short-comings; this was the custom of the service and he would be as much on display as the ship.

At four bells Kydd stepped out of his great cabin to the piercing squeal from the boatswain's call. In full dress uniform he acknowledged the polite report from Standish that His Majesty's Ship *Teazer* was now at readiness for his inspection.

He went to the main-hatchway and stood aside for the boatswain to precede him on deck with a single warning peal, the 'still'. Then Kydd emerged gravely on to the upper deck. With fitting gravity he began in a measured pace to process down the larboard side of the deck, every man still and watching.

Lines from aloft appeared properly belayed and, additionally, the ends were each laid flat in a careful concentric spiral, a Flemish coil. He moved past the bitts to the shot garlands alongside each squat carronade. The gunner watched Kydd's progress steadily: Kydd knew it would be astonishing indeed if the balls were not wonderfully chipped and blacked and the carronades gleaming on their slides but appearances must be preserved and he went carefully through the motions.

The foredeck was in the same pristine state as aft; the lines were not pointed as they were on the holy ground of the quarterdeck where the final four inches had been artistically tapered, but in other ways there was pleasing attention to detail. Here he noted that every rope's end was neatly whipped, in the complex but secure and elegant West Country style, while the canvas grippings of the foreshrouds had been painted instead of tarred.

'A strong showing, Mr Standish,' Kydd allowed. Standish tried to hide his smile of satisfaction.

But professional pride was at stake here; Kydd looked about covertly but there was nothing to which he could take exception. He would have to try harder. Noting the angle of the breeze across the deck he crossed to a carronade neatly at rest on its slide. At the cost of his dignity Kydd squatted and felt under its training bed forward before the waterway and found what he was looking for: wisps of oakum and twine trimmings, wafted there during the work that morning. He straightened and looked accusingly at Standish. 'Ah, sir, I'll be speaking to the captain of the fo'c'sle,' the lieutenant said, with a touch of defiance.

Kydd growled, 'But there's a matter o' higher importance that concerns me.' He held Standish's eyes, provoking in the other man a start of alarm. Kydd went on, 'It is, sir, th' foretop lookout failin' in his duty!'

They snapped their gaze aloft to catch the interested lookout peering down at events on deck, then hurriedly shifting his attention back out to sea. Kydd had known the man's curiosity would probably get the better of him and had deliberately refrained from looking up before. 'Th' mate-o'-the-watch t' inform me how he's to teach this man his duty,' he barked.

In the respectful hush he turned and went down the fore hatchway to the berth-deck. Men were mustered below, in their respective divisions headed by their officers, and stood in patient silence. The swaying forest of sailors filled the space and Kydd picked his way through.

Knowing all attention was on him, he moved slowly, fixing his eyes to one side then the other, looking for a shifty gaze, resentment or sullen rebelliousness but saw only guarded intelligence or a glassy blank stare. He passed along and stopped. 'Why has this man no shoes?' he demanded of Prosser. The sailors went barefoot where they could at sea but mustered by divisions for captain's inspection only shoes would do.

'He doesn't have any, sir,' Prosser answered uncertainly.

'*Why* doesn't he have any?' Kydd responded heavily. The divisional system of the navy was a humane and effective method of attending to the men's welfare by assigning an officer responsible not only for leading his division into combat but as well concerning himself with any personal anxieties his men might have.

Prosser shifted uncomfortably.

'Tell me, why do y' have no shoes?' Kydd asked the man directly.

'I ain't got m' pay ticket,' he mumbled.

'You're fr'm, er, *Foxhound*,' Kydd recalled. 'Are you saying that y'r pay due entitlement has still not come t' *Teazer*?'

'Sir.'

Kydd rounded on Prosser. 'Inform th' captain's clerk that this matter's to be brought t' the attention of *Foxhound* an' report to me the instant this man's account is squared.'

It annoyed him that Prosser, a master's mate, was holding his men at arm's length like that. Only by getting to know them and winning their confidence would he be of value to them – and, more importantly, be in a position to make good decisions when at their head in action. It was no secret that Prosser had been hoping for a bigger, more prestigious rate of ship, but if he was looking for an early recommendation from his captain then this was not the way to gain it.

Aft was where the petty-officers berthed; their mess was in immaculate order, and on impulse Kydd asked that the rolled canvas that would screen them off from the rest should be unfurled. As he suspected, it was richly painted on the inside with a colourful pastiche of mermaids and mythical sea-beasts.

He lifted his eyes and saw Stirk looking at him across the deck; it had been so many years, but some of Kydd's happiest times at sea had been spent with Stirk in a mess such as this. He fought to control a grin and contented himself with a satisfied nod.

The cook's domain was spotless, the morning's salt beef standing by for the coppers. The boatswain's store was trim and well-stowed, and in the sailmaker's tiny cuddy Kydd found a miniature hammock slung snugly fore and aft and in it the lazy-eyed ship's cat, Sprits'l, looking sleek and assured.

Emerging from the cloistered depths of *Teazer* to the more civilised upper realms, Kydd pronounced himself satisfied. As a ship-of-war there was little to complain of and he turned to Standish. 'Rig f'r church, if y' please,' he ordered, and went to his cabin to allow the bedlam to settle that was the tolling of the ship's bell for divine service and the clatter of match-tubs and planks being brought up as pews.

'If ye'd rather . . . ?' Kydd offered to Renzi. The absence of a chaplain meant that the office would normally be carried through by the captain or other officer but Renzi's reputation for fine words would ensure him a respectful hearing.

'I think not,' answered his friend. He added warmly, 'Your good self is much the closer to a divine in this ship.'

The captain's clerk would, however, need to appear in front of the men: on report from Standish, two sailors slowly mounted the main-hatchway and appeared on deck. Every man and boy of the ship's company sat stolidly in a mass facing their captain, who stood by the helm behind an improvised lectern.

Kydd liked what he saw. These were his men, sitting patiently, those who would sail his ship and fight at his word, and on whose skills and courage the success of the commission would directly depend.

He was coming to be aware of several, in terms of their character. Some he knew well, their features strong and comforting, but others were still just faces, wary and defensive. All waited quietly for the ceremony that the Lords of the Admiralty in their wisdom had ordained should take place regularly in His Majesty's ships.

But first Kydd drew himself up and snapped, 'Articles of War!'

'Off hats!' roared Standish.

Heads were bared while the captain's clerk stepped forward and, in a rolling baritone the equal of any to be found on the Shakespearean stage, declaimed the stern phrases to the sea and sky.

'"Every person in the fleet, who through cowardice, negligence or disaffection, shall forbear to pursue the chase of the enemy . . . or run away with any of His Majesty's ordnance, ammunition stores . . . either on the high seas, or in any port, creek or harbour . . . and being convicted thereof by the sentence of a court-martial, shall suffer death . . ."' Duty done, Renzi stepped back.

The two men were brought forward, on report for being slack in stays – Standish wanted the job done speedily. Kydd could only approve of his zeal and sentenced them both to fourteen days in Purchet's black book. Cares of the world dealt with, it was time to address the divine.

A respectful silence was followed by a rustle of anticipation. Kydd knew he was on trial – some commanders would be eager to play the amateur preacher, others flippant and dismissive, but the common run of seamen were a conservative, God-fearing breed, who would be affronted at any kind of trifling with their sturdy beliefs.

'Gissing?' The carpenter's mate stood up with his violin and joined Midshipman Boyd at his German flute. When all was ready Kydd announced the hymn, "O God, Our Help in Ages Past", and the ship's company sang heartily together, the old words to the well-known tune sounding forth loud and strong. It was the sign of a ship's company in good heart.

Kydd went to the lectern, notes ignored – these were *his* men and he knew what they wanted. 'Men of *Teazer* – *Teazer's* men,' he began. There was a distinction and it was rooted in the different allegiances between those merely on her books and those who had found their being in and of the ship. 'Let me spin ye all a yarn.' This got their attention. 'Years ago, when I was in m' very first ship we joined action with a

Frenchy. And as we closed with th' enemy I was sore afraid. But my gun-captain was there, who was older an' much wiser. He was the very best kind o' deep-sea mariner, and he said to me words o' great comfort that let me face th' day like a man.'

His eyes found Stirk's and he saw the studied blankness of expression that showed he, too, had remembered that day.

'"Kydd," he said. "Now, it's certain ye'll get yours one day, but ye'll never know what day this'll be when y' wakes up in the morning. If it *is*, then y' faces it like a hero. If it *wasn't*, then it's a waste o' your life to worry on it."'

Kydd waited for the murmuring to die, then picked up the Bible. 'He's in the right of it, o' course – but it was here all th' time. Matthew, the sixth chapter an' the thirty-fourth verse. "Take therefore no thought for the morrow: for the morrow shall take thought for the things of itself. Sufficient unto the day is the evil thereof."

'Men, should y' need a course t' steer in any weather then th' chances are you'll find it here.'

Portland Bill was the eastern limit of *Teazer*'s area, but it would do no harm to show the denizens that the navy was here. 'T' take us past the Bill an' round to, off Weymouth,' he instructed the master.

There was no real need to pass into the next patrol area, especially with the notorious Race extending out to the Shambles, but this was only bad in heavy weather and it was well known that the King took the waters at Weymouth in summer – what more loyal act could there be than to demonstrate to His Majesty that his sea service was dutifully safeguarding the shores of his realm?

In the bright sunshine the distant wedge of the peninsula seemed too tranquil for its reputation and the irregular rippling over the Shambles was a tame version of the violent tidal overfalls Kydd had heard about. *Teazer* slipped between them and in an hour or so came to off the town, the hands that had been at their recreational make-and-mend, which was customary after divine service, now lining the bulwarks.

More than one telescope was trained shorewards as they slowed and swung with the current but the King was not at home – the squat King Henry fortress showed no colourful royal standard.

'Take us out, if y' please,' Kydd ordered. It would be harder to return now for the wind was veering more to the west, but if they took Lyme Bay in long boards it would not only give the men more time to enjoy their make-and-mend but enable them to raise Exmouth in the morning.

The next day, as they lay off Exmouth for an hour or two it had clouded over; if there were any urgent sightings or intelligence a cutter would come out to them. After breakfast they clapped on sail for the south and Teignmouth, where they did the same thing, heaving to well clear of the bar at the narrow harbour mouth.

Kydd felt a sense of unreality creeping in: this was not war, it was a pleasant cruise in a well-found craft with eighty men aboard who had nothing more to their existence but to obey his every whim. And before him lay only another easy sail south past some of the loveliest coast in England to Start Point, then a leisurely beat back home to Plymouth. When would it pall? When would come the time that *Teazer* had to justify herself as a man-o'-war? And when would he cross swords with Bloody Jacques?

Sail was spread and *Teazer* leant to it heartily; Hope's Nose was their next landfall and beyond it Tor Bay and Brixham. There was just time to go below and do some work, and reluctantly Kydd left the deck.

Renzi was deep in thought at his accustomed place in the stern windows so Kydd left him in peace, settling down with a sigh to an unfinished report. He worked steadily but his ears pricked at sudden shouts on deck and the rapidly approaching thump of feet.

'Sir!' blurted Andrews at the door. 'Mr Standish's compliments and the fleet is in sight!'

'A fleet?' Was this the dreaded invasion?

'Sir! Channel Fleet, flag o' Admiral Cornwallis!'

Kydd threw on his coat and bounded up on deck to find they had rounded Hope's Nose to the unfolding expanse of Tor Bay and come upon the majestic sight of the battleships of the blockading fleet entering their fall-back anchorage.

Looking up, Kydd saw their commissioning pennant standing out, long and proud, at precisely a right-angle from the shore. This meant a dead westerly, so the French in Brest were locked fast into their lair, unable to proceed to sea; the shrewd Cornwallis was taking the opportunity to refit and resupply – for as long as the wind held. Should it shift more than a point or two all anchors would be weighed in a rush and the fleet would stand out to sea to resume its watch and guard. Cornwallis was known as 'Billy Blue': his custom was to leave the Blue Peter flying all the time he was at anchor, the navy signal for imminent departure.

Kydd kept *Teazer* at a respectful distance while the great fleet came to rest. By the laws of the navy he was duty-bound to call on the admiral to request 'permission to proceed', a polite convention that allowed the senior man the chance to co-opt his vessel temporarily for some task.

'Full fig, Tysoe.' Their salute banged out while Kydd shifted into his full-dress uniform and, complete with sword and medals, embarked in the pinnace for the mighty and forbidding 112-gun flagship *Ville de Paris*.

Tor Bay was a scene of controlled chaos. From nowhere a host of small craft had appeared, summoned by an urgent telegraph signal that the fleet had been sighted. Hoys, wherries, lighters and a ceaseless stream of boats plied between the ships. This was resupply: a population equivalent to one of the biggest towns in England had appeared magically offshore and demanded months of provisions, putting into motion a formidably complex system that was timed to the hour.

As Kydd journeyed across to the flagship, constantly at hazard of entangling with the furious passage of the small craft, his boat's crew marvelled at the scene. On each ship they passed, men were thick in the rigging, sending down worn canvas, re-reeving end for end the halliards and braces that had seen so much service in the ceaseless struggle to keep the seas. Lighters were being towed out from the breweries at Millbrook, laden deep with vast quantities of beer, a healthier alternative to water in the casks after weeks at sea; and hoys struggled with all the onions, cabbages and other greens they could carry. That very morning these had been in the ground and hapless contractors were at twelve hours' notice to supply many tons of vegetables.

There was much activity ashore on Paignton Sands, too. Snaking lines of horses and cattle were stretched out over the hills heading towards a series of tents. Around them were piles of barrels and men in frenetic motion. The oxen, driven overland from the depot at Ivybridge, were being slaughtered, salted and headed up there and then in casks on the beach.

It was a telling commentary on the efforts of the nation to provide for its sailors, and a demonstration for all to see of the value placed on keeping this vital battle fleet at sea.

The monstrous sides of the flagship towered up and Kydd felt nervous. This was the commander-in-chief, Sir William Cornwallis, whose iron discipline was chiefly responsible for holding together the fleet in the fearsome conditions of the Atlantic blockade. His sea service went back to the American war – his brother had surrendered at Yorktown – and he had been with Rodney at the battle of the Saintes and served as a commodore in India against Tippoo Sahib.

Kydd mounted the side-steps carefully and was met at the ornate entry-port with the thrilling squeal of pipes and the bored looks of the receiving party. A lieutenant politely doffed his hat while Kydd punctiliously saluted first the quarterdeck, then him, before he strode aft and up to the admiral's cabin.

'Sit y'self down, m' boy,' the great man muttered, rooting about among his charts, then looking up mildly. 'Kind in ye to call.' The florid countenance and bluff ways of a country squire hid a sharp mind and ruthless organiser; the seamen called him 'Billy-go-tight' and stood well clear when he was to be seen pacing slowly, head down, about the decks.

'Seen much sport?' Cornwallis asked kindly.

'Naught but one privateer who gave me th' slip, sir,' Kydd said apologetically.

'Never mind, lad, early days yet. Now, if ye'd pay mind t' me, there's a service I'd like ye to perform as will spare one of m' frigates.'

'Aye, sir.'

A pale-faced lieutenant looked round the door and promptly vanished at Cornwallis's frown.

The admiral turned back to Kydd. 'Do ye find *Immortalité* frigate, Cap'n Owen, an' pass to him a small chest f'r which you'll take a receipt in due form. For y'r information it contains a sum in gold – f'r which I'll take *your* receipt, sir – by which we buy our intelligence.'

'Sir. Er, could I know where she's t' be found?'

'Inshore squadron,' Cornwallis answered testily. 'Who knows? In a westerly, could be anywhere off th' Goulet between the Béniguete an' Toulinguet.' At Kydd's hesitation he growled, 'Ask Flags, an' get some half-decent charts while ye're about it – it's a graveyard o' ships there, an' this has t' be in the right hands main quickly, sir.'

It made sense of a kind, conceded Kydd, resentfully, as *Teazer* left the commotion of Tor Bay astern and stretched out for Start Point. A little brig taken from her lawful duty was far less of a drain on precious resources than a full-blooded frigate, but this took no account of the feelings of her commander at being so casually sent on errands.

On the other hand this was for Kydd and *Teazer* a first time in one of the worst stretches of sea to be found anywhere – rock-strewn and treacherous, the approaches to Brest at the extreme Atlantic north-west of France had claimed the lives of countless English men-o'-war over the centuries. It was a dangerous lee-shore in all but the infrequent easterlies, and no place for the faint of heart.

All too soon the Start was abeam: it might be possible to fetch their objective in one tack but in this cloudy, petulant weather there would be no sightings to fix their position reliably. And the increasing westerly, with a making tide, would result in a leeward drift of an unknown quantity that would make even the best estimations questionable.

Despite the need for dispatch, the only prudent move would be to make a westing sufficient to come about again, and in the morning raise the guardian of Brest, the outlying island of Ushant. Then, knowing their position for a certainty, they could work in closer.

It seemed overly cautious, but Kydd was aware of the little wooden chest with the iron padlock that lay well secured in his bedplace. Much might depend on its safe arrival.

Davies, an amiable master's mate from *Ville de Paris*, had volunteered to act as guide – Dowse had only limited familiarity with the region so the younger man's advice would be crucial. Prosser had made much of his time of service on blockade in the 1790s but this was as a midshipman and, given his brash attitude, Kydd was not readily inclined to take suggestions from him. Any experiences of the lower deck made no reference to charts or coasting pilots and were no better than reminiscences.

The dawn brought with it thin, misting rain driving in from the west in tall white curtains that advanced slowly over a sullen swell to soak the sombre group on *Teazer*'s quarterdeck. As far as could be relied upon, their reckoning placed them some twenty-five miles to weather of Ushant, the traditional fleet rendezvous, but the sea was empty as the fleet was in Tor Bay.

'Helm up,' Kydd ordered, 'Steer east.' The die was cast: they were now sailing directly downwind towards France. They would sight Ushant and shape course accordingly or, missing it, end embroiled in the maze of half-tide rocks promised by their chart.

Kydd went over the arithmetic. The higher he was on the ship, the further he could see. Distance to the horizon in miles was 1.17 times the square root of the height-of-eye in feet. As he stood on the quarterdeck, his eye was about ten feet up, which gave a figure of some four miles. At its highest, Ushant was no more than a hundred and forty feet odd, which by the same calculation gave about fourteen miles. Therefore, adding the two, he could expect to make landfall at eighteen miles off and nearer twenty-three for a lookout in the maintop.

'Get up there, lad,' he ordered Andrews. Another pair of eyes in the tops would never be too many with so much riding on it. But before the lad could swing into the shrouds a sudden cry came from the foretop. *'Laaand hooo!'* The lookout gestured vigorously to leeward.

In a fever of impatience Kydd waited for the land to come within sight of the deck, an anonymous grey shape firming before them. 'Take it south-about,' Kydd told the quarter-master. If it was Ushant they needed to be in place for their southward search and if it was not . . .

Davies came and stood next to Kydd, staring intently. 'Certainly looks the part, sir,' he said pleasantly, as though unaware of the tension about him. 'We'll discover f'r sure when we see him off t' the nor'-west. He has a deep bay there, lookin' all the world like the open claw of a lobster.'

'We used to say "nutcracker" in *Diomede*,' Prosser said importantly. He had taken up position on the other side of Kydd, who didn't reply.

It proved to be Ushant and therefore they had their posi-tion exactly – for the moment. The westerly was holding and beginning to kick up a bit of a sea, although this was probably more due to its disputing with the last of the down-Channel ebb. Kydd fretted at the ragged rain squalls that marched across and lasted for long minutes, bringing visibility down to yards; not only did this make sighting

Immortalité difficult but it hid the dark rocks off to starboard.

'T'were best we made our southing through the Chenal d'Four,' Davies offered, 'We have the slant wi' this westerly.'

Prosser puffed his cheeks. 'In *Diomede* it was always Chenal d'Helle, on account—'

'Hold y'r noise!' Kydd snapped. 'Haven't ye somethin' t' do forrard?'

Leaving the black mass of Ushant astern, they sailed on uneasily until a low line of darker grey spread across the horizon, hardening into a craggy coastline. 'France, sir,' Davies said unnecessarily. Kydd grunted; of more concern to him now was their undeviating approach directly towards it. Detail became clearer as they neared, a wicked, uncompromising cragginess.

The chart had shown an appalling jumble of unconnected reefs and half-tide rocks and had hinted of fierce tidal currents to be avoided at all costs. To thread a safe route through would be a nightmare without help.

'Are ye sure?'

Davies nodded patiently.

'Tut, tut, an' this is a rare moil,' exclaimed Dowse, looking askance at the approaching cliffs, now no more than a couple of miles distant. It was a dead lee shore and all his master's instincts jangled in alarm. His eyes met Kydd's.

'Nothing t' worry of,' Davies said cheerfully, 'Need to keep inshore o' L'Piâtresses, is all.'

The helm went over a bare mile short of the grim heights, but as they made their passage south to parallel them Kydd saw why: at this distance there was a noticeable back wind from the nearby sea-cliffs, which went some way to easing the situation.

Away to starboard the misty sea was full of dismal black crags, white-fringed and dreadful, and after they had passed a stern headland at less than a mile it was evident that they were edging nearer, being crowded ever closer to the coast – suddenly there was no longer any space to wear about or even to tack back to where they had come from.

'I mislike it, sir – no sea room, we can't put back,' Dowse said. 'What if . . . ?'

They were being funnelled between a substantial seaweed-black islet to starboard and a gaunt, twisted headland to larboard, but as they drew in, there was a flat *thump* on the damp air. Kydd heard more and searched feverishly for where the guns were. There must be a battery somewhere atop the lofty cliffs – which they would pass close beneath.

He turned to Davies, who said calmly, 'Pay no mind t' the Frenchy, sir. He's got no notion o' range over water, and in any case, I know a little diversion, this state o' th' tide, as'll take us close in past the Béniguete instead.'

True to his word, *Teazer* found herself picking her way warily past the frighteningly close kelp-strewn islet while the guns thudded away impotently. Another mile, and they were in open water, the dark coastline fallen away to nothing.

'Clear, sir,' Davies said smugly, 'This is y'r Goulet,' he added, gesturing to the tumble of seas stretching away to the left. 'And Brest lies no more'n a dozen miles away there t' the east'd.'

This was all very fine; they had won through the worst to the main approaches of the port but where was *Immortalité*? The little brig-sloop continued across the wide mouth towards the other side but still no trace. And the irritated French might be driven to sending out gunboats.

Picking up on Pointe du Toulinguet on the opposite side,

to the anguish of the master watching the ugly scattering of black rocks stretching seaward for miles, they hauled away across the Iroise towards its natural boundary at the Pointe du Raz and the fifteen miles of reefs and shoals extending straight out to sea.

With a four-thousand-mile fetch, the wind from the open sea had a relentless urge to it that seemed to want to bully *Teazer* ever closer towards the grim coastline. And it was increasing now, with an ugly lop and white horses here and there. The rain had eased to flurries but there was low scud above the ragged cloud.

'Mr Davies?' Kydd asked heavily. It was getting uncomfortable, beam on to the racing seas, and while visibility was improving the doubled lookouts were not seeing any sign of sail.

'Why, y' have to understand, sir, in the inshore squadron we has two jobs to do – tell England when the Mongseers put t' sea, and the other is t' show ourselves anywhere there's a Frenchman, tells 'em they're under eye and it's better for 'em to stay snug in harbour. *Immortalité* could be . . . well, anywheres.'

'Thank you, Mr Davies.' Kydd looked out to the unfriendly sea and back to the forbidding coast. Naval duty was a hard taskmaster at times – was it expected that he comb the seas interminably until he found his frigate? In these dangerous waters, with thick weather promising?

The rocky barrier out from the Pointe du Raz was approaching; decisions would have to be made. To leeward, out of sight from the deck, the sweep of Douarnenez Bay had no port of interest, except possibly the small haven of Douarnenez itself. He was not about to risk entering the bay – Douarnenez! A tickle of memory came: his first ship and he a lowly ordinary seaman smelling gunpowder for the first time. It was here that *Duke William* had clashed briefly with emerging French ships-of-the-line. They must have been taking shelter in an accustomed anchorage – with which the frigate would of course be familiar and might now be reconnoitring.

'We bear up f'r Douarnenez, I believe, Mr Dowse.'

They entered the bay past a prominent foreland towering up to larboard, the bay opening up widely beyond. The further shore would only be in sight from the tops and Kydd gazed up at them impatiently. But – nothing. No sail, no frigate. 'G'damn it!' he blazed.

'Sir! Sir!' Andrews piped from his station on the afterdeck, hopping from one foot to the other. He was pointing vigorously astern. Tucked well into the lee of the foreland just past, a ship lay at anchor, her ensign plain for all to see.

'*Immortalité*,' Davies confirmed.

However, so far downwind there was nothing for it but to beat back to the big vessel. A gun boomed on her fo'c'sle, drawing attention to the challenge that had shot smartly up her halliards. 'Private signal,' roared Kydd to Andrews: thank heaven he had had the foresight to claim these from the flagship before he left and to have the correct signal of the day made up for hoisting every morning.

It soared up briskly: it wouldn't do to trifle with a crack frigate of the inshore squadron. *Teazer* leant to the wind and beat her way over while Kydd decided that he would not stand on ceremony; even a post-captain would not expect him to dress for a visit on this occasion.

As they neared, a twenty-four-pounder crashed out and the sea plumed ahead of their forefoot. At the same time, all along the length of the frigate's gun deck cannon were run out and Kydd found himself staring down the muzzles of *Immortalité*'s broadside.

His mind froze. Then he thought to check again with her ensign – if she had been captured, the French could never fire under false colours – but she still flew an ensign of the Royal Navy.

'Mr Purchet!' bellowed Kydd, his voice breaking with effort. 'Loose the fore topsail sheets this instant!' In a frenzied motion they were cast off and the sail banged and fluttered free. It was the nearest thing to striking topsails, the age-old signal of surrender, that Kydd could think of.

'Clear away the cutter, boat's crew t' muster,' he croaked.

Under Poulden's urgent bidding the men stretched out for the frigate, Kydd sitting bolt upright, his foul-weather gear damp and uncomfortable. As they neared, there was confirmation that this was a vessel of the Royal Navy – sea-worn she might be, but every detail, from the blacked muzzles of the cannon to the fancy ropework round the wind-vane, spoke of a proud sea service.

They came alongside and hooked on, the boat jibbing like a lunatic in the seas that swept the sides of the frigate. Kydd waited for the right moment and jumped for the side-steps, his wet-weather gear tangling and whipping as he climbed up and over the bulwarks.

Two stolid lines of armed marines met him instead of a side-party. A grim-faced post-captain waited ahead and held up his hands for Kydd to stop where he was. 'And who the devil are you, sir?' he grated.

'C-commander Kydd, brig-sloop *Teazer*, at y'r service, sir,' Kydd said breathlessly.

'Prove it!' snarled the captain.

Kydd smothered a retort when he realised that, but for a

bedraggled and threadbare hat, he was in anonymous foul-weather gear – and he had not a scrap of identification on him as a British officer.

He wheeled round on Poulden, who stood rigidly behind. 'What's th' best public house in Plymouth Town? Quickly, man!'

'Th-the Town? Beggin' y'r pardon, sir, but we likes best t' hob-a-nob at th' Portsmouth Hoys, Fore Street in Dock, as serves the best brown ale, but if y' means Old Plymouth, why . . .' He tailed off uncertainly under the ferocious glare of the frigate captain.

There was a brief, unreal silence before the captain grunted, 'Very well. Stand down the marines. Secure from quarters.' He marched up to Kydd and halted within inches. 'Now, sir, do you account for yourself.'

Affronted, Kydd retorted, 'I'm at a loss, sir, why you fired into me.'

The captain kept his eyes fixed on Kydd's and snapped, 'So *you* would not, were you a frigate captain, which I highly doubt will ever be the case? Then, pray, look at it from my point of view.

'A strange and – I observe – foreign-looking sloop sails unconcerned, as though in home waters, straight into Douarnenez Bay, which all good Englishmen do shun. He sees me and, quick as a flash, throws out the private signal, just as if he'd got it by him after capturing one of ours. He puts about impudently and takes his chance to close with me, hoping to catch us off-guard and at anchor, so then he may pour in his treacherous broadsides.

'But he's forgotten one detail.' He paused, giving a savage smile, then went on in a voice of rising thunder, 'If he's of the Channel Fleet, carries their private signals – *then why in Hades is he flying the wrong damn ensign?*'

Too late, Kydd remembered. On her temporary side-voyage for Cornwallis, *Teazer* was flying not the blue ensign of Cornwallis's fleet but the red of Lockwood's command.

Chapter 7

'An' I'm determined on it, Nicholas,' Kydd said, stretching happily in his armchair.

'We have hardly had time to scrape the salt from our eyebrows after our hard weeks on the briny deep, dear brother,' Renzi sighed, 'and here you are proposing we should immediately embark on the rigours of—'

'Not a high occasion as would embarrass th' exchequer, I'll grant ye, more in the way of an assembly or so,' Kydd said comfortably. Becky came in shyly to draw the curtains and departed with a smile.

'Then might we not consider a rout? No expense of a meal at table, quantities of people arriving and departing when they will, wine and jollity on all sides. And, of course, the decided social advantage of there being the opportunity to accommodate more than the usual number so there will be many more in the way of return invitations.'

'Done!' What was the use of maintaining an establishment if it were not to be gainfully employed? 'Who shall be invited? As ye know, *Teazer* will not be in port s' long . . .'

While invitations were agreed plans were put in train. 'I'm of th' mind that a woman's touch might be an advantage,' Kydd said. 'Should I – do y' think that Cecilia is t' be invited?'

Renzi looked up from his writing of the invitations – a bold, round copperplate of impeccable execution – and said, in measured tones, 'She is your sister. It would be singular indeed if you did not ask her. And if by this you make allusion to any feelings I might have entertained for the lady, pray spare me your delicacies – she is quite free to come and go as she chooses, which is her right as a gentlewoman.' His head bent to the writing.

The evening seemed destined for success: all invitations were taken up and Kydd was kept busy greeting the steady stream of guests who showed every inclination to linger.

Cecilia sparkled as hostess; her orange-flower and brandy rout cakes were universally applauded. Becky, under Tysoe's discreet tutelage, mingled with a tray of cordials and wines and it was not long before number eighteen resounded to scenes of gaiety and warmth.

'Ah, Mrs Mullins!' Kydd said warmly. 'Y'r help in acquiring m' residence is much appreciated. Can ye not feel how it likes t' see a party?'

'I do that, Mr Kydd,' she replied, hiding a smile.

'Sir, a Miss Robbins.' It was the hired footman at the door.

'Why, Mr Kydd! So good of you to remember us.' There was movement behind her as she went on, 'Ah, the invitation did mention "a friend", did it not?' she cooed.

'O' course it did, Miss—' Her friend emerged from behind her, stopping Kydd mid-sentence. 'Oh! Er, th-thank you f'r coming, Miss Lockwood,' he managed, then remembered a polite bow, took the proffered hand and escorted her in.

She was in a cream dress of the latest fashion and had taken some considerable pains with her Grecian hairstyle. 'I noticed your ship arrive, Mr Kydd,' she said warmly. 'Such a pretty creature. A brig-sloop, I'd hazard?'

'Aye – that is t' say, yes, she is. *Teazer* is her name.'

'How curious,' she said. Her hazel eyes held his for a long moment. 'Does she suit you?'

Kydd returned the look coolly but inwardly he exulted. How had she known it was his ship unless it had been pointed out to her – or she had been looking out for it? Either way it proved her interest in him. 'Why, Miss Lockwood, there's been three *Teazer*s in our sea service this age but none s' sweet a sailer on a bowline as – as my *Teazer*.'

'How agreeable for you.' She paused and continued softly, 'Tell me this, would you trust your very life to her in a great storm?'

'I would,' Kydd answered immediately. He wondered what lay behind her words, realising that she was using the seafarer's 'she' for a ship instead of the landlubber's soulless 'it'. 'I have afore now, an' conceive I will again, all th' time I'm in English seas.'

'Just so,' she said politely, her eyes still on him. Kydd felt a blush rising. 'Well, Mr Kydd, if I don't see you again tonight let me tell you how much I have enjoyed meeting you once more.'

Kydd bowed wordlessly and, claimed by Miss Robbins, Persephone Lockwood entered the throng. Kydd gazed after her, seeing people fall back in deference to her quality and respectful glances flashed his way.

He resumed his duties, conscious of rising elation. Time passed, and the first guests made ready to depart, among them Miss Lockwood. Should he strike up a conversation before she left? But before he could act she had caught his eye and moved over to him. 'Mr Kydd, thank you for a lovely evening.'

'M-my pleasure, Miss L-Lockwood,' he stuttered.

'I wonder – no, I have no right to ask it of you,' she said, with a frown, a gloved hand going to her mouth.

'Do, please,' Kydd said gallantly.

'Well, since you are so obliging, it does occur to me that you could be of some service to me in a small matter that would really mean a lot.'

'Miss Lockwood, if I c'n do anything . . .'

'It's for my father,' she said apologetically, 'I have it in mind to present him with a painting for his birthday, a marine painting. You see, I'm concerned that it be completely authentic in its sea detail – you've no idea how testy Papa gets when he espies errors in the rigging and so forth. If you could assist me to choose wisely I would be most grateful.'

'Er, yes! I mean t' say, o' course I will.'

'You're most kind. Then shall we meet at the print publisher in Old Plymouth? I've been told he also has some fine sea paintings. Would Wednesday, at eleven, suit?'

'Wednesday, yes,' Kydd blurted. Two days.

'Oh – and this had better be our little secret,' she concluded, with an impish smile.

'Come.' Kydd looked up from his pile of official letters.

'I'll be off ashore, then, sir,' his first lieutenant said boyishly. He looked dashing in his cutaway coat and gush

162

of lace cravat, and held a rakish silk hat as though he was trying to hide it.

'By all means, Mr Standish.' The unwritten custom was that the two officers would take turn and turn about to be out of the ship while at short stay in port. 'An' good fortune with the . . . the entertainments.'

The other flashed a broad smile and was gone.

Kydd bent once more to his task. The constant stream of invoices, dockets, reports and correspondence requiring his sole attention never ceased to amaze him, but any matter skimped or overlooked might rebound at a later time.

'Enter!' he called at a timid knock.

'From ashore, sir,' squeaked Andrews.

It was a simple folded letter from Cecilia.

Dear Thomas – Jane has been lately telling me of your dockyard, and how it is the very wonder of the age. She says that if you are known to a person of conse-quence it is quite the thing to visit at length under escort. You would oblige me extremely if you will indulge my curiosity when convenient.

His dockyard? Kydd smiled. Plymouth, big as it now was, was near dwarfed by the naval dockyard and the vast popu-lation of workers that had grown up around it, but he was feeling restless and an excuse to get away and promenade in the sunshine was welcome. 'At ten, the North Stairs,' he scribbled on the back of the note. She would know where the officers stepped ashore.

She was waiting for him, twirling a parasol and in infec-tious good spirits. 'Such a handsome escort for a lady,' she exclaimed, taking his arm. Since the return of Kydd and Renzi from Terra Australis Cecilia had made a remarkable recovery and was now undeniably in looks, her strong dark features catching eyes on all sides.

'Then shall we spread sail an' get under way, Cec?'

Seamen touched their hats with a grin and a grave ensign of Foot saluted Kydd's gold and blue smartly as they moved off round the wall to the Fore Street entrance. The master porter emerged from his little house and recognised Kydd with a wave, the two sentinels coming to a crashing 'present'.

'This is y'r royal dockyard, then, sis. Seventy-one acres an' three thousand artificers, not t' mention th' labouring men. I dare t' say there are more'n half ten thousand men at work before ye now.'

It gave pause, for the largest industrial endeavour in his home town, the Guildford iron foundry, could boast of no more than a few score and none other in Kydd's acquaintance had more than some small hundreds.

'What a charming chapel,' Cecilia murmured, looking at a trim little edifice just inside the gates.

'Seventeen hundred, sis, William the Third.' An avenue of well-tended lime trees stretched away to a lengthy terrace of fine houses that might well have graced Bath or London. 'An' those are the quarters of the officers o' the dockyard – there ye'll find the commissioner, master shipwright, clerk o' the cheque, all your swell coves. Gardens at th' back an' offices in the front.'

But her eyes were down the slight hill to the main dock area and the towering complexity of a ship-of-the-line in dry-dock. As they approached, the scale of the sight became more apparent: soaring to the skies, her masts and yards higher by far than the tallest building anywhere, it seemed incredible that this great structure was actually designed to move.

Clutching Kydd's arm Cecilia peered over the edge of the graving dock, unprepared for the sheer grandeur of the dimensions of what she saw: the huge bulk of the vessel, the muddy floor of the dock so far below and the tiny figures moving about from under.

'I'll show ye a sight as you'll never forget,' Kydd said. 'Mind y'r dress.' He found a small flight of stone steps with an iron hand-chain that led down into the abyss. 'Come on, Cec.'

Frightened, but trusting, she clung to the chain and they descended, down and down. The sunlight faded and a miasma of mud and seaweed wafted up, thick and pungent. On the last step Kydd called a halt. 'Look now, sis.'

She turned – and caught her breath. In a giddying domination, the colossal green-streaked bulk of the battleship reared above them blotting out everything. As well, it stretched away down the dock on and on, longer than a town street, and the impression of a monstrous bulking poised only on the central keel-blocks and kept from toppling by spindly-looking shores caused a strange feeling of upside-down vertigo.

Kydd pointed past the fat swell of the hull to the further end. 'Those are our dock gates, Cec. I have t' tell ye that the other side o' that is the sea, and where we're stood is usually thirty feet under th' waves.'

'They w-won't open them while we're still here, will they?' she asked, in a small voice.

'Not till I give 'em the order.' Kydd chuckled, but Cecilia mounted the steps back to the sunshine with almost indecent haste.

At the top Kydd could not resist stepping over to the adjacent dock — even bigger, the seventy-four within seeming quite diminished. 'Now this one. It's the biggest in th' world, an' the dockyard has a story about it.

'Y' see when it was built, it was designed f'r our largest ship, the *Queen Charlotte* of a hundred guns. But then the Frenchies built one much bigger, th' *Commerce de Marseille* of a hundred and twenty guns — nearly three thousan' tons. So just in time, they enlarged it an' finished it f'r the war in 'ninety-three.'

He paused for effect. 'Now, ye'll recall in that year that Vice-Adm'ral Lord Hood took Toulon an' much o' the French fleet. So this is sayin' that it's just as well they made their changes when they did, for the first ship t' use the dock was the *Commerce de Marseille* herself!'

Arm in arm they passed the clatter of the joinery work-shops, the rich stink of the pitch house, then dock after dock, each with a man-o'-war in various stages of repair and alive with shipwrightery and riggers.

At a substantial kiln a procession of men were with-drawing steaming planks wrapped in cloths. 'The chippies use th' steam chest t' bend their strakes round th' frames an' fit 'em by eye — that's three curves in one, I'll have ye know,' Kydd said admiringly, remembering Antigua dock-yard in the Caribbean.

'Oh — the poor man!' Cecilia gasped. Peering into a sawpit she had glimpsed the lower individual of a pair who were plying a mighty whip-saw to slice a bole of oak to planks. The one above the trestle bent to saw and direct the cut while his partner, showered with chips and dust as he worked, took the other end in a dank pit the size of a grave.

'All day, an' a shillin' only,' Kydd said, then pointed out

the rigging house. 'You'd not credit it, but old *Tenacious* has near twenty miles o' rope aboard. Goes fr'm your light tricin' line all the way t' the anchor cable, which is two feet round, if ye can believe it.'

Cecilia nodded doubtfully, so Kydd went on, 'Which is sayin' that the crew on the capstan are heavin' in seven tons weight o' cable alone, straight up an' down and stand fast the weight of the anchor.'

Seeing her suitably impressed, he changed tack. 'An' above the riggin' house we have the sail loft. Ye'll know how important this is when I say that we carried more'n four acres o' sail, and if y' stop t' think that we needs so much spare canvas, an' ropes wear s' fast, and multiply this by the hundreds o' ships we keep at sea . . .'

A broad canal crossed their path, running a quarter of a mile straight into the interior of the dockyard. Fortunately it was spanned by a swivelling footbridge. 'This is th' Camber. Right up there we have th' boat pond an' it's also where *Teazer* hoisted aboard her fit of anchors. An' I think I c'n find ye somethin' there tolerably divertin'.'

They turned left towards a stone building a good hundred yards square, bristling like a porcupine with multitudes of tall chimneys. A muffled cacophony of clanking, screeches and deep thumping strengthened as they neared the fitful yellow glare at the glassless windows.

'The smithy,' Cecilia pronounced, seeing an expanse of adjacent open ground covered with hundreds of finished anchors, each set upright and painted black against rust.

'Aye, the blacksmith's shop. But let's take a peek inside.' It was a scene from the *Inferno*: hundreds of men at work on fifty huge forges in an atrocious clamour, white-hot metal showering sparks into the smoky gloom, the dismal clanking of the bellows chains and pale faces darting about with red-hot objects.

'Shall we see th' hammer forge, Cec?' Kydd shouted in her ear. 'Hercules, they call it, an' it takes thirty men to—'

It seemed that his sister would be happy to defer this pleasure to another time, and instead was content to hear that the shop contributed an amazing number of metal objects to be found about a ship-of-war, and that when it was time for anchor-forging the men demanded large quantities of strong ale in place of their usual gallon of small beer, such were the hideous conditions.

The wonders of the dockyard seemed endless. At the mast house Cecilia admired a 120-foot mainmast for a first-rate man-o'-war being shaped from a number of separate pieces to form a single spar ten feet round before it was rolled into the mast pond with a thunderous splash.

At the rope-walk she saw yarns ravelled in the upper storey ready to be laid up together into strands below, and these then twisted mechanically against each other to form the rope. 'A sizeable hundred-fathom cable takes three thousand yarns,' Kydd explained, as she watched.

After the acrid pungency of the pitch house, where she was told about the difference between the two tars to be found aboard ship – one was asphaltum from Trinidad used for caulking deck seams and the other, quite different, derived from fragrant pine-tree resin from the Baltic and was used for tarring rope – she confessed, 'Dear Thomas, I'm faint with impressions. Do let us find somewhere to sit down and refresh.'

It was a little disappointing – there was the wonderful sea stench to be experienced only in the burning of old barnacled timbers to recover the copper and, of course, the whole south corner where so many noble ships lay building on the stocks. And the Bunker's Hill battery, which had a most curious brass gun from Paris . . . But perhaps it would be better to leave some sights for another time.

They walked slowly back to the gate. Cecilia wore a dazed look, and Kydd asked, 'Did you enjoy th' party at all?'

'I did – very much, thank you, Thomas,' she roused herself to say.

'The guests seemed t' have a good time,' Kydd said proudly. 'Did ye notice the admiral's daughter? Persephone's her name,' he added casually. 'So good in her t' come.'

'Oh, yes. It was surprising, I suppose.'

'Well, she was invited b' another lady but, Cec, I think she's interested in me. She asked about *Teazer* an' if she suited me . . . Well, anyway, I thought she was.'

'Dear brother! Hers is a notable family and she's certain to have a whole train of admirers of quite another sort to ourselves.'

'But—'

'Thomas, she's a very nice person, I can tell, but please don't mistake her politeness for anything else, I beg.'

'Miss Lockwood?' Kydd advanced into the upper room of the premises where he had been told she was waiting.

'Why, Mr Kydd! You're very prompt, you know – I'd only just arrived.' She wore flowers in her hair, which complemented her gay morning dress. The only other in the room was an unctuous proprietor, who hovered discreetly. 'What do you think?'

Kydd advanced to inspect the oil. It was a robust piece, a first-rate vessel of another age with bellying sails and two sloops on an opposing course. The man scuttled up and said quickly, 'Ah, Samuel Scott, *A First Rate Shortening Sail* – time of the second George.'

He was cast a withering look and retreated.

'Mr Kydd?'

This was not a time for hasty opinions and Kydd took his time. 'A fine painting,' he began, aware from the discreet price tag that the artist was no mere dauber. 'It is th' commander-in-chief, as we c'n see from the union at the main, an' if I'm not mistaken there is the gentleman himself in the stern gallery with another.'

She peered closer, unavoidably bringing her face close enough to his that he could sense her warmth. 'Ha – hm,' he continued, trying to marshal his thoughts. 'However, here I find a puzzle. The name is *Shortening Sail* but I see th' sheets are well in, an' the buntlines o' the main course are bein' overhauled. If there are no men on th' yard takin' in sail it speaks t' me more of loosin' sail, setting 'em abroad.'

'Mr Scott was well known as a marine artist, a friend to Mr Hogarth. Could it be that he's amiss in his nauticals, do you think?' Persephone asked.

Kydd swallowed. 'Miss Lockwood, if ye'll observe the sea – it has no form, all up an' down as it were. Real sea t' this height always has a wind across it an' you can tell from th' waves its direction, an' this must be th' same as the set o' the sails.'

She waited for Kydd to continue. 'We have here our boats a-swim, which is tellin' us th' seas are not s' great. So why then do we not see t'gallants set in any o' the ships? And y'r sloops – at sea we do not fly our union at the fore or th' ensign at the staff. This is reserved f'r when we take up our moorin's, and—'

'Bravo!' she applauded. 'I *was* right to ask your assistance, Mr Kydd. We shall have no further dealings with this artist.'

She threw a look at the proprietor, who hurried back. 'I can see we have a client of discrimination,' he said, avoiding Kydd's eye, 'Therefore I will allow you to inspect this Pocock,' he said importantly, unlacing a folio. 'A watercolour. LE JUSTE *and the* INVINCIBLE. Should this be more to your taste, do you think?'

He drew it out and gave it to Persephone, who handed it pointedly to Kydd. It was of quite another quality, a spirited interchange between two ships-of-the-line, the leeward Frenchman nearly hidden in clouds of powder-smoke. The liveliness and colour of the sea, a deep Atlantic green, was faultless. 'The Glorious First of June, of course,' the man added smoothly, seeing Kydd's admiration.

'You were present at that, were you not, Mr Kydd?' Persephone put in, to the proprietor's evident chagrin.

But Kydd had been a shipwrecked seaman at the time, held in a hulk at Portsmouth. 'Er, not at that action,' he answered shortly.

'Neither was Papa,' she replied stoutly. 'Yet I do believe you were in another battle besides the Nile.'

'Aye – that was Camperdown,' he said.

'Do you have any oil of Camperdown?' she enquired.

Kydd felt relief: the price of the Pocock was alarming.

'A Whitcombe, perhaps?' the man offered.

Camperdown had been a defining moment for Kydd. Soon after the nightmare of the mutiny at the Nore he had found escape in the blood-lust of the battle, the hardest-fought encounter the Royal Navy had met with during the war. It was there that he had won his battlefield commission to lieutenant.

His eyes focused again; his battle quarters had been on the gun deck and the fight had been an invisible and savage chaos outside, away from his sight and knowledge. However, from what he had heard about the engagement afterwards, it was not hard to piece together the point of view of the painting.

'Yes. In the middle this is Admiral Duncan in *Venerable* right enough, drubbing the Dutchy de Winter in *Fryhide* here. Y' sees th' signal, number five? It means t' engage more closely.' It had been such a near-run battle, with men who had been in open mutiny so soon before. Raw memories were coming to life. 'There's *Monarch* – that's Rear Admiral Onslow who gave me m' step. His family is fr'm near Guildford . . .'

Sensing his charged mood Persephone asked softly, 'Is *this* sea to your satisfaction?'

'It's – it's a fine sea,' Kydd said quietly, 'Short 'n' steep, as ye'd expect in the shallow water they has off the Texel.'

'Then this will be the one. I'll take it.' The proprietor hurried off with it, leaving them alone.

Persephone turned to him with a warm smile. 'So, now I have my painting. That was kind.' She moved to a bench against the opposite wall. 'Do let's rest here for a moment,' she said, sitting down gracefully. It seemed the most natural thing in the world to join her.

'Tell me, Mr Kydd, if you'll forgive the impertinence, I cannot help but observe that you look the very figure of a mariner. Would you tell me, what *was* it that first called you to the sea?'

Kydd hesitated: any information she would have been able to find about his past would only have covered his service as an officer and he was free to say anything he wished. 'I was a pressed man.'

She blinked in surprise. 'Were you really?'

'Aye. It was only at Camperdown I was given th' quarterdeck.' He looked steadily at her, but saw only a dawning understanding.

'Yet you took to the sea – as though you were born to it.'

'The sea is – a different world, way of living. An' – an' it's excitin' in a way th' land can never be.'

'Exciting?'

'Th' feel of a deck under y'r feet when the bow meets th' open sea – always y'r ship curtsies to Neptune an' then she's alive an' never still. You feel, er, um . . .' he finished lamely.

'No! Do go on!'

But Kydd kept his silence: he wasn't about to make a fool of himself before a lady of her quality, and in any event she would discover the full truth of his origins sooner or later.

'Then I must take it that the sea's mystery is not for the female sex,' she said teasingly, then subsided. 'Mr Kydd, do, please, forgive my curiosity, but there are so many experiences denied to a woman and my nature is not one to bear this easily.'

She looked away for a moment, then turned to ask, in level tones, 'If you are a sailor and have a – a *tendre* for ships, what is your feeling when you fire off your great cannons into another, which contains sailors like you?'

Was she trying to provoke him? She must know it was his duty as a naval officer . . . Or was she trying to reach him in some way?

'Well, in course, we see this as th' foe who brings an item o' war forward as we're obliged t' remove, like a piece at chess, an' we fire at it until it is removed.'

'And when you are looking down a musket-barrel at another human being?' She regarded him gravely.

The proprietor bustled up with the parcelled work. 'I have it ready, your ladyship, if you—'

'I shall be down presently,' she said evenly.

They were left alone once more and she looked at him expectantly.

'I fire on th' uniform, not th' man,' Kydd responded.

'Your sword. You stand before a man you would pierce with it. Does it not cross your mind that—'

'I have killed a man – several. That I'm here today before ye is because I did.' What was this about?

She smiled softly. 'I was right. You are different. Is it because you won your place in the world the hard way? Your naval officer of the usual sort would be telling me of duty and honour, but you see through the superficialities to the hard matter without adornment.'

Rising to her feet she straightened her skirt and, in a businesslike voice, went on, 'You are an interesting man, Mr Kydd. Perhaps we may continue this conversation on another occasion. Do you ride?'

The man from London stood up briskly, strode to the centre of the room and looked about. 'Smuggling! If there are any among you who still thinks to puff up smuggling as the stuff of romance, then, sir, I will take the most forceful issue with you. It's a pernicious and abiding folderol that conceals the most frightful consequences to the nation.'

There was intelligence but also animal ferocity in the man's demeanour, and Kydd recalled the respect in the admiral's manner when he had introduced him as an emissary from Whitehall. Kydd stole a glance at Bazely, who wore an expression of studied blankness; the three other captains present seemed either puzzled or bored.

'I see that I shall require to be more direct with you sea officers,' the speaker continued. 'You, sir!' he said, pointing to Parlby. 'How do you conceive this war is being funded? Hey? Where is the means to be found to bestow plentiful vittles and rightful pay on your fine ship? It costs His Majesty some thousands merely to set it afloat. Pray where, sir, is this treasure to be found?'

Parlby started in surprise. 'Why, er, the consolidated funds of the Treasury.'

'Which are entirely derived from?'

'Ah – taxes?'

'Yes?'

Brow furrowed, Parlby hesitated and was instantly rounded on.

'Taxes! And since Mr Pitt's scheme of tax upon income was lately repealed what others are left to His Majesty's government? Naught but a sad collection of imposts on hair-powder, windows, candles, playing-cards – and the dues of Customs and Excise.'

His glare challenged them all. 'If this source withers, the very capability of this country to defend itself is in question. Gentlemen, I have to tell you in confidence that the situation now is of such a grave nature that the prime minister has asked that no pain be spared to control this accursed bleeding of treasure.

'And it is a grievous loss. We find that for every ounce of tobacco faithfully duty-paid, near a pound is smuggled, and three fourths or more of our tea escapes its fair due. When I confide our best understanding is that for every cask of contraband intercepted eight get through, what is this but a ruinous deprivation to the country that it cannot sustain?'

'Just so,' Lockwood rumbled, discomfited by the man's intensity. 'Now, gentlemen, we are asked to apply our best efforts to the suppression of this vice. My orders will reflect this request, requiring you to pursue these rogues with the same vigour as you would a privateer or similar.' He flourished a handkerchief and trumpeted. 'May I remind you that any smuggler taken in the act will suffer seizure of ship and cargo to the interest of the captor . . .'

Chasing smugglers was no way to achieve fame and distinction, but on the other hand, there was a real threat to the nation and the path to duty was clear. 'Sir, are there any parts o' the coast that we should especially watch?' Kydd enquired.

'Devonshire and Cornwall might be accounted as having the worst rascals in the kingdom, sir. They've been at the trade since the time of good Queen Bess, and I don't believe they see reasons now why they should abandon their ways. Polperro and Fowey have been mentioned, and Penzance is far from guiltless, but you will find their kind everywhere you look. Each tiny cove and fishing village has its "free traders" who, in the twinkling of an eye, can turn back into honest fishermen.

'But there has lately been a change, a disturbing and possibly fatal turn. Our best information has it that an organising intelligence is at work along the coast, such that where before we could try to contain and subvert the efforts of an individual village there appears now to be one evil genius who can control and direct the smuggling ventures of all. If we descend on one, there will be a speedy diversion elsewhere and we cannot watch every contemptible little hamlet. The situation approaches dire calamity.'

Penzance harbour was a shimmering expanse under summer sunshine while *Teazer*, anchored in the lazy calm, saw to her domestics. Kydd returned aboard, went below, divested himself of his coat, then gratefully accepted a cordial from Tysoe.

'Be damned!' Kydd threw at Renzi, who sat inoffensively with a book at the stern windows. 'Not as who should say but th' Revenue are a hard crew t' fathom.'

He flopped into his chair and took out some notes. 'D' ye know, Nicholas, as there's a rare parcel o' coves needed t' keep a Customs post? I give ye tide-waiters, boat-sitters, searchers of salt, ridin' officers an' quantities of land-waiters – the rest I forget.'

'How entertaining, brother. Did you by chance learn of how they spend their day?'

'Customs an' Excise? As far as I c'n tell, they're tasked to see that every merchant vessel from over th' seas attends at a full-rigged Customs port, an' there will find the "legal quay" t' land cargo to be assessed. This is where we find our tide-waiters and land-waiters at work t' keep a weather eye open that all's legal an' above board.'

'Legal quay?'

'Aye. This is y'r definition. If freight is landed *not* at a legal quay then, in course, it's contraband and we may seize the villain. But all this'n is your Revenue man earning his daily bread. Where we'll be of use to 'em is in the preventive service – catching the rascals as they come in from seaward to try t' land th' contraband.'

'They have their own officers, I believe.'

'They do, Nicholas – an' a sea service as well. If y' remember, *Seaflower* was Revenue cutter built – monstrous sail area, mighty bowsprit an' the rest. All built f'r speed to catch our smuggler. But they've boats as well, galley built as will take twenty oars, some of 'em, can go against th' wind or chase up a hidden creek. And along shore, there's ridin' officers out on good horses, goin' up an' down the coast atop the cliffs t' spy out what's to see, with more afoot t' call on.'

'They will have their successes, then.'

Kydd looked at him askance. 'They're losin' th' battle, is my supposin' – a sizeable venture has too much hangin' upon it. They're desperate men. Now they're bein' organised. The Revenue is outnumbered – an' just consider. Would you with a wife an' children stand against an armed robber f'r a shillin' a day?'

'Then what's to be done?' Renzi said, putting down his book.

'We're havin' a council-o'-war tomorrow. The Collector has an information as will see us at a landin', an' then we shall have an accountin'.'

'I'm pleased to hear it, brother,' Renzi said mildly, and picked up his book again.

'Er, Nicholas, there is another matter, an' it'll greatly oblige me if ye'd give me y'r opinion.'

'You shall have it. Please acquaint me with the substance of the arguments.'

'It's – it's not y'r regular-goin' philosophy at all, y' should know.'

'Clap on sail and stand on, my friend.'

Kydd hesitated, marshalling his thoughts. 'What do ye conceive a woman's meaning is when she calls you "an interestin' man", Nicholas?'

'In that case I'd expect she'd mean that in some way you have piqued her curiosity, aroused her feminine sensibilities in matters of character, that sort of thing. Why? Has a wicked jade been making her advances?'

Ignoring his friend's tone, Kydd persisted: 'An' if she needs t' know if I ride?'

Renzi paused. 'Do you mean—'

'An' tells me to m' face that I'm different fr'm others – and what are m' true feelin's in a battle?' It seemed so unreal now, the conversation.

'This is Miss Lockwood, is it not?' Renzi said quietly.

'Aye, Nicholas. In th' print publisher's.'

'Then it is altogether a different matter, dear fellow.' He sighed.

Kydd bristled. 'How so?'

'Not to put *too* fine a point on it, you should understand at once that there can be no question of it proceeding beyond the civilities.'

'Why?'

Renzi hesitated. 'I speak only as a friend – a true friend, you must allow. You must take it from me that the higher orders of polite society do view the – relations of a gentleman and lady in quite another way. It is the object of any union to serve, first, a social purpose, in the ordering of the relationships between great families, the arrangements of property and wealth that will ensue and so forth, and in this the wishes of the couple are seldom consulted.

'Any advances made by your good self will therefore be repelled with the utmost rigour, for a young lady must approach any consideration of nuptials with her reputation of the purest hue. A casual dalliance with – with another will most certainly be terminated with prejudice.'

Kydd's expression turned to stone. 'She will—'

'No, she will not. To be brutally frank, I am taking it that your intentions are perfectly respectable. Therefore I must needs put it to you that a marriage of romantic attach-ment is available only to the lower sort. This lady will be expected to conform to her parents' wishes and it is my opinion that it were better you remain agreeable but distant in this instance.'

'She said I was interestin' and, damnit, I'm man enough t' spy when a woman's – when she's lookin' at me.'

Renzi's face was grave. 'Thomas, dear friend, it has been known for a well-born lady to play – toy – with men, and while—'

'Y'r opinion is noted, Nicholas, an' I thank ye for it. I shall take care, but I tell ye now, if my addresses are not disagreeable t' a lady then I will press m' suit if I feel so inclined.'

The Collector of Customs for Penzance closed the curtains of the Long Room. 'I'm sorry to have to ask ye to come at such an hour this night. It'll become clear why later . . .'

Kydd and Standish sat together in the front row; Kydd ignored a quizzical look from his first lieutenant and waited patiently. The rest of those in attendance were hard-featured and anonymous-looking individuals, who were not introduced.

Proceedings opened quickly: it seemed that mysterious information had been received of a run in two nights' time. It promised to be the most daring for months and would involve a degree of deception, but there was apparently one great advantage the Revenue possessed.

'I'll trouble ye for the lights,' the Collector boomed

importantly. One by one the candles were snuffed, leaving the room in heavy darkness. There was the sound of grunts and scraping from the end of the hall, then quiet.

'Stay in your seats, if y' please. I should explain to ye that we have now a gentleman who's in with the free traders and has the griff concerning their plans, which he's agreed to let us know for a consideration. Ye'll understand, o' course, that he'll be requiring to keep his face from ye, so I'll thank 'ee not to ask questions as will put a name to him. 'Now, anything y' may wish to ask?'

From the body of the hall a voice called, 'Where's the run, then?' In the blackness nothing could be made out of the man beyond a vague shape.

'Praa Sands.' The voice was deep and chesty, with little attempt at disguise. 'That's where ye'll see 'em, two nights' time.'

'Praa Sands? Why, that's—'

'I didn't say that's where th' cargo's run ashore, I said that's where you'll see 'em.' He paused. 'See, they'll make a showing an' while youse come a-thunderin' along, the tubs are bein' landed in another place.'

'Where?'

'Stackhouse Cove. Are ye forgettin' Acton Castle only a couple o' hundred yards above? An' at dead low springs there's a strip o' sand will take a boat easy enough.'

Kydd had no idea of the location or its significance but he would find out more later. 'Er, do y' know aught o' the signals they'll use?' he threw into the darkness, an odd sensation.

'Two lights together in Bessy's window 'n' the coast is clear o' the Revenue. Leadin' lights are two sets o' spout lanterns in th' field below the castle. Trouble, pistol flashes. Anythin' else?'

'What vessels can we expect t' see?'

'Ah, well, I can't help ye with that.'

'Who is it organising, do you think?' Standish demanded loudly.

After a slight pause the man replied, 'An' that neither.'

It was quickly settled. As the smugglers expected the Revenue at Praa Sands, that was where they would be, while *Teazer* would lurk offshore at Stackhouse Cove.

Over a convivial draught the Collector pulled out a chart. 'The whole stretch o' coast here – Mount's Bay east from Perranuthnoe to the Lizard – is nothing less'n a nest o' thieving scapegallows. And the worst of 'em you'll find past Cudden Point here, just on from Stackhouse Cove.

'Ever hear on the Carters? "King of Prussia", John calls himself, and he an' his brother Harry have led us a merry dance these last twenty years. Had a bloody tumble with *Druid* frigate once, running in a freight at Cawsand even, and leaving men dead.'

'What's this was mentioned about y'r castle?' Kydd came in.

'Acton Castle? That's John Stackhouse then. The slivey knave knows the Carters well, but claims he's only a-botanising seaweed. I'd like to know as how your seaweed is such a rare business he can set up a castle on the proceeds. It would be a fine thing t' catch him out, Mr Kydd,' he added grimly.

'We'll be ready. Are y' sure ye'll want to stay at Praa Sands?' Kydd asked.

'I don't altogether trust our man – chances are, he's told us it's only a show at Praa while we're off to Stackhouse Cove, and the truth of it is, Praa Sands is where it'll be landed. So, with most of us and the King's ship safely away out of it, they'll be rolling their tubs ashore there. Thank ye, but we'll stay – and know ye'll be doing y' duty at Stackhouse Cove if it's to be the other way.'

There was a warm stillness to the night. They were trying to close with the land in murky darkness. A 'smuggler's moon', a filmy crescent of light, was just enough to make out shapes and movement without betraying detail. That same stillness was robbing the ship of steerage way just when it was most needed.

'Sir, I have t' warn ye – the Greeb.'

'Aye, thank you, Mr Dowse.' Kydd needed no reminding about the evil scatter of crumbling granite that was Basore Point or the particular menace of the Greeb, a dark lacing of rocks reaching straight out to sea for nearly a quarter of a mile.

'Away boats.' If the smuggling gang could try conclusions with a frigate then Kydd was taking no chances. As many as he could spare would go with Standish and lie concealed in undergrowth behind the long, lizard-like Cudden Point overlooking Stackhouse Cove. Others, under Prosser, would take up position on the near side at Trevean.

Teazer left them to it, ghosted back offshore and hove to; it would be impossible to see an approaching vessel until it was upon them – but at the same time they themselves would not be seen. Kydd's plan was to wait until the landing was in progress, signalled by the shore party, and catch them in the act from seaward.

An hour passed in absolute quiet, the slap and chuckle of water along their side and the creaking of timbers in the slight swell the only sounds. Then another: it was difficult to keep men mute for so long but Kydd had warned the petty-officers of his requirement for silence.

A shape materialised next to him. 'A roborant against the night air, dear fellow,' Renzi whispered, proffering hot negus.

Kydd accepted gratefully but out of consideration to others slipped below to his cabin to finish it. 'It sticks in m' throat to see *Teazer* used so,' he growled. 'As fine a man-o'-war as swam, set against a gang of shabbaroons – it's not natural.'

'You were lecturing me sternly only this morning about the country's peril from such blackguards.'

'Aye,' Kydd answered morosely. 'The Collector expects forty or so in a vessel, fifty others ashore t' lift cargo. Is it right to set our seamen in harm's way like this?'

'It is their duty,' Renzi said firmly, 'as it is yours. But do you not think the greater villain is he who funds and orders their depredations?'

'The greater villain's he who buys their run goods. There'd be no smuggling else.'

'Just so. It would, however, be a fine thing to examine these creatures at some length,' Renzi mused, 'in part for the insights we might gather into the sensibilities they violate in order to resolve a response to the claims of their perceived environment.'

'Will we discuss th' philosophy at another time?' Kydd said. 'I'll be returnin' on deck. Could sight th' rogues at any time.'

Midnight approached: still no sign of smugglers, let alone a ship. Wearily Kydd scanned the shore yet again. No lights, no signals. Praa Sands was out of sight behind Cudden Point and therefore there was nothing to indicate whether the landing was going on there, only an inky blackness.

A rocket soared into the night sky from beyond the point. 'Th' shore party! They've seen something. Hands t' th' braces – move y'rselves!' bellowed Kydd.

Another rocket sailed up, this time at a sharp angle out to sea. 'God rot it!' Kydd swore, looking over the side at the pitiful speed they were gathering. But with half *Teazer*'s number on shore nothing could happen quickly.

Still no lights, no signals – and no ship. 'Anyone sees anything – anything a'tall!' But there was nothing.

A chance thinning of the clouds lifted the level of illumination enough to show that Stackhouse Cove was empty.

But two rockets was no accident. Could the landing be taking place on the other side?

Fervently grateful for the fair south-westerly, Kydd brought *Teazer* about and hauled for Cudden Point, which they passed as close as he dared – and at once made out a large two-masted lugger lying inshore, motionless.

'Lay us alongside, Mr Dowse,' Kydd snapped. The information had been false and had successfully lured the two forces away from the true landing-place. But for Kydd's precautions of having men ashore and Standish wisely keeping lookout on both sides they could have landed their tubs safely out of sight.

A musket's flash stabbed the darkness from the lugger, then another, followed by the crack of a four-pounder. Kydd burnt with anger – for such vermin to fire on seamen defending their country!

A broadside from *Teazer* could settle the matter on an instant, but that was not the way it must be. Tysoe appeared with his fine fighting sword, which had seen so much honourable action. In the absence of the first lieutenant it would be Kydd leading the boarding. He shook his head. 'No, Tysoe, thank 'ee, they're not worth its bloodying.' He crossed to the arms chest and took up a cutlass.

'No firing 'less they do,' he roared, and prepared to leap. The firing died away as they neared, and confused shouting came from the shadowy figures in the lugger. 'They're skinning out,' yelled a foremast hand, pointing. A boat was in the water on the other side and men were tumbling into it.

The two vessels came together in a mighty thump and heavy creaking and Kydd jumped down the foot or so to the deck of the lugger, racing aft towards the wheel, followed by a dozen Teazers. 'Secure th' helm,' he ordered, and strode to the side. The boat was in a tangle of panicking men. 'Get out!' Kydd roared.

'Mr Kydd, they're in a mill ashore, sir.' Andrews's voice was cracking with excitement, and as Kydd watched there was a flurry of shots in the shadowy cliffs. 'They're making a fight of it, sir.'

The smugglers had scores of accomplices on shore to carry away the contraband and Standish might be in real trouble if he chose to make a stand. 'Into th' boat, Teazers!' he bawled.

In a frenzy they pulled into the small cove and grounded on a tiny patch of sand. A rush of men met them, but it was cutlasses against cudgels and they broke and fled, scrabbling up the steep, scrubby cliff. In the distance hoarse shouts rose and faded. They were alone.

'Teazers, ahoy!' Kydd bellowed. 'Mr Standish!'

'Sir!' The voice from the spine of the point was accompanied by a crashing of undergrowth and the dishevelled officer appeared, panting but with the white flash of a smile in the darkness. 'A good night's work, I believe, sir.'

'Be damned t' that! Where's their cargo?'

'Oh – ah, it must still be aboard, sir?'

The boat was shoved out into the black depths to return to the lugger. Its crew squatted sullenly on deck. 'Mr Purchet, get into th' hold an' see if there's anything in it,' Kydd called to the boatswain.

'Empty, sir. I already checked.'

Then it could only be at one place. They would have to move fast for if they missed their chance all evidence would be lost. Quickly Kydd gathered a party of men and took the boat back into the little cove. 'After me,' he ordered them, and struck out for the heights.

In the shadowy dark they slipped and scrambled up the rough path to the slopes above, where a stone building stood in darkness. 'You three, wake 'em up an' stand guard upon my return. Nobody t' move an inch.'

Breathing heavily, he headed up towards the massive square bulk of Acton Castle. A single light showed below the central battlements but the rest was in utter blackness.

'With me,' he ordered, and moved forward quickly, thankful to meet the level grass of a lawn. The party hurried across it and stopped at an oddly narrow front entrance. Kydd hammered on the door with the hilt of his cutlass, his men crowding behind. No movement. He banged again, louder – it produced a querulous cry from inside, but Kydd knew that if he could move quickly enough there was no possibility that they could conceal dozens of bulky tubs in time.

'In the name o' the King!' he bawled.

With a tedious sliding of bolts and grating of keys the door finally swung open to reveal the anxious face of an aged servant. 'Mr Stackhouse! Get me Mr Stackhouse this instant, y' villain!'

'He – he's not here,' the man stammered, suddenly catching sight of the men crowding behind Kydd.

'Then get him!'

'I – I—'

Pushing him aside Kydd strode into a hall bedecked with mock-medieval hangings. He looked sharply about, then hailed his party. 'Take position at the doorways, all of ye – smartly, now.'

Kydd pricked his ears: if there was any mad scurrying to hide contraband he would hear it, but the night was still. Then there was movement on the stairs. The light of a candle showed at the top and began to come down.

It was an elderly man in nightgown and cap, who descended slowly. At the bottom he stopped and stared about him. 'Mr Stackhouse?' Kydd challenged brusquely.

The man's gaze turned on him incredulously and Kydd became aware of eyes with the unmistakable glint of authority. 'You!' he grated. 'What the devil do you mean by this, sir?'

There was something about . . . 'Mr Stackhouse, I've reason t' believe—'

'A pox on it! I'm not John Stackhouse, as well you know, sir!'

'Er—'

'Captain Praed, sir!'

Kydd's feverish mind supplied the rest. This was none other than Nelson's senior navigating lieutenant whom he'd last encountered at the battle of the Nile those years ago. He was now a post-captain and, bizarrely, the new owner of the castle.

The next few minutes were a hard beat to windward for Commander Kydd.

*   *   *

The stone building above the cove turned out to be a country drinking den. 'Bessy's tavern, an they swears they know nothin', sir.'

Did they take him for a fool? 'Thank you, Mr Purchet, an' I'll keep a tight guard until daybreak, then search properly.' But the smug look on the landlord's face gave little hope that they would find anything.

Distant hails proved to be the party from Trevean on the other side, who came up breathlessly, agog for news. Savagely Kydd sent them about their business and returned to *Teazer*. It had not been a scene of triumph but he was damned if he'd give up now.

'We carry th' lugger to Penzance f'r inspection,' he grated. Conceivably the vital evidence was still aboard in a cunning hiding-place – false bulkheads, trick water casks and the rest.

In the morning they would search the drinking den; he had fifteen men sealing it off for the rest of the night and nothing would get past them. 'Call me at dawn,' he told Tysoe and fell into his cot fully clothed.

He woke in a black mood. Even the beauty of the unfolding daybreak, as the sinister dark crags were transformed by the young sunshine into light-grey and dappled green, failed to move him: with nothing to show for their efforts there would be accusing stares on their return to Penzance.

The searchers went early to Bessy's and returned while he was at breakfast – empty-handed. Then an idea struck, one that had its roots in a mess-deck yarn, far away and in another time. 'Mr Stirk – Toby – I've called ye here in private t' ask f'r help.'

Stirk said nothing, sitting bolt upright, his black eyes unblinking.

'I'm remembering *Seaflower* cutter in th' Caribbee, a foul night at moorin's off Jamaica, I think it was. Y' had us all agog wi' a tough yarn about a woman an' a ghost. Do y' remember?'

'No, sir,' Stirk answered stolidly.

'I do t' this day, I'll tell ye. Right scareful,' he added, in as comradely a manner as he could manage. 'An' y' happened t' mention then that a long time ago ye may have been among the free traders o' Mount's Bay. I was just wonderin' if that were so.'

Taking his time, Stirk considered and said slowly, 'Y' has the advantage of me, Mr Kydd, an' you knows it. But then I has th' choice as t' what I says back.'

He looked away once, and when his gaze returned to Kydd it was direct and uncompromising. 'Yer wants me to dish m' old shipmates an' that's not possible – but I c'n tell ye that the cat-blash about Mount's Bay was part o' the dit t' make it sound good, as is allowed. I hail fr'm Romney Marsh, which is in Kent, an' it may have been there as I learnt about th' trade, but th' only time I was in these parts was in *Fox* cutter – but north Cornwall, Barnstaple an' Lundy, so . . .'

It had been worth a try. 'Aye. Thank 'ee, Toby.' He allowed a look of sorrow to steal across his face. 'Y' see, I'm vexed t' know just where it is ashore they stowed th' cargo. Seems a hard thing t' up hook an' sail away without we have something t' show for our troubles.'

There was no answering smile.

'Such a pity, o' course. We sail back t' Penzance, having been truly gulled, an' there's the Revenue on th' quay, waitin' an' laughin' at our *Teazer*, a squiddy King's ship as doesn't know th' lay . . .'

Kydd waited, realising he had unconsciously slipped back into fo'c'sle ways of speaking, but there was no response so he rose to his feet. 'M' thanks anyway, Toby – a rummer afore ye go?'

'It's not ashore. Give me a boardin' grapnel an' the pinnace f'r an hour.'

It didn't take long: under the interested gaze of *Teazer*'s company the boat's crew plied the grapnel near where the lugger had been until it snagged. A couple of hands at the line and the first dripping tub broke surface, quickly followed by more, each weighted and roped to the next in a long line.

With a smuggling lugger, prisoners and four hundred gallons of evidence, a well-satisfied sloop-of-war set her sails and left.

Chapter 8

'I 'll have t' leave ye to y'r books, then, Nicholas,' Kydd said, in mock sorrow. His friend was dipping into some musty tomes in the corner of a shop in Vauxhall – or 'foxhole' to seamen – Street.

'Er, ah – yes, this could take some time,' Renzi replied absently. 'Shall we meet later?'

Plymouth was a maritime town, but unlike the noisier Portsmouth, it held itself aloof from the immediacy of a large navy dockyard and fleet, which were safely out of the way in Dock, across the marshes. Instead, it was merchant-ship captains from the vessels in the Cattewater who could be found in the inns on the heights of Old Plymouth – but if any would mingle with the seafarers of a dozen nations, or venture into the rough jollity of their taverns and hide-aways, they could also be found in the rickety antiquity of Cockside and other haunts around the Pool.

Kydd had no wish to be caught up in their shoreside sprees and made his way up Cat Street and past the Guild Hall to the more spacious reaches of the Old Town, which the great sea-dog Sir Francis Drake had called home – he had returned to the Sound triumphant from a voyage round the world loaded with treasure, loosing anchor just a few hundred yards from Kydd's new residence, his first anxious question: 'Doth the Queen still reign?'

It was pleasant to be part of the thronging crowds, to step out over the cobblestones and past the ancient buildings that gave Plymouth such a distinctive character. He stopped to peer into a shop's windows at some gaudily coloured political cartoons.

'Why, Mr Kydd!'

He straightened and turned. 'Miss Lockwood!' He made her an elegant leg, a dainty curtsy his reward.

'Cynthia, this is Commander Kydd of the Royal Navy, and a friend of mine. Mr Kydd, may I introduce Miss Knopleigh, who is – no, let me work it out – a third cousin on my mother's side. Isn't that so, my dear?'

Kydd bowed again, the use of 'friend' not lost on him. 'Miss Knopleigh, a pleasure t' make y'r acquaintance – an' so good t' see you again, Miss Lockwood.'

Miss Knopleigh bobbed demurely to Kydd and said warmly, 'Oh, so this is the interesting man you told me about. I'm so gratified to meet you, Mr Kydd.' She stepped back but continued to regard him thoughtfully.

'We were on our way to Allston's for chocolate – would it be importunate to ask you to join us, Mr Kydd, and perhaps to tell Cynthia a little of your voyages?'

The chocolate was very good; and the ladies applauded Kydd's descriptions of Naples and Nelson, the summit of Vesuvius and the inside of a pasha's seraglio. He felt his confidence grow. She had called him 'friend' – and had introduced him to her cousin. Did this mean . . . ?

'That was most enjoyable, Mr Kydd.' Persephone's skin was fashionably alabaster, but her hazel eyes were frank, round and uncomfortably disconcerting the longer they lingered on him. Kydd caught a ghosting of perfume as she opened her dainty reticule. 'I don't suppose you will be long in Plymouth this time?' she asked, as she took out a lace handkerchief.

'Ah, I – we await a new fore-topsail yard, it being wrung in a blow. No more'n a sennight I'd have thought, Miss Lockwood.'

'Oh, it's so disagreeable when that sort of thing happens.' Then she smiled. 'Well, we must go. Goodbye, Mr Kydd, and thank you for your company.'

Renzi's quill scratching away in the quietness of his cabin intruded into Kydd's thoughts. Was he imagining it or had Persephone meant something special when she spoke of him as 'interesting'? He had detected no furtive glances, no betraying flush of that other kind of interest – but here he was at a disadvantage, for every woman he had known was of quite another quality. The loose rules of engagement with them did not apply here and if he was to press his attentions—

But *did* he want to? Yes! She was the most attractive and accomplished woman he had ever known or spoken to, and she did seem . . .

The cabin felt small and stifling. 'Er, I think I'll take a turn about th' decks, Nicholas,' he said. Renzi murmured acknowledgement and continued to scribble.

The deck was nearly deserted. Standish and most of the men were ashore and Kydd was left alone to pace slowly. Should he make his interest in Miss Lockwood plain? What if he was completely mistaken and she had no interest of *that* sort in him? Would she be furious at an unforgivable impertinence from a low-born – or, worse, laugh him to scorn?

It was galling to be in such ignorance but he knew he was being swept into regions of desire and ambition that made resolution imperative.

A muffled roar of good humour came from the mess-deck below. Jack Tar would have no qualms about action in the situation: cease from backing and filling – clap on all sail and fearlessly lay alongside.

He bit his lip. Renzi would be of no help: he had made his position clear. But there *was* one who might . . .

'Then what is it, Thomas, that's so pressing I must make my apologies to Mrs Mullins at such short notice?' Cecilia said crossly, once they were safely in the intimacy of the drawing room.

'I'm sincerely sorry, Cec, t' intrude on y'r social situation,' Kydd said moodily, staring into the empty fireplace. 'Y' see, I've some thinkin' t' do an' it needs sortin' out of a kind . . .'

She looked at him keenly. 'Of a personal nature, I'd suspect.'

'Aye, sis, private, ye might say. That is – not t' you, o' course.' He shifted uncomfortably. 'Can y' tell me true, Cec, th' answers to some questions, you bein' a woman and all?'

'A lady, the last time I looked,' she said tartly. 'What are your questions, then, Thomas?'

Kydd mumbled, 'If y' aren't goin' t' help me, then—'

'Don't be a silly, of course I will. Although why you don't go to Nicholas with your man problems I really don't know.'

'He's – he's set in his views, is all,' he said, embarrassed. 'This is somethin' I – I need t' ask you, Cec.'

'Very well. Go on.'

'Ah – y' see, I – I met Miss Persephone Lockwood on th' street with her cousin an' she—'

'You're taken with her and, against all my advice, you wish to press your amours!'

'Cec! Don't say it like that. I'm – she's, er—'

'I see. Well, do not, I pray, ask me . . .' She stopped at Kydd's expression and her manner softened. 'Dear brother, it's just that I'd loathe to see you brought low by an uncaring world. Tell me, do you feel for her that much?'

'Cec, I'm thinkin' of her all th' time! She's like no one I've ever met – or even seen afore. She's—'

'How do you conceive her feelings are for *you*?'

'That's what I need ye to advise me on.'

'To tell you what she feels towards you? This is a hard thing, Thomas. One woman's way of showing her inside feelings will be very different from another's and, besides, Miss Lockwood will have been brought up to control her passions strictly. Let me ask you, was your meeting on the street by way of an accident, do you think?'

'Aye, it must have been, for—'

'Then she takes you directly to a public chocolate-house – *mmm*. How did she introduce you to this cousin?'

'Cec, she called me her friend an' the cousin said she was pleased t' meet Persephone's interestin' man, an' looked at me – you know – that way.'

'I really don't understand what you mean by that, Thomas, but it does seem she is talking about you to her friends and this is a good start. Tell me also, does she look at you – do her eyes . . . linger?

'This is gettin' a mort too deep f'r me, Cec, but th' last thing she asked was how long the ship was t' be in Plymouth.'

'The ship?'

Kydd's brow furrowed. 'Well, yes, it was how long *I* would be.'

'Ah,' Cecilia said fondly. 'Then I do pronounce that indeed, brother, she *is* interested in you.'

Reddening, Kydd gave a pleased grin. 'What d' you think of her, Cec?'

'I've not yet had the chance to get to know her – and neither, it must be said, have you.'

'Thank 'ee, Cec, now I know what's m' course,' Kydd said happily.

'Thomas, I've said it before, and I won't again, but after your first task, to win her heart, you must then start all over again to impress her family and friends – become part of her world.'

Kydd nodded wryly, but Cecilia pressed on inexorably: 'We shall suppose you do win her. What is your intent for her? To debase her breeding so that she comes down to your level of politeness, or should it be your duty to strive to attain *her* level of gentility? That she must make apology for your boorishness to her friends, or be proud of your accomplishments?'

'Aye, sis, I c'n see all that—'

'Then first you *must* attend to your speech, Thomas. It is sadly neglected, after all I told you, and is not at all fit for gentle company. Now, this is what you really *must* do . . .'

Kydd lay back in his new four-poster and stared up into the darkness. His talk with his sister had been hard and lacerating. It was all very well to be proud and contented with an outstanding sea career, but women, it seemed, were on the one hand concerned to discover the man that lay beneath, and on the other taken up with foolish notions of what others might think, whether it be in the matter of incomes or appearances of dress and manner.

He had no reason to disbelieve her – she had gone out of her way to express her love and support – but her constant insistence on the niceties of polite behaviour was trying.

Yet Cecilia's words about whether Persephone should make excuses for him or be proud of him were unanswerable. He would have to try his damnedest to wipe away all betraying traces of his past.

Then doubts crowded in – the first of which was the loudest. Was all this vanity? What *proof* did he have that she felt something for him? There were signs that had been pronounced positive but . . .

Just supposing she had indeed been drawn to him, her feelings grew – and then a passionate declaration! Her heart would tell her which was of a truer value, and it would not be trivial details of speech and behaviour or even a humble background. In fact, she knew of his past and it had not in the slightest affected her addresses towards him.

It was possible! If she really wanted him, nothing would be allowed to stand in the way. Her parents – the brother of a viscount and the sister of an earl – would have to be reconciled or be estranged. So for appearance's sake a discreet settlement would be made that would see them setting up a small estate somewhere in the country, a carriage or two and ample servants . . . and, above all, he could appear among the highest in the land with Persephone, Mrs Thomas Kydd, on his arm – even at court, where everyone she knew would be agog to see whom she had married.

Damn it! It was all very possible.

*　　*　　*

Some perversity stopped Kydd telling Renzi when the invitation came; he knew his friend would feel impelled to lecture him on deportment, the graces of the table and interminable other points, for this invitation to a reception in honour of some foreign grandee was a prize indeed – but it was to him alone.

Although at short notice, and thereby again implying Kydd's role as useful bachelor, it was to Saltram House, the seat of Lord Boringdon and unquestionably the finest estate in the area.

Whatever the reason behind the invitation, he had reached the rarefied heights of society. Thomas Kydd – common seaman that was – moving in such circles . . .

The rest was up to him: he had been given his chance, and if he performed creditably, acquitted himself with elegance and wit, polish and urbanity, he would be noticed. Other invitations would come and . . . But for now there was much to take on board.

The coach ground on interminably past the Cattewater to the Plym. He had decided on full-dress uniform; it was expected in this age of war but also it had the inestimable advantage that he would not have to concern himself with the imperatives of high fashion, or the cost – he felt a twinge of guilt when he remembered how he had wheedled Renzi that real bullion gold lace was crucial for a naval captain's full-dress uniform. His friend had glanced at him once, then gone without a word to their common stock of funds. Still, the effect of so much blue, white and deep gold was profoundly satisfying and would stand against anything the *haut ton* could parade.

They crossed the Plym and began the ascent up the final

hill to Saltram. Kydd's heart beat faster; he had devoured Chesterfield's *Guide to Men and Manners*, then consulted Debrett and others in the matter of forms of address and details on European nobility. As always, the *Gentleman's Magazine* had provided plenty of material for small-talk and he had gone to some trouble to acquaint himself with current Plymouth gossip, to Mrs Bargus's surprise and delighted assistance. In the privacy of his bedplace he had assiduously practised his vowels and constructs until Renzi's expression at breakfast told him that progress had been made. He was as ready as he could be.

The spare, classical stateliness of Saltram was ablaze with lights in the summer dusk and a frisson of excitement seized Kydd as a footman lowered the side-step and stood to attention as he alighted. In a few moments he would be entering a milieu to which he had never aspired until now and so much would hang on how he comported himself.

'Commander Thomas Kydd,' he announced to the head footman, attending at the door. It was the largest entrance hall he had ever seen, complete with Doric entablature and a Roman bust set about with panels and carving. The area was rapidly filling with guests of splendour and importance, the candle-light and brilliance an exhilarating backdrop to the scene.

It had begun. He took a deep breath and turned to the distinguished gentleman in the plum-coloured frock coat to whom he had just been introduced. Soon there was move-ment, a general drift inside. 'The Velvet Drawing Room,' drawled his acquaintance. 'Have you been here before?'

'Not to Saltram,' Kydd replied languidly. 'I hail from Surrey originally,' he added, inspecting his cuffs in a lordly way.

'Oh, really?' the man said, interested. 'Then you'd know Clandon?'

The room was impressive: red-velvet-hung walls decorated in the Italian way with giltwood and stucco, and an ornately carved marble fireplace. The babble of conversation rose and fell, the rich foetor of candlesmoke, perfume and warm humanity an intoxicating assault on his senses. He accepted a tall glass from a gold-frogged footman. Furtively he glanced about for familiar faces in the crowded room. 'Ah, yes, Clandon. Splendid place, a credit to the Onslows,' he said casually, and sipped his champagne.

Suddenly the arched double doors at the far end were opened ceremoniously to reveal an even bigger room beyond; a hush descended as a well-built major-domo took position. 'His Grace the Landgraf Karl Zähringen of Baden-Durlach.'

There was a surge forward but Kydd held back while the more lofty dignitaries went in, and made polite conversation while he waited and observed. It quickly became apparent that an equerry was discreetly approaching individuals to be introduced and conducting them forward when the time came.

Then Kydd spied her. Nearly hidden in the throng he saw Admiral Lockwood and his lady before he caught sight of Persephone on her father's arm – a vision in lemon silk and a tracery of cream lace, talking gaily as though it were quite the most ordinary evening. Of course she would be here, he admonished himself. Was this not her world by right?

They were led forward and Kydd saw Lady Lockwood held at a fawning curtsy by a genial gentleman in a splendid hussar's uniform.

Others made their way in, and then the time came for Kydd. He strode into the great room, holding himself proud and ignoring the magnificent pale blue silk-damask walls, the perfection of the Italianate painted ceiling and the blaze of light from the tortoiseshell and ormolu candelabra.

The equerry brought him to a discreet distance but the previous couple had not yet concluded, the man holding forth in florid German.

Eventually they retired backwards, the man giving three short bows, and the equerry murmured, 'Sir, Commander Kydd, His Britannic Majesty's Navy. Commander, the Landgraf Zähringen.'

Kydd swept down in a leg of extreme elegance, practised in his cabin until his muscles ached. 'Your Grace – or, since the happy elevation of your father the Margrave to Elector, should this not be *Hoheit*, sir?'

He straightened to meet raised eyebrows. '"Your Grace" vill do, *Kapitan*, und may I say 'ow rare it is to meet an English who know th' happening in our little kingdom?' His benign features creased with pleasure.

'Thank you, Your Grace. And might I desire you a happy stay in England, the weather being uncommon pleasant this time of the year,' he dared.

'Vy, thank you. May the fortunes of war be kind to you, *Kapitan*.'

Kydd backed from his presence, remembering to bow three times before he turned away in relief and growing exultation.

He was succeeding – and on his own merits! With earnest attention but wandering thoughts he held himself quietly while he heard of the grave consequences of the fluctuations in corn prices in the north country and their probable effect on 'Change.

He looked about him discreetly, and saw Persephone listening politely to a voluble colonel with forbidding whiskers. Then her head turned – and she gazed directly at him. Before he could look away there was a sudden wide smile and a nod of acknowledgement.

Covered with confusion, he bowed his head stiffly and forced his eyes away from her, but his thoughts raced: if he had had any doubt before that he was merely a name to her, it was gone now. In another existence he would have boldly gone across and taken things further, but now he was unaccountably hesitant.

The evening proceeded. A light supper was brought in and everyone found a seat; Kydd practised his small-talk on a ponderous gentleman and simpering middle-aged lady, adorned with ostrich feathers, and covertly noted that Persephone had resumed dutiful attendance on her parents.

'Your Grace, my lords!' Lord Boringdon clapped his hands for attention. 'Pray do indulge me for a moment. The good Landgraf has expressed a keen desire to hear our English entertainments and what better, I thought, than to beg Miss Sophie Manners to oblige?'

The good-natured applause was redoubled when a shy young lady rose and made her way to the pianoforte. There was a scraping of chairs as all manoeuvred to face her. 'A little piece by Mr Purcell,' she announced nervously.

Her voice was pure and sweet but the prolonged tinkling of the melody was not altogether to Kydd's taste. He brightened when a tall soldier in scarlet regimentals joined her to sing a duet, which, in its pleasant intertwining of voices, proved most charming. After rapturous acclaim they sang another. The soldier grinned broadly. 'Most kind in you,' he acknowledged, when the clapping died, and bowed to both sides, then looked directly at Kydd. 'Could I persuade the navy to stand up for us?' he called jovially.

Kydd froze, but a storm of encouragement broke – the Royal Navy was popular in these parts. He cringed, but there was no escape.

He stood, to be greeted with thunderous applause, but was rooted to the spot, speechless at the sight of so many lords and ladies staring at him with expressions ranging from boredom to avidity.

Then he felt a light touch on his arm. It was Persephone. 'Don't be anxious, Mr Kydd – we're all your friends here, you'll see,' she said softly, and then more loudly, 'Mr Kydd will now perform – and I will accompany on the pianoforte.'

She took his arm with a winning smile, and drew him firmly towards the front to a very tempest of support. She sat at the instrument and stretched her fingers, but Kydd stammered in a low voice, 'I d-don't know anything, Miss L-Lockwood.'

'Nonsense!' she whispered back. 'This pretty piece of Mozart's perfect for you. You're a baritone?' Her fingers caressed the keys in an expert introductory flourish and the room fell quiet. 'You shall turn the page for me, Mr Kydd, will you?'

At his stricken face she added softly, 'Don't worry, I'll manage. Just follow the words – they're below the stave.'

He stared down, transfixed. 'It – I can't—!' She looked up at him with sympathy and unconcealed disappointment.

Kydd pulled himself together. 'Thank you, Miss Lockwood, but I've just remembered one – and this I'll sing on my own. That is to say, a solo.'

He stepped forward and faced the august room, the serried ranks of painted faces, the formidable lords and gentlemen, the Landgraf – then filled his chest and sang. It was one of the only pieces he knew well, songs that held meaning and memories but that he had kept suppressed for many years on the quarterdeck.

It came out with deep feeling, the parting of an outward-bound sailor from his true love:

Turn to thy love and take a kiss
This gold about thy wrist I'll tie
And always when thou look'st on this
Think on thy love and cry . . .

The simple melody was received in absolute quiet, Kydd's powerful voice echoing about the room, and soon a soft improvisation from the pianoforte tentatively accompanied it, strengthening and growing in invention as the chorus repeated.

The song finished; there was an astonished silence, and then the room broke into rapturous applause. Kydd dared a glance at Persephone – she returned it with one of delight, her eyes sparkling. 'I rather think an encore is expected,' she said fondly. 'Shall you?'

Kydd obliged with a fo'c'sle favourite, and then his lord-ship and a bemused Landgraf heard a salty rendition of 'Spanish Ladies', Persephone coming in almost immediately with a daring flourish and a laugh.

Now let every man take up his full bumper,
Let every man take up his full bowl;
For we will be jolly, and drown melancholy
With a health to each jovial and true-hearted soul!

While he sang out the old words heartily he saw reactions about the room ranging from delight and amazement to hostility. He dared a glance at Admiral Lockwood and saw him pounding out the rhythm on his knee with a broad smile; his lady, however, impaled him with a look of venom.

Kydd finished the fine sea song to thunderous acclaim and, Persephone at his side, bowed this way and that. 'Well done, Mr Kydd!' she whispered, her eyes shining. 'You were . . . wonderful.'

Kydd's heart melted.

Renzi was sitting by a single candle at his desk when Kydd returned. He glanced up and, seeing Kydd's expression, remarked drily, 'So, the evening might be accounted a success, then, brother?'

'Aye – that is to say, it passed off right splendidly, Nicholas.' He peeled off his coat and flopped into his chair, wearing a broad smile that would not go away.

'And – dare I hazard the observation? – you there saw Miss Persephone Lockwood.'

'I did,' Kydd said sheepishly, and gave a graphic account of events. 'And y' should have been there t' hear the thumpin' applause they gave us at th' end,' he said, with huge satisfaction.

Renzi heard him out, then shook his head in wonder. 'So by this we can see you have achieved your object. You have indeed attained an eminence in society,' he declared, 'and, it must be admitted that at one and the same time you have been able to attract notice, it seems. Though what a young lady of breeding will make of a gentleman who eschews Mozart for "Spanish Ladies" I cannot begin to think.'

'Then can I point out t' you, Nicholas, that it was this same who came an' played for me in the first place, an' it was she who said I should do an encore?' Kydd retorted acidly.

Renzi stretched and gave a tired smile. 'In any event, dear fellow, you are now known and talked about. For good or ill, the society world knows you exist and have made conquest of Miss Lockwood.'

The fore-topsail yard, now promised for Wednesday, would be fitted and squared on Thursday, and Friday, of course, being not a day for sailing to any right-thinking sailor, Kydd would begin to store *Teazer* for a Saturday departure. He called Purchet to his cabin to set it in train.

Only a few days more. Guiltily he was finding himself reluctant to put to sea and he told himself sternly to buckle down to work. Renzi was dealing swiftly with a pile of ship's papers, his pen flying across the pages, no doubt eager to dip into the parcel of books that had recently arrived at number eighteen.

There was now the difficult task of how or indeed whether he should open some form of address to Persephone. Was she expecting an overture from him? Should he ask Cecilia? Or was advice on the best way to woo another woman not quite what one might ask a sister? A knock interrupted his thoughts as a letter for the captain was handed to him respectfully.

Kydd recognised Cecilia's bold hand and smiled at the coincidence, tearing open the seal. Another letter fell out with unfamiliar handwriting. Cecilia went quickly to the subject to his growing astonishment and delight. '. . . and she is wondering if you would wish to accompany us. I really think you should, Thomas – it would get you out of your ship and seeing something of the moors, which are accounted to be some of the most dramatic country in the kingdom . . .'

A ride on the high moor – the wilds of Dartmoor. With Persephone.

The other letter was from Persephone, in a fine round hand, and addressed to Cecilia, whom she had met at the picnic. Kydd's eyes lingered on the writing: it was perfectly executed penmanship with few ornaments, bold and confident. The content was warm but practical – a rendezvous at the Goodameavy stables a few miles north on the Tavistock road, well-phrased advice concerning clothing for ladies and then, in a final sentence, the afterthought that if Commander Kydd found himself at leisure that day, did Cecilia think he might be persuaded to join them?

Cecilia said little on the journey out of town and gazed from the window as they wound into the uplands. It suited Kydd: his thoughts could jostle on unchecked. Would it be a substantial party? The lonely moor was probably a place of footpads and robbers so he wore a sword, a discreet borrowed hanger rather than his heavy fighting weapon. He hoped his plain riding outfit of cutaway dark-brown frock coat and cuff-top boots would pass muster with someone accustomed to the latest in fashionable wear.

Above the trees beyond he could see the rearing bulk of the bare hills that formed the edge of the moor and his pulse quickened. Presently they swung into a lane and stopped in the spacious courtyard of a considerably sized riding stable.

The concentrated odour of horses was heavy on the air as they were handed down, Cecilia finding coins for the coachman. There was no party waiting and he felt a stab of anxiety – his fob watch told him they were on time.

A groom led out a fine Arab that snorted and pawed the

ground with impatience. Persephone, arrayed in a brown riding habit, walked beside it. Her hair was pulled back severely, a few chestnut wisps escaping from her masculine-looking black hat. 'Why, Mr Kydd, I do adore your taste in colour!' she said teasingly, glancing at his coat.

Kydd bowed deeply, aware of Cecilia's respectful curtsy next to him.

'Miss Kydd, it is a pleasure to see you again,' Persephone went on, in the friendliest tone. 'It is tiresome, but the men are so disinclined to make the journey to the moor to ride and I do so love the freedom here. Do you ride much?'

'Not as much as I'd like, Miss Lockwood,' Cecilia said carefully, eyeing Persephone's spirited beast. 'I do find, however, that a morning canter does set the pulse to beating, don't you?' Her mount was a pretty dappled mare of more docile habit than the Arab, and the groom adjusted the robust side-saddle with a slipper stirrup for her.

Kydd's horse was brought out: a powerful-looking mahogany bay, which he approached with caution. Its eye followed his every motion and when he swung up it skittered and snorted, tossing its head, feeling the bit.

'Oh, that's Sultan – do you take no nonsense from him, Mr Kydd. Sometimes he can be a quite a rascal if he gets it into his head.'

Kydd strove to let the horse feel his will and, after some ill-tempered gyrations, it seemed to settle and he brought it next to Cecilia. He stole a glance at Persephone: she looked breathtaking, her handsome straight-backed posture set off by the fall of her habit. 'There will be a hamper and champagne for us at Hele Tor, should we deserve it,' she said. 'Shall we?'

They clopped across the cobblestones of the courtyard

then turned in single file up a leafy lane, Kydd happy to allow Cecilia to follow Persephone cautiously while he rode behind on his fractious steed. The groom with the pannier of necessities brought up the rear. It was now clear that no one else was to join them, and he glowed to think that they must have been specially invited.

The lane stopped at a gate, which Kydd opened and held for the ladies. It led to the open moor, the vast swell of heathland romantically bleak and far-reaching, with only the occasional dark clusters of rocks, the mysterious tors, to intrude on the prospect.

'At last!' laughed Persephone, and urged her horse straight into the wild openness. Kydd's horse whinnied as the others went ahead and he had no difficulty in spurring it on, feeling its great muscles bunch under him.

He passed Cecilia, who was concentrating on finding her rhythm, and quickly came up on Persephone who threw him a surprised but pleased glance, her eyes sparkling. 'Have no concern, Mr Kydd. The footing here is excellent.'

Kydd was having some difficulty reining in his horse and Persephone increased pace to keep with him. She swayed effortlessly in her saddle round rambling patches of furze and laughed into the wind, her cheeks pink with exertion.

Kydd glanced round and saw that Cecilia was trailing, but the groom had stayed with her so he turned back to the reins.

As they cantered further into the moorland Kydd was struck by its wild immensity – not a tree, hedgerow, or building in sight. It was an awesome loneliness – not unlike the sea in a way. The rhythmic thudding of hoofs on the turf came together in a blood-rousing thrill of motion.

A sudden flutter of wings made Kydd's horse rear, its

hoofs flailing, the whites of its eyes showing in terror. He fought to stay aboard, dropping the reins and seizing the animal's mane with both hands as it teetered, then crashed down to leap forward in a demented gallop. Kydd hung on in grim desperation as the horse's panicked flight stretched out to a mile or more. He tried to claw forward to retrieve the flying reins but in vain. Instead he lay along the beast's neck, hoping its pace would slow as its energy gave out.

Eventually Sultan's frenzy lessened and Kydd dared to loose one hand to snatch at the flying reins, then transferred the other, his thighs gripping his mount's sides as he did so. He saw a watercourse of sorts disappearing into a wooded fold and coerced the animal to head for it, hoping the thicker going would slow it.

The first bushes whipped past, then more substantial trees, and the horse slowed. The gallop fell to a canter and then to a trot. With a sigh of relief Kydd straightened, only to be summarily ejected from the saddle as the horse bucked unexpectedly. Kydd whirled through the air and landed in a tangle of boots and undergrowth.

He lay on his back, staring up and panting. A breathless, concerned Persephone came into focus. 'Oh, my poor Mr Kydd!' she said and knelt down, her gloved hand on his. 'Are you hurt? May I help you up?'

'Miss Lockwood,' Kydd managed, and hauled himself to his elbows. 'That damned mutinous beast!' he gasped. 'Which is to say that I should clap him in irons as would teach him his manners to an officer.'

He pulled himself to a sitting position. 'Your pardon while I recover my senses,' he said, pulling greenery from his hair and feeling his leg cautiously.

'Of course.' She sat demurely next to him. 'The groom

will take care of Miss Kydd and I see Sultan is not to be troubled.' The horse was browsing contentedly nearby, on the lush verdancy by the edge of a stream.

Persephone turned to face him. 'You know I am glad to have met you, Mr Kydd. We are both . . .' She dropped her head and toyed with a leaf.

When she looked up, Kydd's eyes held hers for a long moment. As he helped her to her feet they found themselves together in a kiss, which took them by surprise. She froze, then said, with just the faintest quiver in her voice, 'We must find the others now.'

Chapter 9

'Get y'r head down, y' ninny!' hissed Stirk. Luke Calloway crouched lower in the hedgerow as a horse and rider clopped down the narrow lane in the darkness.

'Mr Stirk, an' we're safe now, isn't we?' Calloway said, aggrieved.

Stirk listened for any others who might be coming, then stood up and stretched. 'Shut y' trap, younker, an' do as I says.' Even though they had made it this far, just a mile from the tiny fishing village, they were not safe yet.

Stirk hefted his bundle and they resumed their journey. It got steeper. The village glimmering below was nestled in a coombe, a deep valley with precipitous sides, and seemed shoehorned into a tiny level area.

The lane had become not much more than a path when they finally reached the first houses by a little stream. 'Bless me, Mr Stirk, but th' place stinks,' Calloway protested. A strong, insistent reek of fish was thick in the night air. Stirk stopped and listened again: strangers would be viewed suspiciously in this small community as possible spies for the

Revenue, and all it needed was for some frightened widow to raise an alarm . . . but there was no sign that the inhabitants were in a mind to roam abroad in the dark.

'Where d' we kip, Mr Stirk?'

'First we finds th' kiddleywink,' Stirk snapped.

'Th' what?'

'What the Janners call a pothouse, lad,' he said, looking around. Even a village this size should have two or three. They headed towards the snug harbour and on the far side near the fish-quay buildings the Three Pilchards was a noisy beacon of jollity. Stirk checked about carefully, then he and Calloway passed by a blacksmith's shuttered forge and hastened into the tavern.

It was small but snug, and dark with the patina of age. The aroma of spilt liquor eddied up from the sawdust on the floor and the heady reek of strong cider competed with the smell of rank fish from outside.

The tavern fell silent. Half a dozen weathered faces turned to them, distrust and hostility in their expressions. The tapster approached them, wiping his hands. 'Where youse come frum, then?' he demanded.

'As is none o' y'r business,' Stirk said mildly, and crossed to a corner table from which he could survey the whole room, 'but a shant o' gatter 'd be right welcome,' he said, sitting and gesturing to Calloway to join him.

The tapster hesitated, then went back to pull the ale. One of the men sitting at a nearby table fixed unblinking eyes on Stirk and threw at him, "E axed yez a question, frien'.'

Stirk waited until the ale came in a well-used blackjack, a tarred leather tankard. 'Why, now, an' isn't this a right fine welcome f'r a pair o' strangers?' He took a long pull, then set it down quietly. He felt in his pocket and slapped down a small pile of coins. 'This'n for any who c'n find us some-wheres t' rest. Maybe two, three days, nice an' quiet like, an' then we'll be on our way.' He clinked the coins patiently. After a few mutters with his companion the man came back loudly, 'I knows what thee are – ye're navy deserters, b' glory.'

Stirk bit his lip and then said warily, 'S' what's it t' you, mate? Thinkin' on sellin' us out?'

The man cackled delightedly. 'Knew 'oo ye was, soon as I clapped peepers on yez.' He turned to the other and said something that raised a laugh.

'Ah, but ye'll be stayin' more'n a coupla days, I reckon,' the other added. He had a milky-blue blind eye. 'Else theys goin' t' cotch ye.'

Stirk said nothing.

'What they call yez, then?' the first asked.

'Jem'll do, an' this skiddy cock is m' shipmate Harry.'

'Oh, aye – but if y' wants t' stop here, Mr Jem, we can't have useless bodies a-takin' up room. Thee looks likely lads – done any fishin'?'

'Mackerel, flounder – some hake.' Stirk's boyhood had been the hard life of an inshore fisherman at Hythe in Kent.

It seemed to satisfy. 'Davey Bunt,' the first said.

'Jan Puckey,' the other came in. 'An' t'night I'll see y' sleepin' in a palace, I promise ye.'

They slept in one right enough: in coarse canvas on a bed of nets reeking of fish, in what the Cornish called the 'fish pallace', the lower room of dwellings turned over to keeping the family fishing gear and storing pilchards pressed into tubs.

Stirk rolled over, vainly seeking a more comfortable posi-tion and ruefully recalling that nights at sea in a small fishing-boat were far worse. Had this been a bad mistake, a decision made on the spur of the moment that he would come to regret? And had he been right to involve Luke? The young man knew so little of the wider world.

Stirk was under no illusions of the risk: they were not yet trusted and could be disowned on the spot until they had proved themselves, and in the future . . .

It was all because of what he had done at Stackhouse Cove that night several weeks ago. Mr Kydd had remembered his smuggling reminiscences and seen his knowledge at first hand. Now he had allowed himself and Luke to be landed ashore and, under the pretence that they were deserting seamen, they had made their way to the smugglers' haunt of Polperro to see if they could win confidence and discover something of the unknown genius who controlled the trade.

In the darkness he heard Calloway grunt and turn over; he must be missing his comfortable hammock, Stirk thought wryly.

For Luke it had been the adventure that appealed, but the only reason Stirk had volunteered was the deep respect and, indeed, lop-sided friendship he felt for his captain, whom he had seen grow from raw landman to first-class seaman, then achieve the quarterdeck, and now the command of his first ship. It was unlikely that in trim little *Teazer* they would achieve anything like lasting fame in their duties in the Plymouth command; Stirk was well aware that, without it, the best that could be expected for Kydd was a quiet retirement amid the fading glory of once having commanded a King's ship. He would try his copper-bottomed best to give Kydd a triumph to bear back.

'Thank 'ee, Mrs Puckey,' Stirk said gratefully, to the close-mouthed woman after she had handed him a piece of coarse bread to go with his gurty milk – thin seed gruel.

She said nothing, her dark eyes following his every move.

'Th' first time I've bin fishin', Mr Puckey,' Calloway said respectfully. 'I aim t' learn, sir.'

He grunted. 'You will, son,' he said significantly, and his glance flicked to Stirk. 'Mackerel, y' said.'

'Aye.'

'We'll be out hand-linin' tonight – Boy Cowan says he's a-willin' t' have youse along.'

'Owns th' boat?'

'An' we all has shares in th' catch,' Puckey said firmly.

Stirk finished his bread. 'No business o' mine, cully, but we sometimes hears as Polperro's not a place t' beat fer free tradin'. Why, then—'

There was a sudden tension in the room. Puckey laid down his spoon very deliberately and glared at Stirk. 'We doesn't talk about such here, cuffin. Ye understan' me?'

'O' course. Me bein' in the trade as a kitlin' an' all,' Stirk added quietly, meeting his eyes. There was no response and he bent to his meal again.

A ragged child came up and stood gazing at the strangers. 'Good day, y' young scamp,' Stirk said.

The boy continued to stare at him, then suddenly broke into a chant:

'Mother at the cookpot, Father with his brew
Waitin' for the gennelmen who'll dish the Revenoo!'

Mrs Puckey clapped her hands and scolded him. He disappeared.

It was bright outside as the three men made their way to the quay, the early-morning sun drying the effects of the

219

overnight rain and setting off the little village to gleaming perfection. Gulls wheeled and keened about the fish quay in front of the Three Pilchards while boats bobbed and snubbed at their lines in the harbour.

On each side, the land sloped up steeply with, occasionally, cottages perched at seemingly impossible angles. It was as individual a place as could be imagined, every house set to suit its tiny plot of rock and thin soil, the dwellings of all hues, owing more than a little to shipwreck timbers.

Along the sea-front fishermen were taking advantage of the clear morning light to mend nets and work on tackle. Past the tavern was a jumble of rocks and a final jagged cliff soared at the narrow but picturesque harbour entrance. A short pier beyond the Three Pilchards gave shelter to the inner harbour.

'Well, now, an' here's Boy hisself,' said Puckey, as they reached the level area of the fish quay. 'Mornin', Mr Cowan.'

Cowan was well into his sixties and white-haired, but had a genial manner that gave him a serenity beyond any cares. 'Jan, are these th' noo hands ye told me of?'

'Aye. Jem here, an' that's Harry.'

'Ye've whiffled f'r mackerel, Jan tells me.'

'I did.'

'An' can ye tell me what yarn y' used fer y' snoods?' Cowan asked casually.

'Cobbler's thread, mebbe gut,' Stirk answered, in the same tone, 'an' a long shanked hook if we's expectin' hake.'

Cowan eased into a smile. 'We likes horse-hair in Polperro, Jem. Like t' bear a hand on th' nossil cock, you an' young Harry both?' This was a simple wooden device that twisted together yarns for greater strength into a snood – the final length carrying the hook that stood out from the main hand-line.

Calloway was set to pulling an endless cord passing over a series of whirligigs that were set into a frame to spin hooks with the yarns beneath. Stirk, with a piece of soft leather, took the strands and evened out the twists, lead weights giving it all a momentum. Finally the nossil was detached, and a hook whipped to the line with a mackerel feather. 'There we is, mate,' said Stirk, looking with satisfaction at his finished snood. 'Where's the backin' line?'

Forty fathoms of line looked an overwhelming amount lying in a heap, but Stirk faked it out in six-foot coils and patiently began the task of working a figure-of-eight knot every half a foot, needing to heave the whole length of line through for every knot. These would be where the snoods would attach and it would see him occupied for hours.

Calloway was sent away to help with the barking – dipping nets and sails into the boiling cutch, a nauseating mix of Burma bark and tallow.

'Can't we not fin' 'em some breeks, darlin'?' Puckey said, when his wife came with the noon tea. 'They'll be haulin' fish b' evenin'.'

From somewhere she found smocks, knit-frocks and canvas trousers reeking with old fish-slime, and two seamen were translated on the spot into fishermen. Later, the most important article appeared: sea boots, the like of which Calloway had never seen – huge and thigh-length, they were of hard leather encrusted on the soles with hobnails.

Boy Cowan cocked an eye skyward and, with a seraphic smile, pronounced, 'Mackerel or herring, they a-goin' t' be about t'night. Bait up, boys.'

His work finished until evening, Stirk decided to wander round the narrow lanes to the Consona rocks where the boat-yard was seeing the last touches to a repair on the skipper's boat. 'Which 'un is Mr Cowan's?' he called, to an aproned shipwright working on a vessel propped up in the mud.

The man looked up briefly. 'This 'un,' he said, and went back to his planing. *Polperro Fancy* was lettered on her square transom, and she was a beamy half-decker, well used by the sea and in pristine order. But so small!

'Sprit main?' Stirk guessed, noting the snotter. Without sails it was difficult to make out her rig beyond the single mast and long bowsprit, which, no doubt, would sport at least two jibs for balance and speed.

The shipwright straightened slowly, squinting up at Stirk against the sun. 'An' who's askin'?'

'I'll be goin' out wi' Mr Cowan t'night.'

'Hope they're bitin' for ye,' the man said, wiping his forehead, apparently unwilling to pursue why a complete stranger would be going out to the hard work of the fishing grounds with his client. 'Yes, ye're in th' right of it, we call 'em "spreeties". Y' only fin' luggers at Looe.'

Stirk nodded. Looe, three or four miles away, would have different local conditions, different traditions of boat-building handed down. This fore-and-aft rig was almost certainly to keep as close by the wind as possible when passing through the narrows at the harbour mouth.

He looked again. There was only a tiny cuddy forward and two compartments amidships before the open afterdeck, probably a fish hold and net stowage, and was certainly not suited to the running and concealment of contraband.

'How is she, Mr Butters?' Cowan hailed respectfully from the end of the pier opposite.

'Ready for ye an hour afore sundown,' the shipwright shouted back.

*   *   *

At the appointed time, and replete after a meal of scrowled pilchards and back-garden potatoes, Stirk and Calloway trudged over to their boat. Their hobnailed sea boots crashed on the cobbles but caused not the slightest interest as others made their way down to the harbour, a busy and amiable throng.

The gathering sunset was gilding the hilltops and shadows were lengthening among the tightly huddled dwellings of the village as they reached their craft, now afloat and nudging the quay playfully.

'Ye're a Puckey then, I see,' one said to Stirk, as they jostled down the narrow lane.

Stirk blinked and Cowan chuckled. 'As ye're wearin' a Puckey knit-frock an' all. The women knit 'em in th' family pattern fer their men. If we're misfortunate, makes identi-fyin' the bodies easier.'

They clambered aboard the *Fancy* and were joined by Bunt and Puckey, who seemed to know instinctively what to do as Cowan mustered his fishing gear and set the rigging to rights. The two seamen tried to keep out of their way. Evening drew in, and it was time to join the many boats heading out to the grounds.

Cowan had a last look round, then took the tiller, gave the orders to loose sail and called, 'Let her go then, Davey.' The bowline dropped, and the *Fancy* caught the wind and slewed before crowding with the others through the rock-girded Polperro harbour entrance.

Most fishing-boats stood out to sea towards the setting sun but Cowan, with an inscrutable smile, put down the tiller and, taking the wind astern, the *Polperro Fancy* set her bowsprit for up the coast.

Stirk tried not to show his interest: from seaward, Polperro and its snug harbour was almost completely hidden. So close to the rugged shore he could easily distinguish where run cargoes could land – the sandy coves, small beaches in obscuring twists of shoreline, suggestive caves. No wonder the Revenue was so hard-pressed to cover the coast.

'Here's yourn,' Bunt said to Stirk, handing him a small frame, 'an' I'd get y' line on th' cater here ready, mate.'

The beamy boat was lively even in the slight seas that evening but Stirk knew that its response to every wave meant it would remain dry. He wound the line, ready baited, round the cater frame and waited.

'Mr Cowan, how does y' know where the fish are?' Calloway asked, noting that several of the other boats had turned about and were now following them.

At first Cowan did not speak, his face turned into the wind to sniff gently, his grip on the tiller firm. Then, as they sailed on, there came quietly the distilled wisdom of the Cornish fishery: talk of sea marks to fix favourite sub-sea rocks; the arcane habits of mackerel and ling, conger and pilchard, spur dog and dab; herring shoals square miles in size rising stealthily to the surface at dusk that could be detected by bubbles fizzing upward from below and the faint smell of oil on the surface of the sea, the whole to sink down again at dawn's light. The dexterity of the long-liners and the seiners, the willow withies of the crabbers, the ever-vital pilchard fishing, all were testament to the multitude of hard-won skills of the fishermen.

As the red orb of the sun met the horizon two lanthorns were lit and sails were lowered with a small island barely in sight in the soft dusk. Cowan glanced over the side once and waited for the boat to drift further, the only sound the chuckling of water and creak of gear. He scanned the shoreline for some sea mark, then said quietly, 'This'll do, Jan.'

Obediently Puckey took up his cater and began to lower.

Stirk made to do the same but Cowan stopped him with a gesture. After an interval Puckey grunted, 'Fish is slight, Mr Cowan.'

Small sail was shown to the wind and they ghosted inshore a little way and the sail was doused. Puckey repeated his work, and after a longer time he showed satisfaction. 'Now will do,' Cowan said, and in the increasing darkness their lines went down.

Stirk felt the fish strike, the tugs connecting him with the unseen world far beneath, which must now be a swirl of glinting silver in the blackness as the shoal orbited the unlucky ones jerking on his line, just as they had in those all-but-forgotten days of his youth.

Bunt was first to haul in with a full line; over the gunwale hand over hand, grunting with effort until the first fish jerked into view, flipping frantically. There was a craning to see but Cowan peered over and announced, 'Mackerel, lads, sure 'nough.'

Puckey soon followed, and then an excited Calloway, and before long the midships was a welter of hooks, line and slippery striped fish. Then the work started.

Two hours later the shoal had left and, aching in every bone, Stirk and Calloway were allowed first rest in the stinking confines of the cuddy, only to be woken not long after when the shoal was rediscovered further eastwards.

With eyes strained and sore from the effort of baiting hooks by the faint gleam of a lanthorn, the lines went out again – and again came the toil of heaving in and the messy work of gutting afterwards. All the while they fought a clamping weariness. A lull followed as the mackerel sounded deep again, and then there was blessed rest, but with the suspicion of luminance to the east the mackerel returned and it was to the lines again until the sun's orb rose and the fish sank down once more.

'Brave bit o' fish, Jan!' Bunt said, with tired glee, as the hold showed near full.

'It is that,' Puckey replied, and glanced at Cowan.

'Aye, I'll grant ye,' Cowan said cautiously. 'Shares all roun' – what do thee men say t' these two gettin' a whack?'

The cover was placed on the hold and *Polperro Fancy* made for home. Stirk lay back exhausted; this was a job like no other. However, their readiness to bear a hand must have been noted and their acceptance into this small village would be that much the closer.

Around fifteen boats converged with them in the final entry to harbour on the flooding tide; sails were brailed and they lay to a scull at the transom waiting for room at the fish quay.

They found a place and Stirk bent his back once more in the task of keeping the baskets filled to sway up and disgorge on to the noisy quay where an auction was taking place. For some reason the others in the boat were downcast and when they had finished and taken the *Fancy* to her moorings Stirk asked Cowan why.

'Chancy thing, mackerel fishin' – some days y' finds nothin', other days . . .' He was without his smile as he went on, 'Well, t'day every soul in Polperro – save us – has good luck.' They stopped at the edge of the fish quay and he pointed out a strapping woman with a basket on her back and voluminous pockets filled with salt. 'That's a fish jowter, sellin' our fish all over th' parish. She's sittin' pretty 'cos with everyone lucky the market's flooded and prices go t' the devil.'

He gave a theatrical sigh and added, 'Will we be seein' ye again, Mr Jem?'

* * *

After crumpling into their bed of nets Stirk and Calloway slept until midday, at which point hunger drove them to re-enter the world. Mrs Puckey had seen the boats arrive and land their catch, and her lips were thin.

'What's fer vittles, darlin'? I'm gut-foundered,' Puckey said, sprawling wearily in his chair.

'Teddies 'n' point – what else c'n thee expect?' she muttered, bringing over a pot.

'Th' – the what, Mrs Puckey?' Calloway asked hesitantly.

Puckey grinned, without humour. 'Taties as we grows at the back, an' she'll point out th' meat fer thee in case y' misses it.'

After the thin meal Stirk made his excuses and the two shipmates wandered down to the harbour and the outer pier where they sat leaning companionably against a pile of nets. At first Stirk said nothing, letting the keening of the gulls wheeling over the fish quay form a backdrop to his thoughts. He lay back and closed his eyes, enjoying the warmth of the sun on his aching limbs.

He heard Calloway stir. 'What d' we do next, Mr Stirk?'

He grunted. 'Fer now, cully, I'll allow it's "Toby" till we're back aboard.' But were they getting any closer to uncovering anything to do with smuggling? It was odd, but here the fisher-folk were clearly dirt-poor and hard-working, not as would be expected if they were living high on the proceeds of smuggling.

'Aye, aye, Toby,' Calloway replied, and went on more soberly, 'I don't want t' go back t' Mr Kydd wi' nothing, y' know.'

'As we both don't, mate,' Stirk muttered.

'What d' ye think he'd do if'n he was here, Toby?'

'I don't know what Mr Kydd would do if'n he was here, younker,' Stirk said sarcastically. But of a surety in his place

Kydd could be relied on to find some cunning way through. If there was one thing Kydd had, it was a right sound headpiece that had set him apart from the start, that and the sand to stand up for himself when it was needed.

He didn't want to let the man down: what must it have cost Kydd to claw his way to the quarterdeck and now be captain of his own ship? In a way Stirk took personal pride in this, one of his own gun crew of the past reaching for the stars and getting there.

And besides which, Kydd was a right true seaman, not like some he could put a name to. No, he had to do something. 'Luke, step down t' Mr Butters an' help him. See if y' can hear aught o' this smugglin' – but steer small, cuffin. They's a short way wi' them as runs athwart their hawse.'

He stood up stiffly. There was nothing to be gained from sitting about and waiting. He would take a stroll, see something of the place, keep a weather eye open.

Polperro was as distinctive a fishing village as it could be. Its focus was the small harbour, of course, and the steepest sides of the coombe were bare of dwellings but as he walked he could see that this separated the settlement into a working western side with the fish quay and humble homes, and the eastern area, with more substantial residences.

A charming rivulet ran down to the sea, along which ageless buildings crowded together in a communal huddle. Stirk walked the narrow streets, passing the chapel by the tiny green and one or two humble shops. Nothing in any wise betrayed the presence of smuggling.

Folk looked at him curiously but he could detect no suspicion or hostility. Either Polperro's reputation was undeserved or the Revenue was getting the better of the problem, both of which contradicted what Mr Kydd had been told. It was a conundrum and Stirk knew he would have to try harder to resolve it.

Puckey was outside his house, mending nets. He gave a friendly nod and Stirk went inside for his bundle. Then he had an idea. Carefully he cleared the fishing gear and clutter away from the far corner, exposing the dusty earth floor. He found a stick and brought it firmly across, feeling as he went. Nothing. Then again, a few inches further – and the stick caught. He smoothed the surface and looked closely until he found what he was looking for: a faint line in the dust.

He slipped out his seaman's knife, prodded and twisted until he had the disguised trapdoor free, then swung it up to reveal a cavernous space below. A candle stub in a pottery dish stood nearby. He took a sniff. This hiding-place had been used recently.

He replaced everything and left quickly. Outside, Puckey looked up. 'If thee has th' time, m' wife would thank ye well fer a hand at th' taties.'

She was half-way up the hill, scraping a furrow in the thin soil of a little plot and was grateful for Stirk's help. He didn't mind: without this to sustain them in bleak times they would starve and, besides, it gave him time to think.

They worked on silently until Mrs Puckey stopped suddenly and listened; from afar off there was a faint cry – it was repeated with an urgency that set Stirk's hair on end. 'It's th' huer,' she breathed. 'God be praised!'

'Th' huer?' Stirk asked, in astonishment, as the cry was taken up from windows and rooftops along the steep hill-sides and round the harbour. People hurried from their houses and fields and began to scramble for the lower parts, the cry now plain. 'Hevva! Hevva! *Hevva!*'

'Wha—'

'See?' She pointed down to the rocks that guarded the entrance to the harbour. On the highest Stirk could see a figure capering about, clutching what looked like a tin trumpet through which he kept up his cry.

'The huer! Hue 'n' cry! Get down wi' ye,' she shouted, and pushed past him. 'The pilchards 're here!'

Stirk looked out to sea; below circling and plummeting gannets he saw a peculiar long stain of red-purple and silver in the water extending for a mile or more. With the rest he scrambled and slid until he reached the path and joined the throng converging on the harbour.

A sharp-faced man with an open notebook sized him up in an instant. 'Pull an oar?' he snapped.

'Aye.'

'Volyer,' he ordered, and gestured impatiently at a curious low and broad open boat being readied.

Sitting at his oar Stirk grinned to himself: a gunner's mate brought to this pass! But if he didn't show willing to lend a fist with the rest, his chances of getting near to them would fade.

A net was manoeuvred into the boat and as they pulled out of the harbour the plan was explained to him: the other boat had the main 'stop' net to encircle as much of the pilchard shoal as they could, at which point their boat would close the gap and assist to bring ashore the captives. A third boat, the lurker, would bear the master seiner who would direct the operation.

Stirk knew there would be hard, skilled work before the fish could be landed. They made a wide sweep, carefully approached the shoal from seaward and slowed to a stop. The man on the oar opposite nudged him: the huer on the high rocks had stopped his cries and was now holding a coloured cloth in each outstretched hand which he wig-wagged in a series of signals, watched attentively by the master seiner.

'Give way, y' bastards,' he bawled, throwing the tiller over. Their own boat followed obediently, and Stirk saw they were essentially being directed by the watcher high on the rocks to where the fish were, and the master seiner was deploying accordingly.

At just the right moment and place, the quarter-mile-long stop seine began shooting into the sea along its length in a curve right in the path of the shoal and when it was out the toil of joining the ends together in a vast circle started.

It was back-breaking work, bringing the inert mass of seine net and the weight of uncountable thousands of fish into a vast circle, but that was nothing compared to the unending travail that followed of towing the entire mass to the nearest sandy bottom, Lantivet Bay, where the fish would finally come ashore.

The secluded beach, no more than a couple of miles from Polperro, was crowded with excited people; the boats came closer and just when the mottled black and pale of the seabed glimmered up through the clear water, the master seiner called a halt.

Resting on their oars, the men of the stop seine boat watched as Stirk's companions readied their own tuck net, whose purpose was soon plain. Smaller than the stop seine, it was shot within the larger, then brought tightly together, gathering the catch to the surface in an appalling agitation of threshing fish, screaming gulls and the frantic plunging of stones on ropes to deter escape at the rapidly diminishing opening.

'Lade 'im!' yelled the master seiner, pounding the gunwale of his boat with excitement.

Everyone aboard the volyer threw themselves at the fish. With tuck baskets, broad flaskets and bare hands they scooped them as fast as they could into the boat.

Ashore, children screamed and frolicked, women clustered with baskets and called to their men in exhilaration, and when the boat was finally heaved into the shallows they, too, joined in the glorious mayhem.

The sheer quantity of fish caught was colossal: tons in weight, hundreds of thousands of silver shapes swirling in the stop net, but the master seiner, eyeing the haul, stopped the tuck and declared, 'That'll do fer now, boys.' The rest could safely be left to mill about in the net for later.

'Well, Jem, how d' ye like our fishin'? Sport enough, heh?' The Three Pilchards was in a roaring good mood, fishermen with their immediate futures now secure drinking to their good fortune.

Stirk lifted his pot. 'Decent taut, this'n,' he growled. 'Ye'll have another, Davey, mate?'

'A glass o' bright cider is jus' what I needs,' Bunt answered expansively. 'Fishin' gives thee such a thirst an' all.'

Signalling to the harried pot-boy, Stirk said, 'S' now ye has a right good haul then.'

Bunt leant forward and said earnestly, 'Pilchards mean a brave lot t' us, Jem. As we do say in these parts:

'Here's a health t' the Pope, an' may he repent
And lengthen six months th' term of his Lent;
F'r it's always declared, betwixt th' two poles
There's nothin' like pilchards f'r the saving of souls . . .'

232

Puckey came across and sat with them. 'This is Long Tom Shar, Jem. Thee should know, as fer hake an' conger there ain't a finer hand.'

Solemnly Stirk allowed himself to be acquainted as well with Zeb Minards and Sam Coad, the bushy-browed blacksmith. It was happening – his work in the boats was paying off.

He saw Calloway in one corner in close conversation with a shy fisher-girl still in her pinafore. Stirk winked when he caught his eye and turned back to hear about the hazards and rewards of drift-netting.

Suddenly the happy noise subsided. Two men had entered: these were no fisher-folk and they looked about guardedly. One by one the fishermen turned their backs, the tavern taking on a pointed silence.

'Who're them, mates?' Stirk asked.

Puckey leant over and, in a hoarse whisper, said, 'Bad cess – they's Revenooers, Jem, wished on us t' watch th' harbour. Nobody'll take 'em in, so theys forced t' sleep in a boat.'

One looked at Stirk. Their eyes met and Stirk froze. He knew the man! It was Joe Corrie, in his watch-on-deck in the old *Duke William* and a miserable shipmate into the bargain. If he was recognised it would be disastrous.

Stirk moved quickly. Dropping his head he croaked, 'Feelin' qualmish, mates – have t' be outside sharp, like,' and slipped away through the back door.

As he hurried away from the tavern he noticed that he was being followed. He plunged down one of the opeways, dark, narrow passages between the old buildings along the rivulet. Unfortunately one of the dwellings had swelled with age and he found himself wedged, unable to continue. Shamefaced, he had to back out and his pursuer was waiting. It was the blacksmith Coad. 'Don't y' worry o' th' Revenooers, frien', they's up an' gone. But there's someone wants t' see ye. Do y' mind?'

They returned to the Three Pilchards but this time to a back room where a well-dressed man with dark, sensitive features waited. 'This'n is Simon Johns. His ol' man died last year 'n' now he's lookin' after the business.'

'Thank you, Sam,' Johns said, and gestured to Stirk to take a chair. 'To be brief, I was there in the Pilchards when the Preventives came. Your subsequent actions tell me that you are no friend to the Revenue, no rough-knot sent here to spy among us. And did not our mutual friend Jan Puckey tell me that you're no stranger to free trade yourself?'

Stirk's face was impassive but inside he exulted. 'I may've been,' he said cautiously, looking intently from one to the other.

'May we know in what capacity?'

'Frenchy run wi' tobaccy an' brandy, smacksman on the Marsh, creepin' fer tubs, that kind o' thing.'

'I don't think it wise at this point for you to risk the sea, but we have need still of stout men on shore. Would you be interested?'

'T' nobble a patter-roller?' he said doubtfully. Waylaying an inquisitive Revenue riding officer was not what he had come here for. 'Not as who should say . . .'

'I didn't mean that. We have more than a sufficiency of men to take care of such unpleasantries. No, what would make best use of your seamanlike capabilities would be more the spout lantern . . .'

Stirk grunted. This was more like it – at the landing lights for the cargoes to be run ashore in the right place. 'Aye, I can do it. Pay?'

'Half a guinea on the lantern for the night, another half if there's trouble.'

'Done. Does m' matey Harry find a berth?'

'Mmm. We can find him something. A skinker, perhaps?'

It was just as it had ever been: the familiar tensions and short tempers, suspicion and fingering of concealed weapons. Far out to sea there would be telescopes trained, waiting for the signal that it was this night they were running in the cargo. In the kiddleywink a dozen hard-featured men sat with pots before them also waiting for the word to move.

Stirk had been passed his instructions by Coad only an hour or two before: to make his way with an innocent-looking pair of farmhands driving pigs over the steep hill eastwards to Talland Bay and there wait in the tavern for sunset.

It needed brains and organisation to bring the run to a successful conclusion; even with the consignment of goods assured in Guernsey or elsewhere there was the hazardous journey across the Channel before the landing and then the need to co-ordinate scores of men for the unloading and rapid carrying-off of the contraband.

The little tap-house was remote and near the small beach; a stranger might wonder why so many along the coast were situated so suspiciously but Stirk knew that in the hard life of a fisherman the ready availability of a cheering pot in close proximity to a place to draw up a boat would be appreciated.

Outside, a seaweed-cutter poked lazily about the foreshore, but in his barrow under the pile of kelp two spout lanterns were ready for use, and the several men mowing at the edge of the field were doing so to prepare a signal bonfire.

The sun lowered and Stirk went outside. In the waning daylight he had quickly identified the best approach from seaward in the winds prevailing at the time, past the inshore rocks to the small sandy strip of beach, and made contact with the other lightsman. Together they would set up leading lights, each some hundred yards above the other that the skipper of the smuggling vessel would keep in exact line to ensure a safe approach. The lanterns they would use were enclosed, a long spout fitted to each, however, that would hide the gleam from all but those on whom it was trained.

At last there was action. A body of men arrived in a boat; one had a muffled face and gave brisk orders to the others. Stirk had no difficulty in recognising Johns's cultivated voice. A young farmhand on a white horse was summoned. 'Off you go, lad,' he was told and, to subdued cheers from the men, he dismounted and set off for the coast path, leading it self-consciously by the bridle. It was the signal that the coast was clear of the Revenue.

In the gathering gloom the landing party took shape. Stirk and the other man retrieved and lit their spout lanterns, then took up their positions on the hillside. A gruff man claiming to be Stirk's 'assistant' stood next to him – he was being watched. Shouts in the twilight directed a stream of new arrivals; a loose chain of men was being formed that stretched down from the woods that lay in a fold in the hills behind the tavern.

Packhorses wound down from the hilltop, and a troop of donkeys gathered on the beach. Then gangs of men with blackened faces set off to either side hefting clubs, and the occasional steel of a weapon could be seen. Heaven help the Revenue or Excise man who stumbled upon them: Stirk calculated there must be more than a hundred and therefore the high stakes of a valuable cargo.

So far he had recognised only Johns. Could he be the

leader? Probably locally, but not the evil genius he had been told about who was co-ordinating the whole coast. Doubts crept in. This was a far larger and more detailed operation than he was used to: without asking betraying questions, how would he get to the central figure?

He glanced at the tavern. It was locked and barred; the landlord and tapster would later be able to claim truthfully on oath that they had seen nothing suspicious that night. What was 'Harry' doing? If—

'Lights! Get those lights going, damn it!'

Lifting the clumsy lantern he trained the thing out to sea, making sure it lined up with the two sticks he had placed in front of himself now that the approaches were in darkness. The unknown master of the vessel would cast back and forth until he could see the lights, then begin his run into the unknown, being sure to keep the two lights precisely vertical.

Darkness was now nearly complete, the moon not due to rise before midnight, and it was impossible to make out anything to seaward. Stirk kept up his vigil but if they were surprised by tipped off preventives aided by dragoons he would be taken up with the others and no mercy shown.

His shoulder hurt where the lantern rested but he persevered, keeping the light carefully trained; then a subtle thickening of the darkness ahead became evident. By degrees its form resolved into a large lugger ghosting in. The cargo had arrived.

A rising hubbub was cut short by bellowed orders as the receiving party made ready. Men splashed into the shallows while others drew the packhorses closer. The black shape grew in detail, then slowed and elongated – a kedge had been dropped and the vessel rotated until it lay head to sea.

Stirk lowered his lantern and grinned into the darkness. A successful arrival! It was the feeling he had experienced all those years ago. Now for the landing – a large ship's boat was in the water, loading in minutes, and what looked suspiciously like his volyer had emerged from behind the westward point on its way alongside.

It was matchless organisation; the first boat stroked vigorously ashore and grounded, to be instantly set upon. With not a single light the waiting men were each roped up with a half-anker tub suspended from front and back and sent waddling up the hill in a line. Larger casks were rolled over to the packhorses and heaved into place while the donkeys took two ankers apiece.

The pace quickened. With the tide on the ebb and the moon due to make its appearance there was no time to be lost. Packages – probably tea and silks – were transferred to the saddle panniers of a horse and sent off into the night. Still the casks came ashore. Hundreds were taken steadily into the darkness to some hiding-place in the woods, nearby farms, homes – even church crypts. Holland gin, rum, the finest wines and certainly 'Cousin Jack' – the best Cognac.

It was on a breathtaking scale. By now the casks alone would number considerably more than a thousand and the line of human carriers still patiently trudged on. By morning there would be the best part of ten thousand gallons of the finest spirit safely inland for distribution later and not a penny of duty paid.

The stream lessened; by rise of moon the job was safely complete, the line of men dissipating, the lugger slipping out to sea. Shouts of drunken hilarity pierced the night, and Stirk knew that some carriers had broached a cask and were probably at that moment sucking raw spirit through straws.

It was time to be off. With nothing whatsoever gained for Mr Kydd. He knew now how it was done, much the same as it was in Kent, but the times, places – they would change. The figure behind it – well . . .

Down by the beach he could see Johns paying off the volyer crew and he strode down, waiting for the right moment. 'Er, Mr Johns. A word wi' ye. This is no work f'r a seaman! I feels ready t' sign f'r a workin' voyage. Can y' arrange it, like?'

'Aren't you concerned you may be seen by a King's ship?'

'Well, sir, a smugglin' voyage is always goin' to be inconspictable an', b'sides, it's the only trade I knows, Mr Johns.'

'I understand. I cannot promise a berth, that is not within my gift, but there may be . . .'

Later the following evening Johns took Stirk up Talland Hill to a modest cottage where a single light showed at a window. Inside they were met by a kindly-looking gentleman, who studied Stirk with keen attention.

'The man Jem, sir,' Johns said respectfully, and waited for the inspection to finish.

'Very well,' the gentleman said, and returned to sit at his desk. It was scrupulously tidy, papers arranged squarely and a stand of red and black ink with quills set neatly before him. 'You are a mariner, I can see that – but have you run cargoes 'cross Channel?' His voice was oddly soft.

'Aye, sir. Roscoff in brandy an' silks afore the last war – I knows th' lay, bless ye, sir.'

'And on extended absence from the King's service.'

'I'm free t' ship out with ye now, sir.'

'If you'll recall, sir,' Johns said, 'Privaulx of the *Flyer* is still in Exeter prison.'

'Yes, I know. But I mean to make trial of Master Jem here first.' He stood up. 'My name is Zephaniah Job, you may believe my business interests are . . . many, and I'm sure we can make use of you. Pray wait a moment.'

He left the room and returned shortly with a massive ledger. He opened it and ran his finger down the columns. 'Umm – I see we have *Two Brothers* entered for a Guernsey run in spirits not four days hence. You have no objection to shipping as an able seaman? On good report I can promise an advance later.'

'It'll answer f'r now.'

'By the way, Simon,' Job said quietly, looking at an entry, 'it seems Mevagissey is down for the next moon. Fowey Revenue are getting uppity and I shall want more men in the shore party. See to it, if you please.'

He closed the book and looked mildly at Stirk. 'We shall discover how well you can act, Mr Jem. You'll join *Two Brothers* in Looe two nights hence. Her skipper will have my instructions before then.'

Chapter 10

'Is this the man I saw standing with bloody sword at the gates of Acre? Steals into the enemy's midst in Minorca? Who, for the sake of a romantic tryst, dared the wrath of Gibraltar's town major?' Renzi challenged. 'For shame, Mr Kydd! In the space of less than a day we shall have returned to Plymouth and come under notice, and the object of your admiration will then be wondering whether your ardour yet burns undimmed in her absence. As ladies set such store on these matters you must therefore indicate in some wise that your interest in her is unabated with some – token of your esteem.'

Kydd continued to stare up at the deckhead from his easy chair. It had been an uneventful cruise. Stirk was still away in Polperro and there had been no sign of any privateer, leaving him time to reflect on events ashore. Things had come to pass on Dartmoor that had no explanation other than that Miss Persephone Lockwood had formed an interest in him, which was now personal.

'Nicholas, I – I'm out o' soundings on these matters. Y'

see, I'm concerned that if I . . . press my attentions and you're on th' right tack about y'r ladies playin' with . . . Well, what I'm trying t' say is—'

'Fear not! If the lady wished to toy with you, then what better than before the large and distinguished audience at the princely reception? No, dear fellow, you must try to accept that for reasons which must escape mere men, you have caught Miss Lockwood's fancy.'

'But – but if I . . . pursue her, and . . . it doesn't fadge, then it'll be so . . .'

Renzi snorted. 'Dear chap, do you really believe that you'll be the first to suffer a reverse in the pursuit of an amour? If so, then shall I remind you that faint heart never won fair lady?' He gave a half-smile. 'Besides, I believe that on this occasion you will find the logic unassailable. On the one hand if you hold back for fear of rebuff then, of course, you cannot succeed to win her hand. For the other, if you are active in your addresses and are repelled then you may fail – but equally so you may be gladly received and go on to a blissful conclusion. Therefore only one course is reasonable . . .'

Kydd gulped and pulled the doorbell. He had never been to the admiral's house before and its severe classical frontage seemed to frown at his audacity in visiting simply on a social matter.

'Mr Kydd calling upon Lady Lockwood,' he said, as firmly as he could, to the footman, handing over his visiting card – his name in blue copperplate with an acanthus-leaf border, much recommended by Renzi – and waited nervously.

By the rules of society he could not call upon Miss Lockwood directly: that would never do for a gentleman. He had first to navigate past her mother and he dreaded facing the formidable matriarch. Perhaps the footman would return to announce that Lady Lockwood was not at home to him.

He heard footsteps and braced himself. The door was opened, but by the admiral in comfortable morning clothes. He appeared bemused. 'Mr Kydd, this is a pleasure of course, but may I enquire – Lady Lockwood . . . ?'

'S-sir,' Kydd stuttered. It was not going according to the script that Renzi had patiently laid out for him. The footman should have admitted him to the drawing room where the ladies would be sitting demurely sewing. There would be polite conversation before tea was proffered. He would not stay less than fifteen minutes or longer than half an hour and could not look to seeing Miss Lockwood alone at any time.

'T' be more truthful sir, it was . . . Well, I was hoping to call upon Miss Lockwood to express personally my thanks for the reception.'

The admiral's expression eased with the glimmer of a smile. Heartened, Kydd went on, 'An' to be bold enough to ask her advice in a matter of music.'

'My profound regrets, Mr Kydd, but I have to tell you Lady Lockwood is at the moment somewhat discommoded.' He paused, but then said lightly, 'However, I shall enquire if Persephone is able to receive you. Will you not come in?'

There was no one in the spacious drawing room. Lockwood turned and spoke to the footman while Kydd's eyes were drawn to the fine seamanlike painting in pride of place above the mantelpiece. 'You like it, Mr Kydd? Persephone presented it to me recently – damn fine taste for a woman, I thought. See here – not many artists remember to slack the lee shrouds in anything of a blow and, well, you were present at the action as I remember. A good likeness?'

'Master's mate only, sir – but this is a rattlin' fine piece o' work, t' be sure,' Kydd agreed warmly, peering more closely at it.

Then the door opened behind him. 'Why, Mr Kydd! How kind in you to call!' Her voice was charged with such unmistakable delight that he gave a boyish smile before he remembered his polite bow.

'Miss Lockwood!' Her hair was in fetching curls that framed her face and he found himself looking away while he composed himself. 'Er, I called to express personally my sense of gratitude at your handsome conduct towards me at the reception.'

Another bow could not go amiss and Persephone returned it with a curtsy of acknowledgement. 'And – an' if ye'd be so kind . . .'

'Yes, Mr Kydd?' She looked impossibly winsome.

'Um, that I can ask your advice in the article of polite music, which you consider I might with profit, er – er – take aboard.'

Lockwood had wandered to the other end of the drawing room and was absently looking out of a window.

'Music? Why, of course, Mr Kydd, I should be glad to assist.' She beamed and crossed to the pianoforte, lifted the lid of the stool and pulled out a thick wad of music. 'You have a fine voice, Mr Kydd, I'm sure we can find something . . . Ah, this will always be well received. A favourite of the Prince of Wales.'

She set it on the pianoforte. 'Do come and sit beside me, Mr Kydd. You'll not see the music from there.'

Kydd hesitated. Lockwood had turned to watch but stayed near the window so he moved over to the instrument and discovered that the stool was designed to accommodate two.

'"Sweet Lass of Richmond Hill",' she said, in a businesslike tone. 'It's in two-four time and begins like this.' Sweeping her hands gracefully over the keys, she picked out the tune and sang. 'There! Shall you sing for me now?'

Sitting so close and singing to her, Kydd felt terror mingle with delight.

> '. . . and wanton thro' the grove,
> Oh! whisper to my charming fair,
> 'I die for her I love.'
> O may her choice be fix'd on me,
> Mine's fix'd on her alone!
> I'd crowns resign to call thee mine . . .'

There was the sound of rapidly approaching footsteps and the door was thrown open. Lady Lockwood hurried in, her hair hastily pinned up and face with the barest dab of powder. Persephone's playing faltered and stopped; they both got to their feet.

'Oh! Mr Kydd – it's kind in you to call,' Lady Lockwood said icily. Kydd bowed as deeply as he could, returned with the slightest possible bob.

The admiral moved over swiftly. 'My love, Commander Kydd has called to tell Persephone of his appreciation for the way in which she rescued him at the reception, if you remember. Oh, and if she might have any suggestion as to any music he might hoist in, as it were . . .'

In any other circumstance it would have been diverting for Kydd to witness the look of scorn that words from his admiral received.

'Can that be so?' she snapped. 'And with me lying in bed so ill, and wondering all the time what the commotion was about. Really, Reginald!' Without waiting for a reply she turned to Persephone, who stood with her head hung in contrition. 'Your drawing master will be here at three. You will now allow Mr Kydd to go about his business, Persephone.'

'Yes, Mama.'

'He will no doubt have a list of your suggestions and be satisfied with them. Good day, Mr Kydd!'

Kydd bowed wordlessly and turned to go. Impulsively, Persephone went to him clutching the music and gave it to him. 'Do practise this – for me, Mr Kydd?'

He swallowed. 'That I will, Miss Lockwood.' She curtsied deeply and, ignoring Lady Lockwood's furious look, Kydd left, his heart singing.

'Nicholas! Your note – a matter of urgency concerning Thomas's future, you said,' Cecilia said breathlessly, ignoring Kydd, who was rising in surprise from his favourite armchair next to the fireplace.

'Miss Cecilia, allow me to take your pelisse,' Renzi said smoothly, and handed it to Tysoe, waiting behind her. 'Yes, indeed I did, and I rather fear it might require some action on our part.'

'Nicholas? What's this y' say?' Kydd said, putting down his newspaper.

'Has he – does this concern Miss Persephone Lockwood, do I hazard, Nicholas?' Cecilia asked.

'It does,' Renzi said solemnly.

'Oh! He hasn't—'

Kydd coughed significantly, 'Cec, this is all—'

'He has paid a call on the lady at her home and been received warmly.'

Cecilia's eyes sparkled. 'Did she – has he hopes of a further—'

'That is the matter under discussion for which I fear I have sadly inconvenienced you in the coming here.'

'Oh, Nicholas, of course I'd come! What must we do?'

Kydd blinked in confusion. 'Do y' mean t' talk about—'

'Dear sister, pray let's be seated. There's much we need to consider.'

They sat in the only two armchairs by the fireplace, leaving Kydd to hover. 'If you're about t' discuss—'

'Please be quiet, Thomas,' Cecilia said crossly. 'This is important, you know.'

It was indeed: the principal difficulty lay in the decorous bringing together of the couple in such a manner that would place Kydd to best advantage with respect to other admirers more talented in the social graces than he, so to speak, not to mention the additional difficulties a protective mother might be expected to present.

There was much discussion of Miss Lockwood's probable tastes and proclivities, and the delicacies of conduct that would ensue before a course of action could be decided. Eventually one such presented itself.

'Do you pay particular attention to what I say, Thomas. You will be invited to tea by Jane and her husband, and quite by chance Persephone Lockwood will be present as well. When you see her you will be suitably taken aback, and . . .'

'Why, Miss Lockwood! How surprising to find you here!' Kydd said graciously, fighting down his glee. A warning flash came from Cecilia and he turned to her companion and added quickly, 'And it's always my particular pleasure to meet Miss Robbins. How do you do?'

The parlour was not large and when the ladies had been seated it proved a most companionable gathering. 'I've heard that the moor in July is quite a delightful sight,' Jane opened, with a winning smile at Persephone.

'I would imagine so, Mrs Mullins, yet I would not wish to be without a hat and parasol out in all that open,' Persephone said politely, with a glance at Kydd.

'Perhaps we should venture out upon it at some time,' Mr Mullins said stiffly, clearly awed by Persephone's presence.

'Oh, no!' his wife said in alarm. 'Think of all the wild horses and escaped convicts – it would be far too hazardous, my dear, for a lady of breeding.'

Cecilia turned to Kydd. 'Thomas, would you now please pour the tea?'

'It's my own mixture of pekoe and gunpowder,' Mrs Mullins said proudly. 'Mr Mullins always brings back a pound or two from Twining's in the Strand when he goes up to London.'

Kydd went to the elaborate brass and silver tea urn and did his duty with the spigot. 'Mrs Mullins?' Hard-won lessons on precedence were coming to the fore: Persephone was clearly of the higher quality but Jane was a married lady.

Persephone accepted her cup with properly downcast eyes and Kydd resumed his strategically chosen seat opposite and let the prattle ebb and flow while he covertly took his fill of her.

A lull in the conversation had Cecilia throwing a warning look at Kydd, who cleared his throat. 'Capital weather we're having, don't you think?' he said brightly.

Persephone lowered her cup. 'If we see this nor'-easterly veering more to the west, Mr Kydd, I rather fancy we will soon be reaching for our umbrellas. Do not you mariners so rightly declare, "When the wind shifts 'gainst the sun, trust it not, for back 'twill run"?' she asked sweetly.

Kydd took refuge in his tea.

Mrs Mullins and Cecilia exchanged a quick look. 'Pay no mind to we ladies, Mr Kydd, we do like our gossip,' Jane said, in a determined voice, 'Er, why don't you show Miss Lockwood the new bougainvillaea in our greenhouse, you having been in the Caribbean yourself, of course?'

In the expectant hush Kydd stood, heart bumping, but was so long in choosing his words that Persephone rose and offered, 'I'd be very interested, should you be able to tell me more of such tropical blooms, Mr Kydd.'

They entered the small garden together and Kydd steered his way through the vegetables and ancient fruit trees into the greenhouse and said, in as light a voice as he could manage, 'This is your bougainvillaea, Miss Lockwood, an' I well remember seeing it in Jamaica, and Barbados as well and . . .'

But something was distracting her and she was facing away, not hearing his words. Kydd made a play of looking closer at the plant, then offered his arm to escort her back. Had he done something to offend?

Then she turned towards him and asked, 'Did Mrs Mullins marry in the Caribbean?'

'Er, yes, Miss Lockwood, and my sister was at the wedding.' He cast about for something else to say but no words came and she went on ahead. They wandered a few more steps, Kydd following helplessly, before she stopped and said quite casually, 'Your perceptions of society might lead you to suppose that I should marry as bade, but I can assure you, Mr Kydd, I shall only wed one I care for and cherish. An odd notion, don't you think?'

Was she saying . . . ?

'I – I admire you for it, Miss Lockwood,' Kydd replied hoarsely, as she lifted her eyes to his, her expression softening unbearably. He took a deep breath and said, in a voice that came out harsher than he had intended, 'If you married a – a man who followed the sea by profession, would ye – would you expect him t' leave it? Th' sea, I mean.'

She waited until his eyes held hers. 'No, Mr Kydd, I would not.'

The silence thundered in his ears until she turned and walked slowly to a little grotto of sea-shells set in the shady side of the wall. She looked back at him once and stooped to pick up a shell, which she admired in her cupped hands. 'I believe I will take this to remind me of you, Mr Kydd.'

Renzi scrambled to his feet when Kydd returned, eyes shining, an unmistakable air of excitement about him.

'Nicholas! Ye'd never smoke it! She *was* there an' – we walked together an' talked, and I'd lay out a sack o' guineas t' say before ye that she – she has a takin' for me!' He was touched that his friend was so evidently sharing the same soaring elevation of spirit.

'Felicitations, then, brother, but I trust you will hope to remember your speech in her presence – I am obliged to remark that at the moment it sorely betrays a lack of delicacy.'

Kydd grinned. 'She was wearing such a fine dress, Nicholas. Was it just f'r me? An' her hair, she had—'

Renzi's voice was odd – somewhat charged with emotion. 'Dear fellow, do you know what I have here?' He held up a grubby piece of paper covered with crabbed handwriting.

'Er, no, Nicholas. Pray, do tell me.'

'This,' Renzi said, 'this, dear friend, is the first – the very first evidence from the world that my humble conjectures in ethnical philosophies might indeed possess some degree of merit. This, brother, is a communication from Count

Rumford himself! Praises me for a new insight and encourages me to go further.'

He sat down suddenly and blinked rapidly. 'And – and wishes that when in London I might consider attending with him at the Royal Institution in Albemarle Street.'

To Kydd the name reminded him more of fireplaces but there was no doubting the effect it was having on Renzi. 'Why, that's thumpin' good news indeed, m' friend. Count Rumford himself!'

There was just sufficient Cognac to steady them both, then Renzi was able to say to Kydd, 'I am forgetting myself, brother. Do tell me more of your happy situation.'

'Well, I've been givin' it a deal of thought. I'm t' call on Miss Lockwood, I believe – I have t' return her music, y' see,' he said smugly. 'But not afore I ask Mrs Mullins if she'd help me learn it. I saw a pianoforte while I was there,' he added.

Kydd pulled the doorbell ceremoniously and waited. He was in his most elegant attire: a dark-green morning coat over buff waistcoat and cream breeches, with a painstakingly tied cravat. And the sheet of music tied with a ribbon.

'Sir?' It was the same footman, but he gave no sign of recognition.

'Mr Kydd, to call on Lady Lockwood.'

'Thank you, sir,' he said, with a bow, and went back inside, closing the door gently in Kydd's face. His heart bumping, he heard the footsteps die away. It seemed an age before the footman returned. 'Lady Lockwood is not at home, sir,' he announced, fixing a glassy stare over Kydd's shoulder.

Kydd had seen the carriage in the mews and knew that she had not left the house. 'Then – then Miss Lockwood?' he asked.

'Miss Lockwood is not at home, either, sir.'

'Er, then please to give this to Miss Lockwood,' Kydd said, handing over the music, realising too late that he had just lost his best excuse for calling in the future. He turned on his heel and walked off, thoughts churning furiously.

Cecilia dismissed his fears. 'This is Lady Lockwood being protective, I do believe, Thomas. We shall have to find another way. Now, let me see . . . Jane is being so obliging I think we can ask her to invite Miss Robbins and "friend" once again – this time to a cards evening. She has some tolerably high-placed acquaintances who are martyrs to the whist table.'

It cost Kydd a notable effort to ingest the finer points of whist: the mysteries of the trick, the trump suit and the potential for delicious interplay between the partners, but he was determined to reach the point at which he would not disgrace Persephone.

Time dragged, but eventually the appointed evening arrived and Kydd found himself making inane conversation with a young army lieutenant while the guests arrived. At last he heard Miss Robbins's silvery laugh in the doorway and forced himself not to look round.

'Ah, Miss Robbins,' came Jane's loyal cry. Kydd could bear it no longer and casually manoeuvred round until he could see her. She was with her 'friend' – a diminutive soul with an irrepressible giggle. Not Persephone.

A little later Miss Robbins slipped him a note and whispered archly, 'I rather think you'll want to see this.'

The rubber went on interminably but at its conclusion he was able to excuse himself. He feverishly took out the note – it was to Miss Robbins, thanking her for the invitation to a cards evening, but saying '. . . my engagements at present are such that I find I am unable to accept any invitation for some time to come . . .'

Cecilia's frown as she scanned the words was telling, but Kydd chuckled. 'It's naught but someone tryin' t' flam me, is all. See? This is not Persephone's handwritin'!'

Her expression did not lift. 'That is not the point, Thomas. It's almost certainly from her mother and it tells me that she has set her face against you, for whatever reason.' She bit her lip. 'It will require some thought. I believe I will need to consult Mr Renzi. Is he at liberty to return to land, do you know?'

Kydd thought guiltily of Renzi in *Teazer*, not at his precious studies but loyally accounting for stores come aboard and other ship's business. As captain, Kydd had a perfect right in port to allow the ship's routine to continue in his absence but his appearances on board were now minimal. He knew, however, that Renzi would send for him if there were difficulties.

'He's t' come for dinner tonight, Cec. Do y' not think—'

'No, Thomas, we three will discuss this together.'

It was sobering to find Renzi in so solid agreement with Cecilia on the gravity of the situation. 'Her mother, undoubtedly. In matters of this kind her wishes will prevail, of course. It will be difficult indeed to formulate any plan that might mollify, evoke a contrary tenderness.'

Cecilia asked, troubled, 'Shall he withdraw his attentions for a space, do you think? Allow time for Lady Lockwood to come to an – an appreciation of his qualities?'

'In the absence of any communication between them, there will be nothing at work that will tend to ameliorate her position, I fear. At the moment, dear sister, I am without inspiration . . .'

Kydd got up and paced angrily up and down. 'Belay that wry way o' talkin'! She told me to m' face as how she would not marry as she's bid, only t' one she cares for! Let her lay course where she will an' be damned!'

Renzi steepled his fingers. 'Brother, if she goes against her mother's desires in the matter of matrimony then without question she will lose her portion – her dowry – and your expectations for your position in society will, er, necessarily require revision.'

'And think this, Thomas, can you conceive that with her breeding she will be content to live the life of a – a sailor's wife?' Cecilia said softly.

Kydd stopped and looked at her. 'Yes, I do, sis!' He paused, then said forcefully, 'An' I will show you. I'm going to – to invite her *here* and then th' world will see.'

Renzi's face softened and he said gently, 'Dear fellow, do you think this wise? Her mother will—'

'It's t' be a musical evening an' there'll be – there'll be grand coves attendin' who it'll be unfortunate t' ignore. I'll be askin' Miss Lockwood if she'd assist me with the musical entertainments f'r these important guests. Even her mother c'n see she'll have to come.'

'Grand coves?' asked Renzi. 'And a lavish, therefore expensive, evening?'

There was no dissuading him, however, and Kydd would only hear those whose contributions were in some wise positive; towards midnight the main elements had been hammered out, and on the next day Cecilia began the delicate task of sounding out possible luminaries.

It was not to be a naval occasion – at his rank Kydd could not command the presence of flag-officers – but at the same time there were those in the wider community who would be flattered to attend a fifth anniversary dinner of Nelson's battle of the Nile hosted by one who had been present.

Well before noon Cecilia was back with the satisfying information that should he be favoured with an invitation the worshipful Lord Mayor of Plymouth himself was in a position graciously to accept, as were the colonel and the adjutant of the mighty Citadel that guarded the entrance to Old Plymouth.

It was time to set in train the events of the evening but not before the most important detail of all: Cecilia had demanded the right of wording the invitations, which she insisted must be properly printed on stiff card, albeit at a ruinous price.

They were sent out promptly and Kydd tried to contain his impatience. This would be a most splendid occasion and one that even the most suave and accomplished of the *ton* would not be in a position to mount. He swelled with happiness: as host it was the pinnacle of his achieving in society and to think that . . . *she* would be here to witness it.

The military acceptances were prompt and officer-like, the Lord Mayor's not far behind. But one seemed to have been delayed. Kydd reasoned that Persephone regularly attended such functions as his, and must have many in hand to balance. He waited as patiently as he could.

As the day neared with no word from her he began to fret and to take to his ship as a familiar refuge. It was not until the day before the event that the mate-of-the-watch handed him a sealed message. The handwriting he recognised instantly. For some unaccountable reason he was reluctant to open it on board his ship. He slipped the precious missive into his pocket and ordered a boat.

In the privacy of his drawing room he dismissed the flustered Becky, sat in his armchair and opened it. As if by dictation, the words repeated what he had seen once before, but now undeniably in Persephone's own strong hand – that she was not able to attend and, further, that she was unable to accept any invitation for some time to come.

He folded the paper mechanically and placed it in the centre of the mantelpiece. There was no evident compulsion, no form of words that left any room for hope – and no trace whatsoever of the feelings he had seen in her the last time they had met.

There was something at the bottom of it all, he was sure – but what? Had she changed her mind, reconsidered what it would mean to live in greatly reduced circumstances? Had an unknown suitor cunningly turned her against him with evil words? Was there something in the Byzantine society code that he had infringed and thereby earned her contempt?

He would hear it from her own lips – by confronting her when next she rode on the moor. Shameless bribery of the stable-hands would ensure the time and place.

Kydd heard her arrive. Skulking at the end of the line of horseboxes he listened to her cool voice greet the groom and dismiss her carriage. Her firm steps on the cobblestones approached and Kydd stepped out.

She was on her own, dressed in her usual immaculate fashion, and looked at him in shock. Recovering quickly, she said politely, 'Mr Kydd, what a surprise! You – I hadn't thought to see you here.'

'Why, Miss Lockwood, I did so enjoy our ride together before – do you mind if I join you?'

'I – I do not believe you should, sir.'

Kydd felt the warmth of a flush rising to his face and said huskily, 'Then I should ride alone?'

'As you will, sir. It can be no concern of mine.' She took the reins and prepared to mount.

'P-Persephone!' Kydd blurted. 'W-Why?'

She paused, then looked away suddenly. Then, turning to the groom, she ordered, 'Garvey, I shall walk on ahead for a space. Do you follow on discreetly, if you please.'

Without waiting for Kydd she began to walk rapidly out towards the moor. Kydd hurried until they were side by side, not daring to speak.

'You will have received my regrets for your interesting evening.' She did not look at him.

'I understand, Miss Lockwood.'

It won him a glance. They walked on in silence, the pace not slowing. 'I do hope it goes well for you, Mr Kydd,' she said eventually, in a neutral manner.

'I – we shall fin' someone else t' entertain us, I'm sure,' he said stiffly, his hands in his pockets so she would not see that the fists were clenched.

She said nothing but, after a few moments, slowed. 'Mr Kydd,' she said, turning to him, 'I don't think I ever mentioned my friend to you.'

Confused, Kydd muttered something and let her continue. 'She's quite like me in a way,' she said lightly, stooping to pick a furze flower. 'The same age, as it were.'

'Oh?' he managed.

'But at the moment she has a problem,' she said, in a light tone. 'Which she seems to have resolved, I believe.'

Kydd said nothing, guessing where this was leading and dreading the outcome. 'You see, she met an amiable enough gentleman who might have been considered as a possible –

consort. However, her condition of life is such that her family felt he did not answer their expectations, his connections being decidedly beneath her own.'

She flicked at an errant stalk of furze with her ivory whip and went on, 'She foolishly allowed her feelings to lead her to behave in an unseemly manner and was taken to task by her mother, who forbade her to continue the association.'

'Then you – she—'

'She loves her mama and would not go against her, Mr Kydd. That you must believe,' she said, looking at him seriously.

His gut tightened. 'Can y' say to me – is there another man payin' his addresses to – t' your friend?'

She replied instantly, 'There is none of any consequence who may stand against him.'

Kydd swallowed. 'Then you'll let me say, Miss Lockwood, that I think your friend is – is a shab indeed, if she had said t' him afore that she'd not be wed t' any except she cares for him!'

She stopped, her face white, and rounded on him: 'Mr Kydd, you cannot know what you are saying. Do not speak so.'

'An' if she puts the comforts o' life before her heart's—'

'Be silent, sir! I will not have it said—'

'Persephone, I—'

She took a deep breath and held it for a long moment, then continued sadly, 'Mr Kydd. She – she loves her mother and would not grieve her, but this is not the issue.' She turned away from his gaze and went on softly, 'Mama is right, but not in the way she intends. Shall we suppose they marry, even that her parents are reconciled? Can you conceive what it must cost as she divides her social acquaintances between her own – when she will be constantly in need of explana-

tion for the lack of his own connections at the highest level
– and his, where daily he must find excuse for her airs, her
manner? She could not bear to see *him* put upon so.'

'Oh! Nicholas, it's you. I – I expected Thomas. Er, is he out?'
Cecilia, however, unlaced her bonnet and gave every indication of wanting to stay, though that was contrary to the rules
of polite society, which frowned on unmarried young ladies
attending on gentlemen unaccompanied.

'Good evening, Miss Kydd,' Renzi said quietly, rising but
remaining by his chair.

'I see. Then you have my sincere regrets, sir, should any
now think you to be so far in want of conduct as to entertain the female sex alone . . .' But it brought no returning
smile and Cecilia paused, concerned.

'May I sit, Mr Renzi?' she asked formally.

'If it is your brother you are intending to visit, then I have
to tell you that he has not set foot ashore for the last three
days, and the vessel due to sail on Monday.'

'He—'

'Is in a state of despondency.'

'Poor Thomas.' Cecilia sighed, twisting a ribbon. 'It did
seem so possible, did it not?'

Renzi resumed his chair and blinked. 'I rather think now
it was not a deed of kindness to encourage him to believe
there could be any favourable conclusion to the affair. His
lack of connections damns him in her mother's eyes – an
ambitious creature, I believe.'

'Persephone Lockwood is much attached to him,' Cecilia
said thoughtfully. 'They would make a fine pair together – if
only . . .'

She stood up and paced about the room. 'She will not go

against her mother's wishes, that much is sure. Therefore *this* is the problem we must address.'

'I can only agree in the heartiest manner with your observations on such a match but it is not to be. Do you not consider that, perhaps with some reluctance, you should cease from matchmaking in his case?'

'Why, Mr Renzi, I do believe you have no romantic inclinations whatsoever.'

Renzi held still, his eyes opaque.

'I shall certainly do what is needful to assist Thomas to a blissful destiny − if I can think of any such,' Cecilia said, with spirit, and picked up her bonnet, settling it thoughtfully. Then she stopped. 'There is . . . but this will require that the gods of chance do favour us in the timing and that, when asked, a certain person will grant us a particular kindness . . .' She frowned prettily, and left.

A footman entered noiselessly with a note on a silver tray. The admiral at breakfast was often irascible, and the man spoke diffidently. 'For your immediate attention, sir.'

'What? Oh, give it here, then, dammit!'

Lady Lockwood sighed and continued her criticism of her daughter's needlework but at her husband's snort of interest she looked up. 'What is it, dear?'

'Well, now, and you'll clear your engagements for tonight, m' love! It seems the Marquess of Bloomsbury is giving me the favour of an At Home. Didn't know he was in Plymouth. You remember? I managed an introduction for you at court a year or so back.'

'Oh!' Lady Lockwood said, in sudden understanding. 'The Marquess of Bloomsbury − this *is* interesting, Reginald. Isn't he high in the diplomatic line, as I recall?'

'Yes, indeed. Discreet sort of cove, gets all about the world but likes to do his work in the strictest confidence. Now, I happen to know he has the ear of Billy Pitt himself – and I don't have to tell you, my love, that if I'm to get a sea command he's the kind of man I need to keep well in with.'

'Yes, you must, Reginald. Wasn't he married to the Earl of Arundel's eldest? Charlotte? I must look it up.'

Well satisfied, she turned to her daughter. 'Now, Persephone, the marquess is very important. You will come and be introduced, and remember, my dear, the men will be making high talk and we should never speak unless addressed directly.'

'Yes, Mama.'

'Your tamboured cream muslin will do, and do try to bring those curls more into control – you'll be under eye tonight.'

The Lockwood carriage rumbled grittily to a stop, the footmen hastening to hand down the party. 'Not grand at all – but so in keeping with the man,' chuckled the full-dress admiral, as he took his wife's arm. 'Consults his privacy always. I know he's only passing through – I wonder who's his host? May need to make his acquaintance after he's gone.'

They were greeted at the door by a distinguished butler. 'You are expected, sir,' he was told, and they were taken up the stairs to a small but discreet drawing room.

Outside Lady Lockwood did a last-minute primping of her ostrich plumes and surveyed Persephone once more before they entered. 'Remember, child, a warm smile and special attentions to the host and hostess. We're ready now, Reginald.'

'Admiral Sir Reginald Lockwood, Lady Lockwood and Miss Lockwood,' the butler announced. Wearing her most gracious smile Lady Lockwood advanced to be introduced.

'Sir, may I have th' honour t' introduce Sir Reginald an'

Lady Lockwood, and their daughter Persephone,' their host intoned. 'Sir,' he said, turning to the gaping admiral and wife, 'please meet th' most honourable the Marquess of Bloomsbury and his wife, th' Marchioness.'

The marquess bestowed a smile. 'And perhaps I should introduce you all to my friend,' he indicated the genial man standing to one side, 'who is the Baron Grenville, foreign secretary of Great Britain – if that will be allowable, William?'

'Why, thank 'ee, Frederick. I think it unlikely that Addington's shambles of an administration will survive the winter, and when Pitt takes power again . . . well, I stand ready to take up the burden once more, hey?'

Lady Lockwood rose from her deep curtsy, struck dumb with the effort of trying to come to terms with what she was seeing, while the charming young hostess took the arm of the marchioness and drew her aside. 'Lady Charlotte, I can never thank you enough! You and—' she stammered.

'Nonsense, Cecilia, dear. So good to see you again and, of course, we're delighted to offer Cupid a helping hand. That Grenville happened along was the merest chance, of course.' She gave a fond smile and continued, 'But, then, with Frederick having succeeded his father it seems they have plans in mind for him in the new year. And that will mean . . . I do hope you will not refuse another engagement with us, my dear?'

Cecilia blushed to be so honoured by one whom, as lady's companion, she had always known as Lady Stanhope. 'It will be my pleasure and duty.'

Finally Lady Lockwood came to herself and hissed at the host, 'Mr Kydd! Why on earth – what are you doing here?'

'Lady Lockwood, this is my house and I believe I may entertain whom I will.' It was worth every minute of his recent torments to see her resulting expression.

'A fine part of the country,' the admiral said respectfully, to the foreign secretary.

'No doubt, Admiral – but later. I'm with child to find out from Mr Kydd himself if it's true that he once told Frederick in a boat to pull on a rope or be keel-hauled. Come, sir, tell me the story.' He accepted a glass of Constantia and took Kydd to one side to hear of stirring events long ago in the Caribbean.

A bemused admiral turned then to the marquess. 'Sir, may we know if this is your first visit to the West Country?'

But the marquess had turned to greet an exquisitely turned-out gentleman who had just descended hesitantly from the stairs. 'Why, it's Mr Renzi! Well met, sir! I've heard that your thoughts on the ethnicals of the cannibal islands have met with some success.'

'You've heard? Well, yes, sir, I have been fortunate enough to secure the approbation of Count Rumford of the Royal Institution, who seems to consider my small musings of some value.'

The marquess turned confidingly to Lady Lockwood. 'Mr Renzi, a very learned soul. Mark well what he has to say, madam, for his wisdom in matters academical is only matched by his experiences in the wider reaches of the planet.'

Lady Lockwood could only curtsy mutely.

'Tell me, Renzi, where are you at present?'

'Mr Kydd has had the infinite goodness to afford me lodging at his own residence, sir.'

'Fine fellow, an ornament to his service,' the marquess agreed, then called across to the foreign secretary, 'I say, Grenville, this is Renzi. Do you remember him? Hatchards in Piccadilly and the occasion need not trouble this gathering.'

'Why, yes indeed. Good day to you, Renzi. Have I by chance

yet won you to a proper appreciation of the Grecian ode?'

'Perhaps, sir.' Renzi chuckled, and the three laughed at remembrances of former times and past perils, while Kydd had eyes only for the soft and very special look thrown to him by Miss Persephone Lockwood.

Chapter 11

In Barn Pool, not half a mile south from the pleasant walk round Devil's Point, at precisely ten in the forenoon, HMS *Teazer* went to stations for unmooring. On her pristine quarterdeck Commander Kydd took position, legs braced astride, trying not to notice the promenaders gathered to watch a King's ship outward bound to war.

Everything about the morning was perfection: the deep colours of sky and sea, the verdancy of the countryside in the languid sunshine, the easy south-westerly breeze, the fine seamanlike appearance of the ship he commanded. And the incredible knowledge, which he hugged to himself, about Persephone.

'Take her out, L'tenant,' he ordered. 'You have th' ship.' Even with the small craft lazily at their moorings in Barn Pool and ships passing to and from the Hamoaze, it would not be an onerous task to win the open sea.

'Aye aye, sir,' Standish said smartly, and stepped forward. 'Lay out 'n' loose!' Topmen manned the rigging and climbed out along the yards, sail blossomed and caught. *Teazer* swayed prettily as she got under way, leaving Devil's Point to larboard, but Kydd knew he could not snatch a look for *she* was watching. Possibly even now his image was being scrutinised through a powerful naval telescope.

Rounding Drake's Island *Teazer* heeled to the sea breeze and made splendid sailing south to the wider sea. This time there would be no sordid grubbing about after smugglers – that could wait for now. Today it was a more serious matter: Kydd was to go after the privateer Bloody Jacques, who had appeared off the coast again and slaughtered more innocent men in his predations.

Teazer was under orders to look into every bay and tiny cove, even the lee of islands, from Rame Head westwards – everywhere that the privateer with his uncanny local knowledge might conceivably hide himself. Kydd vowed that when they came upon the rogue he would make sure his career was ended then and there.

But it would be without their gunner's mate. Stirk had not yet returned from his mission to Polperro. Just before they sailed Luke Calloway had straggled back with a painfully written note:

Dere Mr Kydd. Agreable to y^r order, I hav enquyred of the wun you seek and fownd him owt and now I sayle to fynd the hevidance I may be gon won or 2 weaks y^r obed^t Tobias Stirk

Did this mean he had uncovered something? Kydd felt misgivings at the thought of the open and straight-steering shipmate from his days on the fo'c'sle trying to act the spy in the company of a villainous and ruthless gang. But if any had the brute courage and strength of mind to see it through, it was Stirk.

'Course, sir?' Standish asked.

'Oh – er, to weather the Rame,' he replied. Coastwise navigation did not require elaborate compass courses and it would exercise Standish to judge just when to put about to fetch the headland in one board.

Orders passed, Standish returned to stand by Kydd. 'Um, might it be accounted true, sir, what they are saying – please forgive the impertinence if it were not – that, er, you have made conquest of the admiral's daughter?'

Kydd looked at him sharply, but saw only open admiration. 'Miss Lockwood has been handsome enough t' visit,' he said, regretting his pompous tone but finding it hard to conceal his feeling otherwise. 'In company with her parents, o' course.'

'And if my sources are correct – and they're all talking about it – also the highest in the land.'

Now it was to be hero worship. 'That is t' say I knew the marquess before as Lord Stanhope, but his particular friend the foreign secretary Lord Grenville . . .' This was only making it worse. Kydd glanced aloft. 'Is that an Irish pennant I see at the fore-topsail yard, Mr Standish?' he growled, and while it was being attended to, he made his escape below.

'Nicholas.' He sighed as he sat to stare moodily through the stern windows at the dissipating wake. 'It seems th' whole world knows. What will I do?'

Renzi put down his papers with a half-smile. 'It is what *I* shall do that preoccupies my thoughts, dear fellow. In a short space you will be joined to a family of consequence, be in receipt of a fair dowry that will, in the nature of things, have your lady casting about for an estate of worth.'

Kydd beamed. The thought of himself as one half of two was new and wonderful.

'I rather fear,' Renzi continued, 'my *arcadia in urbes* at number eighteen will be a lonely one, even supposing I am able to find the means to—'

'Nicholas,' Kydd interrupted warmly, 'y' will always find a place with us, never fear.'

'I thank you, brother, but I am obliged to observe that when the head of the house proposes it is always the lady who disposes . . .'

They sat in companionable stillness, until Renzi asked, 'May I be informed of the progress of your attachment? Have you made her a proposition?'

Kydd eased into a deep smile. 'There will be time enough f'r that after we return, Nicholas – an' I'll be glad of y'r advice in the detail, if y' please.'

'It will be my pleasure. You will follow the polite conventions, of course – first to seek a private interview with your intended to secure her acceptance, followed by a formal approach to her father requesting approval of the match. There will be some . . . negotiations, at which various matters relating to your post-nuptial circumstances will be—'

Suddenly Kydd felt restless with all this talk. He could contain himself no longer and got to his feet. 'Belay all that, m' friend. I have a cruise t' command. Where's that poxy boatswain?'

That night, under easy sail from the south-west, Kydd crawled into his cot and composed himself for sleep. He tried to shut out the crowding thoughts but they kept coming in different guises, different urgencies.

It was now clear he would wed soon – Persephone had made plain that her father had always approved of him and Lady Lockwood would come round to it, given time. Therefore in the next few months his life would change to that of a married man with a defined and highly visible place in polite society.

Cecilia would be so proud of him. And when he visited his parents in Guildford it would be in a carriage with footmen and a bride of such character and quality – it was such a dizzying prospect that his mind could hardly grasp it.

But what about Persephone? Would he match up to her expectations, be a proper husband with all the trappings of dignity and wisdom, refined tastes, ease of manner in high society? Damn it, was he good enough for her?

It had happened so quickly. Was he ready to exchange self-reliance and the freedom to choose a course of action that had been his way of life until now for the settled certainties of an ordered, prescribed daily round?

Would living graciously and the delicacies of polite discourse begin to pall and he to harbour a secret longing for the plain-speaking and direct pleasures of his old way of life? Would Persephone understand? Or would she be wounded by the betrayal?

He slept restlessly.

Their task was clear and unequivocal: find and destroy the privateer. It would involve a slow cruise westwards, searching thoroughly as they went, while Bazely in *Fenella* sailed in the other direction, east from Plymouth.

Staying close in with the land would be tricky work: each night they would remain resolutely in the offing and resume in the morning. There would be no crossing of bays head-land to headland, only a long tracking round, keeping as close inshore as prudence would allow.

With Rame Head left astern, there was now the sweeping curve of Whitsand Bay under their lee and with all plain sail they set to work. They passed the occasional huddles of dwellings whose names Kydd now knew well, Trewinnow, Tregantle, Portwrinkle: all would have their sturdy fisher-folk, their reckless smugglers and local characters who, one day, would be worthy of Renzi's ethnical study.

Towards the afternoon they had raised Looe; Kydd toyed with the idea of going alongside in the harbour overnight so that Renzi could see the medieval sights there but decided to keep to sea for freedom of manoeuvre; besides which the Admiralty frowned on captains incurring unnecessary harbour dues.

Checking on Looe Island just offshore, he shaped course to continue along the coast: the Hore Stone, Æsop's Bed, Talland Bay – a wearisome progress with the ship cleared and half the company at the guns at all times.

Polperro, Udder Rock, round the questing Pencarrow Head and to anchor in Lantic Bay. It was going to be a long haul. In the early morning they weighed and proceeded once more; Kydd sent Standish in to Fowey for news, but there was none.

St Austell Bay saw them in a slow tacking south to the Dodman; Mevagissey, Gwineas Rocks – all had such meaning now. Mile after mile of rugged coastline, lonely coves, rock-bound islets. Inshore coasters, luggers and yawls wended their way between tiny ports, each vessel a potential enemy until proved innocent. Occasional flecks of sail out to sea could be any kind of craft, from a deep-sea merchantman inward-bound to a man-o'-war on her way to a rendezvous off the enemy coast.

At Falmouth Kydd went ashore to see if there was word, but again it seemed that Bloody Jacques had an uncanny knowledge of suitable bolt-holes and had simply vanished between pillagings.

Wearily he put back to sea, down in long tacks towards the famous Lizard. He decided to wait out the night in its lee for if there was one place more likely than any other for a privateer to lurk it would be at the end of England, where shipping bound up-Channel diverged from that making for the Irish Sea and Liverpool.

The next day, however, the summer sunshine had left them for a grey day and whiffling, fluky winds backing south, and a dropping barometer – sure signs of a change in the weather. After rounding the Lizard, Kydd was troubled to find the seas far more lively and on the back of an uneasy westerly swell; he had no wish to make close search of Wolf Rock and the outlying Isles of Scilly in thickening weather.

Penzance knew of the privateer but could contribute little to the search. Kydd had half expected Parlby in *Wyvern* to be there for he had been sent to the northern coast and might well have put into Penzance. Kydd had his duty, however, and pressed on instead of waiting, dutifully heading for Wolf Rock, *Teazer* taking the seas on her bow in bursts of white and an awkward motion.

In the gathering misery of greying skies *Teazer* found the lonely black menace set amid seething white, cautiously felt her way past and onward into the wastes of the Atlantic. Kydd was determined to clear the Isles of Scilly before the blow really set in.

It was getting more serious by the hour; the wind was foul for rounding the Isles of Scilly from the south, which had the sloop staying about twice a watch in the difficult conditions, but this was not the worst of it. They could not set a straight intercepting course for the islands and because of the resulting wide zigzags against the wind they lost sight of them for most of the time with the danger of an unfortunate conjunction on the next board.

Seamanship of the highest order was now required. Usually a mariner's first concern was to keep well clear of the deadly rocks, but Kydd knew their voyage would be in vain unless they not only made a sighting of the Isles of Scilly but searched closely. This would involve the careful reckoning of each tack such that the last leg would place them precisely and safely to westward of the scattered islands.

The weather was sullen but still clear; however, this could change in minutes. It was now not navigation by the science of sextant and chronometer but the far more difficult art of dead-reckoning, leeway resulting from the wind's blast, the mass movement of the ocean under tidal impetus, contrary currents from the north. The master stood grave and silent, his eyes passing ceaselessly over the white-tipped rollers marching in from the open Atlantic.

Rain arrived in fits and blusters, settling to drenching sheets that sometimes thinned and passed on, leaving the seas a hissing expanse of stippled white that curiously took the savage energy from the waves and left them subdued, rounded hillocks rather than ravenous breakers.

Then the first islets formed, alarmingly close, out of the hanging rain-mist. It was vital to make landfall with precision, and there was only wind direction to orient them. The master told Kydd, 'This is y'r Pol Bank, sir, an' Bishop Rock somewhere there.' There was no disguising the relief in his voice.

The western extremity of the Isles of Scilly. The low, anonymous grey rain-slick ugliness was probably the worst sea hazard in this part of the world. Here, less than a century before, an admiral of the Royal Navy and near two thousand men had died when the *Association* and most of a victorious returning fleet had made final encounter with these isles.

'Nor'-nor'-east t' Crim Rocks, sir,' the master murmured. By now Kydd's dream-like memories of beauty and gracious living were fast fading. The present reality was this waste-land of sea perils and cold runnels of rainwater inside his whipping oilskins.

Thankfully, *Teazer* was now able to bear away round Bishop Rock for her return and, wallowing uncomfortably, she passed close to the deadly scatter of Crim Rocks. The sight of the dark gashes in the seething white caused Kydd to shiver.

To weather off the Isles of Scilly, they could now look into the few possible hiding-places. Most likely were Crow Sound and Saint Mary's Road near the settlements. If the privateer was riding things out there they were perfectly placed to pounce – but a fresh gale was threatening and the master had said that with a sandy bottom both vessels were unsafe in heavy seas and the bird might well have flown.

They had their duty, however, and despite boldering weather strengthening from the westward Kydd looked into every possible anchorage, wary of the baffling complexity of the offshore tidal streams, which, if the master was to be believed, varied by the hour as they wound through tortuous channels and shallows.

When the fat mass of Round Island was reached it was time to return: with winds abaft, a straightforward run to Land's End and the shelter of Penzance. But the bluster from the south-west was undeniably stronger and the swell length-ening, causing a wrenching wallow as the seas angled in from the quarter.

By the time Land's End had been reached few aboard did

not relish the thought of a quiet night in harbour, a cessation of the endless bruising motion. 'Penzance, sir?' the master enquired, gripping tightly a line from aloft.

Kydd thought for a moment, then answered, 'No, Mr Dowse. I'll ask you t' mark the wind's direction. If it backs more into th' south we'll be held to a muzzler if we sight that Frenchman. No – we press on t' the Lizard and anchor f'r the night in its lee.'

His task was to return back up the coast, continuing on past Plymouth into the eastern half of his patrol area, no doubt passing Bazely as they criss-crossed up and down to the limit of their sea endurance. Bloody Jacques had proved himself and could not be underestimated; keeping the seas was their first priority.

Thus, prudently maintaining a good offing, *Teazer* spent the last few hours of the day crossing Mount's Bay, passing the imposing monolith of St Michael's Mount sheeted in misty spray, and shaping course for the Lizard. The seas were now combers, ragged white-streaked waves that smashed beam-on in thunderous bursts of spray and made life miserable for the watch-on-deck.

At last, Lizard Point won, they slipped past and fell into its lee; the worst of the wind moderated and they anchored under steep, forbidding cliffs. *Teazer* slewed about the moment sail was off her and, bow to waves, eased thankfully to her cable.

Kydd waited until the watch-on-deck had been relieved, then went below. There was no hope of any hot food, and as Tysoe exchanged his sodden clothes, he chewed hard tack and cheese, pondering what constituted sea endurance: the ship's state for sea or the men's willingness to endure such punishing conditions. In this fresh gale a stately ship-of-the-line would snort and jib a little, but would essentially move much more ponderously and predictably; a small brig's endless jerky rearing and falling, however, taxed the muscles cruelly. It was physically exhausting to maintain for long and he hoped the gale would blow itself out overnight.

The morning brought no relief: the gale still hammered, with ragged waves trailing foam-streaks in their wake, but *Teazer* had her duty and the anchor was weighed at first light.

'Falmouth, sir?' the master asked. Kydd knew that the men at the conn were listening to every word. It was tempting: Falmouth was but several hours away only and offered spacious shelter in Carrick Roads.

However, in these seas no boat could live, and for *Teazer* to enter the harbour, with its single south-facing entrance, would be to risk finding themselves bailed up. With foul weather clearing the seas of prey the privateer was probably waiting it out in some snug lair, which, if Kydd came across it, would find him helpless. It was worth cracking on.

'We sail on, Mr Dowse. This is a hard man we're after but he's a prime seaman. He won't think aught o' this blow.' At his bleak expression Kydd added, 'An' then, o' course, we can always run in t' Fowey.'

The master said nothing but turned on his heel and went forward. Kydd gave orders that saw them bucketing northwards past the lethal sprawl of the Manacles and into the relative shelter of Falmouth Bay.

They kept in with the coast past the Greeb, and discovered that in its regular north-eastward trend the inshore mile or two under the rocky heights was providing a measure of relief and *Teazer* made good progress. Kydd's thoughts wandered to a way of life that was so utterly different from this one, where the greatest danger was the social solecism, the highest skill to turn a *bon mot* at table, and never in life to know a wet shirt or hard tack.

He crushed the rebellious feelings. There would be time enough to rationalise it all after he had settled into his new existence and had the solace of a soul-mate.

A series of whipping squalls chasing round the compass off the Dodman had *Teazer* fighting hard to keep from being swamped by the swash kicked up over the shoaling Bellows but she won through nobly to resume her more sheltered passage northward.

The Gwineas Rocks and Mevagissey: on the outward voyage they had seen these in calm seas and balmy sunshine. Now they were dark grey and sombre green, edged with surf from the ceaseless march of white-streaked waves. They left Par Sands well to leeward; there was most definitely no refuge for a privateer worth the name beyond tiny Polkerris – they would round Gribbin Head for Fowey.

Easing out to seaward their shelter diminished: Gribbin Head itself was near hidden in spume, driven up by the combers smashing into its rocky forefoot, and *Teazer* rolled wickedly as she passed by.

But was this the right decision? Should they continue? As with so many havens in Cornwall Fowey was south-westerly facing, which was perfect for entry but dead foul for leaving. It would be nothing less than a token of surrender to the elements should Kydd cause *Teazer* to run for shelter unnecessarily.

He sent word for the master. 'Mr Dowse, what's your opinion o' this blashy weather? Will it blow over, do y' think?'

Dowse pursed his lips and studied the racing clouds. There was a line of pearlescence along the horizon to the south in dramatic contrast to the dour greys and blacks above. 'Glass's been steady these two watches,' he said carefully, 'an' it's been an uncommon long blow f'r this time o' the year . . .'

'We go on, then,' Kydd decided.

'. . . but, mark you, the glass hasn't risen worth a spit, an' the wind's still in the sou'-west. Could be it gets worse afore it gets better.'

'So y' think it'll stay like this, Mr Dowse?'

'M' advice t' ye, sir – an' it not bein' my place t' say so – is to bide a while in Fowey an' see what happens t'morrow.'

To continue would be to set out on a long stretch of coast exposed to the full force of the gale and a dead lee shore before reaching Rame Head. But if they did, they could round the headland and enter the security of the enfolding reaches of Plymouth Sound itself and, with its capacious-ness, be able to tack out and resume their voyage whenever they chose.

Yet if they set out for the Rame and the elements closed in, there was no port of consequence before the Sound to which they could resort and there would be no turning back to beat against the gale to Fowey.

It all hinged on the weather.

'Thank you, Mr Dowse, but I believe we'll crack on t' the east'd. I'll be obliged for another reef, if y'please.' Kydd turned to go below; this stretch would be the most extreme and he wanted to face it in a fresh set of dry clothes.

As he passed down the hatchway he heard the quarter-master above comment wryly, 'Always was a foul-weather jack, our Tom Cutlass.'

His unseen mate answered savagely, 'Yeah, but it sticks in me gullet that we has t' go a-floggin' up the coast in this howler jus' so he c'n be with his flash dolly.'

Kydd stopped in shock. It wasn't the resurrection of his old nickname, or that his romantic hopes were common knowledge, but the wounding assumption that he would have another motive for doing his duty. He hesitated, then slipped below.

By Pencarrow Head the force of the seas was noticeably stronger, but Kydd put it down to their more exposed position and pressed on. It was unlikely in the extreme that the privateer would choose this open stretch of coast to lie low but he had his duty and with life-lines rigged along the decks and several anchors bent on they took the seas resolutely on their quarter and struck out for Rame Head.

It seemed that the weather was not about to improve – indeed, within the hour the master was reporting that the glass was falling once more and the wind took on a savage spite, spindrift being torn from wavecrests and *Teazer* reverting to a staggering lurch.

It was getting serious: the rapidity with which the change had occurred was ominous for the immediate future and extreme measures for their survival could not be ruled out. 'Stand us off a league,' Kydd shouted to Dowse, above the dismal moan of the wind and the crashing of their passage. It was the one advantage they had, that essentially they were driving before the wind, with all that it meant for staying a course.

They laid Looe Island to leeward, nearly invisible in the flying murk and began the last perilous transit of Whitsand Bay, which was in the worst possible orientation for the weather, completely open to the rampaging gales direct from the Atlantic and virtually broadside on to the driving surf.

But, blessedly, the grey bulk of Rame Head was emerging from the clamping mist of spray ahead – and directly beyond was Plymouth Sound. At this rate they would make the security of the Sound well before dark. *Teazer* was taking the pounding well, and under close-reefed topsails was making good progress. They could always goosewing the fore and hand what remained of the main topsail – they were going to make it safely to port.

A confused shouting sounded from forward: it was a lookout, now on the foredeck and pointing out to leeward. Kydd saw a lonely sail, deep into the sweep of Whitsand Bay. He pulled out his pocket telescope and trained it on the vessel.

If it was the privateer he could see no way in which he could join action – the seas alone would prevent the bulwark gun ports opening, and on this horrific lee shore – but the snatches of image he caught were sufficient to tell him it was not.

As close-hauled as possible, the vessel was nearly up with the first parallel line of breakers. 'He's taking a risk, by glory,' Standish said.

Dowse came up and shook his head. 'Seen it before,' he said sadly. 'The Rame mistook f'r Bolt Head, an' now embayed, all the time th' wind's in the sou'-west.'

The ship had realised its mistake too late, put about into the wind – and found that it was too deep into the bay. Square-rigged and unable to keep closer to the wind than six points off, the master had no alternative other than to claw along on one tack as close to the wind as he could get the vessel to lie, inching her seaward, and when the end of the semi-circular bay was reached, be forced to stay about and on another reach do the same until the opposite end was reached. Then the process would be repeated yet again.

As Kydd watched, the drama intensified. By the cruellest stroke, the south-westerly was exactly at right-angles to the bay and leeway made by the forced putting about at each end was remorselessly matching the small amount of sea-room gained on each tack. The vessel was trapped: they were doing the only thing possible and it was not enough; but if they did nothing they would quickly be driven downwind on to the pitiless shore.

With a stab of compassion Kydd realised that this cruel state of balance had probably begun at first light when their situation had become clear, and therefore they had been at this relentless toil all day – they must be close to exhaustion, knowing that if they fumbled just one going about, their deaths would follow very soon.

'Th' poor bastards!' breathed Dowse, staring downwind at the endless parallel lines of combers marching into the last broad band of surf.

Standish seemed equally affected. 'Sir, can we not . . .' He trailed off at the futility of his words. It was plain to everyone watching that *Teazer* could do nothing, for if they turned and went in, they themselves would be embayed, and any boats they sent would be blown broadside and overset, oars no match for the savage winds.

Kydd's heart went out to the unknown sailors: they must have been in fear of their lives for hours. How they must have prayed for the mercy of a wind change – only a point or two would have been enough to escape the deadly trap.

He turned on the master. 'Lie us to, Mr Dowse,' he snapped. This would see them hold *Teazer*'s head a-try with balanced canvas and going ahead only slowly, keeping her position. The poor devils in the other ship would see this and at the very least know that there were human beings in their universe who empathised with their fate.

The afternoon wore on; the wind stayed unwavering in the

same direction and the desperate clawing of the other ship continued. It could not last: some time during the night its crew's strength must fail and the sea would claim them. It was so unfair. Two ships separated only by distance: one to sail on to safety and rest, life and future, but the other condemned to death in the breakers.

'She's struck!' someone called.

Kydd whipped up his glass and caught flashing glimpses of an old merchantman no longer rising with the waves or her sea-darkened canvas taut to the wind. Now she was in the lines of breakers, slewed at an angle and ominously still. The foremast had gone by the board, its rigging trailing blackly in the sea, and as he watched, the vessel settled, taking the merciless seas broadside in explosions of white.

Whitsand Bay was shallow; the seas therefore were breaking a long way from shore. The figures that could be seen now crowding up the masts to take last refuge were as doomed as if a cannon was aimed at them.

Pity wrung Kydd's heart: more ships were lost to the sea than to the enemy, but here it was playing out before their eyes. It was hard to bear. But if— 'Mr Standish! I'm goin' t' have a try. Pass the word f'r any who's willin' to volunteer.'

His lieutenant looked at him in astonishment. 'Sir, how—'

'Mr Dowse. Lay us in the lee of th' Rame. Close in with th' land an' anchor.'

The master did not speak for a moment, his face closed and unreadable. 'Aye aye, sir,' he said finally.

Close to, Rame Head was a colossal, near conical monolith, its weather side a seething violence of white seas, but miraculously, as soon as they rounded the headland, the winds were cut off as with a knife.

'Here, Mr Dowse?'

281

'A rocky bottom, sir,' the master said impassively.

'Then we'll heave to. Mr Purchet, away boat's crew o' volunteers an' we'll have the pinnace in the water directly.'

Dowse came up and said quietly, 'I know why ye're doing this, Mr Kydd, but we're hazardin' th' ship ...' As if to add point to his words, *Teazer* swung fretfully under wild gusts volleying over the heights, they were only yards from the line of wind-torn seas coming round the point.

'I'm aware o' that, Mr Dowse,' Kydd said briefly.

Standish approached: he had found a young seaman native to the area. 'Sawley says there's a scrap o' sand inshore where you may land the boat.'

Kydd nodded. 'We're going t' try to get a line out to the poor beggars. I'll need as much one-inch line as the boatswain c'n find.' His plan was to cross the Rame peninsula on foot to the other side, Whitsand Bay, and by any means — boat, manhauling, swimming — get a line out to the wreck. The one-inch was necessarily a light line for they faced carrying it the mile or two to the beach over precipitous inclines.

'After we're landed, recover the boat and moor the ship in Cawsand Bay. We'll be back that way.' This was the next bay round with good holding and a common resort for men-o'-war in a south-westerly.

'Aye aye, sir,' Standish said uncomfortably.

Once more Kydd blessed the recent invention of davits, making it so much easier to hoist and lower boats than the yard-arm stay tackles of older ships. In the water the pinnace jibbed and gyrated like a wild animal, the men boarding falling over each other, oars getting tangled and water shipping over the gunwale. Gear was tossed down and when the men had settled Kydd boarded by shinning down a fall.

They cast off and Kydd called to Sawley. The young seaman surrendered his oar and made his way to Kydd.

The boat rose and fell violently in the seas, and at the sight of the steep sides of the Rame plunging precipitately into the sea it seemed utter madness to attempt a landing.

'Where's th' sand?' Kydd wanted to know.

'I'll go forrard, sir, an' signal to ye.' At Kydd's nod, Sawley scrambled down the centreline and wedged himself into the bow. He glanced aft once then made a positive pointing to starboard.

'Follow th' lad's motions,' Kydd growled. Bucketing madly, the boat approached the dark, seaweed-covered granite, the surge of swells an urgent swash and hiss over the wicked menace of unseen rocks. The hand went out again and Kydd saw where they were headed: an indentation so slight that it was unlikely that the boat's oars could deploy, but there *was* a strip of sand at its centre.

A small kedge anchor was tossed out and the boat went in, grounding hard. It floated free and banged even harder. 'Go, y' lubbers!' The men tumbled over the side and crowded on to a tiny strip of bare sand. Kydd dropped into the shallows and followed.

'Sir, how we's a-goin' t' get up there?' one man croaked, gesturing at the near-vertical slopes covered with thick, dripping furze. Kydd had counted on at least sheep tracks through the impenetrable thickets.

'Sawley, can we get round this?' he called, but the lad was already disappearing into the brush. Kydd waited impatiently; then he suddenly emerged and beckoned Kydd over. Sawley fished about in the undergrowth and came up with the knotted end of an old rope. 'The smugglers, sir – they'd parbuckle the tubs up to th' top wi' this'n,' he said, with glee.

'You first, younker, show us how t' do it.'

Sawley tested it with jerks then began to climb, clearing the rope of vegetation as he went. If it was for parbuckling there must be another near; Kydd found it and followed, the wind, with cruel cold, finding his wet clothes. The men came along behind.

It was hard going, the furze prickling and gouging, and his upper body having to remember long-ago skills of rope-climbing. Eventually he reached a rounding in the hill, a saddle between the continuing slopes inland and the higher conical mass of Rame Head, dramatically set off in the stormy weather with a ruined chapel on its summit.

He mustered his men together; far below *Teazer* was moving away to the safety of the next bay. Out to sea there was nothing but a white-lashed wilderness.

'Gets better now, Mr Kydd,' Sawley said brightly.

Eight men: would it make a difference? They would damn well try! Kydd set off, following a faintly defined track up the slope, pressing on as fast as he could, the ground strangely hard and unmoving after the wildly heaving decks.

They reached the summit of the hill and were met with the renewal of the wind's blast in their teeth and the grand, unforgettable sight of Whitsand Bay curving away into the misty distance, with parallel lines of pristine white surf. The grounded merchantman was still out in the bay, her foremast gone, sails in hopeless tatters, her men unmoving black dots in the rigging.

Scanning the horizon Kydd could see no other sail. They were on their own. He humped his part of the long fake of rope and moved off again, their way along the long summit now clear. He bent against the pummelling wind, trying not to think of the stricken vessel below as they reached a fold in the hills that hid the scene.

'We're goin' t' Wiggle, sir,' Sawley panted.

'Wha— ?'

'Aye, sir. It's a place above th' hard sand.'

They came from behind the hill and looked directly down on the scene. Numbers of people were on the beach watching the plight of the hapless merchant vessel. Would they help – or were the lurid tales of Cornish wreckers true?

Reaching the beach and shuddering with cold, Kydd tried to think. It was heart-wrenching to see how near yet how far the vessel was. At this angle only ragged black spars were visible above the raging combers, perhaps a dozen men clutching at the shrouds.

The wreck was bare hundreds of yards off but in at least ten feet of water, enough to drown in. Every sailor knew that, if run ashore, their end would not be so merciful – the rampaging waves would snatch them and batter them to a choking death as they rolled them shoreward, their only hope a quick end by a crushed skull.

The onlookers stood still, looking out to sea dispassionately. Kydd pulled one round to face him. 'Aren't ye goin' to *do* something?'

The man looked at him. 'They'm dead men,' he said dully. 'What's to do?'

Kydd swung on his men standing behind. He quickly worked a bowline on a bight at the end of the line. 'You!' he said, pointing to the tallest and heaviest. 'With me!'

He lunged into the water, feeling the strength in the surge of the next wave hissing over the beach. He splashed on until another foamed in, its impact sending him staggering. Recovering, he thrust deeper into the waves, feeling them curiously warmer out of the wind's chill. The rope jerked at him. He turned and saw that all eight of his men were floundering behind him, bracing when one was knocked off his feet, then stumbling on.

A lump grew in his throat. With these men he could . . .

A foaming giant of a wave took him full in the chest and sent him down in a choking flurry, handling him roughly until he brought up on the rope and finally found the hard sand under him. When he heaved himself up he saw that only two of his men were still standing, the rest a kicking tangle of legs and bodies.

Flailing forward Kydd tried again, feeling the spiteful urge of the sea as it pressed past him. At the next wave he gritted his teeth and forced himself to stand firm while the force of the water bullied past him unmercifully. As it receded he saw another beyond, even bigger.

The breaker tumbled him down and when he rose his forearm bore a long smear of blood. Trembling with cold and emotion, he had to accept that he and his men were utterly helpless.

He turned and staggered back to the shore, teeth chattering. Along the beach some fishermen had launched a boat, but as Kydd watched it reared violently over the first line of surf, the oars catching by some heroic means. By the third line, though, it had been smashed broadside and rolled over and over in a splintered wreck.

A strange writhing in the surf caught his eye: an unravelled bolt of some workaday cloth. The ship was breaking up and the cargo was coming ashore with other flotsam. The silent groups of watchers came to life and began wading about after it – this was what they had come for, thought Kydd, with a surge of loathing.

His heart went out to the black figures in the shrouds of the doomed ship, giving their very lives for this cargo – and as he watched, one plummeted into the sea without resisting, the last pitiful remnant of his strength spent in exhaustion and cold.

Kydd closed his eyes in grief. A fellow sailor had now given everything to the sea, perhaps an individual whose laughter at the mess-table had lifted the hearts of his ship-mates, whose skills had carried the ship across endless sea miles . . .

A jumble of casks appeared at the water's edge and were immediately fallen upon, but evening was approaching and the light failing. Another figure dropped. Kydd turned away. When he looked again, the mainmast had given way and now many more lives were reaching their final moments. His eyes stung.

There were only three left in the mizzen shrouds when the first corpses arrived. Untidy bundles drifting aimlessly in the shallows, the ragged remains of humanity that had been so recently warm and alive.

As soon as the first body had grounded an onlooker was upon it, standing astride and bending to riffle through its clothes, checking the fingers for rings. It was too much – Kydd fell on the looter shouting hoarsely, until his men ran over and pulled him off.

When he had come to his senses, the mizzen was empty.

'Thank 'ee, you men,' he said, gulping. 'I don't think we c'n do any more here.'

Not a word was spoken as they trudged up the wind-blown slopes, not a glance back. After Wiggle the hill descended the other side into the fisher-village of Cawsand. And out in the bay was HMS *Teazer*. The lump in his throat returned as Kydd took in her sturdy lines, her trim neatness.

They made their way to the little quay and signalled. Even

this far round the Rame the swell was considerable; there were still combers leaving white trails in their wake, but here the sting had been taken from the storm and the boat stroked strongly towards them.

Renzi was there to greet him as Kydd climbed aboard. When he saw Kydd's expression, he offered, 'A wet of brandy may answer—'

But Kydd brushed him aside. 'Mr Standish, I want a double tot f'r these hands. Now.'

He stopped at another thought, but there was no need. In rough camaraderie their shipmates would certainly ensure that each one would be found a dry rig. But one thing at least was in his power: 'An' they're t' stand down sea watches until tomorrow forenoon.' An 'all-night-in' was a precious thing at sea but if any deserved it . . .

He climbed wearily into his cot and slumped back, closing his eyes and hoping for sleep. It was not as if the evening's drama was unusual – it was said that the wild West Country had taken more than a thousand wrecks and would claim many more. Why should this one touch him so?

It was not hard to fathom. Head in the clouds with his recent good fortune and new prospects for high society, he had lost touch with the sterner realities of his sea world. The fates had warned him of what might befall his command should he fail to give the sea the attention it demanded.

A fitful sleep took him, troubling images flitting past. Could he be joined to Persephone in marriage and stay faithful to a puissant, jealous sea? Would she understand if—

He awoke and sat bolt upright, his senses quivering. In the darkness he felt the hairs on his neck rise in supernatural dread. Something was very wrong.

He tumbled out of the cot and stood motionless, listening

acutely. Then it happened. The entire framework of his world was thrown into madness. *Teazer*'s deep, regular sway and heave had stopped. For seconds at a time the deck was frozen at a canted angle, his body unconsciously adapting to the slope, the deckhead compass gimbals quite still.

Then, with an overloud creaking, the sea motion resumed as though nothing had happened. Dumbfounded, Kydd threw a coat over his nightgown and ran for the deck. It was teeming with rain, solid, blinding sheets in the darkness of the night. He heard shouts and running feet.

It happened again, this time preceded by a sickening thump and long-drawn-out groan of racked timbers. In horror Kydd stared into the night, trying desperately to make out the vessel that had driven foul of theirs, but saw and heard nothing. Men came boiling up from below, eyes white and staring as they tried to make sense of what was happening.

Dowse came on deck, also in night attire and hurried over. 'Sir, we're in dire peril. This is a ground sea, sir!'

When the height of a wave exceeded twice the depth of water, a vessel in its trough could actually touch the seabed. In the gale such a swell had developed, and now, with an ebbing tide, they were being dumped bodily against the bottom of the sea. No ship could take such punishment for long before it was racked to pieces.

'Turn up th' hands!' roared Kydd. 'All hands on deck!'

He looked at Dowse. 'T' sail her out, or warp?' But he knew before the words were out that warping or kedging off without boats that could live in white water was not possible. They had to get sail on, and very quickly.

The men began to assemble at their parts-of-ship, the petty-officers loudly taking charge. Standish and then Purchet came to Kydd, their faces white and strained. 'Sir?'

'Get the carpenter t' stand by the wells an' sound 'em every ten minutes. He's t' send word instantly there's sign of a breach.'

He snatched a glance into the dark rigging: *Teazer* had already snugged down for the blow, rolling tackles reeved and double gaskets passed round the courses. This meant that seamen had to move up into the pitch-dark rigging and out along the yards in the driving rain to cut away the gaskets by feel alone, a desperately dangerous thing where a misplaced handhold on an invisible rain-slick spar would mean a sudden fall. And all the time their whole world would be jerking and swaying in crazy motion across the sky.

It was Kydd's duty to order the men aloft. There was no alternative: too many lives depended on it. He did not hesitate. 'Mr Standish, the carpenter t' take his axe an' stand by the cable. I'd be obliged should you take charge in th' foretop while I'll take th' main. Mr Dowse will remain on deck an' give orders f'r a cast t' larb'd and out.'

He demanded of a dumbfounded seaman his belt and knife, then filled his lungs and roared, 'All hands – lay out an' loose!'

Lunging at the main shrouds he swung himself up and began to climb into the blackness and rain. Shaking in the ropes told him he had been followed. Now mainly by feel he found first the catharpings then the futtock shrouds. Calling on skills that had lain dormant for years he swung himself up and into the maintop, then stopped for breath.

Not far behind him others came, crowding up with him into the top. It was madness – he had no call to risk his life up here with the topmen – but it was one way to deal with his feelings.

'Topsails!' he bawled, and reached for the weather topmast

290

shrouds but stopped to peer at the figure first taking the leeward. It was too familiar. It couldn't be – but it was . . . 'Nicholas! You – why are ye—'

'Should we not mount the vaunting shrouds?' Renzi yelled, his face streaming with rain. 'The barky will not wait, I fear!'

Overcome, Kydd ducked round and began the climb to the remote topmast tops. Far above the unseen deck below, he fumbled for the footrope that must lie below the yard and inched his way out on the thin rope, elbows over the sodden bulk of bunched canvas atop the yard. More men came and jostled next to him, the footrope jerking over empty space as he worked free his knife.

The gaskets on the main topsail were plaited and he sawed at them awkwardly while the angle of the wind gradually changed – below they must be bracing the yard round as they worked. Those on deck would be seeing only jerking shadows and would have to judge as best they could the right moment to set the sails.

A harsh judder nearly toppled them from the yardarm. If they could not get away they would be beaten to pieces very shortly and themselves be taken by the sea. 'Off th' yard!' he screamed, for he had noticed the halliards shake; if the new-freed sails took the wind it would be sudden and uncontrollable.

They scrambled for the shrouds and Kydd made his way thankfully to the deck as *Teazer* leant to the blast, then miraculously got under way for the outer Sound.

'Mr Kydd, sir.' The carpenter anxiously touched his forehead. 'An' I have t' say, we're makin' water bad – more'n two foot in th' well.'

It was too much after all they had endured and done that day. 'Thank ye,' he said mechanically, and tried to reason against the cold and tiredness. Without doubt it would be due to seams opening under the crushing punishment of the mass weight of the ship bearing down on the curve of the hull – or worse: whole strakes giving way and the sea rushing unchecked into *Teazer*'s bowels.

To founder out in the Sound in the anonymous night – it couldn't happen! But with no idea where the leaks were and no way to find out in the pitch dark of a flooding hold . . . 'Mr Purchet,' he croaked, 'we'll fother.' This would involve passing sails under the hull in the hope that it would staunch the inflow. 'The whole length o' the ship.'

He turned to Dowse. 'We're not t' make harbour, I believe. Is there any cove, any landing-place – anywhere in th' Sound as we c'n find . . . ?'

The master's face was pinched. 'Er, no, sir. Entirely rock-bound t' the Cattewater.' He hesitated, then said, 'But there is . . . if we stays this side a mite . . .'

Taking in water all the time *Teazer* staggered along before the gale. At a little after four in the morning she rounded to and flung a rope ashore to waiting soldiers, then slewed about close to the little quay of humble Fort Picklecombe.

As if tiring of the fight she gently took the ground and, creaking mightily, settled into a final stillness.

Chapter 12

Renzi held up his *Plymouth & Dock Telegraph* with an enigmatic smile. 'Dear fellow, there's an item here that's of some interest, bearing as it does on . . .'

Kydd began to read what looked suspiciously like a gossip column.

'Our doughty spy, LOOKOUT, once again mounts to the crow's nest in his tireless quest for items of value to pique our readers' interest. He raises his powerful glass and begins his search and it is not long before he spies a particularly gratifying sight. It is none other than that of our beautiful and accomplished *Miss Persephone L—*, the cynosure of every gentlemanly eye, the acknowledged *catch* of the season and the adornment of every gathering of the quality, who is seen to be promenading yet again with the *same* fortunate gentleman. LOOKOUT strains to make out his appearance but is unable to distinguish at such a distance beyond noting that he is in the character of a *naval* person and has an unmistakable air of *Command* about him. Can this be indeed the notorious *Captain Kidd* boarded and taken a prize? Knowing his duty, LOOKOUT instantly sends a messenger post-haste to the *Telegraph* offices advising that space be immediately held over, for it seems the society columns will soon be echoing to the sound of *wedding bells*. He does however beg the dear Reader to consider now the *plight* of the legion of the disappointed—'

He threw down the newspaper. 'What catblash is this?' he growled, secretly delighted that he and Persephone were now so publicly linked. 'They even have m' name wrong, the swabs.'

After *Teazer* had been towed to the dockyard for repairs he had called on Persephone and found that she and Lady Lockwood had gone to Bath to take the waters. The admiral had advised him gruffly that it would not serve his case to go in pursuit and that in the meantime Kydd must bide his time patiently. The difficulty now was to find some occupation that did not bear too heavily on the purse in the coming weeks; on Persephone's return there would, no doubt, be a considerable strain on his means.

As if sensing his dilemma, Renzi got up and stretched. 'If you are of a mind, dear fellow, there is some small diversion in prospect that might serve us both.' He went to the table and picked up a letter. 'I have had the singular good fortune to meet a personable young man named Jonathan Couch, who seems to be somewhat enamoured of our piscatorial cousins. He's shown a gratifying degree of interest in my study and advises that to the enquiring mind there is no need to travel to the cannibal isles to observe man in nature. This may all be got in a wild and picturesque setting not so very far from here.

'In short, he suggests that I base myself there and make my observations at leisure in the countryside round about. He promised to speak to a local squire he knows in the matter of our lodgings and by this letter I find a most generous and open invitation for us both to stay at Polwithick Manor.'

It seemed an agreeable enough plan – Kydd could relax in the quiet and leisurely country surroundings and from time to time assist in whatever ethnical studies Renzi had in mind. 'Er, where is this wild place?'

'Oh, did I not mention it? It is Polperro.'

Polperro? Kydd gave a wry smile at the thought of staying in a smugglers' den . . .

Polwithick was set half-way between Crumplehorn and Landaviddy, with a fine view far down into the steep valley and compact huddle that was Polperro.

'Elizabethan, do you think?' Renzi mused, as they dismounted from their horses; their baggage would follow by packhorse over the rutted tracks that went for roads in this Cornish interior.

The charming manor did seem of an age: a stout jumble of ancient mullioned windows and grey moorstone from the time of the first George, set among ancient yews and hawthorns, blossoms from the neat kitchen garden softening its bluff squareness.

'Come in! Come in, come in – ye're both most welcome, gentlemen!' Squire Morthwen was jolly and red-faced.

'Nicholas Renzi, sir, and this is my friend and colleague, Mr Kydd.'

'A pleasure t' have ye here! It was, er, something in the

philosophical line ye wish to study in these parts, was it not, sir?'

'Indeed. And I'm sure you'll prove of sovereign worth in directing me to where – but this can wait until later, sir. We're under no rush of time.'

They were ushered into a small drawing room where the whole family was drawn up in a line. 'This is m' brood, gentlemen, who're very curious t' see what kind o' visitors come all the way t' Polwithick.

'Now this is Edmund, the eldest.' A tall young man with a studied look of boredom bowed stiffly. 'M' daughter Rosalynd.' A delicate pale maiden with downcast eyes curtsied, but when she rose it was with a startlingly frank gaze. 'And Titus, th' youngest.' A tousled youth grinned at them.

'I know town folk take y' vittles late, but in the country we like t' have ours while there's still light t' appreciate 'em. Shall we?'

The meal in the dark-timbered dining parlour was unlike any Kydd had experienced before. It wasn't just the massive oaken furniture or the rabbit in cider or even the still country wines, but the warmth and jollity in place of the cool manners and polite converse he had grown used to.

The squire, it seemed, was a widower but the table was kept with decorum; the visitors were spared close interrogation and afterwards the gentlemen repaired to a study for port and conversation.

'Well, Mr Renzi, y' mentioned in your letter about ethnical studies in th' West Country. I don't think I can help thee personally with that but you'll find some rare fine curiosities hereabouts.'

Renzi was able in some measure to indicate his requirements but was interrupted by a wide-eyed face peeking round the door. 'Oh, Papa, do let us stay!' Titus pleaded.

The squire frowned. 'Church mice!' he roared. 'Not a squeak, mind!' With three solemn faces hanging on every word, Renzi continued.

It transpired that they were well placed to make comparative study between the way of life of the fisher-folk and that of the country yeomen and, indeed, if Renzi were not of a squeamish tendency, the tin miners along the coast would afford much to reflect upon.

Renzi beamed. 'My thanks indeed, sir! This will provide me with precisely the kind of factual grist I shall need – do you not think so, brother Kydd?'

'Er, yes, o' course, Mr Renzi. An ethnical harvest o' some size, I'd believe.'

Plans were put in train at once: there were horses in the stables for their convenience, and the squire allowed he was modestly proud of an orangery, which, being south-facing, was eminently suited to a learned gentleman's retiring with his books.

Friendly goodnights were exchanged and Kydd and Renzi took possession of their bedrooms; in each a pretty four-poster waited ready, warmed with a pan. It was going to be a fine respite from their recent trials.

After a hearty breakfast, Renzi drew Kydd aside. 'There is a matter . . . that is causing me increasing unease. In fact it concerns yourself, my good friend. It . . . I lay awake last night and could find no other alternative, even as I fear you may feel slighted – and, indeed, cheated.'

Puzzled, Kydd said nothing as Renzi continued: 'You came with me to this place to contribute to the sum of human knowledge in an ethnical examination. It is the first such I have undertaken else I should have realised this before, but in actually contemplating my approach to the persons under study it seems that while I might, over time, be considered a harmless savant, the two of us together could well be accounted a threat of sorts.'

Looking decidedly uncomfortable, Renzi went on, 'Therefore if I am to observe their natural behaviour it rather seems that . . . it were better you remain behind.'

Kydd snorted. 'M' dear fellow, if you feel able t' manage this all by y'rself, then I must find m' own amusements.'

Renzi's face fell, but then Kydd chuckled. 'Pay no mind t' me, Nicholas. If I'm t' be truthful, I'd say that there's nothin' in the world more congenial t' me right now than settlin' t' both anchors in as quiet a place as this.'

It was particularly pleasant to sit in the orangery, a small table to hand with a jug of lemon shrub, and let the beaming sunshine lay its beneficent warmth upon him. He had brought with him Chesterfield's *Advice to His Son and The Polite Philosopher*, which was, in its turgid phrases, agreeably closing his eyes in mortal repose.

The peace and warmth did its work and the memories of the recent past began to fade. Outside, birds hopped from branch to branch of the orchard trees, their song so different from the sound of the sea's rage.

His mind drifted to a more agreeable plane. What would Persephone be doing in Bath? Did taking the waters imply a communal bath somewhere or would someone of her quality be granted private quarters? No doubt Lady Lockwood would come round to things eventually, particularly with Persephone there to explain things. Meanwhile . . .

'Oh! I didn't mean to disturb you, Mr Kydd!' a timid voice called from the door. Kydd opened his eyes and rose.

'No, no, please, don't get up. I only thought you'd like tea and – and I see you already have something.' Her voice was shy but appealing in its childlike innocence, although Rosalynd was plainly a young woman.

'That's kind in ye, Miss Rosalynd,' Kydd said, with finality, hoping she would go away – he was enjoying the tranquillity and those pale blue eyes had an other-worldly quality that unnerved him. But she remained quietly, watching him. 'Y' see, I'm in deep study with m' book,' he explained stiffly.

She approached shyly and Kydd became uncomfortably aware that she had a startling natural beauty, of which she seemed unconscious. 'I'm so curious, Mr Kydd – I've never met a learned gentleman before. Do forgive me, but I've always wondered what they think on when their mind is not in a struggle with some great problem.'

Those eyes. 'Er, I'm really no scholard, Miss. F'r that you need t' ask Mr Renzi. I'm only his – his assistant.' He fiddled with his book.

'Oh, well, if there's any service I can do for you gentlemen . . .'

'Thank you, we'd most certainly call on ye.'

She hesitated. Then, with a smile and a curtsy, she left.

It was no good. She had ruined his rest so he took up Chesterfield. The Latin tags annoyed him and the convoluted prose of half a century before was tedious. Yet if he was to hold his place in the highest society he should know the rules by heart, and soon. He sighed and ploughed on.

Renzi returned in high spirits. 'Such richness of material – it's striking to see the variation in responses. And the philology – it would give you pause should you see what I've gleaned

299

from their rustic speech. A splendid day, and tomorrow I'm promised an old man of a hundred and five years who can remember Queen Anne's day . . .'

At the evening meal Kydd left it to Renzi to deflect the polite enquiries concerning where they had come from. It would probably cause alarm and consternation if ever it reached down to the nest of smugglers below them that an active commander, Royal Navy, was taking his ease so close. And, of course, he did not want to hazard the trust Renzi had established with the local folk.

In the morning Renzi was off early, leaving Kydd to his orangery once more. Just as he had settled in his easy chair there was a shy knock and Rosalynd entered, then stood before him. 'Mr Kydd, I don't believe you're a learned gentleman at all.'

Kydd blinked and she went on, 'I saw you last night when Mr Renzi was telling about his *word fossils* and I could swear you had no notion at all of what he was saying.'

'Ah, well, y' see, I'm a friend of Mr Renzi's who assists when called upon,' Kydd said weakly.

She laughed prettily. 'You see? I knew you weren't. You're much too – too, er . . . May I be told who it is you are, sir?'

It was unsettling, but her innocence was disarming and he could not help a smile. 'No one of significance, you'll understand. I'm just a gentleman o' leisure, is all, Miss Rosalynd.'

Looking doubtfully at him she said, 'I do believe you're teasing me, sir. You have the air of – of someone of consequence, whom it would be folly to trifle with. You're a soldier, Mr Kydd, a colonel of some high regiment!'

Kydd winced. 'Not really,' he muttered.

'But you're strong, your look is direct, you stand so square – it must be the sea. You're a sailor, an officer on a ship.'

He could not find it in him to lie and answered, with a sigh, 'Miss Rosalynd, you are right in th' particulars, but I beg, do not let this be known. I've just endured a great storm an' desire to be left to rest.'

'Of course, Mr Kydd. Your secret shall be ours alone,' she said softly. In quite another voice she continued, 'I really came to tell you that the first Friday of the month is the fair and market in Polperro. If you like, I'd be happy to take you. Of course, Billy will come with us,' she added quickly, dropping her eyes.

'Billy?'

'That's what Titus wants us to call him. He hates his name.'

A country fair! It had been long years since he had been to one – but Chesterfield beckoned. 'Sadly, Miss Rosalynd, I have m' duty by my books an' must decline.'

'That is a great pity, Mr Kydd, for your friend left before I could inform him of it, and now there is no one to tell him about what he might have seen.'

Kydd weakened. 'Mr Renzi – you're right, o' course, it would be a sad thing should there be no one t' report on it. I shall come.'

'Wonderful,' she said, with a squeal. 'We'll leave after I put on my bonnet – will that be convenient to you, Mr Kydd?'

They set off for Polperro on foot. 'I hope you don't mind the walking – we should take a donkey shay but I do so pity the beasts on this steep hill.' The Landaviddy pathway was a sharp slope down, and Kydd thought of their return with unease.

'It's so lovely in Polperro at this time of the year,' Rosalynd said wistfully. She went to the side of the path and cupped her hand. 'Just look at these yellow flowers. It is the biting stonecrop come to bloom. And your yellow toadflax over here will try to outdo them. We call it "butter and eggs",' she added shyly.

Titus hopped from one foot to the other in his impatience to get to the fair. They descended further, the rooftops below now in plainer view.

'I do love Polperro – there's so much of nature's beauty on every hand.' A rustle of wings sounded on the left and a small bird soared into the sky. 'A swift – we must make our farewells to him soon. Do you adore nature too, Mr Kydd?' The wide blue eyes looked up into his.

'Er, at sea it's all fishes an' whales, really, Miss Rosalynd,' Kydd said awkwardly, wishing they were closer to their destination.

She stopped and gazed at him in open admiration. 'Of course! You will have been all round the world and seen – you'll have seen so much! I do envy you, Mr Kydd.'

He dropped his eyes and muttered something, turning away from her to resume walking. He had no wish to be badgered by this slip of a girl when his thoughts were so occupied with the challenges of high society.

Well before they reached the village Kydd's nose wrinkled at the unmistakable stench of fish workings, but Rosalynd seemed not to notice. The muffled sound of a band mingled with excited voices floated up to them and when they reached level ground a glorious fair burst into view.

There were stalls with toys and sweetmeats, penny peep-shows, the usual story-tellers holding audiences agog with lurid tales. Despite himself Kydd felt a boyish thrill at the gaudy scenes, the village lads decorated with greenery and the lasses in their gay ribbons and gowns.

Then, preceded by terrified children, a bear lurched down the street and round the corner a dragon breathing real fire progressed, opposed by brave boys baying at it with fishermen's foghorns. Titus ran forward. 'The gaberlunzie man!' he shouted. The cloaked performer was executing risky tricks with sulphur matches while a tumbler and juggler tried to distract him.

'To the green!' urged Rosalynd, touching Kydd's arm. 'There's always a play!' The village was a dense network of narrow streets and they emerged suddenly on to a tiny open area nearly overwhelmed by close-packed buildings. There, on an improvised stage, a seedy band of players declaimed to a rapt audience.

On the way back, Kydd paid twopence to a fiddler for a gay twosome reel danced by a masked youth and maiden, while the three each ate a filling Cornish pasty to keep hunger at bay. A quick visit by the Goosey Dancers ended the day and they wended their way back up the steep pathway.

They walked slowly, Titus going ahead. 'It's been so good to have visitors,' Rosalynd said quietly. 'We don't get many, you'll understand.'

Kydd murmured something and she gave him a quick glance. 'You may think us simple folk here, Mr Kydd, but we are blessed with many things.' She bent and picked a flower. 'Here – so many pass by this. It is the bridewort and is provided by nature to give us an infallible remedy against the headache.' She pressed it on him, her fingers cool. He lifted it, feeling her eyes on him as he smelt it. 'Mr Kydd, it's been such a lovely day – I do thank you.'

Renzi seemed strangely unmoved at the news of what he had missed. His notebook was clearly of compelling interest and Kydd left him to his aggregations. For himself, he could feel the sunshine and placidity working on him, and the trials of the recent past were fading.

But something was unsettling him – the girl. Rosalynd was at odds with any other he had met and he was at a loss to know how to deal with her other-worldliness, her communing with nature, the innocence born of the seclusion of this place from the outer world . . . and her ethereal loveliness.

What about her was so different, an only daughter in a household of men? Her detachment from the usual cares and preoccupations of the world? He checked himself: this was no fit subject of concern for one about to be wed.

He declined her invitation to explore the village and buried himself in a book, then found, to his surprise, that he felt put out when she accepted his refusal without comment. On the next day when Titus came to extend her hesitant offer to accompany them on their visit to the fisher-folk he accepted instantly.

She was wearing a plain linen morning dress and bonnet, and carried a basket. 'This is so kind, Mr Kydd. I'm going to visit Mrs Minards. You see, we lost a boat in the big gale and her husband was not found, the poor soul.'

Kydd winced. If *Teazer* could find herself between life and death, then what of the little fishing-boats?

'They have such a hard life, Mr Kydd, you have no idea. Hurry, please, Billy, Mr Kydd is waiting.'

It was the Landaviddy path again, but this time they stepped out purposefully. 'When something like this happens it's so difficult to know what to do.'

'That there's somebody in the world who knows an' understands will be comfort enough,' Kydd said warmly. She flashed him a look of gratitude.

It was a pretty village. The small harbour was central with its piers and little fishing-boats in rows on the mud. However, the nearer the fish quay they went, the meaner the cottages.

At the edge Rosalynd stopped to fasten on pattens, over-shoes that would protect her own from the fish-slime.

'Good mornin', Miss Rosalynd,' a buxom lady with a fishing basket hailed, looking curiously at Kydd.

'And a good morning to you, Mrs Rowett,' she called back gaily, with a wave.

They reached the open space in front of the Three Pilchards, and squeezed down a passage to the rickety cottages behind. A dull-eyed woman came to the door of one, then broke slowly into a tired smile. 'Why, Rosalynd, m' deary, there's no need to—'

'Nonsense, Mrs Minards. I'm only come to make sure there's enough to go round.' A child wandered in, lost and bewildered.

Kydd felt an intruder: the thin cobb walls, two rooms and pitiful furnishings spoke of a poverty he had never been witness to. The calm acceptance by this new widow of the sea's pitilessness and her future of charity shocked him.

After they left, Kydd asked Rosalynd, 'What will she do now, d'ye think?'

He was startled to hear a sob before she answered. 'To – to know your love will not ever return to you in life is the cruellest thing, Mr Kydd.'

They walked out to the brightness of the day and she said, with an effort, 'I suppose she will go wool-washing at Crumplehorn. It pays quite well although the work is dirty.'

At a loss, Kydd kept pace with her. She stopped suddenly and turned to him with a smile. 'Mr Kydd, I'm going to show you my most favourite place in Polperro. Come along!'

She hurried to the corner of the row of cottages and found a neat but narrow path winding up high in the rocks.

'Oh, do we have to?' Billy said.

'Yes, we do! Now, get along up there, if you please.'

Kydd, however, found sixpence for him to spend afterwards as he liked, which won him a firm friend.

When they had toiled up a short slope and reached a spur of rock they were rewarded with a dramatic view: the length of the harbour with its impossibly narrow entrance, the two mighty formations of rock, like a gigantic lizard's spine, and stretching in a vast, glittering expanse to the distant horizon, the sea.

'There!' she breathed. 'All the rest of the world is out there. The elephants of India, the palace of the King, even that horrid Napoleon. All you have to do is get on a ship and you can go there – anywhere.'

Kydd was touched; for him the far horizon was a familiar sea highway to every adventure and experience of significance in his life so far, and he had perhaps taken for granted the freedoms it gave.

She pressed him: what *was* life like for one who sailed away over that horizon? What changes in character, what deep feelings were involved? Kydd hesitated at first but he was soon opening to her parts of himself that had remained closed to everyone else, including, it had to be faced, Persephone. Rosalynd was reaching him in a unique way.

Renzi arrived back late and somewhat rumpled. 'Gurry butts and arrish mows.' He sighed. 'Such a richness in diversity to the same urgent imperatives. You'll recall the islands of the Great South Seas – the savages there . . . Please know that this is proving a most satisfactory first expedition.'

'As I c'n see, Nicholas,' Kydd answered, over his port, 'an' I wish you well of it all.'

Renzi looked at him fondly. 'I am aware, dear fellow, that

this is hardly an enthralling adventure for your good self and it is on my conscience that—'

'No, no, Nicholas! I am findin' th' peace an' tranquillity a fine solace,' he said, 'And th' family is, er, takin' good care of me.' Renzi would probably not understand if he mentioned his pleasant walks with Rosalynd.

'You should ask them to show you about Polperro,' Renzi said encouragingly. 'I passed by yesterday, a most curious place.' He accepted a restorative drink and continued: 'Some might find its fragrance less of sanctity and more of fish, but I was amused to read a most apposite inscription above the door of one such pallace: *"dulcis lucri odor"*, or "This be the sweet smell of lucre."'

Kydd grinned. 'Your Ovid, then.'

'Perhaps not. The wit who placed it there was probably thinking of Vespasian, that most earthy of emperors who actually said, *"pecunia non olet"*, "Money does not reek", a most practical view, in my opinion.'

The next day Kydd and Rosalynd visited Jan Puckey's fish pallace; it was diverting to see the speed and skill with which the women balked the pilchards. They were placed in an earthenware 'bussa', tails in and heads out in an endless spiral of salted layers, two thousand for the Puckeys' winter consumption alone, with the oil pressed from them fetching a good price.

Afterwards they took a picnic atop the medieval ruins of Chapel Hill. Rosalynd spread a cloth and took out country goodies from her basket. 'I do hope you'll have these – I don't know, really, what you like,' she added shyly.

With mutton pies and saffron cake happily tucked away, Kydd lay back contentedly on the grass and closed his eyes in the warm sun, waiting for yet another question about the wider world but none came. She sat close to him but seemed quiet and affected, staring away over the sea.

At last she broke silence. 'When will you leave, Mr Kydd?' she asked, in a small voice.

'Oh, er, I suppose that'll be when Nicholas has had his fill o' things t' see,' he said off-handedly.

'Oh.'

An awkward silence grew; Kydd got to his feet. 'We'd better be back,' he said, dusting himself down.

'Oh – not straight away, please,' she cried. 'Do you see there?' she said pointing to the cliff edge. 'It's a path that follows all the way to Fowey and there are enchanting prospects to be had.'

'Well, where's Billy? Absent fr'm place of duty – we'll keel-haul him!'

But she had already moved away. He hurried after her, across the grass and on to the narrow track that found its way along the ragged edge of the coast, the sea beating against the rocks a precipitate hundred and fifty feet below.

'Rosalynd?' he called. She did not stop until she had reached a fold in the cliffs.

He caught up and said, 'Miss Rosalynd, you should—'

She turned slowly and Kydd was astonished to see the glitter of tears. 'M-Mr Kydd,' she choked, 'I b-beg you – please don't forget me.'

'Wha—?'

'I d-do assure you, I will never forget *you*.'

Kydd was unable to think of anything to say.

'You – you've changed me,' she said, choked. 'I can't be the same person any more.'

'I – I—'

'It's not your fault, Mr Kydd. I've been living here quietly and thinking it's the whole world and then . . .' Her hands twisted together. 'You see . . . it's nothing you've done – it's all my fault – b-but I've found I care for you more than is proper and now you'll get in your ship and sail away from me and . . .' She buried her face in her hands and wept.

Struck to the heart his hands went out to her. She reached for him with a tearing sob and clutched him fiercely, weeping into his chest.

Appalled, but deeply touched, he stroked her hair, finding himself whispering meaningless phrases while the storm of emotion spent itself. Then she wrenched away from him and sought his eyes. 'I love you, Mr Kydd – I love you so much it hurts me. There! It's said!' Her fingers dug painfully into his arms until the moment passed. She kept his gaze, then added, with a shaky laugh, 'And I don't even know your name.'

Kydd stepped back in dismay, caught up in his own chaos of feeling. He turned away, and saw Billy standing, staring.

They made their way back in an uncomfortable silence; at the manor Squire Morthwen was waiting for them and, seeing his daughter's condition, demanded an explanation. He listened stonily as she declared she had been upset at Billy's absence, thinking he had taken a tumble over the rocks and been swept away. The squire looked sharply at Kydd.

Rosalynd excused herself from dinner; Kydd endured until he could get away to the privacy of his bedroom, then flopped on to the bed, his thoughts running wild.

By morning he knew what he had to do. No decent man could stand to see such sweet innocence betrayed; he had been blind and stupid not to realise that what had been to him a pleasant time in the company of an enchanting young woman might mean rather more to her. It had to end. 'Nicholas, I do think I should go back an' see how *Teazer* is at the dockyard.'

Renzi's face fell.

'That is t' say it will only be me, o' course. You should stay an' take aboard a full cargo o' your ethnical facts afore returning.'

'You are bored and vexed by idleness while I garner my harvest of particulars,' Renzi said suspiciously.

'No! No, Nicholas, it's just m' duty, is all.'

There was no prospect that *Teazer* would be away to sea in the near future. A survey had found started strakes and displaced frame timbers, nothing that could not be put right but the dry-docks were occupied by important units of the fleet and *Teazer* would have to take her turn.

Kydd returned to number eighteen, sending Mrs Bargus and Becky into a fluster, but found it the worst of places to be. He sat alone in the drawing room, staring into the fire with nothing to divert him from his brooding thoughts.

It was unfair: Rosalynd had invaded his consciousness and threatened his ordered life, but now her image seldom left him. The wide innocence of those dreamy blue eyes, her beauty, her direct, even intimate, way of talking – he was tormented by her. And he had to do something about it.

Time was not the answer: after several days, her presence was as real as ever. Why could he not put her from his mind?

It was not his way to shy from a difficulty: the only way to deal with the situation was to confront it. He would ride out to Polperro and dispose of it once and for all by the simple device of seeing her again; then he would surely realise she was a pretty slip of a country girl, with whom he had found it agreeable to pass the time on a leisure visit, nothing more. That would finally lay to rest his unreal images of a girl who never was.

His knock at the door was answered by the pleasant maid-servant. No, the squire was out; at this time every day he visited his tenants. Mr Renzi? He was chasing his ethnicals again.

'I'll wait f'r the squire,' Kydd said, and was ushered into the snug drawing room where he had first set eyes on Rosalynd. He pulled himself together and settled in a chair to await the squire's return as in all politeness he was bound to do.

The door squeaked and Rosalynd hurried in, incredulous. 'Mr Kydd!' she cried, her face lighting with joy. 'You came back! You came back for me!'

She flew across the room and embraced him. 'My dear man, my dearest sweet man . . .'

Kydd looked into her brimming eyes and his arms went round her to hold her close, his hands caressing, cherishing. His eyes pricked and a lump formed in his throat, for now it was plain that he was facing the greatest trial of his life.

'So you've done well by y'r particulars in Polperro, I see,' said Kydd, eyeing Renzi's careful piles of notes.

'Indeed – and enough to keep me in thought for a long time to come. Such variance! I would never have conceived it that—'

'Nicholas – um, might we talk for a spell?'

'Talk? Oh, yes, fire away, old fellow.' He left his notes reluctantly and came to sit with Kydd.

'Nicholas. There is − er, that is to say, I have a problem an' I was hoping you'd give me a course t' steer.'

'Oh? Please tell.'

'Well, it's all shoal-water navigation f'r me, but y' see, Nicholas, um . . .'

'Dear fellow, do clap on more sail or we'll not make port by dinner.'

'Er, you see, Nicholas, I − I find my affections have, er, been engaged by Miss Rosalynd.'

Renzi sat bolt upright as though his hearing was in question. 'Do I understand you correctly? You have formed some species of taking after Squire Morthwen's daughter? A − a lusting for her?'

Kydd reddened. 'I can't keep her out of m' mind, no matter what I do.'

'Then you had better find a way, my good friend.'

'This is my problem, Nicholas. Is it right t' wed a lady while thinking of another?'

'Are you telling me in all seriousness that you are allowing a casual obsession of the moment to interfere with your marriage to one of the most eligible scions of society? This is nothing but rank idiocy!'

'And if it's more than − *a passing fancy*, what then?'

'Good God, man!' Renzi spluttered. 'I do believe you've taken leave of your wits!' He quietened with an effort. 'Be advised, my friend, that if you still hanker after the woman, in higher society these matters can be arranged discreetly enough. Your Prince of Wales enjoys the attentions of his paramour where he will and—'

Kydd's face tightened. 'Damn it, Nicholas! You're so high on morality an' conduct, where's your advice t' me now?'

Renzi's expression hardened. 'You're forgetting yourself. A

gentleman by definition is concerned with graces and appearances – politeness and urbanity above all. If it's the case that you're unable to control your coarser spirits then the least you can do is conduct yourself with discretion.'

Kydd fought back anger. 'An' I'll remind you we're talkin' of a fine lady here – what of her?'

'She will accept it, in course – as one of breeding she will be first concerned with the respectability of her family and heirs. You will not find a difficulty there, I believe.'

'You – for th' sake of *appearances* you'd take a wife an' lie with another?' Kydd choked. 'Then I pity my poor sister.'

Renzi went white. 'Let me remind you, sir,' he said dangerously, 'it is *you* who are discontented with your lot. I do strongly advise you consider your position carefully and put an end to this ridiculous posturing.'

'Thomas, my dear, so good to see you again. How are you?' Cecilia poured the tea and regarded her brother with undisguised affection. 'The talk in town is all about your brave deeds in the storm. You really should take more care – it's so very dangerous in a gale.'

'Yes, sis,' Kydd said, accepting his cup.

'And how's Nicholas? You've both been gone for so long on your expeditions.'

'He's well, Cec, but why I'm here is, er, I need y'r advice.'

'Oh, don't worry about it! A wedding is really the concern of the womenfolk. They'll see everything is right on the day.'

'No! It's – it's not that. Y' see, um, something's happened.'

Cecilia saw his set face and sat up. 'Then you'd better tell me about it, Thomas,' she said quietly.

In the bare telling it sounded so thin and illogical. When he had finished Cecilia said nothing, staring at him, troubled.

'Now, let me be clear about this, Thomas. In just a week or so you have discovered deep feelings for this Rosalynd that cannot be denied.'

'Aye,' Kydd said miserably. 'It happened so quick, Cec, an' it's knocked m' feelings askew.'

'This is very serious, Thomas.'

'I know,' he whispered. 'Can I ask it, sis – is it right to marry one while thinkin' on another?'

Cecilia looked at him sharply, then melted, leaning to clasp his hands in hers. 'You dear sweet boy, you know the answer to that.'

She drew out her handkerchief and wiped a tear, then continued in a practical tone: 'So, now there are decisions to be made. And these are, it seems to me, one of three: cast Rosalynd out of your mind and marry Persephone; continue with the wedding to Persephone and make other arrangements for Rosalynd; and the last is to cast out Persephone and be wed to Rosalynd.'

Kydd said nothing, gazing at her as if mesmerised.

'You might consider delaying in the hope that your feelings change?'

'I – I feel it worse every day.'

'I see. Then we must find a resolution, and for this, I believe, I must ask you some hard questions.'

Kydd nodded and braced himself.

'Do you love Miss Lockwood?'

'She's the most handsome and intelligent woman I've ever met, an' that's the truth.'

'Do you *love* her?'

Wretchedly, Kydd tried to escape Cecilia's accusing eyes. 'Look, Cec, it's not that, it's – it's that when I see Rosalynd she's such a tender innocent an' I want to love her an' protect her, but Persephone, she – she doesn't need me t' protect her. She's strong an' knows things and . . .' The lump in his throat made it difficult to carry on. 'And Rosalynd is care-free an' loves simple things – I don't feel I have t' be polite an' play a part all th' time.' Tears pricked. 'She talks t' me and I c'n feel her words inside me . . .' Sobs choked him.

'Thomas! Listen to me! There's a terrible flood coming and you must save one and lose the other. Only one – who is it to be?'

Kydd shook his head in anguish.

'You must answer!' she demanded forcefully. 'Soon one will vanish from your life for ever – for ever! *Which one will you miss the most?*'

The tears were blinding but Cecilia spared him nothing. '*Which one?*'

'Rosalynd!' he shouted hoarsely. 'It's Rosalynd I can't bear to leave.' He stood in agony, tears coursing down his cheeks. 'I can't help it! God help me, Cecilia, I can't help it.'

She held him while the storm passed, saying nothing but rocking him slowly.

When it was over he stood away from her, his fists bunching helplessly as he fought to regain his composure. 'I – I'm sorry, Cec,' he gulped, 'We – we men are a lubberly crew when it comes t' this sort o' thing.'

'Dear sweet brother, please don't say you're sorry. This is all because you're such a good man – you see?' She sighed and looked at him lovingly. 'You've answered your own ques-tion and, to be frank, it's not altogether a surprise to me.'

Kydd swallowed.

'Yes – do you mind if I say something very cruel to you, Thomas?'

'If y' must, Cec.'

'I do believe that you've been infatuated not with Persephone Lockwood but with what she is, the world she comes from, all that pomp and finery. And the pity of it is that, of a certainty, she loves you.'

There was nothing he could find to say.

She went on gently: 'This is why you must tell her yourself, Thomas – she's a fine woman and at the least deserves this.'

'I will,' he agreed.

'So, now we must consider the future.' She got up and began to pace up and down the room. 'I gather you have not spoken to her father yet?'

'No,' he said huskily.

'Have you an understanding with Persephone?'

'I was t' ask for her hand when she returned from Bath.'

'Very well. Then there is no question of a breach of engagement but the world will believe there is an understanding – your attachment was much talked about.'

She stopped. 'Do you intend to marry your Rosalynd?'

Kydd gave a shy smile. 'If she will have me, Cec.' The idea broke on him like thunder and he felt nothing but a soaring exhilaration.

His elation seemed to vex Cecilia. 'I don't believe you can conceive what an upset this will cause, Thomas,' she said, with the utmost seriousness. 'It will be gossip in the salons for ages to come. Can you not see? The daughter of a family of the first quality and known at court, an acknowledged beauty, and turned down by a penniless commander for a simple country girl?'

Kydd still stood in an attitude of the greatest happiness, while Cecilia continued grimly, 'Her family will be mortified – they will seek to destroy you in society. They will have you damned at every polite gathering in the land. No one will dare invite you for fear of offending – you'll be an outcast just as you're about to enter at the highest level. And your sea career – you cause mortal offence to your admiral and he will take his revenge, I'd believe.'

It stopped Kydd, but only for a moment. 'He can't turn me out of my ship, sis. I've now got someone t' care about, and I'm going to do m' copper-bottomed best t' see she's proud o' me – and be damned to any who'll stand athwart m' hawse. An' in the meanwhile, Cec, I'll be with my Rosalynd, an' raising our family.'

The hoofbeats of his horse thundered in Kydd's ears as he tried to grapple with the enormity of what he had just done.

Immediately on her return from Bath he had requested an interview alone with Persephone. Shocked by the reversal of what she had expected, she had nevertheless remained calm and controlled, standing nobly to hear what Kydd had to say.

He had spoken woodenly, forcing himself to look at her while he delivered his words, and then had been nearly undone by her calm reply: as she had before answered his own challenge truthfully, she now simply wished to know if another had secured his affections.

His face was streaked with tears at the memory of her parting words, to the effect that she understood and was grateful for his frankness, for she could never have given her heart to one who could not promise his own.

He had fled.

It was now a completed act. With dread and joy he was riding across the hills to Polperro – to Rosalynd. Out of one world and into another. He had propped a note to Renzi on the mantelpiece and had left the storm to break without him.

317

A straight stretch of road opened ahead and instinctively Kydd whipped his mount into a frenzied gallop, needing the wild motion to work on his emotions. Whatever else in the world happened, he was now riding to lay his heart before Rosalynd Morthwen and seek her hand in marriage.

In a flood of feeling he brought the exhausted horse to a crashing stop before the manor, and slid to the ground. At the old windows faces began to appear but Kydd would not have been stopped by the devil himself and strode forward.

'Mr Kydd?' The squire himself answered the door and eyed Kydd's dusty, wild appearance apprehensively. A manservant and stable-hand hovered protectively behind him.

Kydd made a short bow. 'Sir, my business is brief. I beg th' favour of some small time with y'r daughter – alone.'

As the import of his request penetrated, a disbelieving smile appeared. Then, by degrees, it spread until the squire's face grew red with heartfelt pleasure. 'By all means, m' boy!' he chortled. 'Do wait a moment, if y' please.'

Inside, excited shouts were urgently shushed and there were sounds of running feet. Then the squire appeared again at the door. 'Do come in, sir.'

Kydd entered and stopped; she was standing rigid in the centre of the little drawing room, her eyes never leaving his.

'Miss Rosalynd,' he said, in a voice charged with emotion, 'I come to speak with y'r father on a matter of the highest importance. Y' see, I've come to see that, um, m' feelings for you are, er . . .' He was reddening and the words he had prepared fled at the reality of the impossibly lovely creature before him. There was nothing for it. He flung himself on to one knee and choked out, 'Rosalynd – will ye wed me?'

* * *

'It's an ox-roast! I'll stand for nothing less!' The squire's roar cut across the excited babble. With Rosalynd sitting shyly beside him, his hand securely over hers, Kydd's heart was full to bursting. Tears only a whisker away he endured the friendly jests of her brothers and dared to steal another look at her. It was beyond mortal belief that this sweet creature and he would go forward as one for the rest of their lives.

Rosalynd suggested they take a walk together. However, it seemed that the proprieties were still to be observed and Titus was called to accompany them. In the event, the embarrassed lad went on ahead until he was all but out of sight. They walked slowly together in silence, Kydd anxious that the magic spell might be broken and Rosalynd by his side, with a soft, dreaming look.

'I – I believe we must make some plans,' he said finally, in a low voice.

'Yes, my – my dearest,' she whispered. 'If it does not inconvenience you, I would wish to be married as soon we may. Banns will be called for three Sundays at the parish church and it – it would make me very happy if we could be wed on the fourth.'

She bestowed on him a look of such love that it quite unmanned him. He crushed her to him. 'We shall,' he croaked.

In a daze of happiness he walked on, the world in a blur, reality at his side. Their steps had taken them down to the village – to Polperro, which to Kydd now was more dear than anywhere on earth.

'Why, Miss Rosalynd!' Mrs Puckey's dour face was now wreathed in smiles. 'I never did! We'm all been wonderin' who ye'd end with!' She looked with keen interest at Kydd.

'This is my intended, Mrs Puckey. He's Mr Kydd,' she said

proudly. News must have spread in the village at breakneck speed.

Others arrived to share in the moment. 'Bejabers, Mr Kydd, but ye be one of us now, then.'

'Mr Bunt, please! He only asked me this morning!' laughed Rosalynd. 'And I did so accept him,' she said softly, with a sideways glance at Kydd.

They moved on, noting the makings of a huge driftwood fire even now enthusiastically under way on the foreshore of the harbour before the Three Pilchards, and continued through the streets.

A small shop caught Kydd's attention: it offered the services of a shade-maker. 'My dearest, if you would indulge me, I have a yen . . .' he said.

Each in turn sat in a darkened room beside a paper screen and candle while the artist went laboriously round the shadow with a pencil. Afterwards a dextrous flourish with the pantograph saw their silhouettes reduced magically to black miniatures, then charmingly encapsulated in two gilt-edged lockets.

Kydd slipped his into the inner recesses of his waistcoat where it settled in a glow of warmth.

'My love – do let me show you Talland Bay. It's so enchanting!' Rosalynd urged.

Then as they passed a modest cottage on the hill she propelled him towards it. 'This is someone I'd like to meet you – a man who's been so good to the village. He came as a schoolteacher, and since he's been here he's prospered in business, but he's always helped people in trouble, taken care of those on hard times and – oh, do come!'

The kindly old gentleman blinked with pleasure at meeting Rosalynd's chosen and pronounced words of benevolence upon them. 'It's good t' meet ye, Mr Job,' Kydd said sincerely.

They left the village by the Warren and followed a girdling cliff path far above the sea and right down into the next bay. 'There,' she said, as their shoes crunched in the sand.

Kydd couldn't help but note it was a very secluded beach, ideal for landing contraband. 'In the navy, Polperro bears a reputation for smuggling as hard as any,' he murmured.

'I know, dearest, but please believe me, the fisher-folk and villagers are not your smugglers. They only fetch and carry for small coin, and who can blame them when the fishing is so uncertain? No – the villains are those who put down fifty pounds to invest in a cargo from France and pay others to face the danger.'

Kydd said nothing, thinking of Stirk somewhere at sea in a smuggling lugger on his dangerous mission to find evidence.

'See here,' Rosalynd said, stooping to a pile of misty dove-grey and violet pebbles. She lifted one up to show him. 'Aren't they lovely?'

'Not as fair as you, my dear Rosalynd,' he said, and kissed her tenderly.

Talland Church was a little further on, up a remarkably steep hill, which left them both panting at the top. 'This is where we'll be married,' she breathed, holding both of his hands. 'And the fishermen's choir will sing for me and the bells will ring so loudly . . .'

It was a striking church with a wondrous view of the bay. Mellow with age, it nestled into the Cornish hill as though it had grown from it, the bell-tower set apart from the main edifice but linked with a coach-roof. And there they would be joined together for ever.

As they returned Kydd found it hard to deal with the forces pulling on his soul. Here was his future – there lay his past. A gathering black cloud of social ruin was waiting, and this simple sweet soul knew nothing but her new-found happiness.

She stopped at the sea's edge and turned to him with a smile. 'When will you take me to visit your ship? I'll be so proud. Will the captain allow me, do you think?' she added anxiously.

'He will, I promise,' Kydd said softly. Then the dark clouds returned to edge about his happiness. Who knew what lurked in wait for him?

'Er, th' ship's in dock for repair after th' storm. We'll have time later.' But there was a larger issue that had to be faced. She had the right to know what he – they – were headed into: the unjust social retribution that would be visited on her innocence, the friendless, harsh new world after Polperro.

'Rosalynd, my very dearest. I have t' tell you something as will touch on our future.' He swallowed and continued: 'Before I met you, there was a lady called Persephone, an' she and I . . .'

Chapter 13

Kydd could not throw off his sense of foreboding as the coach drew closer to Plymouth. Rattling along the last mile it curved round to stop on the foreshore, which had once been a favourite sight, with the long spread of the dockyard on the opposite shore, and sail on the river. Now, as he waited for the Torpoint ferry, it seemed hostile and foreign.

He gazed over the half-finished vessels and the ships in for repair. To his astonishment he saw *Teazer*, with just her lower masts but to all intents and purposes out of dock and in completion.

Hailing a returning wherry he hurried out to his ship. Standish was there, impassively at the salute, but with few others about the decks.

'How is th' ship?' Kydd asked him.

Standish doffed his hat formally and said coolly, 'Wanting masts and stores only, sir.' The implied rebuke was barely concealed.

Kydd turned abruptly and went to his cabin. 'Ah, Nicholas!

We're afloat again. Have you your sufficiency of ethnicals, do y' think?'

Renzi rose from the table, his manner cold and detached. 'Here are the returns for stores demands. You should be aware that in your absence eleven men have deserted. And we have received an instruction from Admiral Lockwood that the instant you returned aboard you were to present yourself at his office immediately.'

'Thank you,' Kydd said, with as much dignity as he could muster. 'I will go now, o' course.'

'Get out!' Lockwood roared at a frightened clerk, when Kydd had been announced. 'You too,' he savagely snapped at the flag-lieutenant. Lockwood strode across and slammed the office door. 'How dare you, sir? How dare you show your villainous face in public after your unpardonable behaviour towards my daughter?'

'Sir,' Kydd said stiffly, 'there was no engagement.'

'But there was an understanding!' Lockwood shouted, his face white with fury. 'As well you knew, sir! You have been dishonourable in your intentions. She is upset – quite undone – and I will not let it pass. As God is my witness I will not let this go.'

Kydd swayed under the blast.

Suddenly Lockwood turned and stamped over to his desk. He waved a copy of the *Telegraph* at Kydd. 'Have you any conception of the ruination you have caused my family? The distress this has caused my beloved wife? No? Then read this, sir! *Read it!*' Kydd took the newspaper.

Our intrepid spy, LOOKOUT, climbs aloft to the crow's nest in his unceasing quest for those furtive proceedings of the world most likely to surprise and concern the public. He trains his powerful telescope and before long a most *lugubrious* sight catches his eye. Readers of a delicate disposition should now avert their eyes for what must follow is a heartrending tale of *desolation* and *woe*. A comely maiden stands weeping, and to LOOKOUT's astonishment and *anguish* he sees that it is none other than our fair *Miss Persephone L*—, who when she last graced this column was expecting the joyful sound of wedding bells. What is this? he asks, bewildered, and turns his glass around and about. Aha! Can this be the reason? The dashing and notorious *Captain Kidd* has vilely abandoned her and is now making wicked advances to another. And who is it for whom he has spurned our lady of quality *Miss L*—? None other than a simple country girl with no prospects but a *saucy figure*. Can it be believed? We can only beg our Readers to contemplate the feelings . . .

Kydd reddened. 'Sir, this is no—'

'You've shamed us to the whole world, sir!' bellowed Lockwood, 'And cast my dear wife to her bed with mortification. And I can assure you I'll see you in Hades before I let it rest.'

Kydd stood rigid as he continued: 'And when I'm finished there won't be a soul in the land who'll think to let you pass their door! And as for your sea service, I promise you, my report to their lordships concerning your fitness for command will spare not a single detail. None, sir!'

'Sir, this is monstrous unjust,' Kydd said thickly.

'Your ship has been at moorings these last two days awaiting her commander. This is intolerable and demonstrates to me a complete and utter contempt for your position as a commanding officer. Permission to sleep out of your ship is therefore revoked – you understand me, sir?'

'Yes,' Kydd ground out.

'What was that?'

'I understand, sir,' Kydd said, suppressing his anger savagely.

'Then, if you find the time, perhaps you might bring your command to sea readiness. I have a special service in mind.'

The midshipman of the boat quailed under his captain's fury, and as they returned to *Teazer* Boyd gave his orders to the crew in a hushed voice.

Kydd had come to a cold, hard understanding of how things now were. He had chosen his path – and it had cost him dearly. The dream-like past, with its promise of elevation to the heights of gentility and aristocratic privilege, was now but a memory. All he had to look forward to was the remainder of his commission in *Teazer* before the admiral's malicious actions took effect at the Admiralty, then gentle penury for the rest of his life.

But it would be with Rosalynd. He clung to the radiance of her laughing image, his eyes misting. Be damned, it was worth it – a hundred times worth it!

'Um, sir – we're alongside,' the midshipman said uncomfortably.

'I c'n see that, blast you,' he said, and clambered inboard over the bulwark. 'Send f'r the sheer hulk, we're taking in masts,' he snapped at Standish. 'Now, sir!'

He plunged below and sat in his chair, breathing heavily. 'Tysoe!' he roared, 'Brandy!'

Renzi glanced up from his quill, face blank.

Kydd glowered at him. 'As y' said! An' I'll thank ye not t' preach it!'

Renzi looked at him for a moment, then said coldly, 'I'm sorry to hear it.'

'I don't think you are,' Kydd said venomously. 'You're satisfied t' see me on a lee shore, now I've made m' choice.'

'I take no pleasure from your predicament.'

'Then why the wry looks?'

'Since you ask it, I believe you have done yourself a grievous harm – no, hear me out for I shall say this once only.'

Kydd's expression tightened as Renzi went on remorselessly, 'It has been too rapid, too precipitate. It is my firm belief that taken, as you no doubt are, by one of nature's children, you have progressed too far in your acquisition and appreciation of the higher arts of civilised conduct, and later you will find yourself quite unsatisfied and morose with your lot, shackled to one for whom the graces will mean so little.

'And why you have seen fit to throw over without thought a gentlewoman of such incomparable quality as Miss Lockwood, with all it means for your hopes of entry into society, I simply cannot conceive.'

Kydd glared at Renzi. 'Have y' finished?'

'That is all I wish to say.'

'Then hear me now, f'r I'll say this only th' once.' He tossed back his brandy in one. 'I don't expect ye to reckon on it, but when I came up wi' Rosalynd, all m' world has gone like – like a dream, a wonderful dream.' He saw Renzi wince at the return of his old ways of speech but didn't care.

'I – I love th' girl.' He gulped, 'I didn't know love would be like this'n. It's wonderful – an' so terrible!' He grabbed the bottle and splashed more into his glass. 'An' this I'll tell ye today, *it's Rosalynd an' no other*, so help me!'

Renzi spoke in an icily neutral tone: 'Then there seems no

point in continuing this conversation. You are besotted of the moment and will take no advice from anyone. We are of different minds on the issue and I, for my part, can see no reason to change my view of your unfortunate situation.'

He took a long breath. 'Therefore I offer the termination of my services aboard *Teazer*. If you so desire, I shall shift my berth out of this vessel tonight.'

Kydd felt stifled by the ship. He knew the signs, the sly looks, seamen listless in their duties, the lack of respect in their eyes – his men had taken against him.

It could be anything: there would be lofty criticising on the mess-deck, arguments. But counting heavily against him from the point of view of the seamen before the mast was *Teazer*'s conspicuous lack of victories in battle. Was he unlucky? A Jonah?

But the real reason, he knew, was deeper. He had had the chance of marrying into the world of the aristocracy, with all the prestige it would have given the ship, and had somehow botched it, settling for a simple country lass. It brought into question his judgement as a man – and, by implication, as their commander.

Two more had gone over the side as they were getting in the masts, knowing that no one could be spared to chase after them. *Teazer* would be putting to sea in the next few days and she was falling apart. Standish was cool and aloof, and the master had retreated into monosyllables. Even Tysoe was reproachful and distant, clearly put out because his hopes of a prestigious situation in the future had been dashed.

It had cost Kydd dignity and patience to beg Renzi to remain, and there was no guarantee that it would last. But with Renzi set against him he had now not a single friend or confidant to whom he could turn.

He burnt with the injustice of it all, but he was helpless. Forbidden to sleep ashore, there was, however, nothing to stop him setting foot on land for a little while so he ordered his boat.

At the hard he saw two lieutenants in conversation. On seeing Kydd they stopped, then deliberately turned their backs to continue their exchange. It would demean him to take them to task, and he passed them, wounded. Were the officers of the fleet now taking sides?

A casual naval acquaintance, in plain clothes, stopped and looked at him with frank curiosity, and a pair of ladies in Durnford Street passed him primly enough but then broke into excited chatter.

Number eighteen was no longer a snug haven. His estrangement from Renzi cast a pall over their lodging, and when Mrs Bargus came in to find whether to set the fire it was with a disapproving air.

But there *was* one who would understand, Kydd hoped. His spirits returned as he summoned the housekeeper. 'Here, Mrs Bargus, find a boy an' tell him t' deliver a note this hour.' A reply came back by return:

Dear brother – I have to get this off, so please do forgive if I'm short. I'm so truly sorry to hear of your trouble, but right at this time I don't think I can be seen with you, Mrs Mullins taking on so. You will understand, won't you? And I don't think I want to go on board your ship and see Mr Renzi there until things are settled. Do keep well, and next time I see you I hope it will be with Rosalynd.

* * *

Kydd felt the world closing in on him. The only thing now in his universe that had any meaning was Rosalynd. Her softness, the clear sweetness of her voice – only she mattered. He sat back and let warm thoughts of her take him away.

It was getting towards dusk, and as he readied himself to return to the ship there was a hesitant tap at the door below and voices as Mrs Bargus answered.

'I, um, was passing.'

'Bazely! S' kind in ye! Please draw up a chair – brandy?'

'Not now, thank 'ee,' he said, without his usual breeziness. 'I can't stop for long. *Fenella* puts out on the morning tide. To the east'd,' he added.

'Well, now . . .' Kydd tried to think of talk, but Bazely cut him short. 'I came, er, to see if there's anything I can do for ye,' he said uncomfortably.

'Do for me?'

'Now you've come up against things, an' all. You'll know what I mean.'

Kydd was touched beyond measure. Bazely had risked the admiral's displeasure and his career by visiting him. 'That's so good of ye, Bazely. It seems there's not s' many wish t' stand as my friend. I'm sorry we didn't find time ever f'r a ran-tan ashore.'

'One of us has to keep the seas while the other sports it in harbour, m' old cock. It's the way of it. I recall y' took a hammering off Whitsand while we was snug at two anchors in Tor Bay.'

'Aye. Well, it's right good of ye t' call. I might yet have a need.' A soft look spread on Kydd's face as he added, 'An' I'll have ye know, wherever Rosalynd and I fetch up, you'll be first across th' threshold, m' friend.'

*   *   *

HMS *Teazer*'s orders were waiting for her captain when he returned aboard. A single page, delivered by a lieutenant under signature. It was far from elaborate; the 'special service' was nothing more than the instruction to resume smuggler-hunting, to remain on station without leaving, at his peril.

It was a cynical move: by one easy stroke, and appearing to be in earnest about a serious problem, Lockwood had ensured that Kydd would find neither glory nor notice; it was a sentence of sea toil and drudgery, flogging up and down the coast after fast and elusive smugglers, who seemed to have second sight.

When *Teazer* finally put to sea it was with a scratch company, the Impress Service finding seven resentfuls, a new gunner's mate, with Stirk presumed lost, and discontent rippling out from the quarterdeck after their fate was revealed.

How things had changed. *Teazer*, his fine ship of which he had been so proud, was now the focus of his troubles; and she was not the lovely creature she had been. He had not been able to find the funds to smooth away the raw marks of damage and repair with expensive varnish and had had to accept the utilitarian dull black of the dockyard which disfigured and besmirched her bright-sided hull.

They rounded the Rame westwards past Whitsand Bay; they were the same places as before but now they seemed indifferent, going about their unseen everyday business while *Teazer* sailed endlessly offshore.

But one held special meaning: almost hidden from seaward the snug village of Polperro came up under their lee – he would have given almost anything to land there, but even the most compelling reason would be misinterpreted. And as he could not travel from Plymouth and return in a day, and was unable to sleep out of his ship, it would be impossible to visit Rosalynd.

Kydd had to possess himself in patience for the twenty-four days that remained before they would be finally together and be satisfied with the precious locket. Polperro was left gradually to sink astern.

Days followed other days; Renzi had retreated into formality and spent time in Kydd's cabin only on ship's business. Standish affected a cynical correctness that preyed on Kydd's nerves, but he hugged to his heart the knowledge that now every day was one closer.

He took advantage of a mild south-easterly to call on the Collector of Customs at Fowey. As usual, he heard a litany of missed landings, fruitless swoops, the outrageous ease with which operations were co-ordinated, and views on the complete uselessness of the Royal Navy, but nothing to help his quest.

The gig set off to return to *Teazer* and Kydd spotted seamen crowding together at the foremast about one man. It wasn't until he was aboard that he could see Tobias Stirk was at the centre of attention.

Only Standish knew the real reason for Stirk's absence and Kydd took savage delight in not asking him to the cabin to listen to any adventures, instead ordering him to take the ship to sea.

'Good t' see ye, right fine it is!' Kydd said, in unaffected pleasure. 'Th' best sight I've had f'r a sennight, y' must believe.'

'An' it's right oragious t' be back, Mr Kydd,' Stirk growled.

Kydd felt a rush of warmth. 'Ye'll have a rummer for y'r bones,' he said, then found glasses and a bottle.

He saw Stirk looking up at him with his steely eyes as he

poured and, for some reason, felt defensive. 'Not as who's t' tell, Toby, but it's been a hard beat for me these last weeks,' he tried to say lightly. 'Only t' say, there's been a mort o' trouble over me bein' spliced t' the wrong lady and, er, y' may hear rum things about me,' he finished lamely.

Stirk watched him levelly as he took a pull at his drink, then set the glass down and said carefully. 'Sorry t' hear of it, sir.'

'Aye,' Kydd said. There had been a time when he could have unburdened his soul to this man but that was far in the past and they were separated in any friendship by the widest gulf that could exist in a ship. He topped up Stirk's glass. 'Then I'll be pleased t' hear of y'r adventuring now, Mr Stirk.'

There was a glimmer of a smile. 'And ye'll be interested in *these*,' Stirk grunted, as he tugged off his shoes and retrieved some folded papers. 'Fr'm Guernsey.'

Kydd scanned them quickly. One was a form of cargo manifest but in essence showed orders to tranship specified freight to an English ship, openly listed contraband. It was countersigned – by the guarantor.

'It's Zephaniah Job o' Polperro,' Stirk said bluntly. 'Runs it all, even sets 'imself up as a bank t' guarantee to the Mongseers which supplies th' run goods.'

Kydd brought to memory the kindly face of the Mr Job he had met: could he really be the same man?

He looked at another paper; a letter-of-credit with the same beautifully executed and perfectly readable signature with an ornate flourish in the exact centre below it. Zephaniah Job.

'A very fly gennelman, Mr Job. Has s' much ridin' on the cargoes he's taken over th' business o' gettin' it ashore himself. Organises th' lot fr'm a master book 'e keeps.'

So that was how—

'Now, Mr Kydd, if ye has th' book an' matches it there t' the sailin' times, even a blind Dutchman'll have t' say as how he must by y' man.'

'How—'

'That's 'cos I know where 'e keeps th' book. It's in his house, f'r I seen him get it quick, like, so it must be there. An' if ye'd rummage his house, why . . .'

Kydd sat back in admiration. Then he said, 'This letter-o'-credit, it's worth a bucket o' guineas an' I'm thinkin' th' owner was vexed t' lose it. May I know, did, er, y' come by much trouble in th' gettin' of it?'

Stirk said nothing, fixing Kydd with an expressionless stare.

'Come now, Mr Stirk, y' must have a tale or two t' tell.'

There was no response and Kydd knew he would never learn what had taken place.

Stirk stood. 'I'll go now, sir,' he growled.

'This is a great stroke, an' there'll be a reward at th' back of it. I'll see y' square on that, Mr Stirk,' Kydd said warmly.

'No, Mr Kydd. I doesn't want any t' know – ever, if y' unnerstands me.' Stirk had done what he had for Kydd, but he was not proud to have deceived those who had befriended him and Luke.

Kydd bounded on deck. The sunshine felt joyful on his face.

Standish looked at him curiously. 'Did the rascal find out anything of use, sir?'

Kydd smiled. 'A rare enough set of adventures, I'll grant, but nothin' o' value.'

'Ha! I didn't think it. He's had a holiday on the King's account and lines his pocket in following his old ways. That sort don't know the meaning of honour.'

Kydd's smile vanished. 'That's as may be. F'r now we have

a pressing task. I've had intelligence fr'm the Collector in Fowey that will mean we c'n lay our hands on this smuggler-in-chief.'

'Why, sir, if that's so then—'

'We crack on all sail conformable. I'm not goin' t' miss the chance to settle th' rogue.' He could have alerted Fowey to send a Revenue party to arrest Job but this opportunity was too good to miss. When he succeeded where all others had failed, Lockwood would be furious but would have no alternative but to thank him publicly and release him from this drudgery.

'Er, where . . . ?'

'No more'n a league ahead, Mr Standish. Polperro!'

HMS *Teazer* rounded to and anchored in four fathoms off the little fishing village. Much too big to enter the tiny harbour, she made a fine picture so close in and Kydd thrilled to think that Rosalynd might be among the curious sightseers come to see why a King's ship had disturbed their morning.

But they were there for a stern purpose. 'Eight men – Poulden in charge. Cutlasses, two muskets.' He did not expect difficulties but if Job had men of his own it would be prudent to mount a show of force.

The pinnace stroked for the harbour entrance, eyes turning at the dramatic flare of rocks that was the Peak. Ashore, people hurried to stand along the rugged heights to watch the drama.

'Th' fish quay,' Kydd ordered his coxswain. A small boat scrambled to get out of the way and people crowded there when it could be seen where they were headed.

'Hold water larb'd, give way st'b'd.' The pinnace swung and headed in. 'Toss y'r oars!' Looms were smacked on thighs and oars thrown vertical as the boat glided in to the quay. Excited faces peered over the edge and Kydd adopted a suitably grave expression as he climbed up to the top, his men behind him.

'Form up,' he snapped, clapping his cocked hat firmly in place. 'Shoulder y'r arms.' There were gasps from the jostling onlookers as the seamen drew their cutlasses and rested the bare blades on their shoulders.

The crowd's noise died as they watched, wide-eyed. There was a jostling movement and suddenly Rosalynd was there – fear and delight in her features. 'Thomas!' she called, and flung herself forward.

'Hey, Miss! Y' can't do that!' Poulden said, scandalised. 'That's the captain!'

'The captain!' she squealed, eyes shining. 'But he's *my* captain!'

'Er, hmm,' Kydd said gruffly. 'M' dear, I have m' duty t' do, if y' please.' He was conscious of a growing hubbub as he was recognised under his gold lace, and there were open grins among his men. 'If ye'd wait f'r me . . .'

'I'll be here for you, my very dearest!' she breathed. A hug turned into a kiss before Kydd, crimson-faced, could march the men off, the crowd surging after them.

He knew the way: they swung across the little bridge and up the pathway, the nervous agitation of the throng echoing in the narrow lane as they speculated loudly on their destination. At the modest cottage he hammered on the door. 'Open th' door! In the King's name, open!'

Unrest spread as the people realised what was happening; Job was popular in Polperro. Kydd raised his hand to knock again but the door opened and a bemused Job emerged, blinking in the sun. 'Gentlemen? Ah, Mr Kydd, is it not?'

Kydd felt a wave of misgiving at seeing him again. A powerful smuggling gang-master? If Stirk was wrong . . .

'Let's be inside, sir,' he said firmly. There were angry shouts from the crowd, but Poulden and one other entered close behind and shut the door.

'I've reason t' believe . . .' Kydd began. It sounded so theatrical, and the mild-mannered Job stared at him in alarm. 'Right, Poulden. Y' know what ye're lookin' for – go to it.'

'What? You can't do that, sir! What are you doing?' Job shrilled, as Poulden went into the room described by Stirk. 'There's the accounts of years in there – they'll be sent all topsy-turvy. Oh, do stop him, Mr Kydd, I beg.'

But it was too late. Poulden came back with a great volume and placed it on the table in front of Kydd. 'Behind th' dresser, sir.'

Neat columns: names, dates, cargoes. Consignees, special instructions, ships, times, places. It was more than enough. 'Zephaniah Job. I arrest you f'r – f'r doin' smugglin', contrary t' the law. Ye'll come with us t' Fowey – now.'

Iron handcuffs were produced. Job was now calm, almost serene. 'This is my home village, Mr Kydd. It would oblige me extremely should you permit me to go on board your vessel unfettered, sir.'

'Your word?'

'My word.'

There was something disturbing about his imperturbability but Kydd allowed his request and they stepped outside.

The crowd was restless. Shouts and jeers met them and a stone whistled past Kydd's head. 'Go,' he told Poulden, and the party set off quickly for the quay, seamen with naked blades to each side of him and the prisoner. Catcalls sounded above the tumult; cries of anger and betrayal.

They reached the quay and the pinnace made ready. Rosalynd stood back, her face pale with shock.

'Bliddy spy, that's what y' came 'ere for!' screamed Mrs Minards, in Kydd's face.

'Aye! Not fit f'r a Polperro lass, he ain't!' spat Puckey, and the mob took it up. Grim-faced, Kydd told Job to get into the boat and turned to face the crowd, seeing Rosalynd tear free and run to him sobbing.

'I had t' do my duty,' he said huskily. Fish entrails slapped against his coat, soiling Rosalynd as well.

She composed herself. 'You must always do your duty, my love. Go now, and I'll be waiting for you.'

'Sir?' Poulden said anxiously.

'S-soon,' was all Kydd could trust himself to say to her, before he turned abruptly and went down into the boat. 'Give way,' he said, in a low voice, and as they made for the open sea, he twisted round to keep her in view as long as he could.

He should have considered it more, Kydd thought bitterly. Job was a benefactor to the village, well liked and, most importantly, a regular employer of tub carriers and lookouts. Kydd had angered the folk of Polperro, antagonised the very place that had made him so welcome, and now his world of happiness had contracted to just one person – whom he had unthinkingly made an outcast among her own people.

'Sir?' Standish entered, unsure. 'Ah, Mr Job is asking for a word with you in private, sir. I did tell him it was improper, but . . .'

'It is. Where is he now?'

'In irons, sir. I thought it—'

'In bilboes? A mort hard on a man o' years, Mr Standish. Bring him t' me, I'll hear him out.' For some reason he had an odd regard for the man.

'I do apologise f'r my lieutenant, Mr Job. He's zealous in th' King's service, y' must understand. Now, what c'n I do for you?'

Job settled himself. 'You will believe that my course is finished, Commander, but I should like to say to you here that there is a service I can yet do for my fellow man, which it would render me much satisfaction to perform.'

Kydd kept a noncommittal silence.

'And it has to be admitted, its doing must stand me in good stead for anything that must follow for me.'

'Y'r service?'

'Yes. You will no doubt have heard of that vile privateersman, Bloody Jacques.'

The hairs on Kydd's neck pricked. 'I have. What can y' tell me of the villain?'

'I want you to remove this evil creature from the high seas, sir.'

'Your jest is in bad taste, Mr Job,' Kydd said.

'Let me explain,' Job said evenly, 'You may have noticed that his knowledge of these coasts is exemplary. This is no coincidence. I can tell you now that I know him well, but as Michael Haws, resident as was of Looe – a species of turncoat, as it were, in his own interest.

'In the past I have had occasion to employ him and his lugger in – in trading ventures, but since the resumption of war he has taken the character of a French privateer in order to prey more profitably on our richer trade. In short, a pirate, owing allegiance to none.'

It was incredible – if true.

'He wears a dark beard, adopts a rough manner, all this is to hide his identity, of course – and the selecting of victims on the deck of captures to run them through as an example to the rest, why, this is nothing more than disposing of those he knows, and fears might later bear witness against him.'

'This is fine information, Mr Job, but I—'

'I will lead you to him. The rest I leave to you.'

'Well, gentlemen,' Kydd said, with relish, unfolding the chart of St Austell Bay on the table. 'Thanks t' our guest Mr Job we're at last one jump ahead o' Mr Bloody Jacques. We have th' same information that he has – there's t' be a landing at Pentewan Sands this next night.' He let the news sink in and went on, 'The villain's goin' t' be waitin' to take th' smuggler, an' when he makes his move we want t' be there to make *ours* on *him*. And mark this, if y' please, I'm not goin' t' spare this poxy villain. He's not y' usual privateersman, he's a mad dog an' must be put down.'

Standish looked grave; the others remained impassive.

'He's not about t' give up without he takes it out of us. I don't need t' say it, but he'll not be offerin' quarter an' therefore I do see it as a fight t' the finish. I'm sorry t' see *Teazer*'s company put t' hazard in this way, but I know you'll see th' need.

'Now. I don't want t' lose this chance so I've given it a lot o' thought. I'd like y'r comments afterwards.' He glanced at Renzi, sitting at a small table and taking a record, but he realised there would be no discourse in the old way with his friend.

However, Kydd was satisfied he was thinking as Bloody Jacques was. The smuggler would be running fast and direct

340

across the Channel, for with every sail hostile there would be no point in prolonging exposure. Therefore his course would be generally from the south-east, given the easy westerlies that had prevailed these last few days.

But it would be in the last few miles only that the smuggler's position would be guaranteed. Where could a privateer lurk unseen? In the almost north-south trend of St Austell Bay to the Dodman, with Pentewan in the middle, one place stood out above all others: Black Head, to the north. This looming mass of granite standing well out could comfortably conceal a dozen vessels within a mile or so of the sands. Not passed from the south-east and with all attention in the smuggling craft on the dangers of the landing, the privateer could close in from behind with deadly ease.

'So it's t' be Black Head. Are we agreed?' A murmur about the table he took to be consensus and went on, 'Then I want t' be in position close in to Charlestown harbour at dusk t' be ready to drop down on 'em at th' right time.'

From seaward, Kydd hoped that HMS *Teazer* at anchor looked for all the world like a merchant brig waiting out the tide to enter Charlestown, but aboard her, preparations for the night went on apace.

It was going to be that hardest of battlefields, the sea at night, with all that it meant for the accuracy of gunfire and distinguishing friend from foe in combat on a strange deck in the pitch dark. With most certainly a larger crew in the privateer, the odds were shortening fast.

But their duty was plain and there could be no hanging back; there would be many sailors along the Cornish coast who would bless their names before the night was out – or not, should they miss this chance.

'Sunset, sir,' Standish said, in a low voice.

'Very well,' Kydd said briskly. 'Hands t' quarters and prove th' lookouts.' It was not impossible that Bloody Jacques could arrive at Black Head from the north. It was now just a waiting game.

The run ashore was timed for after dark and before the moon rose. The land in shadows lost its character and faded into gloom. Lights began to wink on ashore. Kydd lost sight of the tip of Black Head; it was time to get under way.

It seemed so at odds with the lovely scene, it should have been a time of serenity, perhaps a promenade in the warmth of the evening, hand in hand – he thrust away the thoughts.

Tysoe brought his treasured fighting sword. He acknowledged curtly and fastened it on. 'Man th' capstan – quietly now.'

The anchor broke ground and they ghosted out into the blackness. The tension began to work on Kydd, but at the back of them was the thought that he so much needed this success, for Rosalynd's sake. The pirate-privateer captured as well as the smuggling chief: it would secure his standing, no matter what Lockwood could contrive.

'Still! Absolute silence in th' ship!' Somewhere out there was the bloodiest foe on the coast – or not. If this was nothing but a wild-goose chase he would have Job back in irons instantly.

'Sir!' Andrews whispered urgently.

The midshipman's more acute hearing had picked up something. Kydd strained – then heard a regular series of tiny wooden squeals, precisely as if the yard on a lugger was being hoisted up the mast. And the sound came from closer in to the land: if this was the privateer he must have superlative knowledge of the coast. They rippled on through the calm water trying hard to catch a betraying clue, knowing Bloody Jacques would be keeping his own silence. But if that was indeed yards being swayed up, the pirate was hoisting sail to make his lunge.

A sudden thickening in the gloom to starboard was Black Head – the lugger was not there. Damn the blackness to hell!

From about a mile ahead Kydd heard a sudden cry of alarm. Then a ragged chorus of shouts carried over the water, followed by a pistol flash or two. Kydd's heart leapt as he willed *Teazer* on in an agony of impatience.

He heard more shots and the clamour of edged weapons rising, then falling away. It wasn't until long minutes later that they could see dark shapes on the water: two, close together. Kydd's strategy had been simple: he would close on the privateer, fire, and board in the smoke and surprise. The one thing he was relying on in this risky attempt was that half of the enemy would be away subduing the smugglers.

On *Teazer*'s deck the boarders were ready with bared steel. Standing next to the wheel Kydd tried to make out the situation – then he saw movement, separation. The larger vessel was detaching from the smaller. There was a cry – they had been seen! A swivel gun banged uselessly at them into the night, then a larger carriage gun was fired.

The vessel's angular lugsails were sheeting round urgently to the light westerly, but at this point of sailing a lugger's ability to sail closer to the wind was of no advantage since it was boxed in to the land, and *Teazer* was no mean sailer on a wind. As they drew nearer, the shape foreshortened as it bore away south for the open sea. The smaller was endeavouring to make sail as well but the smuggler could be dealt with later, if it was still there – after they had put paid to Bloody Jacques.

The wind freshened as they plunged south, all to *Teazer*'s favour, exulted Kydd, for they were only a few hundred yards astern. A conclusion was certain if it held or strengthened. A little after midnight the moon rose, its silver light picking out the lugger in pitiless detail. *Teazer* grew nearer and Kydd realised that, with a reduced crew, his opponent had no scope for fast manoeuvre.

The Dodman stood stern and massive in the moonlight when they fore-reached on the lugger. If only Rosalynd could be there, Kydd thought – but this was his world, not hers: she would take no pleasure in seeing him about to hazard his life. It cooled his battle-fever: from now on, he realised, he had to consider two, not one. But had not her last words to him been, 'You must always do your duty'?

'Stand by, forrard!' he roared. The carronades were loaded with alternate ball and canister; there could be no reloading in this dark.

Teazer's bowsprit inched past the lugger's stern. Beside him Standish was watching, his hand working unconsciously at the hilt of his sword.

'Fire!' A split second later a twenty-four-pounder carronade blasted, its gunflash overbright in the gloom. At thirty yards' range there was no missing and in the moonlight leaping splinters could be seen as the ball struck home.

'We have him, damme!' Standish yelled in glee.

If they could do their work before the Dodman and the open Atlantic – but then, without warning, it all changed. There were frightened shouts in the lugger and it sheered up into the wind, sails banging and ropes all a-fly. Then the yards began to drop. It made no sense.

Standish looked at him. 'Sir, I do believe he wants to yield.'

It was impossible but the lugger had doused all sail and

344

lay submissively to await her conqueror. 'Board an' bring that rogue before me, Mr Standish,' Kydd ordered.

His lieutenant returned quickly. 'Sir. I'm so sorry to tell you – but this is the smuggler, the other the privateer.'

Many smuggling craft were lugger-rigged as well and often of sizeable proportions. In the heat of the moment Kydd had forgotten this – and he had lost Bloody Jacques.

'My commiserations on the events of the night,' said Job, smoothly, not at all disobliged to be summoned before his captor at such an hour.

'T' damnation with that! Do you check y'r book an' tell me where there's t' be another landing. He'll want t' satisfy his crew after tonight, I'll believe.' Kydd handed over the heavy tome.

Job adjusted his spectacles. 'Why, there's a landing tomorrow, at Portloe.'

'Around the Dodman only. So we'll be there as well,' Kydd said, with satisfaction.

Job looked up with a small smile. 'And at the same time another – at Praa Sands.'

It would be impossible to watch two separated locations at the same time. 'Seems t' me you're in a fine way o' business, so many cargoes t' land,' Kydd growled.

'Not so much, Mr Kydd,' Job came back. 'These few days of the month are the choicest for running goods. A smuggler's moon; one that does not rise until the work is done and with a good flood tide to bear it ashore.'

Kydd made up his mind. 'Praa Sands is nearly up with Falmouth. I'll choose y'r Portloe as is now so convenient f'r the scrovy dog.'

*   *   *

Overcast, with the same westerly veering north, it was a perfect night for free trading in Veryan Bay and thus Portloe. But there seemed nothing close to the little port that would serve to conceal a predator, the jagged hump of Gull Rock to the south probably being too rock-girt to lie close to.

They tried their best but their long and stealthy creep from seaward was in vain with not a sight of their prey. Either they had chosen wrongly or, after his recent experience, the privateer was more than usually vigilant and had slunk away.

And, it seemed, there were no more landings in prospect. Their alternatives were now few, the scent run cold. Job was summoned once more; there was just one question Kydd wanted answered. 'If Bloody Jacques is not a Frenchy, as y' say, then tell me this. Where's he get his ship refitted after a fight? Where's he get his stores an' such? An' what I'm asking is, he must have a base – where is it, then?'

'A fair question,' Job said. 'Since Guernsey won't have him, he's taken to seizing whatever he wants from small fisher villages. Simply appears at dawn, sends a band of ruffians to affright the people and takes a house while his men do disport aboard.'

'Go on,' Kydd said grimly.

'He chooses carefully – only those villages far from others, with poor roads out so he's no worry of the alarm being raised quickly, and a sheltered anchorage for his vessel. Stays for only a day or two, then disappears again.'

It was getting to be near impossible to lay the pirate a-lee, but Kydd was resolved to put an end to him. He dismissed Job and sat down to think.

He had now come up with Bloody Jacques twice and had

always found him a cool and reasoned opponent. The violence and cruelty in no way prevented him being an able, resolute seaman and enemy. So what the devil would he do now?

Lie low out of the way and wait for *Teazer* to tire of the chase. Where? Beyond her normal patrol limit – not to the east and the old, well-served and prosperous ports but to the rugged and remote west. Beyond Falmouth and even Penzance – to the very end of all England.

Land's End, where he had given Kydd the slip so easily before? Or perhaps further beyond? The chart gave few details of the region, for its wild majesty was of no interest to seafarers, who feared the ironbound coast. He peered closer – no ports to speak of; he remembered the precipitous cliffs, the dark menace of subsea rocky ledges and the rolling waters of the Atlantic meeting stern headlands.

Further round was Cape Cornwall with offshore banks and shoals aplenty: but before that a long beach was marked. Surely the fisher-folk had a village somewhere along it?

They had, and it was called Sennen Cove. Round the coast from Land's End, it was tucked into the end of the beach under high cliffs and guarded from sea intruders on one side by the sprawling Cowloe reef, and on the other an easy escape to the north with these westerlies. The nearest authority of any kind was miles away over scrubland. Ideal, in fact, for such a one as Bloody Jacques.

In some way Kydd was sure that this was the place – he could *feel* it. And this time there would be no mistake.

He could crowd on sail and bring *Teazer* round the headland, then fall on the privateer; but what if they were seen by a lookout atop the cliffs and Bloody Jacques slipped to sea again? It couldn't be risked.

A night attack? Problematic, and there was the hideous danger of the Cowloe reef in darkness. Boats, swarming round the point? Just one gun in the lugger would cause horrific casualties before they could close, and in any case they would find themselves hopelessly outnumbered.

This needed thought – the kind that was generally sparked when he and Renzi talked together . . . but Renzi was not available. He would have to find a plan on his own.

It was something Job had said: Bloody Jacques's practice was to go ashore and take a house. That was the answer. Kydd knew he could not simply sail in and send a boat ashore with the lugger crew looking on, but there was another way, and he set *Teazer* after her quarry.

As long as the weather held. If there was even a slight heave, one of the more common Atlantic swells rolling lazily in, it would be impossible. On this day, mercifully, there wasn't and mere waves would not worry them.

With *Teazer* safely at anchor, bare yards south of the extreme tip of Land's End, her cutter pulled away by the last light of day with as many men as it could hold, those at the oars cramped and swearing, but it was less than a mile they had to pull.

Close in with the rearing crags, gulls rising in screaming clouds at their intrusion, they stroked northward, with wicked rock formations standing out into the sea from the precipitous heights. Kydd's eyes were scanning urgently: before it got dark he had to find a place on this utterly rockbound coast to land and discover a means of ascending the cliffs. No one but a madman would think to land here.

At the base of the rockface all along the shore there was a narrow ledge of tumbled boulders and sea-rounded stones washed white by the slight seas. They proceeded just off the line of breaking waves, the cliffs prettily red-tinted by the setting sun with occasional deep, shadowed caves and natural archways, the pungent smell of rotting seaweed wafting out.

Then he saw it: a deep cleft between two bluffs. 'Hold water!' Kydd said, in a low voice. While the boat rocked, he examined it as closely as he could. It was probably eroded by water run-off from above, and therefore a possible way up.

Bringing the cutter about he took it as close as he dared to the shore. With little swell, there was no real danger of the boat rising and falling on to the rocks waiting under it. He splashed over the side into the water and stumbled ashore over the mass of stony boulders towards the cleft. It was in the sunset's shadow but nearer to it, he could see that even though it was choked in places with loose stones it wound up steeply out of sight and, as far as he could tell, to the top. It would do.

He brought his men ashore and sent the boat back. There was nothing more to do but wait for the dawn.

Shivering, stiff, and conscious that he had spent a night under the stars on unyielding stones, Kydd awoke. Others stirred nearby. It was calm and with a slight mist. Impatiently Kydd waited for the light to improve so they could make a move. But when they did reach Sennen Cove, would Bloody Jacques be there?

'I'll be first, Mr Stirk,' Kydd called quietly, looking back over his men as he hurried past. They were not many, but he was relying on the likelihood that only a few would be trusted ashore from the privateer.

349

If any words were to be said, now was the time; but Kydd could find none in the face of what they were about to do. 'Let's finish th' job,' he said, and began to climb.

It was hard going, a scramble on loose pebbles and dust, then hard-edged rocky shards. They heaved themselves up like topmen, shifting hand or foot only when the others had good purchase. All the time the light strengthened allowing them to see the appalling drop that was opening beneath them to the sea below.

Then the cleft angled to the left and shallowed. The going was easier, and almost before they knew it, the slope gentled and the ground levelled out.

Kydd moved cautiously. There was every reason for Bloody Jacques to post a lookout here: there was a view both to Land's End on the one side and the broad sweep of beach on the other.

And there was indeed a sentry. He was sitting on a ledge of rock gazing out to sea, a clay pipe going peacefully – with a musket across his knees. Kydd dropped to the ground.

The man had to be silenced: the musket would sound the alarm. But in a paradoxical way Kydd was comforted. This was proof that he was right. Bloody Jacques was here.

Stirk slithered up next to him. 'Mr Kydd,' he whispered hoarsely, gesturing to himself and then to the lookout. Kydd nodded, and Stirk scrambled to his feet. He stood swaying for a moment, his hands clamped piteously to his head as though it were about to burst, then fell to his knees.

There was a shout from the man, but Stirk shook his head and crawled further, then stopped to dry-retch into the dust.

The lookout shouted again, thinking him another of his crew, betwaddled after a riotous night. He put down his musket and came over irritably.

Stirk exploded into life, barrelling into the unfortunate man and, with a snarl, lofting him over his shoulder. The sentry crashed on to the edge of the cliff, his fingers scrabbling hopelessly, and slithered over with a despairing cry.

Now they had only to cross a quarter-mile of barren heath-land, then descend into Sennen Cove. They hurried along silently and emerged on to the bluffs overlooking the neat little village and the beach. There, nestling within the flat blackness of the reef, was the three-masted lugger they had sought for so long.

There was no early-morning activity aboard and, indeed, none in the village, from what could be seen. If Bloody Jacques was in a cottage, which one? Was he still aboard his lugger – and preparing to sail?

A track led at an angle to the side, which soon wound into thick, concealing furze. Kydd plunged down.

Surprise was their only advantage: they did not carry muskets, which would have hindered them on the climb, and pistols in the belt could well work loose and drop. They were going into the attack armed only with bare steel.

It seemed impossible that their awkward, skidding haste down the track had not been heard in the huddle of cottages just below, but Kydd could detect no alarm. Should they risk everything on a mad dash to the centre of the village or keep out of sight of the lugger and search the houses one by one?

As they came upon the first dwelling he could see that this was no longer an alternative. There were men untidily asleep on the sand, others no doubt elsewhere. Should he spread out his own men in a search or keep them defensively together?

'Stay with me!' he hissed, and stalked out into the narrow

street, sword in hand – his precious fighting blade, which had been at his side on countless occasions of peril, a fierce comfort.

Standing four-square, his men behind him, he bellowed, 'Bloody Jacques! I have ye now! Come out an' yield y'self to me!'

His voice echoed off the silent buildings. 'Commander Kydd! In th' King's name, surrender y'self!' There were tiny movements at the windows of some cottages.

Shouts rose from the beach. How many were there?

'We have ye surrounded, y' villain! Come out an' show y'self!'

'Sir – th' lugger! She's gettin' a boat wi' men ashore!' They would soon be overwhelmed; Kydd's men could barely hold their own against those who had come up from the beach.

'Y' last chance afore I come in an' tear ye from y' bed – Mick Haws!'

Behind him a door crashed open and Kydd wheeled round. With an animal roar, a giant of a man in shirt and breeches threw himself towards him, a monster claymore in his fist.

Kydd braced himself, his sword at point. The claymore came down in a mighty sweep, meeting Kydd's blade with a jarring smash, numbing his arm. But he was not intimidated: such a heavy weapon was unwieldy and slow – the fight would be over soon.

However, it had been a blind – Bloody Jacques held a smaller blade in his other hand, which swept round in a savage thrust to Kydd's groin. He parried awkwardly, the action bringing them close, and caught the other man's rank stench. He became aware that the fighting round him had become general. Clashes of weapons, cries of pain. But he dared not lose concentration. He tried to turn his parry to a tierce, but it was savagely deflected.

More sounds of fighting, blade on blade, pistol shots. Kydd felt his opponent's desperation but what if the lugger crew reached them before . . . ? However, Calloway had kept a cool head, and when Bloody Jacques had been flushed out he had done his duty. With a sudden hiss and whoosh, Kydd heard their signal rocket soar skyward.

There was a groan of pain, more shrieks. From his men? It was only the fine balance and superbly tempered steel of his weapon that enabled him to withstand the savage battering that followed, the demented onslaught with which Bloody Jacques was trying to overwhelm him.

But suddenly the tide seemed to have turned: cheers and jeering broke out, strengthening as the sounds of battle diminished. Clearly the privateersmen had realised the significance of the rocket – that a King's ship was in the vicinity. They were throwing down their weapons, which, no doubt, were swiftly snatched up by Kydd's men.

'If ye'd stand clear, sir.' Kydd could not afford to take his eye from his opponent but he knew what Stirk intended to do. However, a musket ball to the throat was too easy an end for this man.

'Belay that,' he called breathlessly, between blows. 'He's t' pay . . . at th' end . . . of a rope!'

That goaded Bloody Jacques into a furious, reckless assault that sent Kydd stumbling, then falling full-length backwards. In an instant the man threw himself forward, but Kydd had sensed this coming and thrust out with his foot. Bloody Jacques fell – squarely on to Kydd's waiting blade. It was all over in seconds. Kydd drew himself to his feet and looked around breathlessly. In the mêlée the men of *Teazer* had

suffered lightly. Bloody Jacques and several of the privateersmen lay still, the others huddled together in meek
submission.

'Well, Mr Job, and as you've been of such rousin' assistance
to us, I'm sure that—'

'Ah, Mr Kydd. I've been meaning to talk with you about
this. You see – and please forgive if I'm brief in the article
of explanations – there may be reasons why it should be
more expedient for you to set me at liberty, as it were.'

Kydd slumped back, amazed at the man's effrontery. 'Pray
why should I do that?' he said.

'I'm sure this will go no further, Mr Kydd? Then I should
inform you that my business interests are near – and far.'

'If you're thinkin' t' offer me—'

'Sir, I shall speak more clearly. In my trading ventures –'

'Smugglin'!'

Job allowed a pained expression to appear. '– in which it
is plain I have made my mark and thereby gained the respect
and trust of many disparate parties, which necessarily includes
the French authorities, it would appear that His Majesty's
government has found me of some utility in actions of a
clandestine nature. These might include the passing of agents
and others into and out of France in the character of smuggling crew – do not, I beg, press me for details.'

'Go on.'

'I cannot go further, apart from suggesting that your
admiral in the strictest confidence consults a Mr Congalton
at the Foreign Office as to whether, in fact, it is a good idea
that I be taken up as a common smuggler. If I am unsup-
ported, I may of course be instantly taken and cast into
prison.'

His confident smile implied there was little danger of that.

'And, dare I mention it, sir, your reputation with your admiral afterwards will be as high as if this were public knowledge.'

To put before Lockwood that not only had he laid hold of the smuggler-in-chief but that he was privy to secrets at the highest level would be sweet indeed. 'I'll need y' word on it.'

'You have it, Commander.'

'Then I'll take ye back to Polperro while we check th' details.' Kydd chuckled drily. 'I may be wrong in th' particulars, but I have th' feeling that this day I may have destroyed Bloody Jacques, but I've also got rid of a business competitor for ye.'

Renzi sat in the boat next to Kydd. On the other side Job was serene and confident. Renzi had agreed to come to Polperro only because Kydd was in such fine spirits and had begged that he pay his respects to Rosalynd. He did not dislike the girl, it was not her fault that Kydd had been so hopelessly lovestruck: it was simply such a waste and one that, so obviously, Kydd would come later to regret.

They reached the fish quay. Renzi stood back while Kydd helped Job up and sent him on his way.

'Lay off an' wait,' Kydd ordered the boat's crew and, with a broad smile, added, 'We won't stay, Nicholas, don't y' worry.'

They stepped off briskly for the Landaviddy path. Instinctively Renzi felt uneasy: it was peculiar that so few people were about. They walked on and even the few seemed to be scurrying off. Did they think Kydd was looking for someone else?

A fisherwoman stopped, a set expression on her lined face.

Then she turned and hurried away. It was deeply unsettling. In a low voice Renzi said, 'There's – something afoot. I don't know . . .'

Kydd looked about with a frown. 'Where's th' people?'

They were both unarmed: should they return immediately to the boat? Had there been a French landing? It could be anything.

Then there was movement down the path. 'Titus – Billy! What's happenin', y' rascal?' called Kydd.

The lad approached unwillingly, his face white and strained. Kydd stiffened. 'Something's happened,' he said. 'Something bad,' he added, with a catch in his voice and forced the lad to look at him.

'She's gone, Mr Kydd.'

Kydd froze rigid.

'We – we buried her yesterday.'

For long seconds Kydd held still. Then he stepped back, his face a distorted mask. 'No! No! Tell me . . .'

'I – I'm s-sorry.'

'No! It can't . . .'

He turned this way and that as though trying to escape and an inhuman howl finally erupted. *'No! Noooo! Dear God in heaven, why?'*

The sexton was at the church gate. He gestured across the graveyard to the freshly turned earth. Kydd stumbled there blindly and dropped to his knees at the graveside.

'Damnedest thing,' the sexton confided to Renzi in a low voice, 'On passage to Plymouth for t' get her weddin' rig – a fine day, an' out of nowhere comes this black squall an' they overset. Over in minutes, it were.'

Renzi did not reply. He was watching Kydd and, as his

shoulders began to shake, he knew that the man was as alone in the world as he had been when they had first met, a desperately unhappy pressed man in the old *Duke William*. And now he needed his friend . . .

Without a word he went to him.

Author's Note

As I began to gather my thoughts for the author's note for this, my eighth book, I could not help but think how lucky I am to have Tom Kydd! Because of him and his wonderful world of the sailing man-o'-war, so many aspects of *my* life have been enhanced.

Becoming an author has meant that I have met people from many walks of life all over the world – certainly in my previous profession as a computer software designer it would have been unlikely for our paths to have crossed: there are far too many new friends and acquaintances directly attributable to Thomas Kydd to acknowledge here, but I know I'm enriched by them all.

Then there is the location research each January for the upcoming book. This has taken me to locales ranging from the Caribbean to Gibraltar and further. I visit each country with the specific goal of stripping away the trappings of modern life and building up a picture of the late eighteenth and early nineteenth century – the particular sights, smells, colour, the food, ways of life there in general. Some places still retain much of what Kydd would have seen, in others it is more difficult to peel away the layers – but that is the challenge . . .

To my surprise I realise that this is the first book set in home waters – I hope I've been able to do justice to what I've found to be as wild and exotic a location as any, with such spectacles as the incredible complex of the Plymouth naval base and dockyard. Certainly, in those pre-factory times it was the wonder of the age, employing many thousands of men, when most industries counted their workers in scores. No one in England lives far from the sea and a strong and abiding relationship with Neptune's Realm is a national characteristic, but it is perhaps in the West Country where the maritime heritage is strongest. Since time immemorial, the sea has provided food and transport links between isolated communities, and with hundreds of miles of rocky coastline, and winter storms equal to any, it has also been the graveyard of so many ships.

As usual, I owe a debt of gratitude to the many people I consulted in the process of writing this book. Probably foremost among these is my life's partner Kathy. As well as her professional input at all stages of the books, she functions as a *reality manager*, keeping the trials of everyday life at bay and enabling me to immerse myself in my research and writing.

Space precludes mentioning everyone but I would particularly like to convey special thanks to the people of the picturesque fishing village of Polperro in Cornwall, notably ex-fisherman Bill Cowan, former harbour-master Tony White and historian Jeremy Johns. I was honoured when the trustees opened the Polperro Museum especially so that I could view the wonderfully intricate models of local fishing vessels under sail crafted by shipwright Ron Butters.

My thanks, too, to Richard Fisher, who organised a special tour of Stonehouse Royal Marine Barracks; the Long Room, where Kydd attended the ball, still stands tall within the complex.

And lastly, as always, I must acknowledge the contributions of my literary agent, Carole Blake, marine artist Geoff Hunt RSMA, publisher Carolyn Mays, editor Alex Bonham – and all the team at Hodder & Stoughton.

Long may Kydd's voyages continue . . .